"The way Linden weaves her characters and various intricate plots together is at once delightful, edifying, heartwarming, and, believe it or not . . . even hilarious at times."
~Susan Peek, author of the best-seller *Saint Magnus, the Last Viking* and other saint stories

"With its strong pro-life message, *Life-Changing Love* will open the doorways to many great conversations about what love and life are all about."
~ A.J. Cattapan, author of the award-winning book *Angelhood*

"*Life-Changing Love* is a poignant tale about the beauty of life and the importance of being yourself. It is well-written and compelling, inspiring me to finish it within a few days. . . . threads are tied together seamlessly, as they form a love letter of life that God has given us."
~ Gina Marinello-Sweeney, author of *The Veritas Chronicles*

"You'll love Roland West, Caitlyn, and the cast of *Life-Changing Love* as they experience the heartache, trials, and pitfalls of courtship and dating."
~ Cynthia T. Toney, author of *10 Steps to Girlfriend Status*

SILVER FIRE
PUBLISHING

LIFE-CHANGING LOVE

A novel about dating, courtship, family, and faith.

By Theresa Linden

Dedication:

This book is dedicated to every young person who longs for authentic love and who strives to put God's will above their own, trusting that Our Lord always gives more than we ask or imagine.

Acknowledgments:

I wish to express my gratitude to the people who saw me through this book, especially Carolyn Astfalk, Don Mulcare, and Susan Peek whose encouragement and assistance with this manuscript blew me away. I hope my beta readers and those who read advanced copies know how much I appreciate their help, too. I also wish to acknowledge the love and support of my husband and three boys, without whose understanding and support this book would not be possible.

Chapter One

Caitlyn

All Nature seems at work.
Slugs leave their lair —
The bees are stirring —
birds are on the wing —
And Winter slumbering in the open air,
Wears on his smiling face a dream of Spring!
And I the while, the sole unbusy thing,
Nor honey make, nor pair, nor build, nor sing.

~"Work without Hope"
by Samuel Taylor Coleridge

Fourteen-year-old Caitlyn Summer stared, transfixed. She had sucked in a breath three seconds ago but still hadn't exhaled.

The other kids—sitting packed like sardines on the couch, loveseat, and floor of the Summers' cozy living room—hadn't seemed fazed. They continued gazing attentively at the courtship speaker, a young lady whose smiling face radiated joy.

Caitlyn had thoroughly enjoyed the talk. Courtship reminded her of Jane Austen stories, of ladies in frilly gowns and gentlemen on horseback. But then the woman said, "The couple get to know each other by spending time together only in groups or with their families." And Caitlyn had sucked in that breath.

Groups? Families? No, that wouldn't work. Caitlyn slunk down in the rocker recliner and twirled a long tress of her red hair in front of her face. Her life flashed before her eyes. No guy would want to practice courtship just to see her, especially not the boy she liked.

She exhaled. She would live out her years alone and die an unmarried woman. What was the word for that? Oh yeah, *spinster*.

A shadow moved on the wall behind the courtship speaker then someone knocked on the frame of the screen door.

Caitlyn jumped up, the chair squeaking and her eyes snapping to the time displayed on the cable box. The meeting should've ended already. She turned to her mother, who sat on a chair pulled from the dining room. "Mom, I'm gonna . . ." She pointed to the screen door.

Mom glanced at her watch and nodded.

Caitlyn stepped over legs. All eyes swiveled to her. Then kids pulled out their phones, probably checking the time or their latest text message. The speaker stopped talking and turned to Mom. Mom mumbled something about the next meeting.

Caitlyn pushed open the screen door and stumbled out onto the porch, stubbing her toe on the threshold. The fresh air cooled her cheeks and neck, and a grassy smell tickled her nose.

"I thought your meeting would be over by now." Zoe, in sandals and white shorts that drew attention to her long, tan legs, sat on the porch rail. She turned and glanced at the cars in the driveway, her silky black hair cascading over one shoulder.

"Yeah, me, too." Caitlyn sighed, admiring Zoe's grace and beauty, a hint of jealousy flickering inside her. Her shapeless, rail-thin body and wild red hair couldn't attract a fly.

Voices came from inside, several people talking at once. Someone laughed. Several more laughed. *The meeting must be breaking up.* Soon the kids, most from the Catholic youth group, would stampede from the house.

"Come on." Motioning for Zoe to follow, Caitlyn thumped down the steps and cut across a front yard littered with toys.

"So how'd it go?" Zoe came up beside her, taking long steps like a runway model.

"It was nice." Caitlyn stepped over a green ride-on toy and into a tangle of jump rope. "I wish you would've come." She shook her foot free and sort of staggered into the backyard, heading for the painting area she'd set up this morning.

Upside down cardboard boxes in the freshly-mowed grass, near the flowering turtlehead Chelone, served as tables. A long, low box held tubes of acrylic paint, paintbrushes, a jar of water, and Cool Whip lids that she used as palettes. Her 4-by-6-inch canvas lay out on the bigger box, the crumpled paper towel next to it hopefully hiding it from Zoe.

"What could I possibly learn from your courtship meeting? I've had boyfriends since junior high." Zoe, the only child of professional parents and the most attractive and self-possessed girl Caitlyn knew, did seem to have the boyfriend thing down pat.

"Courtship is not the same as having a boyfriend," Caitlyn said, "or dating. It's a different way of doing things." Eyes on her painting, she doubled her steps. She hated for people to see her unfinished work.

"What's that?"

Caitlyn's heart skipped a beat. She lunged and snatched the miniature canvas then turned to face Zoe, holding the canvas behind her. "What's *what?*"

Zoe pointed to another upside down box, a little one that held the model for Caitlyn's painting . . . a bumble bee corpse that Caitlyn had positioned just-so.

"It's a bee." Caitlyn brought the canvas from behind her back and hugged it to her belly. "I thought it would look nice in my picture."

Zoe wrinkled her nose. "But it's dead." She sat in the grass and stretched one leg out, now looking like a model posing for a shoot.

"David found it by the fence when he was trying to sneak into the neighbor's yard." Her little brother seemed obsessed with getting into their garden lately.

"And you decided a dead bee would be a good subject for your painting?"

"Well, it's not dead in my painting. See?" She gave Zoe a glimpse of the painting then sat cross-legged next to her. "It's hovering by a pink turtlehead Chelone blossom, its little wings fluttering as it tries to get nectar."

"Okay. I'm sure it'll look great." Zoe smiled, her honey brown eyes sparkling in the sunlight. "So tell me about the meeting. Will you have to follow a bunch of rules now? I always thought someday we'd double date."

"Rules?" Caitlyn sucked in a breath again. "Well, there are certain principles to courtship." That wasn't the same thing as rules, was it? "It's about putting things in the proper perspective, the proper order."

"What order?"

"Oh, you know." She neatened the paints and brushes. "Like finding yourself first, thinking about where you're headed, and knowing how to get there." It had all made sense to her when the lady explained it. Perfect sense. Except for that one detail.

The screen door slid open. One of Caitlyn's younger sisters and little David ran out.

"Close the screen door!" Mom screamed.

"My truck!" David toddled toward ten-year-old Priscilla.

Priscilla stood on the back patio holding a muddy yellow truck. "I told you it was in the house . . ." The cold smile and tilt of her head made her resemble Mom in parent mode. ". . . where it's not supposed to be."

David shrieked.

Caitlyn sighed. A shy boy would never feel comfortable around *her* family.

"Anyway, I know who I am," Zoe said. "And I know what I want. Don't you?"

Caitlyn shrugged. She loved Jesus, her family, and her life. And she knew what she wanted long term: she planned to get married and fill the house with bouncing babies and cuddly children. Short term . . .

She exhaled and allowed herself to think about him. Roland West. The sweetest, most mysterious boy in ninth grade. Dark eyebrows over piercing gray eyes, an unnaturally pale complexion—particularly appealing to the vamp girls, not that she was one of them—and the hint of a smile. He rarely spoke to anyone, yet still managed to grab girls' attention. He'd gotten her attention the moment she'd laid eyes on him.

School had just begun. Mom had told her she couldn't attend the annual camping trip with her friends. After screaming her head off in protest, to no avail, Caitlyn had stormed from the house and all the way to the downtown square. There she paced back and forth. Unbeknownst to her, Roland watched from the steps of St. Michael's Church. She wouldn't have ever known if she hadn't been so clumsy. In the middle of questioning God, she flung out an arm, shot a look heavenward, and smacked into a pair of bikers. They all tumbled to the cement. Roland came to her rescue, stopping her heart as he did so.

She brushed her lips with a dry paintbrush, liking the tickly sensation. Could Roland be the one for her . . . her future husband?

Caitlyn's heart sank. As shy as he was, how would she ever get to know him? Maybe Zoe was right and courtship had too many rules. Could she miss her future husband because she had to practice courtship?

"I'll tell you one thing I don't want anymore." Zoe flipped her hair off one shoulder. Her mouth became a straight line. She had no need to say more. They'd been best friends since kindergarten. Caitlyn could read her.

"You're kidding," Caitlyn said in her most sympathetic voice. "You guys broke up?" She wasn't really worried. Zoe, like every other popular girl in school, would have another boyfriend within the week. With the exceptions of square dancing in the third grade, her brother David, and Peter, who didn't count, Caitlyn had never even held a boy's hand.

"We're taking a break." Zoe gave a sly smile, stretched her arms out behind her, and leaned back.

"So you'll go camping with me?" Caitlyn dropped the paintbrush, excitement making her hands fly up and her eyes pop. Zoe had never gone on the annual camping trip. Roughing it was not her thing, she'd always said. This year was different. She'd claimed she wanted to go but that her boyfriend held her back.

"I thought you weren't going camping," Zoe said, "that you had to go to a wedding."

"My cousin backed out, so I'm free to go." Caitlyn shouldn't have been smiling. She felt sad for her cousin. Caitlyn had never seen her more bubbly than when she announced the wedding. The break-up probably devastated her. But, boy, this year's camping trip had Caitlyn excited.

This camping trip might be the answer. If Roland decided to go, they could get to know each other without having to worry about courtship rules. Her friend Peter was supposed to call today and let her know. "What time is it?"

"What?" Zoe pulled a cell phone from a back pocket. "Oh, I have to get going." She stood. "I'll call you later, okay?" She sauntered back around the side of the house, her silky black hair billowing out with every step.

Caitlyn sighed. Did she even stand a chance with Roland?

She grabbed her Cool Whip lid palette and lifted the wet paper towel she had put over it to keep the paint blobs from drying. Was she too young to be so interested in a boy? "High school is where you find your bridesmaids," the courtship woman had said, "not your husband."

Caitlyn rinsed her brush and reformed the tip, ready to add final touches to the flowers before she started on the bee.

The screen door slid open.

Caitlyn spun to face it. Maybe Peter had phoned.

Stacey, her youngest sister, stepped outside clutching an armful of superhero action figures. She never had liked dolls. Stacey skipped across the yard, headed for little David, who was burying his truck in the sandbox.

Oh, Peter, hurry up and call.

Caitlyn rolled her brush in pale pink paint then touched it to the canvas with gentle strokes. The flower should appear delicate but irresistible, full of something more than eye could see. Painting the bee, the living, fluttering creature in pursuit of the flower's alluring nectar, posed a challenge for her. She typically painted still life and landscapes. She had no experience with bees.

Did bees even like turtlehead? She'd seen them come around, but they never seemed to get inside the blooms. Not only did she know nothing about bees, she had little knowledge of flowers.

The screen door screeched open.

Caitlyn jumped, jerking the brush. The flower on the canvas now had a horn that she needed to remove before it dried. She sighed.

"Telephone," Mom said. "I think it's Peter."

Chapter Two

Roland

Heart racing and thighs burning, Roland West pumped the pedals of his mountain bike as if a demon pursued him. He imagined he heard the Lexus crunching down the two-mile, winding, gravel road that led home. Who would make it to Forest Road first?

Speeding toward the edge of the woods, he noticed too late the branch of a yellowing Witch Hazel bush that stretched across his path. It scratched his cheek as he passed. He winced but maintained his speed. He expected his actions to have consequences.

The road came into view. Just after rush hour. No cars either way. Standing, he pedaled harder, crossed the road, and made a beeline for the Forest Gateway Bed & Breakfast, the home of his friend and fellow freshman Peter Brandt. A single car waited in the driveway, a dented black Ford Taurus.

Good. Leo was prompt.

As Roland turned up the driveway, he squeezed the brakes and the bike swerved. Clinging to the handlebars, he jumped off and let the bike veer around him.

A rear window of the car lowered and Peter's pink face poked out. "Come on, come on, hurry!"

Roland let his bike fall and darted to the other side of the car. Trying to catch his breath as he got in, he gagged on the odors of burning oil and leather air freshener.

Peter greeted him with a grin and a fist bump. Foster laughed. Leo's only acknowledgment came in the form of an outstretched, palm-up hand.

Leaning back, Roland struggled to stuff his hand into the front pocket of his black jeans.

"Kill the headlights, dude." Peter tapped Leo's seatback. "This is a covert operation."

Leo waited until Roland slapped the money into his hand before choking the lights. He examined his payment, shoved it into a chest pocket, and peered in the rearview mirror. "I wanna know who we're following."

"Ah, whaddya need to know for? We just need money." Foster, who sat in the front passenger seat, reached up and rubbed Leo's blond crew cut. Leo swatted him. Foster yanked his hand back.

"There he is!" Peter scooted forward, clutching the driver's headrest.

The Lexus sped past, its silver coat shining under the setting sun, its taillights matching the pink-streaked sky.

Roland's heartbeat quickened. The car headed toward town. But to what destination? Maybe he didn't want to know.

"Go, go, go." Foster spun his hand in a circular motion. "Drive!"

Leo revved the engine, shifted into reverse, and peeled out of the driveway with a squeak of the tires.

"Not so fast." Foster shook a hand at Leo. "We don't want him to see us."

"Who's *him*?" Leo slowed a little. "I'm driving. I should know."

"Turn your lights on, dude," Peter said. "We don't want to get pulled over."

Roland was amazed at Peter's courage, bossing Leo like that. Maybe he assumed Foster would take the edge off Leo's temper. Then again, Peter never seemed to use caution.

Leo glared at Peter through the rearview mirror before obeying.

"He's turning," Foster shouted, whacking Leo's arm.

"I can see he's turning. I'm not blind." Leo sneered.

As the car rounded the corner, Peter faced Roland and stared for a moment before speaking. "So, where do you think he's going? What do you think he's up to? And why are we following him?"

Roland watched the Lexus's taillights as it turned again. He shrugged.

"Not gonna tell me, huh?" Peter's jaw twitched. "Fine. Keep your secrets, for now. I'll get you to talk eventually."

"There he goes." Foster jabbed the air.

"I can see that." Leo slammed his palms against the steering wheel then cranked it for the turn. "Man, I'm not an idiot. I'm older than all of you."

Peter grinned. "Older . . . but not necessarily smarter."

Leo muttered something, his eyes oscillating between the rearview mirror and the windshield. He was nicknamed The Dumb Ox, a name a good Catholic wouldn't even appreciate, though St. Thomas Aquinas had it first. He got the name largely due to his size. He had an incredible bulk, most of it muscle. But the name also reflected his perceived intelligence. He answered questions after a long delay, if he answered at all.

If he wasn't the only kid they knew with a license and a car . . .

They passed the downtown square and turned onto a residential street. Roland's attention drifted to the little yellow ranch house on the corner. Maybe Caitlyn would be outside. Maybe she'd see them.

Her green crystalline eyes flashed in his mind, her angelic smile, her copper tresses . . . He sighed and calmed a little. She had a way of doing that to him. There was something about her—

"What?" Foster's voice came out high, tearing Roland from his vision. "He's turning again."

The left turn signal flashed, but the Lexus turned right.

"Think he's on to us?" Peter grinned, his face beaming with sheer delight. Sometimes he seemed absolutely nuts, thrilled over things others would fear. He couldn't have gotten the quality from his parents, his father a rugged, level-headed forest ranger, his mother a compassionate and organized woman. Maybe his younger autistic brother's bizarre behaviors drove him to it.

"This way only goes to the backside of some stores," Foster said.

The Lexus passed a gas station and drove behind the grocery store at the end of a strip mall.

Leo stopped in the parking lot.

"What're you doing, man?" Foster wailed on Leo's arm. "He went back there."

Leo leaned on the steering wheel, stared for a moment, then pointed toward the corner of the grocery store. "See the sign? It says *deliveries only*. We can't go back there."

"*He* went back there." Foster's freckled face turned red.

Roland shook his head. What did Foster care? He didn't even know the mission. Maybe he just loved a good adventure.

"Go!" Peter slammed the headrest.

Leo glanced to either side before throwing the car in drive. He rolled behind the grocery store into an enclosed area of loading docks and dumpsters. His mouth fell open. "Oh, man!" He slammed the brakes hard.

Roland smacked into Foster's seatback.

"What?" Peter craned his neck. "What's your prob—"

The Lexus pulled out from behind a dumpster, heading for them. It stopped. The driver's door flew open and out jumped Roland's older brother Jarret. He strutted toward them, one hand rubbing his stubbly chin and the other clutching a pipe-wrench, *try me* written on his face.

"Shoot, shoot, chicken spit," Leo said, throwing the car in reverse. "You didn't tell me . . ." He cranked his head to peer over his shoulder as he backed the car up. "You didn't say . . ."

Roland stared, dumbfounded. Jarret never wore ripped jeans or dingy shirts. The fashionable, rich-boy image meant everything to him. What type of kids had he been hanging with? What foul things did they do? Jarret must've been totally lost without his twin brother Keefe.

As Leo's car whined backing up, Jarret stopped and took a wide-legged stance. A slow, crooked grin stretched across his face. He slapped the wrench against his palm and gave a slow nod.

"Go, go, go!" Peter and Foster said together.

Leo threw the car in drive, floored it, and did an about-face with a screech. Barreling out onto the road, he pounded the steering wheel and grumbled under his breath. "So, that's why you didn't tell me." He shot everyone a furious look, Foster getting the longest one. "I'm gonna have Jarret West after me now."

Peter faced Roland. "Think he knew it was us?"

Roland shook his head and leaned back. His body relaxed for the first time since he had set out. Peter kept staring at him, so he added, "Don't worry; it's too dark to see inside the car."

"Worry? Me? I'm not worried." Peter raised his voice and eyed Leo. "*I'm* not afraid of Jarret West."

"Why are you following him anyway?" Leo peered at Roland through the mirror.

"Don't worry. We don't need to know. Roland paid us," Foster said in a calming tone.

"Think Jarret knows my car?" Leo spoke low.

Foster mumbled a reply. Leo said something about not wanting to ride the bus to school. Foster said something else.

"Maybe we followed too closely." Roland stared out the window at the purplish sky.

"Not to worry, my secretive friend." Peter leaned to whisper, "I know a better way to follow him. We can keep some distance, not be seen."

~ ~ ~

Roland sat on the end of Peter's unmade bed watching Peter work at his cluttered desk.

Peter looked back and forth from a page of instructions to the small black box in his hands. "So, are you gonna tell me why you're stalking your brother, or not? I mean, I think it's only fair if I'm gonna be helping you out here—"

"All right, fine." Roland bit his lip, trying to think of the best way to explain it without making Jarret look bad. "Before my father decided Keefe would go on *my* Italy trip . . ." He still felt a bit of resentment even though he'd made it impossible for Papa to take him as originally planned. ". . . Jarret begged me not to tell on him."

"Begged you?" Peter whispered, grinning and probably trying to picture it. Jarret wasn't one to beg. He threatened, manipulated, sneaked. And this particular request was more of a friendly threat, anyway, than actual begging.

"Papa—I mean, my father said if he found out Jarret was responsible for any of the stunts I pulled two weeks ago, he would send Jarret away." Roland had never gotten in more trouble in his life, though none of it was his fault, really. It all started when he had overheard Jarret scheming about the Italy trip and had confronted him. Roland ended up taking a beating, getting locked in the basement, then running away and staying at Peter's house without permission. A couple days later, he returned home and Jarret locked him up again, not letting him out until after school. Of course, he had to serve detention for skipping school. Then there were the cigarettes, and Papa's missing coins . . .

"Sent away?" Peter's eyes flashed with hungry curiosity. He reached for a screwdriver and closed the black box.

Roland clasped his hands and leaned forward. "Yeah, my father threatened to separate him and Keefe, his twin, by sending him to private school or to live with my father's friends in Arizona."

Peter chuckled. He always seemed to enjoy gossip. "You should've told on him. You didn't do anything wrong, but you took the fall. I don't get it. If you'da told, then you'd be in Italy and he'd be in Arizona. It'd be a perfect arrangement."

Roland shrugged. Maybe he should've told, but he'd felt compelled to *cover his brother's sin with the mantle of charity*, to put it in the words of a little-known saint named Conrad, to whom he'd recently developed a devotion. He'd known he would lose out on the Italy trip, but he hadn't considered that Papa would take Keefe and leave him alone with Jarret. "I didn't want him separated from Keefe. Because after he threatened me—"

"Begged you." Peter grinned.

"Whatever. He told me Keefe was his conscience."

Peter's smirk faded. "Oh. And Keefe's gone. Yeah, that could be bad." After another glance at the black box, he tossed the screwdriver into a toolbox on the floor.

"I feel responsible for the way things turned out."

"You shouldn't. Whether you told or not, Jarret would now be separated from his twin, right? Separated from his conscience." His grin returned.

"I guess so." Roland stood and paced to the window. "But I'm worried about him. Since they left, he's been gone every day after school. And he comes home late. Where does he go? Who's he with? What're they doing?"

"Hmm. For a kid without a conscience, the possibilities are endless."

He turned to glare at Peter. "Well, I'm glad you're amused. But I'm not."

"Don't get so touchy, man." Peter held up the shiny black box and waved his brows. "Soon your questions will be answered." He slapped the device into Roland's hand.

It was a four-inch black box with a panel on one side. It didn't look like much.

"You'll need to get this inside your dad's Lexus. That's the car Jarret uses, right?"

Roland chewed his bottom lip and nodded. "You sure this thing will work?"

"Of course it'll work. My transmitter worked, didn't it? I've been working to get a greater tracking distance. If he gets outside the range, we'll have to search for him, I guess. But this'll send a signal when we're close enough, about a quarter of a mile."

"A quarter of a mile? That's it?"

Peter's eyes narrowed. He snatched the tracker back. "Yeah, that's it. Tracking devices using radio frequencies typically get three hundred to five hundred feet. I'm talking a quarter of a mile. It's not a GPS device." His face flushed.

"Sorry." Roland lifted his hands as a gesture of peace. "Fine. It's fine."

"So, when are we doing it?"

"Tomorrow." Roland stared blankly out the window. He'd have to plant the tracking device in the Lexus some time tonight or early in the morning. Without getting caught.

Chapter Three

Keefe

From the balcony of their fifth-story, luxury hotel room—cell phone to his ear—Keefe West feasted his eyes on the sea of red-tiled roofs and pale buildings of Florence, Italy. A red dome rose up in the distance. He couldn't wait to see what it belonged to. When would Papa let him loose to explore the area?

They'd arrived in Florence after dark a few days ago, but Papa had kept him busy with online research and phone calls while he met with dealers. They had taken all their meals in the hotel restaurant, so the view from the balcony was all Keefe had seen of the city. Still . . . it was amazing.

He had traveled often with his family, and each place had something to offer, but he had never left the continental U.S. Being an ocean away from home, in a city so unlike any he'd ever seen, made him feel different inside. He felt free—not that it made sense. Free from what? He felt like he'd woken from a coma or as if life just began. His soul sang with a sense of adventure.

Keefe stepped back from the balcony railing, sat in a wrought iron chair, and closed his eyes. A soothing breeze blew his dark curls into his face. It carried the scent of a woman's flowery perfume. Indistinct chatter and laughter came from somewhere below. God, he was blessed to be here.

How had he lucked out, being chosen by Papa to go on this trip? Papa had originally wanted Roland to go. Roland always threw himself into work, helping Papa with assignments, so it only made sense that he should've been the one. Jarret had messed it up for Roland, making him look bad, blaming him for things he hadn't done, and even getting

Nanny to believe the lies. Roland could've defended himself and explained his side of things. He had barely made an effort. Why? It didn't make sense. If he had, he'd be here right now, gazing down at the awesome view of clay roofs and antiquated buildings. He'd have loved it.

Keefe's eyes snapped open, his guilt in the situation weighing on him. He'd wanted to tell Papa before. But when Papa chose him to go on this trip, he hadn't wanted to blow it. Now his conscience nagged him to come clean.

He glanced at his cell phone then stuffed it into the back pocket of his chinos. Why wouldn't Jarret answer his phone or call? The second Papa had announced Keefe would go on the trip, Jarret had grown distant and angry. Sure, it took him a long time to get over things, but that was over a week ago.

The balcony door slid open, and a sheer white curtain blew out, flapping against Keefe's legs and the wrought iron chair. Papa stepped outside backwards, lighting his pipe.

"Did you talk to Jarret?" Keefe scooted his chair over a few inches.

Papa shook his head, holding the pipe to one side of his mouth while smoke seeped out the other. Lowering the pipe, he leaned his forearms on the balcony railing and made a sweeping gaze of the view. "I spoke with your nanny and Roland. Everything's fine over there. I wouldn't worry about Jarret. It takes him a while to haul in his horns."

Keefe nodded. "It's seven hours earlier back home, right?"

"Yup. It's about seven-thirty there now. Maybe he's in the shower."

Keefe shook his head. Jarret wasn't in the shower. He knew exactly what his twin did and when. Jarret kept a strict morning routine: wake at five-thirty to work out on the weights, then shower, breakfast, and off to school by seven-forty.

"I remember being here with your mother."

Keefe's ears perked. Papa rarely spoke about Mama since her death many years ago. "Here? Did you stay at this hotel?"

Papa nodded and stuffed the pipe into his mouth. Years under the sun as an archaeologist had made him tan and weathered, but he always had an air of distinction, a cool composure that rarely wavered. As he gazed out over the city, his deep blue eyes seemed to view something else, some memory or impression of the past.

"How long were you two in Italy?" Keefe longed to know more, but he'd have to tread lightly to get Papa to keep talking.

A smile flickered on Papa's lips, fading when he glanced at Keefe. "Several months." The cold look in Papa's eyes said the conversation was over.

"What did you two do here?" Keefe wanted to ask, but Papa never said more than he wanted to, and prodding soured his mood.

Keefe took a breath. Might as well get the confession out and give his conscience a rest. "Papa, there's something I need to tell you."

Papa's eyes shifted to him.

"I, uh . . . It's about Roland." Keefe shoved the curls off his forehead, trying to think how to word it. He should probably just blurt it out. "I really shouldn't be here. Roland should. I want to explain what happened two weeks ago, what I did."

Papa lowered his head and adjusted his cowboy hat. "No, son. Let's leave that be. I know that situation was a mite different from what it appeared, different from what you boys told me. I know Roland had very little guilt in the matter. But I respect his decision to . . ." He looked Keefe dead in the eyes. ". . . cover for his brothers."

Keefe swallowed hard. So Papa already knew. Papa knew he had some share in the guilt.

"Each one of you needs to think for yourself and not go along with things that are wrong or questionable. You need to learn to fish on your own hook." Papa's gaze sharpened, piercing a deep place in Keefe's soul. "You need to find yourself, Keefe. That's why I brought you with me."

A breeze ruffled Keefe's hair. He shifted in the cool, wrought iron chair. With a glance and a few words, Papa had laid his soul bare and exposed his weakness. Papa was right. He did need to find himself. He had gone along with Jarret, for good or bad, all his life. Until now, he hadn't considered it a weakness. Jarret needed him. How many times had he talked Jarret out of making bad choices? Jarret had even told him that Keefe was his conscience. What would Jarret do without his guidance?

As if by impulse, Keefe reached for his phone. Why wouldn't Jarret call him back?

Papa spoke before Keefe drew his phone out. "I'll need to see the list of museums, dealers, and buyers." Even before they'd left for Italy, he'd had Keefe compiling lists. Their mission was to locate and reacquire the collection of antique paintings that once belonged to the Giodarno family. The collection had been with the family for generations until a frivolous young heir decided to liquidate it to support his lifestyle.

"We'll be spending the afternoon and the next few days making visits," Papa said.

Glad for the change of topic, Keefe stepped inside to get the list. With wall-sized frescoes of mythical battle scenes, high ceilings, and ornate antique-style furniture, their hotel room was a step into the past.

"What about the churches and cloisters?" Keefe said, his voice sounding loud in the quiet hotel room.

"We'll get to those." Papa spoke from the balcony. "On the weekend, we'll head over to Bagno di Romagna."

"Where's that?" Keefe flipped through folders until he found the one with the lists.

"About fifty miles due east. But we'll have to wind around some mountains to get there. So, about a two-hour drive. We'll stay one night at least. There're a few people and an old basilica we'll need to visit."

Bagno di Romagna meant nothing to Keefe, but the two-hour drive meant he'd have an opportunity to get in touch with Jarret . . . if Papa didn't have him working on something in the car.

Chapter Four

Caitlyn

Roland and Caitlyn didn't have a single class together. It hardly seemed possible, and it wasn't fair. They did, however, share the same lunch period, though he often sat at the back of the school property, hidden behind an old maple tree. She sat with him once, shortly after they'd met. They'd talked on and on, connecting as if they'd known each other a lifetime. That was before she accidentally leaked one of his secrets to a group of gossipy girls, a terrible rumor spread about his deceased mother, and he stopped talking to her. She'd apologized through tears and he'd forgiven her, he *said* so anyway, but he'd been shy around her ever since.

Zoe pushed open a door to the back schoolyard and held it for Caitlyn. "It's chilly." She zipped her white sweater and sauntered toward the picnic tables. "I don't get why you want to eat outside every day. What's wrong with the lunch room? We always eat in the lunch room when it's cold outside."

Caitlyn stumbled along behind Zoe, trying to keep up without dropping her lunch. "It's not that cold. It's perfect. Besides, don't you just love the fall? I always want to eat outside in the fall. *You* always want to eat in the lunch room."

Zoe glanced over her shoulder and threw Caitlyn a coy grin. "So, why are we doing things your way now? Don't I always get my way?"

Caitlyn giggled. Zoe did always get her way. Caitlyn had considered herself to be flexible, like a sapling content to bend with the wind. Things were different now.

Zoe said something, but Caitlyn didn't catch it. Hoping to spot Roland, she peered at the old maple tree.

He didn't appear to be out there today. Now that she thought about it, he hadn't gone out there on lunch period since his brother Keefe left for Italy. Caitlyn scanned the school grounds.

Off to the left, kids played basketball. Girls and couples strolled along the building. Smoke traveled from around the corner of the building, the smokers' hangout. A few kids sat at picnic tables. Where was Roland?

"I can't believe I agreed to go," Zoe said. "Do you think I'll regret it? You know how I love my Keurig and taking a bath in lavender oil."

Caitlyn skipped a few steps to catch up. "Go where?"

She looked at her, smirking. "You aren't listening to me at all."

They neared the picnic tables. "Sure I am. What'd you say?"

Zoe laughed and sat at the only picnic table not littered with acorns and leaves. "I was talking about camping. I can't believe I agreed to go on this silly camping trip of yours."

"Silly? It's not silly. It's fun. You'll love it. It'll be a once-in-a-lifetime experience." Caitlyn couldn't wait. Peter had said Roland was going, so she would have an opportunity to hang out with him without having to worry about courtship practices.

"So who are you scouting for?"

"What?" Caitlyn walked around the picnic table and sat across from Zoe, immediately opening her lunch. Her stomach had growled all through Algebra class, and she couldn't wait to get something into it. "What makes you think I'm scouting for anyone?"

"I know you're looking for someone." Zoe turned suspicious eyes to Caitlyn. "Who is it? A guy?" She opened her insulated, designer lunch bag, that looked more like a purse, and pulled out a container with a pink lid.

Caitlyn grabbed a sandwich wrapped in newspaper from her brown paper bag. Mom had run out of sandwich bags, but Caitlyn was too hungry to let it embarrass her. "I wish you didn't know me so well. How's a girl to keep a secret?"

"You can't keep secrets from your BFF." Zoe's honey-colored eyes sparkled in the sunlight.

"Fine. You're right." Caitlyn meant to admit whom she was looking for, but she couldn't stop shoving her sandwich into her mouth. The turkey roll and Swiss on Italian bread with mayonnaise and pickle tasted so good today. Besides, she hated to tell Zoe whom she liked. It was laughable that she hoped someone as hot as Roland would be interested in her.

Zoe grabbed Caitlyn's lunch bag. "Tell me or I'm eating your lunch."

Caitlyn laughed. Zoe only ate healthy food. She would die before eating what she'd find in the bag: chips, cookies, and a Twinkie. "Okay, I'll tell you. But you have to promise not to tell anyone."

"You know I won't tell. We're best friends."

They stared at each other for a moment.

"Okay, I promise." Zoe tossed the lunch bag to Caitlyn.

"Do you know Roland West?"

A smile spread across her face. "I know him. He's in most of my classes."

Caitlyn huffed. *It figured.*

"You like him?" Zoe leaned across the picnic table, smiling.

Caitlyn nodded, regretting her confession and wondering if Zoe was about to laugh at her. "Out of my league, huh?" She ripped open her lunch bag, dug out the Twinkie, and wrestled with the wrapper.

Zoe sat straighter and folded her arms, a sly smile on her face. Her gaze clicked to some point behind Caitlyn. She shook her head. "No, he's not out of your league . . . Is he Goth?"

"Goth? No, he's not Goth." Despite herself, she instantly felt defensive. "He just likes dark colors. It's not like he wears make-up or has piercings or does strange things to his hair."

Zoe shrugged. "I swear he was wearing black nail polish last week." She continued staring at something behind Caitlyn. "He does *something* to his hair. It's so full and wavy."

"That's just the way his hair is. Some people have naturally wavy hair." The more Caitlyn talked, the more defensive she knew she sounded and the more her face burned. She really needed to chill. Zoe was entitled to her opinion. "My hair curls naturally." Caitlyn shoved the Twinkie in her mouth to keep from further defending him.

"Well, if you really like him . . ." Zoe's eyes shifted to Caitlyn again. ". . . you'd better think of a plan to get his attention."

"We're fwends aweady," Caitlyn said, mouth stuffed.

Zoe cleared her throat and her gaze shifted again to the point behind Caitlyn. "You're not the only girl attracted to him."

Caitlyn lost her appetite just like that. She swallowed hard and took a swig of water. "You like him?"

Zoe's gaze shot to Caitlyn, and she laughed. "No, he's too shy."

"Someone else told you they like him?"

"No."

"Well . . . then how do you know?"

Zoe nodded towards whatever she had been staring at over Caitlyn's shoulder, so Caitlyn turned to look.

Roland, dressed in black jeans and a black denim jacket, leaned against the smokers' corner of the school building. Mya Taylor, dressed in a cute plaid skirt and no jacket, leaned next to him.

Second only to Zoe, Mya was the last girl Caitlyn would want for competition. Caitlyn was plain, bone thin, and had a full head of untamed red hair. Her every movement led to an accident or disaster. Mya was a clone of Marilyn Monroe. She idolized the actress, copying her laugh, her hair, her clothing style. Guys fawned over her.

And there she stood, fawning over Roland West.

Chapter Five

Roland

In a thin strip of woods that separated the older neighborhoods from the newer ones, Roland sat on his bike, leaning on the handlebars. And waiting. Caitlyn's house was just down the road. She might even be outside. He wouldn't risk glancing though, not with Peter beside him. Peter always had something sarcastic to say when Roland looked her way. Roland wasn't in the mood for it.

Peter sat on his bike with one foot on the ground. He fidgeted with the black box he claimed would pick up the signal of the tracking device Roland had hidden in the Lexus.

Hiding the device hadn't been easy. Jarret spent little time at home, and he guarded the keys to the car. Roland had planned to make his move early in the morning while Jarret worked out with his weights in the basement, but his alarm clock hadn't gone off. The sound of the bathroom door slamming had woken him. Then the shower blasted. Roland tumbled out of bed, bolted to Jarret's room, and swiped the keys. Heart pounding in his throat at the fear of Jarret catching him, he'd dashed for the garage. Twice he dropped the keys while trying to unlock the door . . . only to discover it hadn't been locked. Then he couldn't decide on the best place to hide the thing, so he shoved it under the back, passenger-side floor mat. He raced through the house and back upstairs.

By that time, the shower had stopped. And the instant Roland mounted the top step, the bathroom door swung open and Jarret emerged in a towel. He saw Roland standing there with his mouth hanging open and his hands behind his back.

"What's your problem?" Jarret had said.

Roland gave no reply. Feeling doomed, he just gulped.

"Why do you look like that?"

"I, uh, I wanted to talk to you." Roland had backed into Jarret's bedroom and tried to slip the keys onto the dresser, but they dropped to the floor.

Jarret glanced at them but not suspiciously. "So what d'ya want?"

"Uh . . . I was wondering if, um . . . Want to ride the horses with me after school? They could use the exercise."

"Can't." Jarret stooped for the keys and tossed them onto the dresser. "You should though. And brush Desert. She needs a good brushing." Desert was Jarret's horse and he usually took good care of her, spending more time grooming and exercising her than Roland or Keefe did their horses.

"What're you doing after school?" Roland asked.

"None of your business." He shoved Roland from the bedroom. "I'm glad you're taking care of the horses. Mr. Digby don't exercise them long enough. Better get dressed if you're riding to school with me." He closed the door.

Roland had exhaled, hoping Jarret hadn't suspected anything.

As Roland sat on his bike, he desperately hoped Peter's tracking device would work and they could keep enough distance to avoid being caught.

"You really think this is the best place to wait for him?" Roland twirled a foot pedal with the toe of his boot. "What if he doesn't come this way? Maybe he doesn't go to the same place every day. And what if he sees us when he drives by?"

"Relax, little buddy, and stick to the shadows. The way you're dressed, all that black, you're like the Invisible Man." Peter peered down at his own mustard-yellow sweatshirt then rubbed his chest. "I should-a changed when we got home from school, but you were in such a hurry. I'm like a traffic light. Anyway, if I'm right, Jarret was headed this way until he realized we were following him. Leo, the big goon, he'd never make a good spy. He practically rode Jarret's bumper. Did you see Leo at school today?"

"Sure. I saw him."

"Did you talk to him? He's really mad." Peter smiled. "He said Jarret was out in the school parking lot looking over cars. He's worried Jarret's gonna come after him once he recognizes his car. Think he will?"

"Probably. He doesn't like people in his business."

"I bet Leo starts taking the bus to—"

The black box strapped to Peter's handlebars beeped.

"Ha!" Peter lifted a foot to the pedal. "Game on." Peering through the woods, he inched his bike forward.

Roland rolled to where he could see the road. A moment later, the silver Lexus sped by and slowed at the intersection. Jarret turned left where he had turned right the other night.

"When I'm right, I'm right." Peter led the way from the cover of the woods and out onto the street.

"What's down that road?" Roland pedaled up beside Peter, his eyes on the intersecting road.

"New neighborhood, I think. Maybe your brother has a new friend, a new conscience." He smirked.

They turned left riding side by side. Newer, two-story houses lined the streets on their left, older houses and empty lots on the streets to the right. The Lexus was nowhere in sight.

Peter tapped his tracking device. The beeping had stopped. "He must've turned here. He's got to be over a quarter of a mile away."

"So how's that supposed to help us? We can't keep up with a car on our bikes."

Peter threw up a hand. "Chill, man. You West boys are so impatient. Some things you just have to wait for."

They pedaled past a few more streets when the beeping sounded again.

"Told ya." Peter gave a cocky grin. "Patience, my friend, and we'll find him." His grin vanished, and his eyes opened wide. "Shoot! Maybe we ought to turn around."

Roland turned to see what Peter saw. His gaze snapped to the Lexus halfway down one of the older streets, backing toward them. Jarret caught them again.

"I'm outta here." Peter whipped his bike around, skidding one tire.

Roland rode over a curb and dropped his kickstand in the grass.

"Are you crazy?" Peter did an about-face and rode up to him.

"I'm going to talk to him. He saw me already." Roland swung a leg over his bike and waited as the Lexus stopped and the driver's door flew open.

Jarret climbed out of the car and gave Roland a nod, inviting him over. Dressed in gray sweatpants and an old black concert t-shirt, he leaned against the car and lit a cigarette.

"No way." Peter shot a laser beam of hate across the street, at Jarret. "Don't go to him. Get back on your bike."

"I'm just gonna ask what he's been up to." Roland stepped off the curb.

"Well, been nice knowing ya." He rode his bike several yards back and turned to watch.

Roland chuckled, but his humor died when he made it across the street and got within spitting distance of Jarret's sneer.

"Following me, huh?" Cigarette in hand, he picked something off his tongue then spit to the side.

Roland shoved his hands in his jacket pockets. "Hi, Jarret."

"Were you in the black Taurus following me the other day?"

"Uh . . . yeah."

Jarret took a hit off the cigarette and gazed into the distance, probably considering how to retaliate. It would probably hurt.

"Since Keefe's been gone," Roland forced himself to say, "you haven't been yourself. I'm worried about you."

A combination of annoyance and amusement flashed in Jarret's dark eyes.

Roland's breath caught. Jarret had a temper only Keefe knew the secret of cooling. What would Keefe say if he were here now?

Jarret pushed off the car and straightened. "Didn't you already ask me where I've been going?" He closed the little distance between them with slow steps.

Roland resisted the urge to back away. "Uh . . . yeah."

"What answer did I give you?" Jarret stopped inches away and blew smoke in Roland's face.

"You said . . ." Coughing from the smoke, Roland made a move to step back, but Jarret grabbed his shoulder. "I guess you said it was none of my business."

Jarret leaned and whispered in Roland's ear. "That's right and now you're gonna remember it." He drew a fist back and slammed it hard into Roland's side.

Pain shot through him. He groaned, cracked his knees to the pavement, and doubled over. He reached for the car to pull himself up, but the car door slammed and the Lexus sped away.

"Hey, you all right?" Peter jogged to him and squatted. "Your brother's a jerk, man. And I hate to say I told you so, but . . ."

Clutching his side and trying to shake off the pain, Roland forced himself to his feet. "I'm all right. He just gets mad when—"

A car whined, the Lexus backing up the road again, coming toward them.

"Get outta the road!" Peter shouted, dragging Roland by the arm.

The car squeaked to a stop near them, and the driver's window lowered. "You want to know what I'm up to?" Jarret shouted over the heavy metal blaring from his radio. "You really want to know?"

Roland stepped forward, but Peter dragged him back. Roland nodded to Jarret from where he stood. "Yeah, I want to know."

"705 Bradberry Lane. That's what I'm up to."

"Who lives there?"

"Nobody lives there, not yet." Jarret peered through narrowed eyes, but at least he was talking.

Roland yanked his arm from Peter and approached the open window. "So what're you doing there?" Roland said.

"I'm helping someone." An eyebrow twitched, and his eyes held a look of challenge. "Find that hard to believe?"

"No, I-I don't know. Helping someone do what?"

"You're always judging me, thinking I'm so bad. I'm just helping the Finns build their house."

"You're helping build a . . . ?" Roland tried picturing it. What did Jarret know about building a house? "Who are the Finns?"

"They go to your church. Don't you know them?" he said, his tone accusing.

"No." Roland had only recently returned to Sunday Mass, attending the church they'd gone to as a family years ago. He knew almost nobody there, just the kids who went to River Run High.

"I know the Finns." Peter came up beside Roland. "They're a big family. Homeschoolers. Lots of kids. I get the impression they're kind of poor. I guess I remember someone saying they'd outgrown their house and were building another. I didn't know they were doing the work themselves."

The car lurched forward. Jarret stared ahead blankly. "It's cheaper that way." He turned his eyes on Roland again. "If you care so much, why aren't you helping them? I'm sure they could use all the help they can get." He gave a cold grin and took off.

Roland stared, dumbfounded.

"Wow. So that's a major shock." Peter kicked a stone into the curb. "Your brother's helping people. Doesn't seem possible, does it?"

"No." Roland held his aching side as he gazed down the street. "Think we should help, too?"

"I don't know. Feel up to it after that sucker punch? Let's go to Caitlyn's. She's just down the road. Of course, you already know that. I saw you looking for her as we passed." He grinned.

"I was not."

Chapter Six

Caitlyn

Mya, of all people, liked Roland. Beautiful, bubbly, blonde Mya Taylor just had to like Roland West. Caitlyn couldn't stop thinking about it as she stood out in the backyard. It so distracted her that she only heard half of what Zoe said over the cordless phone from the kitchen, and she only pushed her little sister on the swing with half of her regular enthusiasm, and she only kept half an eye on Stacey and David in the sand box. It was a good thing Mom had little Andy in the house. He would probably have rolled off into the neighbor's yard unnoticed.

"So, is there? Should I bring them? Please say *yes*," Zoe said over the phone.

"I'm sorry. What'd you say? Is there what?"

"You're not even—"

Priscilla lurched back in the swing, burst into song, and rammed Caitlyn with her head. The phone slipped. The screen door opened and David, covered in sand, stepped a foot up into the house.

"Wait, David. Stop!" Mom would kill her. Caitlyn dropped the phone into her skirt pocket and dashed for David.

"I go potty," David said, desperation in his tone.

"Just . . ." Gripping his wrist, Caitlyn slapped sand from his shins. ". . . one . . ." She brushed sand off his hands and arms. ". . . second." She ruffled his hair, finding it relatively sand-free. "There. You can go in the house."

She turned to find Stacey and Priscilla digging in the landscaping.

Caitlyn sunk her hands in her hair, turned heavenward, and groaned. Then she remembered the phone in the pocket of her skirt. And Zoe.

She dug the phone out and pressed it to her ear. "Hello? Zoe?"

"Oh my word," Zoe said. "Do you live in a zoo? It sounds crazy over there."

Caitlyn made threatening gestures to get the girls back into the sandbox where they were allowed to dig. They ignored her. "It is crazy. It'll calm down after dinner. What were we talking about?"

"I was talking about my blow dryer and flat iron, wondering if your campground has electricity. You, however, were distracted, and I doubt it had anything to do with your siblings."

Determined to get Stacey out of the landscaping, Caitlyn stomped over, grabbed her ponytail and tugged. Stacey whined but got up and slunk to the sandbox. Priscilla made a mean face, propped muddy hands on her hips, and followed Stacey.

"Why do you think I'm distracted?" Caitlyn said to Zoe.

"I don't *think*, I *know*. It's Mya. Just when you get a crush on someone, she zeroes in on him. I know I'm right."

Caitlyn hated to admit it. Was she that transparent? Did Roland know she liked him? He probably liked Mya. Mya was going camping, too. Why had she invited her? "Do you think it's wrong to un-invite someone to something?"

Zoe laughed. "You don't have to worry about Mya."

"I don't?"

"No. Roland already knows you. He's your friend, right? Maybe he even likes you the way you like him. You just need to find out. But you should probably find out before Mya finds out how he feels about her."

Caitlyn groaned. If Roland had the slightest interest in Mya, Caitlyn didn't stand a chance.

"Cait-lyn," Mom sang through the back screen door. "There's someone at the front door."

"I'm watching the kids," Caitlyn shouted, feeling defeated. "Can't you get it?"

Mom opened the screen door, a dishtowel in her hand and Andy on her hip. "David's in the house. Your sisters will be fine. Besides, it's for you. It's Peter and one of his friends."

"One of his—" Caitlyn's eyes popped. Her heart skipped a beat. She pressed the phone to her ear. "Zoe, I have to go. I think Roland's at the door."

"Well, get to work, girl."

Caitlyn handed Mom the phone as she stumbled into the house. Then she saw them. Sure enough, Peter and Roland stood on the other side of the front screen door. On the way to the door, she smoothed her dress and hair. Something gritty . . . Oh! She still had sand on her hands. She took a second to shake her hair out then pushed open the front screen door.

"Hi," she said in a strange whispery voice that she'd never used before.

Peter gave her the once-over and smirked. Something on her was out of place, but he probably wouldn't tell her *what* until later.

Roland looked only at her eyes. "Hi." He spoke in an equally whispery voice.

They smiled at each other for a full second, Caitlyn's heart going wild.

"What took you so long?" Peter plopped down in one of the two lawn chairs on the porch. "Sit down, Roland. She's not gonna invite us in. It's chaos in there."

Roland blushed and sat on the top step of the porch. His hand shot to his side, a sudden look of agony crossing his face.

"Are you okay?" Caitlyn asked, concerned.

"Me?" Roland glanced from Caitlyn to Peter, giving Peter a look she couldn't interpret. "I'm fine."

Peter laughed. "He just got sucker punched by—" Eyes on Roland, he shut his mouth and raised his hands in a gesture of surrender.

Caitlyn hopped up to sit on the porch rail. She wished she'd been watching Roland so she could've seen what look or sign he gave to make Peter shut up.

"Who punched you?" she asked Roland. "Do you hurt? Do you want some ice?"

He shook his head. "I'm all right. It was nothing." He averted his gaze, which Caitlyn took as his way of saying he didn't want to talk about it.

"Are you thirsty? Can I get you something to drink?"

"We're not staying long," Peter said, still smirking as if he were up to something. "We're resting up."

"Resting up? For what?"

"Hey . . ." Peter's expression turned serious. "Did you know the Finns were building a house?"

"The Finns? From church?"

"Yeah. We're going over there. We're gonna help."

"You are?" A wave of jealousy struck her. Peter planned to help Roland with a project. "Can I help? What are you going to do?"

Peter and Roland exchanged glances.

Roland shrugged. "He never said."

"Who never said?" Caitlyn asked Roland.

"Jarret," Peter answered. "Jarret's over there. Helping. Weird, huh?"

"Why is that weird?" She looked from one to the other.

"You don't know Jarret," they said together.

"Hey, did you talk him into going camping?" Peter asked Roland.

Roland shook his head. "He says he has too much to do." His gray eyes flickered as if something occurred to him. "Do you think he meant working on the house?"

Peter nodded. "Yeah, that's where he's been going in his grungy clothes, right? He's working on their house all this time, and here we're thinking he's up to no good. Kinda makes you feel like a judgmental scab, don't it?" He grinned.

Roland shifted his position but still held his aching side. "Yeah. Maybe if we help get the work done, he'll go camping with us. I know he misses Keefe." He gazed out at the road.

Caitlyn's heart melted. "Can I help, too?" She slid off the porch railing and dropped down by Roland. "If we all help, it'll get done that much sooner."

She immediately thought of a whole bunch of people who would love to help. The Catholic youth group!

They had recently taken the name Fire Starters which, understood in light of Luke 12:49, was the perfect name for their group. *I have come to bring fire to the earth, and how I wish it were blazing already!*

A few weeks ago, they had only eight regular members. Since last week, they had over twenty, not even counting their non-Catholic friends who sometimes joined them. This all happened after Dominic Miato, a friend of Peter, was miraculously healed through the intercession of Saint Conrad. Caitlyn had witnessed the miracle herself, had even been a part of it, and she still couldn't get over it. Dominic had lost the use of his legs in a car crash and had been in a wheelchair for years, until just last week. Roland and Peter got the idea of praying for him using a relic of the saint. Caitlyn had joined them, and before their very eyes, Dominic had stood up and walked. *Actually walked!* Every time Caitlyn thought about it, her heart skipped. She couldn't stop telling people. Not that she had to. Everyone knew Dominic. He always drew attention, racing down the school halls in his wheelchair. So when he walked into school last week, everyone was amazed.

The youth group had been on fire ever since, growing in members, praying more, praising more, and helping with more projects. They believed God had set a fire in their hearts and their job was to pass it on, thus the name *Fire Starters*. Would Mr. Finn mind a group with that name helping on his house?

Chapter Seven

Caitlyn

As Caitlyn rubbed a sheet of sandpaper against a patch of drywall mud on a wall in the dining room, she pondered the goodness of God. A few days ago, the Finns were worried about making the dates on their house contracts. Now all that had changed. In addition to Peter, Roland, and Caitlyn, a good number of Fire Starters came to help. In fact, so many people had shown up to work on their house that Mr. Finn walked around in a state of near shock, not sure what to do with himself.

Caitlyn's motive for helping wasn't as pure as others, like Roland and the Fire Starters—and even Jarret, who seemed unbelievably kind all of a sudden—but she considered this opportunity a gift from God.

Like a dream-come-true, she had worked by Roland's side for the past three days, staining doors, painting walls, and raking dirt in the back yard. It had made her feel shy, being so close to him. But one of the principles of courtship was to develop friendships, right?

Of course, if he ever *actually* wanted Caitlyn for his girlfriend . . . then what? Panic. Would he have to ask her parents' permission? Would they have to spend their time together playing Monopoly with her sisters? *Oh well.* One step at a—

"Hey."

Caitlyn turned to see Jarret West standing directly behind her.

He wore a fluorescent orange tank top, ripped jeans, and a blue bandana over curly hair. Drywall mud streaked his stubbly jaw and his forearms. The first day they came to help, Jarret told everyone he'd spent most of his time at the Finn's taping and mudding drywall and how he'd developed an impressive skill in such a short time. Mr. Finn agreed with Jarret's boastful self-appraisal, adding that Jarret had almost singlehandedly mudded every room in the house once the professional drywall installers had shown him how. Of course, Mr. Finn had something nice to say about everyone's work. Caitlyn couldn't imagine anyone doing any wrong in his eyes. He was so happy to have the help.

"Is something wrong?" Caitlyn said.

Jarret nodded, one eyebrow cocked, his expression saying she should know better.

Caitlyn glanced at the wall she sanded, not sure what it should look like. It was her first sanding job.

He laid his hand on hers, the one holding the sandpaper, and made her sand the wall in a circular motion. "You can't go side to side. You make ruts that I'll have to go over with more mud. Go round and round."

Caitlyn swallowed hard, wishing he'd take his hand off hers. Where was Roland? "Okay. I got it."

He let go, and the hint of a smile passed his lips. "Good." His gaze dropped to her skirt and stayed there as he spoke. "Ain't you got any jeans? You're a little dressed up for dirty work."

"I've got jeans." She found herself saying, "They're new though, and I've never really worn them before. My best friend gave them to me for Christmas last year."

She should've just said *yes*. She didn't owe him an explanation.

Jarret chuckled. "I'm sure you've got something other than a dress to wear here."

Caitlyn looked at her skirt. Tan with pale flowers and a few bleach stains, made of thin, woven cotton, it hung down past her knees. She'd bought it over a year ago from a second-hand store, not realizing it had a big slit in the side. But it was so comfortable she kept it anyway. "It's a skirt, not a dress, and it's old. I wear it around the house, especially when I clean."

"You've worn a skirt here every day. What's wrong with jeans?" His upper lip curled on one side. He probably thought she was strange.

"Nothing. I just don't wear them." Why should she have to explain herself to him? So she only wore skirts and dresses. So what? If she wasn't the only girl in the dining room, he probably wouldn't even be talking to her.

His gaze bounced all around her face then lingered on her mouth.

Did she have something on her lips? Powder from sanding maybe? She wiped them and checked her finger. White drywall dust covered her entire hand, except for the tip of her finger. She huffed, knowing she'd just transferred white powder to her mouth.

He smirked and reached toward her face. "Want me to get that for you?"

Irrational panic swelled inside her. "No!" She backed into the wall. Then facing away, she wiped her mouth with the inside of her t-shirt neckline. When she turned back, Jarret was already stooping over a bucket of drywall mud on the other side of the room.

Deciding to check her face in a mirror, she dropped the sandpaper, wiped her hands on a rag, and headed for the bathroom.

Pushing the door open with her hip, she stepped into the cool, dark room and sighed. The lights flickered on automatically. The workers had finished the bathroom first. With its bright walls, shiny white porcelain, sparkling fixtures, and pale turquoise tiles around the tub, she could stay in it all day.

She looked herself over in the huge, spotless mirror over the sink. Fine white dust covered her hair and top. Not wanting to mess up the bathroom, she let it stay, but she did wash her mouth and hands. Then she stepped from the peaceful bathroom and set out in search of Roland and Peter.

Caitlyn strolled back through the entryway, avoiding the dining room, and passed through a group of chatty, giggling girls in the kitchen.

Before she rounded the corner, Peter's voice came from the family room. For some reason, she stopped and listened.

"I tell you he's out there hitting on her."

"I'm sure she can take care of herself," Roland said. "What're you worried about?"

Caitlyn dared to peek. The family room looked great, having received a final coat of warm blue paint and new beige Berber carpet yesterday. Roland faced the far window and scraped off new-window stickers. Peter stood on a ladder, holding a little bucket and a small paintbrush, touching up the creamy trim.

"Worried? I'm not worried," Peter said. "I'm just saying. You've never admitted it, but I can tell how you feel about her. You really don't care if Jarret hits on her?"

Caitlyn sucked in a breath and withdrew from view. Were they talking about her? Peter could tell how Roland felt about her? How *did* he feel about her?

"He can try all he likes. He's not her type," she heard Roland say, his tone confident. "Is he? You've known her longer than me. I don't think she'd like a guy like him."

The ladder squeaked. "Well, why take any chances? Do you like her or not?"

"Sure, I like her."

Caitlyn's heart leaped. Then she heard Peter say, "Why not make her your girlfriend before someone else does? She's not exactly ugly. Clumsy, yes. Silly, sure. But not ugly."

Heat slid up her neck. She glanced into the kitchen to make sure no one noticed her spying.

Peter thought she was pretty? *Really?* In all the years they'd known each other, growing up as close as siblings, he'd never once hinted that he thought she was pretty. In fact, he always made fun of her appearance, comparing her long red hair to Raggedy Ann's and saying she was thinner than a toothpick. He had an endless supply of rude comments about her.

Roland spoke again, and Caitlyn's heart sank. "I'm only fourteen. I'm not ready for a relationship right now."

"Well, maybe *she* is. Maybe she wants a boyfriend."

Roland made no audible reply, but Caitlyn didn't wait around to hear more. Tears threatening to burst forth, she took off for the bathroom again. Roland didn't like her like that. He didn't want her for a girlfriend.

Caitlyn closed the door behind her, hid her face in her hands, and fell onto her knees before the light clicked on. Before the first tear fell.

Chapter Eight

Keefe

Keefe stared at the 15th century, tri-fold panel before him, awestruck. The strap of his leather document bag dug into a shoulder sore from carrying the bag around all day. He readjusted the bag, but he didn't want to move away.

He'd never seen more artwork in his life than he had in the past couple days. They had visited a dozen museums, churches, chapels, palaces and even a castle, each with collections or galleries of artwork. The paintings ranged from the 13th to the 18th centuries, works of Italian Renaissance artists, and works of foreign artists, mostly German, Flemish, Dutch, and French. He recalled some of the names from an Art Appreciation course, artists such as Titian and Raphael, Michelangelo and Leonardo. He had seen a few of the paintings before, in books and calendars or on the Internet, paintings such as the *Adoration of the Magi* by Lorenzo Monaco and several paintings of the Blessed Virgin Mary.

He and Papa had met with several dealers and museum officials. They'd gone through files on computers, in filing cabinets, and in archives, and searched gallery warehouses. Too bad they recovered only one painting from the Giodarno family's collection. Only one. It was a still life of fruit and pitchers, and they had to fork over the dough for it. Papa was not happy.

The strap shifted back to the sore spot on his shoulder. A strange feeling stirred his soul, an inner prompting. He'd felt it before when they had stepped into the first museum on their list, the Uffizi Gallery, the oldest museum in modern Europe. It dated back to 1581. Strolling through corridors decorated with frescoed and sculptured ceilings from the 16th and 17th centuries had put him in an introspective mood.

In fact, each exhibition room he ventured into, each painting or sculpture he gazed upon drew him deeper into the mood. For some reason, it kept striking him that God had given awesome talents to men and that using these talents, artists directed men to God.

Keefe hadn't given the spiritual side of life much thought until now. His twin's moods and schemes had always consumed his attention. He knew Jarret inside and out, his hopes and goals, what made him happy, what made him mad . . . But Keefe knew little of himself. He'd only wanted to cooperate with Jarret in order to subdue his unrulier passions and keep him on an even keel.

But who was *he*, Keefe West? What talents had God given *him*? What had God called him to do? A desire to know these things welled up inside. His mind soared above him.

"Keefe."

Papa's voice snapped Keefe back to the moment. He breathed.

"Remember why we're here." Papa came up behind him, rubbed his shoulder, and spoke low. "I have one more gentleman to speak with, then we'll get lunch. I need you to make a phone call." He pulled a paper from his pants pocket and stuffed it into Keefe's shirt pocket. "I need you to change our appointment time with Romano, the dealer. We'll be an hour late. Make sure that's okay with him."

Keefe nodded. Then, for the first time since arriving in Italy, his cell phone rang. It echoed in the exhibition room, making him wish he'd set his phone on vibrate.

Papa's brows lowered. "Who's that?"

Keefe checked then smiled at the familiar number. "It's Jarret."

Papa's eyes narrowed. "You can talk to him later. I need you to make that phone call now. And make it outside. You can't use cell phones in here."

The phone rang two more times before Keefe answered it. "Hey, Jarret," he said, watching Papa make his exit then looking for the way to the courtyard.

"Hey." Jarret stretched out the word, sounding nonchalant.

"Are you done being mad at me?"

"I'm callin' you, ain't I?"

"Yeah, yeah, you are. I'm glad. It's been way too long." Keefe stepped outside and strolled across the courtyard into a patch of sunlight. "What've you been up to? Getting yourself in trouble?"

"Na. Work. Too much work."

"Work? You?"

Jarret chuckled. "Yeah, I've been helping this family work on their new house."

"You're kidding? What family and why?"

"I have my reasons."

Jarret laughed. "What're you up to out there? Did you get me that shirt?"

"The shirt? No, I haven't gone shopping. Papa keeps me busy with phone calls and stuff. We've been touring museums the past couple days."

"You gotta have time for shopping. If I were there, I'd be shopping. Make sure you get me that shirt. I want it to be just like Roland's favorite, the one Papa got him last time he went to Italy."

"You mean the one you destroyed?" Jarret had been so jealous when he discovered Roland was going to Italy that he ripped apart the shirt Papa had given Roland.

"That's the one." He sounded cheerful.

"I'll see what I can do. Maybe I'll get one for Roland, too."

"No. That'll blow my whole reason for getting it. And you're not gonna *see* what you can do. You're *getting* me that shirt. So promise me now, and I'll tell you why I'm working on that house."

Even four thousand miles apart, Jarret could still manipulate him. But he did want to know. Keefe shook his head, lamenting his own weakness as he caved in. "Okay, I promise to get you the shirt. Now tell me what you're up to."

"I want a car. You know I've got some cheese saved, but it's nowhere near enough for what I want. I moaned to Papa about it. And he said he'd pay the balance if I helped the Finns get in their new house.

He probably thinks the job will keep me out of trouble while you guys are gone. But that's a sweet deal, ain't it?"

"Yeah, wow. You're getting a car?" A twinge of jealousy struck him. They were twins, after all. If one got something, shouldn't the other?

"Hey, you ain't got room to complain. You're in Italy and I'm not. And hey . . ." He snickered. "Our dear little brother found out what I was doing—but not why, of course—and he and all his friends came over to help. So guess what. Job's almost done. Hello, new car."

"That's great. I guess. Roland doesn't know about the car?"

"Heck, no. He thinks I'm doing a good deed."

"Keefe!" Papa came up behind him. "Did you get our appointment changed?"

Keefe lowered the phone. "Uhh."

Chapter Nine

Caitlyn

Caitlyn stepped on a pile of clothes and reached for something on the shelf in her bedroom closet.

Zoe sat on Caitlyn's bed, watching. After school, she had come over to help Caitlyn pack for camping.

Caitlyn didn't have a cool, sporty, black and hot-pink duffle bag that one could carry by hand or wear as a backpack, like Zoe did, but she did have a choice. She could borrow either Mom's 1970s purple duffle bag with the word "DUFFLE" all down the side or her flowered carpetbag with the leather handles. Caitlyn tossed both of them onto the bed, collapsed next to them, and sighed.

Zoe laughed and brushed the hair from Caitlyn's face. "You're so pathetic. I've never seen you like this."

"Which bag should I use?" Caitlyn sat up. "Which one doesn't scream *dork* but only whispers it?"

"I like them both."

"Oh, that's great. Then can I use yours?"

"No." She picked up the purple duffle bag and dropped it in Caitlyn's lap.

Caitlyn moaned and returned to the closet. She stared, blinking for a moment. Due to the shortage of room in their three-bedroom, ranch-style house, and due to her begging for and getting her own bedroom, her brother's clothes took up half her closet space. Every time she went to pry something of hers out, she had to remind herself that she did in fact have her own bedroom. Mom and Dad were kind enough to squeeze all of her brothers and sisters into the big bedroom so she could have the little one all to herself.

"We're going camping tomorrow," Zoe said. "You told me how much fun I would have, so I cast all my doubts behind me, and I'm going. You should be excited. But here you are moping around, moaning and groaning."

Caitlyn sighed and searched through the clothes on hangers. Where was her denim jumper?

"Are you going to tell me why you're so miserable? Or do I have to guess?"

"Oh, I don't know." She found the gray ribbed sweater that she wanted to wear and wriggled it free. "I have no reason to be moody. It's not like I can really have a boyfriend anyway, not with all the new rules. I'm just supposed to work on friendships right now."

"I knew it. It's about Roland. Do you think Mya's won? Just because you saw her standing next to him at lunch? Because that doesn't mean anything. It doesn't mean he likes her just because she obviously likes him."

"No, that's not it." She yanked the denim jumper and a long khaki skirt out of the closet and tossed them onto the bed.

"Well, then what?"

Bringing a white, long-sleeved t-shirt with her, she approached Zoe. "Roland doesn't want me for a girlfriend." She flopped onto the bed.

Zoe suppressed a giggle. "How could you know that? Did you ask him?"

"No, I heard him. He said, *I'm only fourteen. I'm not ready for a relationship.*"

"You heard him? How?"

Groaning and moving with great effort, she stood up again. "It doesn't matter how I know. I was being nosy, eavesdropping. Peter told him he should make me his girlfriend, and he said *no*. That's all that matters."

She leaned against the clothes in the closet. They were so tightly packed that they easily held her body weight. "I finally meet the most handsome, mysterious, and sweet guy in the whole world, and he wants nothing to do with me."

"He's fourteen? Aren't you fifteen?"

"Not yet. Next month I will be. Don't you know my birthday?" She sounded offended though, given the greater issue, she couldn't have cared less.

Zoe joined her at the closet. "Where are those jeans I gave you for Christmas?"

Caitlyn pointed to her dresser. "I was so worried about all the courtship principles that I have to follow, him being so shy, but here he doesn't even like me at all."

"Of course he does. Don't be a quitter." Zoe opened the bottom drawer and lifted David's pants off Caitlyn's never-worn jeans. "Just because he thinks he's not ready for a girlfriend, doesn't mean he doesn't like you." She brought the jeans to the bed. "Like you said, he's shy. Maybe the whole girlfriend-boyfriend thing scares him." She sat on the bed again.

Caitlyn joined her, knowing she was about to receive great advice. When it came to boys, Zoe always knew what to do.

"You need to show him that having a girlfriend isn't so scary of a thing."

"I do?"

"You do. And if you don't, Mya will. Mya and Roland are in several of my classes and, let me tell you, she's after him. She tries to walk with him between classes, sit by him in class . . . And she hangs on his every word, though I admit he has few. She's not going to give up just because he thinks he doesn't want a girlfriend, and neither should you. Here . . ." She reached for one of the miniature paintings that sat on Caitlyn's nightstand.

Caitlyn loved making little paintings. She struggled with history class, so sometimes she painted a scene to help remember things.

Zoe handed Caitlyn a battle scene. "You can't accept defeat before the battle has even begun."

Gazing at the painting, she sighed and almost laughed. Though it wasn't funny. If the painting Zoe chose was an omen, defeat was imminent. "This is the Battle of the Alamo. We lost that one."

"Oh." Zoe snatched the painting from Caitlyn's hands and tossed it over her shoulder. "Forget the Alamo. This is a battle you're going to win." She grabbed the jeans and stuffed them into the duffle bag. "I'll help. You just listen to me. Mya's going camping too, right?"

"Yes. I invited her before I knew she liked Roland. She's even sleeping in our tent. You never answered when I asked you before. Do you think it's wrong to un-invite someone?"

"It's too late for that. We just have to prepare. Don't worry."

Mya for competition. Caitlyn dragged herself to the mirror on the closet door.

Peter once compared her to a longhaired, red tabby cat. The image had stayed in her mind, haunting her whenever she looked in the mirror. Her long, red hair hung in curls and waves that easily turned into clumps and tangles. The layers often made it fall in her face. Her green, round eyes had the same naïve, crazy look of a cat's, Peter had said. Even her mouth, too narrow but with full lips, reminded him of a cat's little mouth.

Meow. Maybe Roland liked cats.

Zoe came up beside her, making Caitlyn automatically compare them. Zoe, with tan skin, silky smooth black hair, thick lashes, and thin shapely lips, was all sophistication and beauty.

"See? You're gorgeous," Zoe said. "The only reason guys don't hit on you is because you never flirt with them. Or if they do hit on you, you misunderstand and get offended. Plus, you're clumsy." She opened another dresser drawer. "We probably can't do anything about that. You've always been clumsy, so we won't worry about it."

"We won't?"

"No. Do you have any make-up?"

"Make-up?"

"If you want Roland, you're going to have to do just as I tell you."

$$Chapter\ Ten$$

Roland

"Bug off, twerp. I'm not going."

Jarret, back to his old self and his designer clothes, breezed through the house, a stack of car magazines on his hip.

Refusing to take *no* for an answer, Roland followed. After school, Roland had gone straight to Peter's house to go over last minute camping details. Then he'd hurried home to invite Jarret again. He'd felt bad about misjudging Jarret and wanted to change things between them. Why did they have to be either strangers or enemies?

He had hurried home for nothing. Jarret wasn't there. Jarret hadn't pulled into their four-car garage until well after Nanny hollered, "Suppertime."

"Why not go? What else do you have to do?" Wanting to make eye contact, Roland tried to keep up.

Jarret darted toward the front hall. This was not the ordinary route one took when going from the garage, clear across their castle-type house, to the kitchen. It was a straighter shot going through the family room and the great room.

"When I asked you before," Roland said, "you said you had too much work to do. You meant working at the Finn's house, didn't you?"

Jarret sneered. "Yeah, well, now I'm working on something else." He stopped at the door to the Digbys' suite and pounded on it.

"Come on. Go camping with us. It's just over the weekend. You love camping."

Jarret made a sarcastic snort then curled his lip. "I hate camping. Besides, we always took a camper, slept in beds. I ain't sleeping on the ground and eating burnt hotdogs all weekend long." He raised a fist to the door again.

"The Digbys are in the dining room. It's time to eat."

Jarret took off down the front hall, rounded the corner, and didn't stop until he reached the dining room doorway. "Uh, Mr. Digby, hey, I'm not going camping. So you can get my gear out of the car."

Mr. Digby sat at the far end of the table, hunched over a plate of food, holding his fork aloft. He looked up through droopy, cow-like eyes. "You're not? But I thought—"

"I'm *not* going." Jarret took off for the stairs before Nanny could tell him to sit down and eat dinner.

Once he reached his bedroom, he would close the door and Roland's chance to change his mind would end.

Jarret's way of handling the mildest annoyance: walk away, close the door— unless he was in the mood for a fight. He never talked things out. If he went camping, though, he wouldn't have any doors to close.

Roland imagined the two of them sitting by a campfire, turning marshmallows into torches, and talking all night. *If only*. It would be so nice to get along.

Mounting the steps by twos, Roland passed Jarret and breezed into Jarret's bedroom first. His bedroom was a showcase of antique furniture, artwork, and flashy decorations in red, purple and gold. Anything he wanted, he got, one way or another.

Roland crossed the room and peered out the window. Mr. Digby's car sat in the circular driveway, the trunk open. The Digbys, who had lived with the Wests ever since Roland could remember, planned to spend the weekend with their family. If Roland couldn't convince Jarret to go camping, Jarret would have the house to himself. And that could mean trouble. As popular as he'd become at River Run High, he might even consider throwing a party. If he did and Papa found out, Jarret could end up in private school or sent to live with Papa's friends in Arizona, as Papa had threatened to do last week when he suspected Jarret had been up to no good.

"You can go now." Jarret spoke like one dismissing a servant. He sat on his bed, leaning against a mound of silky pillows, flipping through a magazine. "And you can tell Nanny I already ate."

Roland rested a hand on the bedpost. "I really want you to go camping."

Jarret looked up from the magazine. "Yeah, I get that impression." He jerked his head to indicate the door. "Go."

Shaking his head in annoyance, Roland left the room. After sitting sullenly through dinner with Nanny and Mr. Digby, it occurred to him what he had to do. So he went straight for the phone in the kitchen.

"What?" Peter's voice screeched through the phone. "You're kidding me. Who cares if he goes? You don't need him to have fun. We'll have a blast. Besides, I thought you two didn't exactly get along. It should be a relief to be somewhere without him."

"Yeah, yeah. But I don't want things to be like that. I'm going to see what Jarret's up to this weekend and hang with him."

"Maybe he doesn't want you to *hang* with him."

"I'm sure he doesn't, but I'm going to try. We're brothers. Why can't we be friends?"

"Good luck. I wish you'd change your mind. Who's gonna sleep in my tent now? Mom'll probably put Toby in my tent." Peter rambled on about the troubles his autistic younger brother Toby had caused on past camping trips.

Mr. Digby happened to be sitting at the kitchen table during the phone call, glancing up from his lemon pie and giving Roland squinty looks. When Roland hung up the phone, Mr. Digby cleared his throat. "Did I just hear you say you ain't going camping neither?"

Jarret sauntered into the kitchen and stopped mid-stride.

"Uh, sorry, Mr. Digby," Roland said. "I can get my own camping gear put away."

"Nah, never you mind. I'll see to it." He scraped his chair back and abandoned his empty pie plate.

Jarret stormed to the bar counter and up to Roland. "What's this? What's he going to do?"

"I'm not going camping."

"You're not going camping? Why?" His eyes grew wide and hard.

"I'm staying with you. It'll just be me and you in the house. Maybe we can do something fun."

Jarret's mouth opened. His eyes narrowed and his lips wrapped around a word, but then he closed his mouth and shook his head. "No. You're going camping. It's just gonna be *me* . . ." He jabbed a thumb at his chest. ". . . in the house."

"Why? What've you got planned?"

"None of your business. Is Papa paying you to spy on me? You got some arrangement with him?"

"What? Of course not. Why would I have an arrangement?"

"Yeah, right." He stormed from the kitchen.

Roland sighed and slumped over the counter. This wasn't going to be easy, but he wasn't giving up. There must be something he could say or do to change Jarret's—

"Hey." Jarret leaned a shoulder against the doorframe. "If Papa didn't tell you to spy on me, what's your deal?"

"I-I want to be your friend. Keefe's not here. I thought you and I could hang out, talk or whatever. What you did at the Finn's . . . that was nice. And it's true, I never thought you'd do something like that. I guess I thought you'd been out doing something, you know, stupid."

Roland slid off the barstool and stepped toward Jarret. Courage grew inside him. Where did it come from? In a flash, he knew. Ever since Saint Conrad had come into his life, he'd felt different, driven to help no matter the personal cost. He could help by prayers. In fact, he'd taken up praying for Jarret and Keefe every chance he got. And he could do this. He could help Jarret. If he could only get the words out right.

"But I was wrong and I'm sorry. I'm sorry for judging you. Growing up together, I feel like I've seen only one side of you." He glanced down, remembering Jarret's past cruelties and ashamed of himself for not having looked deeper. ". . . not your good side. I feel like I don't even know you. But I'd like to."

Jarret's mouth twitched. He nodded, looked Roland over twice, and left the room.

Roland slept uneasily, his mind going over what he had said, what Jarret probably thought of him, and what he could possibly say or do to make Jarret his friend, or at least keep Jarret out of trouble. He regretted having misjudged Jarret. Still . . . he couldn't shake the feeling that Jarret, left to himself, would find trouble.

Chapter Eleven

Keefe

Keefe swung open the door to the Tuscan restaurant and stepped outside. A pleasant feeling of excitement and expectation grew within him. *At last!* After a late dinner, Papa had finally cut Keefe loose, given him leave to explore the streets . . . provided he made a few *assignment-related* phone calls to people in the states.

With the time difference, they often had to wait until evening to reach people. Keefe had made most of the phone calls in the restaurant lobby, though he'd spent more time speaking with Jarret, trying to talk him into going camping with Roland. It had taken a while to convince Jarret that Roland didn't have ulterior motives. Then Keefe had to assure Jarret that he'd still have plenty of time for car shopping before they returned from Italy. The conversation ended on a sullen note, Keefe sensing Jarret's residual jealousy over the trip.

Weaving around other pedestrians, Keefe scanned his surroundings.

Every hour of the day in Florence created its own unique masterpiece. At this hour of the evening, the two- and three-story, old-world buildings had turned to silhouettes, dark against a purplish sky. A crescent moon hung over one horizon, clouds painted orange with the last hint of sunlight over the other. Pleasant voices carried. People strolled along angled cobblestone streets, past shops and cafés with welcoming light and heavenly aromas.

Keefe inhaled slowly, letting the delicious air reach the corners of his lungs. Someone sold leather nearby and someone else coffee. He could go for a steaming cup of espresso right now. It just might hit the spot.

The aroma of sweet, fresh-baked bread traveled to him, and his mouth watered. Maybe he could get one of those savory loaves he'd tried the other day—What was it called? Oh yeah, a prosciutto bread. That stuff was good. He took another deep breath and sighed.

No, he didn't want to eat. He wanted something, though. *Needed* something. He couldn't quite put a finger on what he needed, but the feeling wouldn't go away and even seemed to increase moment by moment. Perhaps the strange introspective mood that had struck him in the museums had deepened. The sights and sounds of Florence called him to explore not only what they had to offer . . . but also things inside himself.

Explore he would.

Keefe glimpsed his reflection in a tall window he passed. Silver mannequins in men's designer clothing stood on the other side. Keefe stopped. *Jarret. The shirt.*

Men's clothing stores lined both sides of the street. Since they planned to leave for Bagno di Romagna the next morning, this might be his only chance. Jarret would never forgive him if he didn't come home with the shirt.

Keefe stepped through the columns that flanked the first clothing shop.

Four shops and an hour later, Keefe gazed at himself in a thick-framed, fancy triple mirror. He had finally found it, the white, slim-fit, button-front, designer shirt with the zippered chest pocket. It looked exactly like the one Papa had gotten Roland. It fit tighter across the chest than a standard dress shirt, emphasizing his broad shoulders. Jarret would like it. Roland had looked good in it, too, though he had probably worn a size too large.

"You look-a spectacular." A meticulously dressed, gray-haired attendant stood behind Keefe, clasping his hands and smiling politely. "If-a this is not-a you, we have uh many other styles from which to choose." He immediately produced a white shirt and held it up for Keefe to see.

The attendant was right. The shirt wasn't Keefe style. In fact, standing before a fancy, triple mirror in a men's designer clothing shop, with an attendant waiting on him, wasn't him either. He had done it countless times with Jarret, but he had felt more like an attendant than a customer.

"Or-a this?" The attendant waved another shirt in the air.

"Thanks, but I think I'll just take this one. It's perfect. Oh, and another one in the slate color." Jarret wouldn't approve, but he just couldn't go home without something for Roland, too.

As he returned to the cobblestone street, he checked the time. He had spent more time in the shops than he realized. Thankful that he had a good sense of direction, he sped his steps back to the hotel.

Papa sat out on the balcony, smoking his pipe, the breeze carrying the fruity aroma into the room. Keefe tossed the shopping bags onto the bed and sat down to kick the tennis shoes off his hot feet.

A moment later, Papa stepped in, his gaze snapping to the bags. "Shopping, huh? What'd you get?"

"Uh . . . something for Jarret." He should've just said *some shirts*.

Papa grimaced. "Get anything for yourself?"

Keefe ran a hand through his hair. "No. I didn't really want anything, but I remembered Jarret asked for something." He felt guilty, sounded defensive. What difference did it make if he bought something for Jarret?

"Did you make those phone calls?"

The two phone calls he had forgotten flashed to the front of his mind. "Oh, shoot." Maybe that explained the feeling he couldn't identify.

Papa shook his head. "Talk to Jarret?"

"Yeah."

After a deep breath—Papa's attempt to control his temper—he let loose. "No more phone calls to Jarret. I brought you along to help me. You're going to help me."

The muscles in Keefe's forehead tensed. "But what if he needs to talk to me?"

"He doesn't need to talk to you. He's a big boy. He can take care of himself."

Some of Jarret's recent ideas played in Keefe's mind. Jarret counted on Keefe to rein in his wilder impulses before they got him into too much trouble. In fact, Keefe could not recall a single time Jarret had independently turned his mind away from a bad idea.

"Jarret needs me."

"Jarret doesn't need you."

"He does." Without words or explanations, they had always understood each other. "We've always been together. It's not the same with him and Roland. He's probably lonely and—"

Papa whipped his cowboy hat onto the bed with a violence befitting of the scowl on his face. "I don't care a continental what *you* think Jarret needs right now. You need to worry about yourself. As twins, you've always been hand in glove with him, so I understand if you're having a bit of separation anxiety, but this has got to stop. You spent every waking hour of the first few days here trying to call him. Now that he's talking to you, you're on the phone with him more than a cow chews its cud. I don't want to think I got me the wrong pig by the tail, bringing you instead of Roland. Are you even keeping up with your school assignments?"

Papa had a good eight years of college education and could communicate as intelligently as any doctorate-holding man, but when he got riled up, he had a tendency to use cowboy talk. His father and grandfather, both men of little formal education, had run a cattle ranch, so maybe that manner of speech came from them. Papa hadn't followed in their footsteps when he became an archaeologist, but he held to the cowboy look and, when angry, the talk.

"My school assignments? Oh, yeah. Sure." He hadn't given them a single thought.

"Give me the list." Papa stuck a hand out. "Who haven't you called?" He glanced at his watch. "It's what, two o'clock in California?"

Keefe fumbled through one pocket of his chinos then another. He found the list next to the receipt from the men's store.

Papa snatched it from his hand and scooted out to the balcony.

Keefe flopped onto the bed and gazed up at the floral design on the high ceiling. Papa was right. He did need to worry about his own responsibilities. And he needed to find himself. If he only knew how to look, he would find something of himself here in Italy, of that he was certain.

Papa stuck his head back in the room. "You can talk to Jarret once in the evening before bed, and that's it. No more shopping for him."

Chapter Twelve

Caitlyn

Standing behind her family's van, Caitlyn draped two plastic grocery bags loaded with miscellaneous camping supplies onto David's arms. "Follow Stacey and Priscilla," she said. "And tell them that's the last of it."

David toddled off in the general direction of their campsite.

No sooner did Caitlyn slam the van door shut when Zoe's mother pulled up. Two car doors flew open, and out popped Zoe and Caitlyn's new archenemy, Mya.

"Oh, this is going to be fun!" Mya squealed. She dropped her sleeping bag and pink duffle bag, clasped her hands together, and glanced around. She wore shorts, sandals, and a baby-pink t-shirt, all entirely inappropriate for camping. She'd think so, too, when the mosquitoes came out, or if she decided to actually take a hike through nature.

Caitlyn had dressed in layers, a pale-blue cotton shirt under a turquoise button-front shirt, old hiking boots, a long denim skirt, and bug spray.

Zoe, in jeans and a soft brown sweater, sauntered up to Caitlyn and nudged her. "Sorry," she whispered. "Mya asked for a ride. What could I say?"

"No. You could've said *no.*" Caitlyn narrowed her eyes, pretending to be angry.

"You're the one who invited her."

"I know." Caitlyn sighed.

After promising her mom that she'd come right back to help set up their tent, Zoe, Mya, and Caitlyn took a walk to check out the area.

People milled around everywhere, setting up tents or just goofing off. Kids from school, families from church, and others she didn't know. Peter and his dad had done a wondrous job. At one site, a dozen lawn chairs surrounded a big stack of wood and a fire pit with a little welcoming fire. A short distance from that they'd set up two rows of picnic tables, enough seating for the entire group to enjoy meals together. Peter's mom, Mrs. Brandt, and a few other moms spread out red-checked tablecloths and placed citronella candles on them to keep them from blowing away.

Mya stopped to talk with the moms while Caitlyn and Zoe strolled a short distance away, toward the road. Tags with familiar names marked campsites on both sides of the dirt road, as far as Caitlyn could see.

Excitement raced through her veins and made her want to jump or scream. She couldn't wait to see the bonfire area and more of her friends. Where was Peter . . . and Roland?

"Hey, Caitlyn!" Peter came up behind her.

"Oh, Peter!" Without thinking, she turned and flung her arms around him. She rarely ever hugged him, so he gave her a funny look.

"Sorry." She backed up and brushed his shirt. "I'm just so excited to be here."

He slapped her hand away. "Yeah, you're weird. But this is cool, huh?"

She leaned and whispered, "Where's Roland?" Then she glanced to see if Mya heard her. Mya stood watching a group of Fire Starter boys wrestle with a seriously old tent.

"Oh, he's ghosting." Peter peered over his shoulder.

His younger brother Toby ambled around tree trunks, his gaze apparently fixed on sunbeams streaming through the canopy of leaves. He wore a shirt with his full name on the front, and he carried a long stick. While only nine years old, he had the body of a twelve-year-old but the behavior and speech of a three-year-old.

"Hi, Toby," Caitlyn said.

Toby turned his big brown eyes to her but made no reply. He did that sometimes. The new surroundings probably overwhelmed his autistic mind.

Caitlyn looked at Peter again. "What do you mean *ghosting?*"

"He's not coming."

Her heart crumpled. "Not coming? Why? But you said he was. I thought we all helped with the Finns' house so his brother could come, too."

Toby shuffled toward Peter, whining, "Go fishing," in a pathetic voice. He latched onto Peter's arm and hung on him.

"I don't know." Peter tried shrugging Toby off but with no luck. "Don't ask me about it. I guess, Jarret didn't want to go so he decided not to go, too."

"Who?" Mya came up behind Peter.

"Roland." Peter pushed Toby away. "Stop hanging on me. Go find Mom."

Mya's smile turned into a pout. "He's not camping with us?"

"No." Peter motioned for them to follow. "I set up the girls' tent over here."

Caitlyn trailed the others. All the jittery excitement that had coursed through her veins whenever she'd thought about camping and Roland had gone.

"What do you think?" Peter flung out an arm and turned up a palm, indicating a big blue-green tent with yellow trim and screens on every side.

"It's taller than me," Mya said, making a beeline for the zipper door.

Caitlyn forced herself to smile. "Thanks for setting it up."

Zoe crawled in after Mya. Their giggles and voices carried as they talked about who would sleep where and how hard the ground felt.

Caitlyn watched them for a moment through a screened window then set out for her family's site. She still had to help set up their tent.

Peter went with her. "You should see what we did up on bonfire hill. We got—" His head spun. Then he took off, bolting toward the dirt road where a silver car had stopped. "Hey, you made it anyway," he shouted. Resting his arms on the open passenger-side window, he spoke with the passengers.

Unable to identify the car, Caitlyn stopped watching and strolled alone to her family's site to get the tent setup over with.

A few seconds later, the car crunched down the road, making a little dirty cloud. Peter shouted to someone and laughed.

Caitlyn sighed and reached for a tent pole. She hoped her enthusiasm would return even without the prospect of spending time with Roland.

Fifteen minutes later, Caitlyn stood next to her dad, both of them admiring the old tent they'd put up in record time.

"Well, that doesn't look too bad," Dad said, eyeing it strangely.

Caitlyn was about to comment on the bent tent stakes and frayed guy lines when a shadowy figure caught her attention. Her gaze traveled to the dirt road. And through the trees, she saw him.

Roland West!

Her mouth fell open, and her heart stopped.

For a moment, everything seemed to move in slow motion. A breeze played in the waves of his hair. A beam of sunlight reached his face, making his skin dazzling white against his gray hooded jacket. With Peter on one side and Jarret on the other, he strode across the dirt road, headed her way.

Caitlyn ran her hands through her hair and wiped the front of her skirt as she ran to Mom. "Mom, hey, can I go now?"

Mom's brows creased then her gaze shifted and she smiled. She probably caught a glimpse of the guys. She wouldn't have known Caitlyn's interest in Roland, but she knew Peter was her friend. "Fine. Have fun. I'll see you for dinner."

When Caitlyn turned, the guys had stopped their approach and stood in a circle. Mya had joined them. All pink, shapely, and blonde, she bounced on her toes and threw her arms about, gesturing wildly to emphasize whatever silly thing she had to say. Peter looked away, head shaking and eyes rolling, but both of the West boys gave her their full attention.

Zoe appeared at Caitlyn's side. She folded her arms. Her eyes gleamed like bronze spears in the sunlight. "Let the battle begin."

"What battle? How can I win against her?"

"You're not allowed to think like that. Come on. To the tent."

Caitlyn followed Zoe, stumbling on roots and lagging behind because she couldn't keep her eyes off Roland and Mya. Roland hadn't looked Caitlyn's way once.

A few minutes later, Caitlyn emerged from the tent wearing skinny, distressed jeans; Zoe's new hiking boots; and a fuzzy, forest-green sweater. Zoe had put gel or something in her hair, saying Caitlyn needed it to keep the long curls together. But Caitlyn refused the make-up. It just was not her, and it always made her eyes water. She could only imagine it causing more problems than good. Of course, slim, distressed jeans weren't her either.

Caitlyn tried not to feel self-conscious as she followed Zoe through the trees. Everyone wore jeans. Why shouldn't she? No one would think a thing of it.

They found the boys—and Mya—engrossed in conversation at the picnic tables. Jarret sat atop one, Mya on a bench, and Peter and Roland stood facing them. No one noticed their approach until Roland cocked his head to one side. He couldn't have heard their footsteps over Peter's and Mya's loud voices, but he did seem to sense them. He turned to face them, and his mouth fell open.

Zoe and Caitlyn joined the group.

Peter and Roland both checked Caitlyn out, Peter with an obvious stare, Roland with glances. Having never seen her in jeans before, they probably wondered why in the world she wore them now. And why jeans that emphasized her skinny legs. Maybe they even suspected she wanted to impress someone.

Caitlyn's cheeks burned. Feeling fake and exposed, she wanted to run back to the tent.

"Jeans, huh?" Peter's eyes snapped to hers. He grinned and gave a knowing look.

Mya stood and stretched. Roland stopped staring at Caitlyn, his gaze turning to Mya then to his brother.

"What else would she wear camping?" Jarret sounded annoyed, rude even. He gave Caitlyn an approving nod, his eyes roaming over her in a way that increased her discomfort.

"She usually wears dresses," Peter said, his tone mocking, ". . . even camping, if you can believe it."

"Skirts," she said but not loud enough for them to hear. She wished they would talk about something else. She shouldn't have put on the jeans. It was a bad idea. It really wasn't her, and this wasn't the attention she wanted. Yes, she wanted Roland to like her, but not for the way she filled her jeans.

"So what are we going to do out here all weekend long?" Mya bubbled, everyone turning to her.

Caitlyn exhaled. For the first time in her life, she appreciated Mya's talent for drawing attention.

"Are you kidding me? Haven't you ever gone camping?" Peter, always quick to enumerate the joys of camping, rattled off a list of all the fun things they could do.

Zoe leaned close to Caitlyn and whispered in her ear, "Aren't you going to introduce me to Roland's brother?"

"No," Caitlyn whispered back. "I don't know him that well."

"Well, he's cute," she whispered, eyes on him.

Caitlyn turned her back to the others and whispered to Zoe, "He's trouble." He was in the eleventh grade and new to River Run High, but he already had a bad reputation.

Zoe turned her back on them, too. "How can he be trouble when you told me he volunteered to help some guy build a house for his family? He sounds nice." She glanced over her shoulder and gave a flirty smile. "And he's so hot."

"Yeah, but he flirts with everyone. Are you really interested in someone like that?" Caitlyn looked him over, trying not to be obvious.

Jarret wore faded jeans ripped at the knees, black boots, an oversized red hoodie, and a black cord necklace. He had the hint of a goatee, and his hair—dark, curly, and worn in a ponytail—seemed very important to him. It looked as though he'd spent a lot of time on it, maybe even using some sort of hair product. And the way his dark eyes moved over Zoe, he totally looked like he fit the rumors.

"What are you girls talking about?" Mya, all silliness and bubbles, invaded their huddle.

"Nothing," Caitlyn snapped.

"What's *his* name?" Zoe nodded to indicate Jarret.

"That's Jarret, Roland's brother. He has a twin just as cute." Mya, not respecting their secretiveness, blurted it all out. She might as well have invited him to their huddle.

"You talking about me?" Jarret grinned, looking pleased.

"I have an idea," Zoe whispered to Caitlyn, her eyes still on him. "Why don't we—"

"Where's Toby?" Mrs. Brandt shouted. She jogged up to Peter and grabbed his arm, worry in her eyes.

Peter glanced to either side. "What? I sent him back to you."

"You were supposed to be watching him."

"I'll help find him," Caitlyn said. "Where have you looked?"

Mrs. Brandt welcomed Caitlyn's offer and soon Zoe, Mya, and Roland had offered, too.

"You girls take the mile-long trial." Peter pointed at it. "Me and the West boys will take the longer trails."

"Not me," Jarret said. "I got something to do."

"Why not you?" Roland looked calm but sounded miffed.

"I got something to do."

"What can you possibly have to do that's more important?" Roland growled, almost under his breath.

"You guys don't really need me for this, do you?" Amusement flickered in Jarret's eyes. He glanced to either side then reached into the front pocket of his hoodie. "I'm sure you can handle it." He pulled out a pack of cigarettes.

Roland stepped up to him and said something Caitlyn couldn't hear, but anger showed in his posture. Jarret hopped off the picnic table and stood face to face with his brother. They locked eyes. Were they going to fight?

"Forget about him." Peter grabbed Roland's shoulder. Peter was one of the biggest instigators Caitlyn knew, but he also had a way of rising above conflict.

Yielding to Peter's prompting, Roland turned and stepped away from Jarret. Then he muttered something to Peter.

A heartbeat later, Jarret lunged and flicked the back of Roland's head.

Roland jerked to face him.

Jarret laughed, challenge in his eyes.

Roland stood glaring for a second. Then he shook his head and walked away.

Roland and Peter went one way, Zoe, Mya, and Caitlyn another. They explained their mission to the boys from the Fire Starters and other friends they came across. Soon they had a scouting party, two and three to a group, all searching for Toby.

Their path crossed Peter and Roland's once. Peter was frowning, his face pink and sweaty. "Did you see him?" He kept cracking his knuckles.

"No." Caitlyn shared his anxiety.

Roland and Caitlyn exchanged sympathetic, worried looks. She hated that Toby was lost, but she liked working toward a goal with Roland, the way they had at the Finn's house. They were doing something for somebody else. They both cared. It felt good. She wished she and Roland could've been searching as a team, but she forced that selfish thought from her mind. They had to find Toby.

Zoe grabbed her hand and they continued down the trail. She took long steps, pulling Caitlyn along, until they gained a good distance from sandal-footed Mya.

"Don't worry," Zoe said. "We'll find Toby. Everyone's looking for him. The woods don't go on forever."

Maybe they didn't go on forever, but the Black Hills Forest was over a hundred miles long and over sixty miles wide, Peter had always boasted. Having a forest ranger for a father, Peter knew these things. And there were cliffs, canyons, gulches, fast streams, and deep lakes. Not to mention the wild animals. Caitlyn comforted herself with the thought that Toby had probably found something he liked and was standing still, fixating on it at this very moment. Someone would find him any minute now, and they'd all return to the campground where they could laugh about it while enjoying hotdogs around the fire.

"Once we find him, here's the plan . . ." Zoe peeked at Mya over her shoulder. "You and Roland. Me and Jarret. We'll do things together. We'll rent paddleboats and take walks." She smiled, her eyes sparkling.

"But Roland doesn't want a girlfriend." Caitlyn glanced at Mya. She had stopped and stood balancing on one foot, dusting off the other. She waved at Caitlyn, as if to say she was fine, before sliding her foot back into her sandal.

"We'll all just be friends," Zoe said. "I'll make suggestions for things to do. You'll second them, and we'll casually invite the West boys along."

"I don't know." It sounded too much like dating. Would she be allowed? Maybe if it were more of a group . . .

"You'll see. He'll like being your friend so much that he'll no longer be afraid of having a girlfriend."

"What about Mya?"

"Hmm. We'll come up with something." Zoe walked on, silent and thoughtful.

Chapter Thirteen

Jarret

Jarret took a few steps down the trail, glanced to make sure no one saw him, and then slipped into the woods. He leaned against a tree with a thick, knotted trunk and lit up. Taking a long drag off the cigarette, he began to relax. He exhaled and watched the smoke billow into a beam of sunlight and dissipate.

Camping no longer seemed like such a lame idea. A change of environment. A whole lot of girls. A way to keep his mind off Keefe playing it up in Italy. And something to do until he could get his first car. He hated waiting. But if he had to wait, he might as well have a distraction.

Too bad Keefe couldn't be with him. It felt wrong, them being apart. It really felt wrong, Keefe experiencing something he wouldn't experience for a long time. If ever. He should've been the one to go to Italy. If only Jarret's plan had worked.

His body tensed. He took another slow drag off the cigarette and let the smoke seep out his mouth and nose the way he'd seen it done in old movies. Then he shifted to a more comfortable spot on the tree trunk and stuck a thumb in his belt. His fingers brushed his cell phone.

What was Keefe doing now? Had he gotten the Italian shirt for him? He'd better have. Jarret flicked his cigarette to the ground, snuffed it out with the toe of his boot, and pulled up Keefe's number. The phone rang five times before Keefe answered.

"Hey." Jarret tried to sound indifferent though it made him jealous to hear the street sounds in the background.

"Hey, Jarret. What's up? Are you at the campground?"

"Yeah, yeah, I took your advice and I'm here. I didn't tell Roland I changed my mind until this morning. I banged on his bedroom door, all ready to go. I think I woke him out of a dead sleep." He laughed, remembering the stunned look on Roland's face. He'd been so flustered he didn't even shower, just dressed and jumped in the car, probably afraid Jarret would change his mind.

"Mr. Digby sure was annoyed."

Keefe laughed. "Mr. Digby? Why should he care?"

"Ah, he'd been carrying our camping gear back and forth from the basement to the car all day."

Keefe laughed again. "Poor old Mr. Digby. You ought to treat him better. But I'm glad you're there instead of all alone in the house. So how's it going?"

Someone off to the right called Toby's name.

Jarret slunk around to the left side of the tree. "It's all right. A lot of hot girls here." Maybe that would make Keefe jealous.

"Oh yeah?"

"Yeah, and I'm really into one of them. I think she likes me, too." Girls liked him. Keefe knew it. The fact had made him envious on more than a few occasions in the past. Being identical twins did not make them equally appealing to girls. "Who knows? Maybe me and her will get together, you know, maybe she'll be my first." That would make Keefe mad, make him wish he were here.

"Your first? What do you mean by that?" Keefe sounded worried.

Jarret grinned, pleased with himself. Yeah, Keefe was wishing he were here, wishing he could talk him out of the idea. "You know what I mean."

"I hope you don't mean what I think you mean."

Jarret twisted the toe of his boot on the cigarette butt, grinding it apart. His twin knew him well enough. He wouldn't be able to think of anything else. He would just keep wishing he hadn't gone to Italy, wishing he could be here to stop him.

"Jarret?" Keefe paused. "Don't go doing anything stupid. Don't go doing anything you'd be sorry for."

"Why would I be sorry for that?"

Keefe huffed into the phone, the way he did when something annoyed him and he didn't know what to say about it. "So what's everybody doing right now?"

"Nothing much. Some kid went missing. Everyone's looking for him."

"Wow. Who?"

"I don't know. Peter Brandt's little brother. I guess he's autistic and likes to wander."

"Aren't you looking for him, too?"

"No."

"Why not?" he shouted, making Jarret pull the phone from his ear. "Jarret, go look for that kid."

"More than two dozen people are looking for him. They don't need me."

"Yes, they do. Now go." A muffled sound came over the phone, as if Keefe had covered the phone to talk to someone. "Look, I gotta go. Let's talk again. I'll call you later. Help find that kid."

Jarret gritted his teeth as he ended the call. But he pushed off the tree and cut over to the trail, having in mind to do what Keefe commanded. Keefe was right. He should've been helping.

Distant voices sounded to either side. "Toe-bee . . . Toe-bee!" So Jarret strode down the path behind the campsites, the path that led to the river. It would've been one of the first places anyone would've thought to look, but at least he could say he made an effort.

Not being one to drag his feet, he strutted along at a good pace, fondling his pack of cigarettes as he neared the river. He'd wait until he got to the bank before he actually lit up, a reward for forcing himself to do something he didn't want to do.

Reaching the riverbank, he tapped a cigarette from the pack and dug the lighter from the pocket of his hoodie. No sooner had he lit up and exhaled a puff of smoke, when he glimpsed something strange on the rocks in the middle of the river.

The river was wide, a good forty feet across, and deep in places, at least according to Peter. Boulders peppered it. Water rippled in patterns around the largest boulder, a long and lumpy thing in the middle of the river. Something hung low off one side, something resembling a . . . shoe?

The cigarette slipped from Jarret's hand. Dread filled him. He crept to the edge of the riverbank, squinting to get a better look.

The strange object was gray and shaped sort of like a tennis shoe. It hung near the surface of the water, so it might have been something the river dragged up onto a jagged edge of the boulder. It could've easily been a trash bag or other piece of garbage. A good-sized branch stuck out the other side of the boulder, so things obviously caught on it.

Jarret sighed. He had no need to suspect the worst. For all he knew, someone could've found the boy already. Then again . . .

He scanned the area, finding himself alone at the river. He had no one to get a second opinion from, no one to advise him, and no one to go into the river and check in his place. If he didn't check, no one would.

"Hey!" he shouted, cupping a hand to the side of his mouth, "Hey, kid! Toby!"

The shoes, or whatever they were, didn't move.

"Toby! Is that you? You out there?" Feeling stupid for shouting at a boulder, he scanned the area again. He saw no one. If he was really going to do this, he should hurry: find a way out there, take a peek, and get back before anyone came around.

Other boulders littered the river, smaller ones that he could possibly use like a bridge to get out there. Chances were he'd end up wet. He glanced down at his new black Dupree boots and sighed, disgusted.

He snatched his cell phone, wallet, pack of cigarettes, and lighter from his belt and pockets. "If that's you, Toby . . ." He set his possessions on a dry rock. ". . . and you're making me come out there and get you . . ." He stepped onto the rock closest to the river's edge. ". . . you're gonna be in a heap of trouble."

A good leap got him to the next rock. Six more rocks would get him to the boulder in the middle of the river. Three jumps later, halfway to his destination, he saw the object clearly. Dirty, gray tennis shoes and—

His gut turned.

Skin. Ankles stuck out of the shoes, and the shoes hadn't moved at all. How would the kid have gotten out there? What could've happened to him?

Jarret attempted to glimpse the riverbank, but the rock under his feet shifted. If only someone else would come by. The last thing he wanted to do was find a-a-a body.

Teetering, he threw out his arms for balance. His gaze latched onto the ripples in the river.

Up and down. Rolling, rolling. His head grew light.

He couldn't do this. He wanted to pivot around and check the distance to the rock he had leapt from, but the horizon tilted. Besides, he had come this far. He should just do it. There was no one else.

Taking a breath, he locked his gaze on the next rock and forced himself forward. Now he stood where a jutting edge of the boulder hid the shoes, and the next rock set farther away than he cared to jump. He stooped, preparing for it. With a deep breath, he leaped.

His left foot landed first. And slid. No way was he gonna let himself get wet! He threw his arms out, but he still went down. His right knee and palms cracked hard on the rock with a jolt of pain. He let loose a stream of curse words as he steadied himself and got to his feet. Legs trembling, he jumped to the last rock. He made it to the boulder.

The constant motion of the river had worn a network of cracks and crevices into the five-foot long, chest-high boulder. He used them to climb to the top.

Then he saw him.

Toby lay stretched out on his tummy on the low, flat side of the boulder, all but hidden from the riverbank. Clutching one end of a long branch and dangling the other end in the water, he seemed oblivious that he had company.

"What're you doing, kid?"

Toby squinted up at Jarret. "Go fishing with me?" He had a high, childlike voice.

"Are you kidding me?" Jarret sneered. The kid acted like he hadn't a care in the world. "Don't you know every man, woman, and child in the campground is looking for you?"

Toby stared.

Did he understand English? "Come on. We're going back."

"No. Toby fishing." Toby returned his gaze to the stick in the water.

"Fishing, my foot," Jarret mumbled, glancing at the riverbank. Of course, no one was there. "Didn't you hear people calling your name? Why don't you answer? Don't you know your brother's looking for you?"

"Peter?"

"Yeah, Peter. Come on."

"Peter go fishing?"

"Yeah, that's right. Peter wants to go fishing with you." If that's what he wanted to believe, what it would take to get him back to land, well then, sure. Jarret reached a hand to the kid. "Toss the branch and come on."

Toby got up without help and put the branch behind his back. Only his shoes were wet, so he must've come over on the rocks.

"You a good jumper?" Jarret climbed down the way he had come up, using the narrow footholds.

Toby climbed to the top of the boulder and sat where Jarret had been.

With little room to maneuver, Jarret leaped for the nearest rock. His foot landed well, but his torso kept going. He had to jerk himself back to avoid toppling over. How would Toby ever make it?

Stick in hand, Toby eased himself down the boulder and stood with each foot on a little ledge. Slowly, he turned around, still clutching the stick.

"Why don't you lose the stick? You gonna be able to jump over here?"

Toby tilted his head, face to the woods.

Jarret leaped to the next rock and turned to coax Toby. "Well, come on."

Toby stared at the woods.

"Come on and jump." What was his deal? This was gonna take all day. "You made it over here, so you must be a good jumper."

"Good jumper?"

"Yeah. Drop the stick and let's see ya jump." He tried to sound peppy, like a kindergarten teacher, but irritation eked out in his tone.

"*My* fishing pole." Toby put the stick behind his back again, lurching forward.

"Careful!" Every muscle in Jarret's body tensed. "We don't want to get wet, so let's be careful. Now, come on and jump." He pointed to the rock.

Toby squatted a little, then he did it. He leaped and landed squarely on the rock, making it look effortless.

Jarret exhaled. "Good, good. Let's keep going." He leaped to the next one, and Toby followed. A few more leaps and the miserable situation would be over. He couldn't wait to give Peter a piece of his mind, maybe even a piece of his fist.

Landing on the next rock with ease, he opened his mouth to say something to encourage Toby.

From behind him came a shriek, a splash, and a spray of cold water.

Jarret spun around in time to glimpse Toby's hair and one hand before they disappeared under the water. Was the river that deep? Maybe he could get to his feet on his own. Maybe he could swim. Maybe he—

Jarret dove in after him. The cold water hit him with a shock. A current pushed against him. He opened his eyes.

Toby flailed in the greenish water. Not far. A few feet away.

Fighting the current, Jarret pushed through the water. He wrapped an arm around Toby's chest from behind and dragged him to the surface.

Toby gasped and spluttered.

Jarret struggled to keep Toby's head above water as he swam a few feet. His boot brushed the riverbed. He continued on a bit more until he was sure Toby would find footing.

"Stand up!" Anger came out in his tone. "Put your feet down. You're okay."

The second he let go, Toby thrashed in the water and gasped.

"Stand up!" Jarret wrapped his arms around Toby, forcing him to settle down. A few steps later, he lessoned his grip.

Toby grabbed him. Eyes on the woods and hands latched onto Jarret, he sloshed through the cold water. The instant they reached dry land, he began sniveling and breathing funny.

Jarret led him to big boulders in the shade and made him let go. "You're okay," he snapped, heart beating wildly, body trembling. His boots were ruined. He was drenched from head to toe. He did not want anyone seeing him like this.

He climbed the boulder Toby leaned against, peeled the wet hoodie off his cold body and wrung it out. The water formed a puddle and ran down the side of the boulder. "If you were my brother, I'd beat you for this. In fact, I just might—"

"Toby!" Peter dashed out of the woods, Roland at his heels.

Toby flung himself into Peter's arms and bawled.

Roland jogged to Jarret, relief on his face. "Thank God! What happened? Where'd you find him?" He looked Jarret over. "Are you okay?"

Jarret sneered, ready to answer with a snide remark, when Mya, Zoe, and Caitlyn burst onto the scene. They ran to Toby and Peter but every one of them glanced at him, too.

Caitlyn approached him first, followed by Zoe. "Wow, you found him." Their eyes held something like awe.

Jarret's anger subsided. "Yeah." They didn't need to know how begrudgingly he had done it, only that he *had* done it. *He* rescued Toby. "He was out there." He covered his cold chest with one arm and pointed to the boulders in the river. "Fishing."

"We looked out here. We didn't see him," Peter said, still coddling Toby. He had taken his jacket off and wrapped it around trembling Toby's shoulders.

"He was lying on the flat side of that boulder, the big one." He pointed again to indicate it. "His shoes were sticking out."

Roland and Peter mumbled to each other.

"Did you guys fall in?" Mya said. He'd seen her in school. She always came across like a girl who'd ask the obvious.

"Yeah."

"You look cold." She eyed his bare chest.

Roland unbuttoned his jacket. "Here take my jacket?"

Cold as he was, he accepted it and jumped off the rock to put it on.

"Well, let's get them back," Peter said. "And I need to call Dad. Who's got a cell phone?"

Jarret let Peter retrieve his phone, wallet, cigarettes, and lighter, glad that he had set them somewhere safe before going after Toby. Then he let Peter use his phone. And why not, he was a real hero.

Peter stared at him, frowning and pink-faced. "Thanks, man. I don't know how to thank you for something like this. Anything could've happened to him. He could've drowned. You . . . you saved his life."

Jarret's throat muscles tightened, making it impossible to speak, so he only nodded and walked away.

Chapter Fourteen

Caitlyn

Caitlyn stopped at the second row of picnic tables, cradling four bottles of ketchup and one of mustard, two saltshakers and a hot sauce, ready to complete the condiment arrangements . . . when her eye caught him.

Roland stood with the others. Practically everybody in the campground had gathered around the campfire. Roland smiled.

Her heart swelled with emotion. A saltshaker rolled from her arms to the table. She sighed. If only he'd meant the smile for her. People blocked her view, so she couldn't see whom he looked at. Probably Jarret. Roland must have felt pride and admiration. They all did.

On the way back from the river, Zoe had walked beside Jarret, asking him questions and hanging on his every word. Mya ran ahead to get towels—Zoe's idea. Roland had given Jarret his jacket then carried Jarret's wet shirt. As the other searchers got word of Toby's rescue, they converged by the campfire, flocking around Jarret and wanting the details. Jarret must've retold the story ten times, each time with a little more enthusiasm, an added joke, or a detail he'd neglected to mention earlier. He finally put his hands up and said he needed a shower.

Poor Toby. He'd clung to Peter's arm all the way from the river to the campsite, repeating in a sorrowful voice, "Toby go home." Mrs. Brandt finally took him home.

Somewhere in her mind, Caitlyn knew that God had been with Toby, keeping him safe. God must've had a reason for letting him wander off. He knew they would find Toby and that Jarret would rescue him. He knew all things.

Caitlyn carried salad bowls to the picnic table and found herself scanning the group by the campfire. God knew all things. He already knew her future husband. Her gaze flitted from face to face.

Being two months shy of fifteen and four years from graduation, she really shouldn't have, but she thought about it all the time. She loved children and wanted to be a mother. She knew, for a fact, someday she would marry.

Mindlessly, she reached for a bag of barbequed potato chips and ripped it open. *Please, Lord, direct the steps of my future husband.*

Roland had been glued to his brother's side since the rescue, but she couldn't find him now. Half a dozen boys, all from the Fire Starters, stood in a circle talking. Mya's laughter carried over the chatter. Where was she? Girls sat in lawn chairs around the campfire. Other teens walked nearby. Someone ran. Zoe and Jarret stood amongst the trees just outside the campsite, deep in conversation.

When Mya laughed again, Caitlyn saw her. Blonde curls shimmering under a patch of sunlight. Eyes lit with joy. She and Roland stood together behind the group of Fire Starters. His back was to Caitlyn, so she couldn't see the expression on his face. Did Mya's flirting embarrass him, or did he like it? If he liked flirty girls like Mya, he wouldn't like Caitlyn.

Caitlyn sighed. Maybe she wasn't his type.

She carried the open bag of chips to the end of the row of tables, hoping for a better view. If only she could see his face.

"Caitlyn," Dad hollered from the grill.

The bag slipped from her hands, chips spilling onto the picnic table. Caitlyn blushed as if caught doing something wrong. "Yes?"

Mr. Brandt and Father Carston, their parish priest, stood with Dad, each of them holding a red plastic cup. "Why don't you get our guest of honor?" Dad used a spatula to point to Jarret.

"Okay." Caitlyn scooped chips back into the bag, rounded the picnic tables, and weaved through the crowd. Her gaze drifted to Roland and Mya.

Mya giggled. Roland stood with his hands in the front pockets of his jeans. They both stared at something on the ground.

A few steps later, Caitlyn saw what held their attention. *Peter.* The goofball lay on the ground, squirming, clutching his chest, and moaning ridiculously. Mya's laughter reached hysteria. Roland laughed, too, in his own restrained way. Then he turned his head.

His eye caught Caitlyn.

Her face warmed and she tripped. She couldn't play it off—they were less than ten feet apart—so she came over.

Roland gave the hint of a smile. "Peter's telling us how his father rescued a man from a coyote last year."

"Peter exaggerates," Caitlyn said.

Peter continued to tell his story, from the ground, but Roland looked at her.

"We're ready for lunch," Caitlyn said. "I'm getting your brother."

"Oh." He glanced toward the strip of trees between campsites, to where Jarret and Zoe stood.

Caitlyn walked away to fulfill her task, watching her step this time. She imagined she felt Roland's gaze, but he could've been staring at his brother.

Jarret leaned a shoulder against a tree. Zoe rested a palm, shoulder high on the same tree. Her eyes shifted to Caitlyn. Jarret glanced over his shoulder, his hand swinging to his side. Had they been holding hands? She hardly knew him.

"Are you guys hungry for lunch?" Caitlyn said. "We're waiting for the guest of honor."

Jarret grinned and pushed off the tree. "I guess that's me."

"I'm starved." Zoe slunk past Jarret, giving him a subtle smile, and linked arms with Caitlyn. "After lunch we're going on the paddleboats."

"We are? Who's *we*?" They cut through the crowd.

Zoe glanced over her shoulder. Jarret strutted along behind them. "All of us," she said then she whispered, "Remember the plan."

"But look . . ." Caitlyn nodded to indicate Roland and Mya. Mya motioned for Roland to follow her to the table. Roland—Caitlyn could gag—obeyed.

"Hurry." Zoe walked faster. "You'll sit next to him."

Zoe and Caitlyn had almost reached the picnic tables. People pushed past them, someone bumping Caitlyn. Groups of friends took seats together, filling up the closest row of tables within seconds.

"Don't worry. We'll sit over there." Zoe dragged Caitlyn to the other row. The parents had already claimed the tables nearest the grill. Little kids climbed onto the benches near them. Caitlyn's sister Stacey sat towards the middle of the row, inching over every time another friend joined her.

Caitlyn turned to find Roland.

Zoe jerked her hand. "Sit. Quick."

They plopped down onto a half-empty bench, staking their claim at a table. Zoe gave a triumphant grin. But they still didn't have Roland at the table.

Jarret stooped over a cooler then sat across from Zoe. "Wanna Coke?" He slid dripping cans to her and Caitlyn.

Teenage boys with the Fire Starters sat on either side of him, one of them patting his back, the one directly across from Caitlyn. The one in Roland's seat.

Caitlyn frowned. Still . . . no one had taken the seat next to her, on the side opposite Zoe. Roland could sit—

Someone bumped her on that side.

"Sorry, Caitlyn." Stacey had scooted all the way to her, friends on her other side, leaving no space for Roland.

Lips pursed and a scheming look in her eyes, Zoe glanced up and down the table. Few empty seats remained.

Then along came Roland, Mya at his heels.

"Hey, have seat," the Fire Starter across from Caitlyn said to Roland. "You probably want to sit by your brother." He jumped up.

"Well, that was nice," Caitlyn said aloud to no one in particular.

Zoe leaned on her shoulder. "Perfect."

Roland stared at the empty seat then looked at Mya.

No! Caitlyn could've screamed! *No chivalry. Let her find her own seat.*

"There's room for us both," Mya said, lifting a bare leg over the bench.

An uncharitable thought concerning splinters and bare skin came to Caitlyn's mind. She dismissed it at once. She wasn't like that. She really wasn't. *Oh, why did Mya have to sit there?*

~ ~ ~

"Come. On. What are you doing?" Zoe opened her eyes so wide the whites showed around her honey-brown irises. She glanced over her shoulder at Jarret as he walked away. "Remember the plan?"

Caitlyn shrugged. She had an armful of dirty serving dishes, a pan of soapy water in her scope, and no intention of joining the group. "I told Mom I'd help clean up."

Zoe's eyes grew wider. "Can't we do that later?"

Jarret shouted, "Come on, Zoe," and disappeared down a trail. Most of the kids had gone off, some to play football, others to the paddleboats. Roland got swept away with the Fire Starters . . . and Mya.

"You go ahead. I'll catch up."

Zoe huffed, flipped her hair as she turned away, and sauntered toward the trail Jarret had taken.

Caitlyn strolled to the dishwashing station and stooped to position her armload on a stack of dirty dishes. A serving spoon slipped from the table, smacked against her skirt, and landed on the ground.

Today, for the first time ever, she had not enjoyed lunch. Why had she invited Mya? Mya spent the whole time bumping into Roland, giggling at every little joke, and speaking in her whispery Marilyn Monroe voice. Caitlyn couldn't bear another moment of Mya and Roland.

She couldn't compete with Mya. She wasn't bubbly and flirty, and she didn't dress to draw attention to her body. Caitlyn brushed her skirt where the spoon had touched it, glad she'd slipped away and changed out of the jeans. Long ago, she'd made up her mind: she wanted a guy to like her, knowing the real her.

Her foot kicked something on the ground. *Oh yeah, the serving spoon.* As she squatted for it, the hair on her neck bristled.

A hand latched onto the spoon and snatched it before her finger touched it.

"Can I help?" A voice in her ear. Breath on her neck.

She gasped, and her heart flopped in her chest.

Roland squatted beside her, his gray eyes sparkling in a mottled beam of sunlight. He handed her the spoon.

"You want to help *me*?" She glanced to either side, expecting to see Mya.

They stood up together. Alone.

"Yeah." He lowered his head and spoke in a low, spellbinding voice while peering up at her through magnetic steel-gray eyes. "Actually, I've got an ulterior motive." Without explaining, he broke the connection and stepped to the tub of rinse water.

"You can help, but you have to tell me your ulterior motive." Caitlyn dunked a few dirty dishes into the soapy dishwater and grabbed the scrubber.

"Okay, but you can't tell."

Her heart fluttered. He wanted to share a secret with her! "I won't tell." She scrubbed a plate in the warm sudsy water.

"I'm hiding." He took the soapy plate from her hands and plunged it into the rinse water.

Although he was a guy of few words, Caitlyn expected him to say more. She scrubbed and scrubbed the hotdog plate, waiting for the rest of his explanation. "Aren't you going to tell me who you're hiding from? I am, after all, letting you help me wash dishes."

Roland glanced at her. "Okay, well . . ." He set the first plate on the towel next to the rinse tub and took the hotdog plate, even though she was still scrubbing it. "I'm sure she's very nice."

She listened, waiting for him to go on, dying for him to say her name. *Mya. You're hiding from Mya! You don't like her!*

"Who do you mean by *she*?" Caitlyn dared to say.

He stared blankly into her eyes for a moment. Then he looked away. "I don't want to say." He took the spatula from her, but she had only been holding it. He glanced at it, at the black charred gunk on the blade, and gave it back.

Gazing at the spatula, she debated pressing him further. Could he mean Mya? Or did some other girl like him, too?

He took the spatula from her again and the scrubber. "I'm sure she's nice. I'm sure she'd be a good friend." He leaned close, not making eye contact but bumping her arm, and submerged the dirty spatula in the soapy water. "But I think she wants to be more than friends."

Caitlyn sucked in a breath. She flashed back to the Finn's house, to eavesdropping on Peter and Roland. *Peter's voice: "Why not make her your girlfriend . . ." Roland saying, "I don't want a girlfriend."*

She frowned. "And you don't? You don't want to be more than friends?"

"Not really. I'm not . . . I'm not ready for that." He faced her, a playful glint in his eyes. "You want to hide out with me?"

. . . not ready for that. . . . hide out with . . . ? She stared at him, her mind reeling as she tried to understand his motives. "I . . . um . . . sure."

$$Chapter\ Fifteen$$

Keefe

Keefe sat in the front passenger seat of the Mercedes, Papa's rental, rubbing his chin and searching his memory. Tall evergreens cast long shadows on the lonely road. A tile-roofed house of pale stones and arches sat back from the road, between a vineyard and a field. Blue hills stretched across the distant horizon.

"You worried about something?" Papa, driving with a single palm on the steering wheel, gave him a sideways glance. Wind blew through his open window, ruffling his graying hair.

"Worried? No, er, yeah. I think I forgot to do something."

"Like what?"

"I don't know. Can't remember." The thought had plagued him for the past half hour, ever since they'd left their hotel room. A phone call? No, that wasn't it. He'd snuck off to call Jarret first thing in the morning but got no answer. Papa hadn't given him any work this morning. No, it definitely wasn't a phone call.

He lifted his arm and sniffed his armpit. No. He remembered deodorant. It was something else, something important. Or . . . maybe . . . a warning. Yeah, it almost felt like a warning, like something critical would soon happen to him.

No. He sneered at the idea. It was probably nothing. He hadn't slept well. He just needed rest. Keefe reclined the seat and took a slow, deep breath.

"Yeah, why don't you relax?" Papa said. "We've got an hour and a half yet. Take a nap."

It was a two-hour drive to their destination, Bagno di Romagna. They had set out from Florence around ten o'clock, the morning sunlight shining at an angle that gave the city a gloriously ancient appearance. Keefe pictured the great Renaissance men up early and hard at work . . . Michelangelo, in his twenties, with a chisel in his hand as he sculpted David . . . Vasari painting one of his awe-inspiring masterpieces at the request of the Medici family . . . Michelozzo designing the Palazzo Medici palace . . .

"I feel like we've missed something, too," Papa said. He hadn't had much to say since they hit the road. They had faced too many dead ends on his assignment. He was probably frustrated. "I don't mind those museums where stored collections are arranged in chronological order or by schools of art. They make the job easier." Papa shook his head. "But those ones with pieces stashed in one storeroom or another . . . no particular order, where you almost seem to stumble across pieces by accident . . ."

He shook his head again. They had found only one more of his client's collection and had gained very few leads. "I have a good feeling about Bagno, though."

"I don't." Keefe lowered his window to catch a breeze. The turbulence in his soul had moved to his chest. He sucked in a deep breath of sweet, fresh air. Why wouldn't the feeling pass? Something was coming. Something was going to happen.

Closing his eyes, Jarret's face flashed in his mind. Maybe Jarret needed him, needed his counsel. Sometimes they sensed things about each other even over a distance. He could predict Jarret's moods as easily as a weatherman could predict a storm. Did that explain the feeling? The warning?

Why hadn't Jarret answered his cell phone this morning? Why hadn't he called back to tell him if the lost boy had been found? Was he serious about making some girl his first? He'd regret it. Somewhere inside, he knew right from wrong. Maybe he only said it to make Keefe worry. Or maybe he didn't care about doing the right thing. Jarret cared about himself. He knew himself, who he was and what he wanted.

A twinge of envy disturbed Keefe. Every day in Italy made it clearer. He had no idea who he was or what he wanted. At age sixteen, two years from adulthood, shouldn't a guy know what he wanted out of life, what was important to him? Maybe the inner turmoil had nothing to do with Jarret or forgetting something or lack of sleep. Ever since visiting the museums, excitement and expectation had coursed through his soul, building daily as if preparing him for something.

A gentle breeze blew through the window, soothing him. He sighed, slouched down in the seat, and pulled his hair over his eyelids to cut the light.

Preparing him . . . for something . . . What about Jarret? Jarret had Roland . . . No. Never listened to Roland. Roland should've been here in Italy . . . Michelangelo with a chisel in his hand . . .

~ ~ ~

Keefe's head jerked. He snapped his eyes open.

A strong breeze flung locks of hair across his face. The road curved like a snake preparing to strike. Papa drove fast—too fast!

Keefe's stomach leaped. He latched onto the dash.

Papa chuckled. "Did you have a nice nap?"

"Are we in some kind of hurry?" His stomach twisted at the view: a sharp drop to his right, a road lower down, and green mountains beyond. He tried focusing on the mountains.

Papa rounded another curve, picking up speed. "Eh, we're a bit behind schedule. But that's your fault. So hold onto your lunch. I don't want you shooting the cat in the rental."

"You're blaming me? I'm not driving. Aren't there speed limits out here?"

"We got a late start on account of you." Papa rounded another curve, the road going steadily downward.

"Me? What'd I do? I didn't think we had a schedule."

Papa threw a sideways glance. "This isn't a leisure trip. We have appointments in Bagno di Romagna. With you sneaking off to call Jarret this morning, we got a late start."

Keefe's face warmed. He thought Papa had bought his excuse when he'd said he needed some air.

"We're almost there." Papa took his eyes off the twisty road. "When we get into town, I'm going to the basilica, and you're going to make phone calls. We're supposed to meet with two people today. We have an appointment with one, which you'll have to change since we're going to be late. The other hadn't set a time. Give them the option of today or tomorrow."

"Okay. Where're you going to be?"

Papa took his eyes off the road again and smirked. "Aren't you listening to me? I'm going to the basilica. Catch up with me there."

"How will I find it?"

Papa grinned, amusement in his eyes. "Can't miss it. Look for the clock tower. It's not far from our hotel."

"Watch the road!" Certain dread overcame him.

~ ~ ~

Bagno di Romagna, Italy.

Rivers and lakes, lush hills and mountains surrounded the town. Nearby forests gave the air a pure, clean scent. Fresh thermal waters made it a famous thermal resort.

Keefe gazed out the open car window, soaking in the peaceful energy.

They drove down a road bordered with low rock walls and decorative bushes. People strolled along clean sidewalks under the shade of trees. Pale buildings with red-tiled roofs, arched walls, and flower boxes under windows added to the old-world beauty of Bagno. The place gave a feeling of health, life, and renewal.

Papa left Keefe at the hotel so Keefe could make phone calls.

White sunlight flooded through the glass balcony door of their second-story hotel room. Beds, square and tightly made. A shiny wood floor. The room had a clean, antiseptic feel to it.

Keefe sat on the bed and flipped through folders, searching for the names and numbers of the people he needed to call. He wanted to explore. He really did. But the turbulence in his soul wouldn't allow him to rush for anything.

He grabbed the landline, punched the first number, and stretched out on the bed.

~ ~ ~

After making the second call, he hung up the phone and sat up.

What was Jarret doing now? Given the time difference between Italy and South Dakota, it would be early morning there. He couldn't call, and he shouldn't think about it.

Keefe returned the phone to the dresser and went to the bathroom to freshen up.

His hair hung to his shoulders in a mess of dark, wild curls. He hadn't bothered fixing it back today, and the wind had had its way with it for most of the two-hour drive. Running his fingers through it, he met with tangles. With a shrug, he pulled it into a ponytail and splashed water on the top and sides.

During the whole trip, he had rarely scraped a razor over his jaw, but he could only see a trace of growth, not enough to bother with. So he brushed his teeth, renewed his deodorant, and set out.

The mild, high-seventy-degree weather refreshed him. Most of the people he passed on the sidewalks smiled or nodded. He nodded back. He kept his eyes open for the clock tower, thinking he ought to see it rising above other buildings. After strolling down a few streets and not seeing it, he finally asked directions.

"Santa Maria Assunta?" the old man he had stopped repeated. He pointed over his shoulder. "Sì, è nella piazza."

A few minutes later Keefe stood in the piazza.

When Papa had said *basilica*, Keefe pictured the spectacular Florence basilicas, each one a masterpiece of Renaissance architecture. He hadn't pictured this, and only after verifying it with two passersby could he believe it.

The Basilica of St. Maria Assunta, while massive in size, was an old and unassuming building. It had a medieval Romanesque façade of uneven gray bricks, a few high narrow windows, a circular window in the front, and there—the bell tower. Tall and reaching to the clouds, the bell tower cast a long shadow on the piazza.

Keefe mounted the steps, yanked open the door in the arched Romanesque doorway, and stepped inside. A sign with the words *miracolo* and *eucaristia* hung in the vestibule.

As he entered the nave, he stopped trying to translate the sign. Simplicity, silence, and a strange peace surrounded him.

People, probably waiting for Mass, sat in plain brown pews. Several high arches opened to nooks on each side, where long white candles burned before statues and pictures.

With an eye for Papa's client's collection, he gazed at the few Florentine works of art in the church: a colorful nativity in a gold frame, a terracotta relief, a polychrome statue of a female saint . . . No, Papa wouldn't have much to look through here. Maybe they had other pieces in a—

His heart skipped a beat at what he saw next, and he found himself drawn forward for a better look.

Upon the altar stood an ornate reliquary of silver and gold, but he couldn't make out what it held. Everyone else seemed used to it, seemed to know what it meant. What did it mean? Why was it on the altar?

He inched down the main isle, eyeing the reliquary, a strange anticipation growing within him with each step.

No one appeared to notice him. No one made a sound. All eyes seemed fixed upon it. Upon what? He drew nearer, nearer until he realized what he saw.

Blood! The reliquary displayed a white linen cloth with drops of what looked like fresh blood. Why would there be—

All else faded from view. The silence deepened. Golden, pulsating light appeared like a great halo around the bloody cloth. The light expanded to the extent of his peripheral vision, inviting him spiritually to the Blood.

Suddenly, nothing else mattered. Keefe neither could nor wanted to look away. No one needed, now, to tell him upon whose Blood he gazed.

The golden light pulsated around him, through him. Waves of merciful love washed over him.

He fell to his knees, transfixed by the penetrating gaze of Christ. God loved him. Loved him. As if he alone existed in the world. The Lord had been waiting for him for so long, waiting, finally drawing him here to this place to show him this sign of His love.

His Precious Blood.

Christ loved him so intensely that He came down from heaven and shed His blood to save him.

Keefe yielded to the gentle waves of Christ's love. Motionless, silent, gaze fixed—

A hand landed on his arm.

Keefe gasped but couldn't break his gaze.

"Keefe." Papa stooped beside him and whispered in his ear, "Come on into the pew."

How long had he been kneeling here? Keefe yielded to his father's prompting, letting Papa lead him to a pew in the middle of the church.

The golden rays faded and disappeared. The miraculous bloody cloth remained on the altar, but Keefe lost the profound awareness of the Lord's presence. The feeling had moved inward, so he bowed his head and let Jesus speak to his heart.

"I am with you always."

The words reverberated deep within his soul. Then, surrounded by a mantle of mercy, Keefe saw things of himself, things he hadn't wanted to but needed to see, things long hidden, long ignored. Sorrow welled up inside, and he wept.

~ ~ ~

Sometime later, they left the church in silence. Once outside, Papa had said one thing about it and never brought it up again.

"I felt it, too."

Disjointed thoughts scrambled through Keefe's mind, but it wasn't something he wanted to or even could talk about. Not yet. The experience had touched him too deeply, had been too profound. Words could not describe it. Somewhere inside he felt a determination to return the love he had only begun to realize God had for him.

"Listen," Papa said, standing by a huge decorative planter outside the church. "I need to talk to someone at the rectory. Why don't you take a walk? What time is our appointment?"

"Uh." Keefe struggled to reign in his thoughts. "Four o'clock. And the other appointment's tomorrow at noon."

Papa nodded. "That's fine. Meet me at the hotel at three." He strode back to the church.

Having no idea what to do with himself and hours to do it, Keefe walked. It would feel good to stretch his legs and breathe the fresh air. On the other side of the piazza, he came to a road and a sidewalk that ran along a river. He passed hotels, a playground, park benches, and long strips of grass, all the time moving farther from the river.

When he reached the end of town, to where only fields stretched out in the distance, he decided to head back, but then something stirred his soul.

He closed his eyes and turned his heart to God. The love of God, the Spirit of God, spoke to him without words.

Wanting to return love for love, on impulse he whispered a promise. *I will listen to Your voice. I will live knowing You are with me and that You love me, knowing that You shed your blood for me. I will not forget, no matter whom I'm with or what temptation I face.*

He made this promise, knowing well that Jarret would be his greatest source of temptation. He could no longer go along with Jarret's bad schemes just to keep him from doing worse things.

Keefe turned and headed back.

Chapter Sixteen

Caitlyn

"I think we're all done here," Mom said, smiling at Roland and Caitlyn.

After washing the camp dishes, Roland and Caitlyn had helped Mr. Brandt and Mom with little things like taking the garbage to the dumpster, getting ice, and rearranging camp chairs. Roland barely spoke two words except for a polite *Yes, ma'am* or *Yes, sir*, which made Caitlyn like him that much more.

"Appreciate the help," Mr. Brandt said, "but you probably want to catch up to the others. Where are they now? Paddleboats?"

"Yeah, um . . ." Roland stuffed his hands in his jacket pockets and gave Caitlyn a communicative sort of glance that she didn't understand. Maybe he didn't want to catch up to the others. They were, after all, hiding.

"I don't want to go on the paddleboats. Maybe we'll just take a walk," Caitlyn blurted out, hoping she'd read Roland right.

Mom blinked. Had it occurred to her, just now, that Caitlyn liked Roland?

Mom stared. The courtship principles probably began scrolling through her mind. Would she say no? She wouldn't know that Roland had no interest in having a girlfriend.

Mom blinked again. Then she smiled. "Why don't you take the girls? I'm sure they'd love to go exploring."

My sisters? Priscilla was ten years old and Stacey seven. Caitlyn would have to watch them, and if they did catch up to the others, they wouldn't be able to do anything. She opened her mouth to protest.

"Sure, Mrs. Summer." Roland nodded at Caitlyn. "They can come."

The four of them set off down a path under the shade of quaking aspen and paper birch trees. There couldn't be more beautiful woods than those in South Dakota's Black Hills. Roland and Caitlyn strolled without words. Priscilla and Stacey lagged a few yards behind, talking incessantly.

A few minutes into their walk, Roland stopped. He looked from Priscilla to Stacey. "You guys want to sneak through the woods?"

Stacey giggled. Priscilla squinted up a Roland. They whispered to each other then faced him again. Priscilla nodded.

Roland nodded. "There's a little trail here." He pointed. A skinny ponderosa pine stood at the entrance of a deer trail. "Maybe if we're quiet, we'll see some animals."

Roland took the lead, moving like a Sioux Indian, stepping on rocks and bare patches of ground, making no sound at all.

Being quiet didn't come naturally to Caitlyn or her sisters. Her sisters hadn't stopped talking, and their voices sounded louder under the thick canopy of leaves.

"Look, Priscilla, a beetle."

"Caitlyn, can I keep this rock?"

"I think Indians used to live back here . . ."

"Shy Ann Indians."

"No, Dakota Indians."

"There's no such thing. It's Lakota Indians."

"No, it's not. It's not South Lakota. It's South Dakota."

A branch snapped under Caitlyn's boot. Roland glanced. She must've stepped on every branch or twig in her path. She stumbled twice, shrieking each time.

After a while, Roland stopped and turned around. Caitlyn's sisters stopped talking and looked at him. He shoved his hands in the front pockets of his jeans, which Caitlyn began to think he did when something made him uncomfortable. "Maybe we can sneak better, quieter."

Pricilla and Stacey nodded, peering up at him.

"And you." His steel-gray eyes swiveled to Caitlyn. "See the rocks?" Big, smooth rocks littered the landscape. He glanced in the direction of one.

Caitlyn nodded.

"Try to step on those. And when you need to step on the ground, watch for twigs."

"Watch for twigs?" She continued nodding.

"Yeah. Don't step on twigs. People can hear you a mile away."

"Oh, I . . ." She pressed her lips together. Her clumsiness wouldn't push him away, would it? "Sorry."

He gave her a little smile.

Her heart did a little dance.

She tried to follow his advice, creeping along silently for some time. Then it happened. She knew it would. A rock she hopped onto expecting to land silently was not a rock at all but rather a big hollow branch partly covered in pine needles. It gave way under her foot. She sailed forward, flinging her arms out to catch herself. Pine needles cushioned her fall.

She lay on her face, stunned.

"Are you okay?" Roland stooped beside her.

Humiliated, she moaned and buried her face in her arms. "I'm sorry. Everyone in the forest probably heard that." She glanced to catch his expression.

He smiled and stuck out his hand. "That's okay. You were doing great until . . ."

Caitlyn took his hand. "Yeah. I'm a bit . . ."

"Caitlyn's clumsy," her sisters said together then giggled behind their hands.

Roland stifled a laugh as he yanked her up. He pulled a pine needle from her hair.

Still holding his hand, she used her other hand to check her hair. More pine needles. Leaves. Something she couldn't identify. Embarrassed, she offered a shy smile.

Stacey and Priscilla guffawed without restraint.

Roland chuckled, too. Holding hands and laughing, they picked dead leaves and pine needles from Caitlyn's hair, bonding for a moment. Then their hands drifted apart and they moved on.

Before long, scaly-trunked ponderosa pines rose up all around them, and the woods thinned. They walked on a pine needle carpet. A grassy area and the glistening lake showed through the farthest pines.

They soon reached the edge of the woods that overlooked the lake and the paddleboats.

"Let's stay behind the trees," Roland said, leaning against one and squinting at the lake.

Stacey and Priscilla giggled, each finding their own place from which to spy.

Paddleboats drifted on the shimmering lake. Caitlyn couldn't make out most of the people in them, but Mya's shiny blonde hair and Peter's golden hair stood out. They shared a paddleboat. Caitlyn laughed. She could almost see Peter's eyes rolling. "That girl's such a diva," he said whenever he heard her talk in her whispery voice.

"Peter must've got stuck with—" Roland shut his mouth and gave Caitlyn a wary glance.

Then they cracked up together.

They watched the paddleboats for a few minutes, until Caitlyn's sisters broke out in an argument over a little white rock. Roland suggested they move on.

"I'm hungry," Stacey said.

"Me, too," Priscilla said, eyes on Roland. "Which way goes back?"

"It's probably close to dinnertime," Caitlyn said.

Roland nodded and took the lead again. Caitlyn followed, picking her steps carefully, attempting to make no noise and to avoid another embarrassing fall.

Before long, they stepped out of the trees and onto the site with the campfire and lawn chairs. Voices sounded and a feminine laugh rang in the air. Mya's laugh?

Roland leaned and whispered in Caitlyn's ear, "Um, hey . . . See ya later."

Caitlyn turned to Roland.

He was gone.

The group returned. They traipsed onto the campfire site and dispersed. Some headed for the bathrooms, others sat at the picnic tables and camp chairs. Peter wandered through all the campsites then came and sat next to Caitlyn at a picnic table.

"Where's Roland?" His mouth curled up in a crooked grin.

Caitlyn made a casual glance to each side. "I don't know."

"Why didn't you go paddle-boating?"

She shrugged. "Not interested."

"Was Roland with you?" His grin grew slyer.

Not sure if Roland wanted anyone to know what he'd been up to, she played dumb.

Later, she made her sisters promise not to talk about it. Roland never showed up for dinner, and his brother Jarret disappeared after they ate. Both of them reappeared after everyone gathered around the campfire. Roland didn't sit near her, but he threw a couple of glances her way, leaving her to wonder . . . Did he like her as more than a friend?

~ ~ ~

The next day, Caitlyn wore her denim jumper and felt much more herself. Yesterday's sneaking with Roland left her with a happy spirit. Toby and Mrs. Brandt had returned, increasing her joy, and so everyone went fishing in the afternoon. Jarret and Zoe wandered off by themselves twice, taking long walks. Caitlyn noticed them holding hands once. She sighed. Mom would never let her go off alone with Roland.

Roland gave most of his attention to Jarret, and the rest to Peter, though Mya clung to him like an old dryer sheet. She, in her yellow board-shorts and striped shirt, seemed to have renewed her efforts to gain his attention. She sat next to him at every meal, walked with him when the group went hiking, and hovered by him at the river.

Caitlyn's happy spirit diminished.

Evening drew near. The air grew thick with anticipation so tangible it gave her goose bumps. Everyone looked forward to the bonfire, the best part of the annual campout. The boys had gone off with Mr.

Brandt after dinner to set it up. The girls cleaned off picnic tables, washed dishes, and prepared snacks.

Under a sky streaked with yellow and orange clouds, they carried blankets and coolers through aspen, birch, and pine trees down the path that led to Bonfire Hill—the name they had given the hill some years ago. Music and loud voices carried though they couldn't see the hilltop through the trees. The hill inclined gradually to a flat top of mown grass. In the middle of it stood the wood for the bonfire, tall and awe-inspiring. People had already arranged blankets and lawn chairs around it.

Zoe stopped at a distance from the other blankets, closer to the edge of the woods. She knelt gracefully to arrange her red plaid blanket. "Come sit by us. Put your blanket there." She pointed.

"Us? You look like you're all by yourself." Caitlyn arranged her blanket a few feet away.

"Jarret and me." Zoe sat on her blanket and leaned back on her outstretched arms, smiling to herself. Relationships with boys came so easily for her. Was it her appearance? Her confidence?

"Yeah, I figured." Caitlyn crawled across her old ratty blanket, trying to smooth out permanent wrinkles. "Roland will probably sit with Mya." Giving up on having a smooth blanket, she sat cross-legged and scanned for Roland.

"Yeah, she's been attached to him all day," Zoe said. "You need to work harder."

"How can I? She's like a barnacle, always clinging to him. Besides, I don't even know where he is." Caitlyn continued scanning.

The adults had set up snack and beverage tables on the opposite side of the bonfire. Quite a few kids—but not Roland—hung out with them. Mr. Brandt, Peter, and two other boys stood in a circle by the pile of extra wood for the bonfire. The one with his back to her wore black jeans. Roland?

She squinted, leaning in for a better view. *No.* It wasn't Roland.

Most kids hung out at the bottom of a slope, watching a DJ set up. Someone in that group of kids jumped two times. White-blonde hair caught a slanted beam of sunlight.

Caitlyn's jaw tensed. *Mya.* She glanced from head to head and face to face, searching for Roland.

Then she exhaled. Mya was with other girls. No boys. No Roland. Maybe he wouldn't show up at all.

The sky turned purplish-pink. A few stars popped out. Grass rustled nearby.

Caitlyn turned to the sound.

Jarret strolled over, hugging three bags of popcorn. "Hey," he said, handing Caitlyn a bag.

"Thanks," Caitlyn said, somewhat amazed that he'd thought of her.

Jarret shuffled to Zoe. Her eyes lit up. She tucked her hair behind her ear and scooted over to make room for him on the blanket. He sat down and handed her a bag of popcorn. They whispered to each other. They looked good together, happy, natural.

Did Caitlyn really want to sit all by herself next to a new couple?

The sky grew darker. Lawn chairs and blankets filled up. Time dragged on. Roland did not appear to be anywhere on Bonfire Hill. Someone shouted and everyone grew quiet. It was almost time for the bonfire.

Peter strutted from around the pile of wood, walking proud as a rooster, a microphone in his hand. "Can anybody hear me?" His voice came loud and clear through the speakers.

"Get the fire started!" someone shouted, and a few kids hooted and clapped.

"All in due time, my friend, but first . . . a little story."

Someone in the crowd booed but was immediately hushed by Caitlyn and a few others. All eyes went to Peter. This was his moment. He traditionally told a story. Then, at a dramatic moment, he would start the fire in a unique way.

"There was a girl," he said, his voice lower than usual.

Tingles broke out on Caitlyn's arms. She couldn't take her eyes off Peter as he paced with the microphone. His obsession with electronics made her think he had something cool rigged up, something to outdo last year's performance.

"She wanted to go to the high school dance, so she bought a new dress. It was all sparkly and red and she looked hot in it."

A few guys made catcalls.

Peter laughed. "This was going to be the best night of her life. But the girl's mother didn't want her to go to the dance."

Zoe and Caitlyn happened to look at each other. Caitlyn smiled. Mom and the courtship rules came to mind. Would Caitlyn be able to go to dances? She didn't see why not.

"Their preacher had said the dance was for the devil."

The kids sitting by Father Carston made comments that Caitlyn wished she could've heard. Father Carston said something back, and they all laughed.

"The girl nodded to her mother," Peter said, "but she was still determined to go. So that night . . . she sneaked out. Now, normally, no one noticed her. So she was surprised when she became the center of attention. Guys fought with each other to dance with her, dance after dance. Finally, she broke away and went to get some punch. There was a sudden hush and the music stopped . . ."

Caitlyn braced herself. The way he paused, she thought sure the bonfire would burst into flames, but it didn't.

"When the girl turned . . ." Peter glanced over his shoulder. ". . . she saw a good-looking man with jet-black hair and black clothes standing next to her. *Dance with me*, the man said. The girl said *yes* and let him lead her out onto the dance floor. Music sprang up at once, and she found herself dancing better than ever." Peter spoke louder and quicker.

Caitlyn straightened, again thinking it would happen soon.

"The man spun her round and around. She gasped for breath, trying to step out of the spin. But he spun her faster and faster. Her feet burned, and the floor melted beneath her. Faster and faster, he spun her. She feared she would burst into flames. Then a cloud of dust blew up around them, hiding them from the crowd." He spoke slow and low. "When the dust settled . . . the girl was gone." Head down, he paused.

Caitlyn's heart thumped in expectation. Perhaps now he would light it. But she'd been wrong two times before, so maybe—

"POOF!" Peter flung his arms up. Flames burst from the top of the tepee of firewood.

Caitlyn gasped. A few girls screamed. Then everyone spoke at once and applauded. A self-satisfied grin flashed on Peter's face.

"Can I sit here?"

A shiver ran through Caitlyn at the sound of Roland's voice.

Stepping from the shadows, he sat down beside her. He wrapped his arms around his raised knees and smiled.

"Of course." Caitlyn smiled back, her heart thumping madly. "Where did you come from?"

Before Roland could answer, Peter's loud voice snagged Caitlyn's attention. "The man in black," he said, "bowed once to the crowd and disappeared. The devil had come to his party, and he spun the girl all the way to HELL." Peter raised a hand dramatically to show he had finished. Everyone clapped.

"Let the party begin!" he shouted, and people clapped louder. He handed the microphone off to someone and jogged over to Caitlyn and Roland.

"Man in black, huh?" Roland said as Peter crouched beside him in the grass.

"Eh, don't get tight. It's just a story. I'm sure you're not the devil." Peter grinned, nudging Roland.

"So where's Mya?" Peter waved his brows at Roland.

"How should I know?" Roland said.

"Oh, I don't know. Maybe because she's been attached to you all day."

Roland gave Caitlyn a sideways glance and opened his mouth to speak.

Peter slapped his arm and jumped up. "Yeah, well, anyway, I'll be back." He dashed off, leaving Roland and Caitlyn alone.

They didn't speak, but sitting together felt comfortable. Roland watched the bonfire awhile, but then his gaze traveled to Zoe and Jarret. They sat close but not touching, though Jarret leaned in whenever he spoke to her. She whispered back, tilting her head and stroking her long black hair.

"I feel bad, that's all," Roland said.

"What?" Caitlyn snapped her gaze to him.

Facing the bonfire, he made a little head shake. Then he sighed. "I've been judging him, and he's been proving me wrong." He glanced at Caitlyn, so she nodded.

"It's just . . . He used to always be up to no good, at least in my mind." He ran a hand through his gorgeous black hair, his gaze still on the fire. "But maybe I've been wrong about him. Or maybe he's changed. I should give him the benefit of the doubt."

"You mean because he said he wasn't going to help find Toby, but he did, and he was the one to find him?"

He nodded. "And the Finns. He never told me where he was going, what he was up to, so I assumed . . ." He glanced at Caitlyn.

"You assumed he was up to no good?"

He nodded again, this time locking gazes with her.

"I wouldn't feel too bad, if I were you. Do you pray for him?"

"What?" A smile flickered on his face, then a serious look replaced it. "Yeah, I've been asking Saint Conrad to . . . you know, to change his heart. I pray for Keefe, too."

She smiled. "That's good. So just start over with him."

He looked away and whispered, "Yeah, I think I'll try."

They both watched the bonfire, now, joy tingling inside Caitlyn. Roland had come to sit by her! He seemed to trust her and wanted to share things with her. If only she had something more profound to say. If only she had anything at all to say. But then again, it didn't feel necessary, and Roland looked content now, no longer glancing at his brother.

"There you guys are."

Caitlyn's joy shattered at the sound of Mya's bubbly voice.

She bounced over and stood blocking their view of the bonfire. "I got some hotdogs. Want one?" She plopped down next to Roland and offered him a hotdog.

"No thanks."

She shoved one into his hands anyway. "I wanted to get drinks, too, but I don't have enough arms," she said to Roland, all sweet and whispery. "Want to come with me?" She took the hotdog from Roland and handed his and hers to Caitlyn. Then she stood and offered him her hand.

Roland took her hand and stood up, but his eyes turned to Caitlyn. "You want a drink?"

Caitlyn shrugged. "Okay." He could've asked her to come, too. She sighed, watching them walk away. At least she'd had a few minutes with him. Mya would probably monopolize him for the rest of the night. He went with her willingly enough. Maybe he'd started liking her attention.

Chapter Seventeen

Caitlyn

Mya, Zoe, and Caitlyn left the well-lit, moth-infested bathroom and stumbled through the grass. They directed the beams from their flashlights in the general direction of their campsite. The moon shone bright and round overhead. Crickets, frogs, and bugs chirped and croaked all around them, a noisy serenade.

Caitlyn took a deep breath and let it out slowly. She loved camping.

"Where do you think the guys went?" Mya whispered.

"Jarret didn't say," Zoe said. "Roland came over and whispered something to him, and they both went off into the woods."

"Peter and Dominic came up to Roland, first, and whispered to him," Caitlyn said. "Peter's always up to something." They tried waiting for the guys to return, or at least for the bonfire to burn itself out, but sleepiness overcame her. She just wanted to change into pajamas and crawl into a sleeping bag.

Mya shuffled closer to Zoe. "Is Jarret your boyfriend?"

Zoe glanced over her shoulder at Caitlyn before answering. "I don't know. Not officially. But he told me all these things he wants us to do together."

Mya whispered, "Like what?"

"Well . . ." She looked at Caitlyn again. "Do the Wests really have horses? And do they really live in a big house? I told him our house is big, but he said it wouldn't compare to his."

As private as Roland was about his home life, Caitlyn couldn't believe Jarret was so open. "Um, I guess."

Zoe stopped outside the tent and shined her flashlight in Caitlyn's face. "You guess? Don't you know? You said you went over there once."

She *had* gone there, not long ago, to apologize for accidentally starting a rumor at school about Roland. She'd had to beg Peter to show her the way. Her first glimpse of their awesome house still lingered in her mind. Turrets and battlements, black gated windows and a huge front door. They lived in a castle.

"Has he invited you over already?" Caitlyn asked.

Zoe smiled and gave a look that answered Caitlyn's question. He had.

Mya unzipped the tent.

Caitlyn crawled in after her. She shoved her toothbrush into her duffle bag and unzipped her sleeping bag. She left her flashlight shining on a wall of the tent so they could see.

Zoe zipped the tent and sat on the end of Caitlyn's sleeping bag, the air mattress squeaking under her. "Jarret never said when, just that he wants me over."

Mya giggled then spoke in an awestruck tone. "Wow. You're Jarret West's girlfriend. Has he kissed you yet?" Dressed in a yellow nightshirt, she sat atop her sleeping bag, arranging a blanket over her legs.

Zoe smiled. "Maybe."

Mya squealed. "I wish Roland would kiss me. Do you think he likes me?" Her pale blue eyes snapped to Caitlyn as if she had no clue that Caitlyn liked him, too.

"Roland doesn't want a girlfriend," Zoe said.

Mya scrunched her face. "How do you know? Maybe he—"

Something scraped the side of the tent.

Mya drew in a sharp breath.

Caitlyn giggled. "Don't worry. Haven't you ever camped out before? It was probably an acorn or a twig falling from a tree."

"Zoe." The quiet voice came from directly outside the tent.

Everyone's eyes popped. They exchanged glances. Zoe slid off Caitlyn's sleeping bag and crawled to the door of the tent. "Who is it?"

"Who do you *think* it is?" whispered a guy. "Come out."

Caitlyn would've been offended by his rude tone and made some snotty reply, but not Zoe. She unzipped the tent, stuck her head out, and whispered something to him. Then she said to Caitlyn and Mya, "I'll be back," as she slipped sandals on.

"Wait," Caitlyn said as Zoe crawled out. "Who is it? Where are you going?"

Zoe zipped the tent shut. She and her visitor whispered back and forth for a moment. Then silence.

"I'm sure it's Jarret." Mya stretched out on her side and propped her head on her hand.

"She shouldn't go out there with him at night." Caitlyn crawled into her sleeping bag, glad to finally rest her head on a pillow. She left the flashlight on and shining low on the corner of the tent so Zoe could see when she got back. A bug outside tapped the tent where the light shined.

"Why not?"

"Just the two of them? Alone?" Mom would have a cow if she ever did that. A boy and girl shouldn't be alone together, she'd say. It just opens the door to trouble. She was probably right but maybe not for everyone.

"I'd go, if it were Roland."

"I wouldn't," Caitlyn said. *Would I?* If Roland ever did want her for a girlfriend, would she turn down his offer for a midnight stroll? If she did, would he take it as rejection and dump her? What if he wanted them to be alone sometimes and she always said *no*? How long would he put up with that? Would he be willing to follow so many rules? If she did things Mom's way, the courtship way, he would have to. A relationship would be easier, less restrictive for him, with other girls. Like Mya.

Watching the shadow of a long-legged bug that stood motionless on top of the tent, Caitlyn shook her head. "Why can't Jarret see her in the daytime?"

"You don't understand because you don't like anyone right now." Mya lay back and let out a long, wistful sigh.

Caitlyn's blood simmered. Was Mya that blind? Had she no clue that Caitlyn also liked Roland?

"I do," Caitlyn said. "I do like someone."

Mya lifted her head. "You do? Who?" She sat up, wrapped her arms around her legs, and gazed wide-eyed at Caitlyn.

If she couldn't figure it out for herself, why should Caitlyn bother telling her? What would Mya do if she knew? Redouble her flirting efforts? Certainly not give up. Did it even matter? Roland didn't want a girlfriend. But she did love being his friend and maybe . . . after some time . . .

"I like Roland."

"What!" Mya whipped her pillow at Caitlyn. "You can't like him. I like him."

Caitlyn whipped the pillow back, hitting Mya squarely in the face.

"That's not fair. You know I like him," Mya whispered loudly. "I liked him first. You can't like him, too."

"Well, I like him, too." Caitlyn rolled onto her side, facing away from Mya, but then the tent door unzipped so she rolled back.

Zoe crawled in, smiling.

Mya flicked her flashlight on and shined it in Zoe's face. "What did he want?"

Squinting, Zoe snatched the flashlight from Mya and shut it off. "He wanted to take a walk, that's all, but I said *no*. So he just told me goodnight."

Stretching out again, Mya let out another wistful sigh. "I wish Roland would've told me goodnight." Then she bolted upright, a scowl on her face. "Did you know Caitlyn likes Roland?"

Chapter Eighteen

Keefe

Keefe twisted pasta on his fork with no intention of eating it. His appetite had waned before he'd finished half the plate, maybe because he had something on his mind, something he needed to say.

Papa, taking his time, had put away every bit of his pasta, sausage, fresh bread and cheese, and fried zucchini . . . though he hadn't looked interested in his dessert, a fruit-topped panna cotta.

Setting out early, hours early, they had taken a ten-minute drive from Bagno di Romagna to a nearby municipality for an appointment. Papa, having assumed the leisurely disposition of the locals, had gone directly to a restaurant where he planned to remain until the appointment.

Papa leaned back in the patio chair, wine glass in hand, and gazed off in the direction of a nearby pond. When not actively working, and sometimes when he was, Papa often had a faraway look in his eyes and seemed lost in thought, perhaps going over plans, but more than likely returning to a memory from his past. Some memory of Mama.

Voices carried from people below the patio and Papa's gaze shifted.

Keefe took the opportunity to speak. "Papa, I'd like us to go to church again."

Papa stared a moment before answering. "It's less than five miles from here. Take a walk. You've been useless on my appointments anyway. I don't know where your head is." He smiled and leaned across the table to muss Keefe's hair. "Really, I don't need you for this appointment, so go take a break."

105

"I'm sorry. I know my mind's been somewhere else." Keefe yanked the band from his hair so he could fix what Papa had messed up. "I guess my concentration is worse now than back in Florence. I bet you're wishing you'd taken Roland instead of me."

Papa chuckled into his wine glass and downed the last sip.

"But I didn't mean the Basilica of Saint Mary. I meant, I want to, I mean . . . Could we start going to Mass on Sunday?"

Papa coughed, set the empty glass down, and patted his shirt pockets. Papa had stopped going to church after Mama died. Maybe he blamed God for taking her so young, or maybe going to Sunday Mass brought back too many memories. With the exception of Roland, who recently began attending Saint Michael's Church with friends, they hadn't been since.

He brought out his pipe and tobacco. "You're sixteen. You want to go to Mass, go to Mass. You hardly need my permission for that."

Keefe needed to say more. Would he be out of line? He had many things he needed to change in his life, none of them easy. If he didn't start now, when would he? He pushed back the doubt and steeled himself for Papa's reaction. "I'd like you to go, too. I think it was wrong of us to stop going."

Papa grimaced, his blue eyes squinting into the tobacco pack. "Yeeeah, I suppose you're right." Pipe in hand, he stood and shook his pant legs down over his boots. "I'll meet you back at the hotel around dinner time."

Watching Papa descend the patio steps then stroll through well-manicured grounds toward the lake, Keefe decided to head back to Bagno di Romagna. Maybe he would visit the basilica again. He had something to sort out in his mind.

He needed only to take a single road to return to Bagno, but the way it twisted and curved made him think he might somehow get lost. So after walking for ten minutes, when he happened by a parked car that he thought was a taxi, he tried to find the driver.

Two men smoking cigarettes stood under the awning of a nearby restaurant. They both looked him over as he approached. One mumbled to the other. They laughed.

"Is this your taxi?" Keefe pointed, wishing his Italian wasn't limited to *Where is the bathroom?* and *Do you speak English?*

The less friendly looking of the two men, thinner and dressed in a suede jacket and jeans, stepped forward. He glanced at his watch, said something in Italian, then gestured to the right and left. The other man chuckled.

Assuming he wondered where Keefe wanted to go, Keefe said, "Bagno di Romagna."

The man repeated him and said a few more things in Italian, annoyance showing in his attitude. He raised a hand and rubbed his fingers together while he spoke.

"Yeah, I've got money." Keefe reached for his wallet.

The driver's mouth curled up in a crooked grin. He glanced at his watch, gestured toward the taxi, and mumbled something else, this time with a more resigned tone.

As the taxi rolled down the twisty road and a warm breeze blew, Keefe's mind returned to the basilica and to what God had done for him. The promise he had made came to him.

I will listen to Your voice. I will live knowing You are with me and that You love me, knowing that You shed your blood for me. I will not forget, no matter whom I'm with or what temptation I face.

God's presence overwhelmed him for one fleeting moment. He decided he would turn his promise into a prayer and remind himself of it daily lest he forget. Making the promise felt important to who he was, who he would become, but somehow incomplete. There must be some way of cementing it, like married people exchanging rings or religious putting on habits.

Just then, the wind blew a curl of his hair into his eyes, and he knew what he would do.

He ran his hand over his hair. His hair. He kept it long like Jarret did, down to his shoulders. Jarret was determined to let his grow halfway down his back. They had hair like Mama's and that made it special. It felt like a connection to her in some mystical way. But it had also made Keefe vain. He liked the way girls looked at him when he wore it free. And he had wasted time admiring himself in the mirror, though not to the same degree as Jarret.

Within ten minutes, they reached the edge of town. Keefe leaned forward. "Hey, do you know where I can get my hair cut?" He pointed to his hair.

The driver glanced over his shoulder and made a polite examination of Keefe's hair. "Bella e lunga."

Keefe made pretend scissors with his fingers. "I don't want it long anymore. I want it cut." He cut at his hair. "Haircut."

"Ohh. Negozio di barbiere." The man nodded and started talking as if Keefe could understand him.

A moment later, the taxi stopped and the driver, still talking, gestured to one of the buildings in a piazza, a two-story with dark green shutters and a heavy, carved door.

After paying the driver a considerable sum of money, Keefe stepped inside to cement his commitment to the Lord with a tangible sign of his promise.

It had taken him several tries to get the barber to understand what he wanted. His phone kept ringing while he was trying to explain, so he'd shut it off. The barber kept combing Keefe's hair and running his fingers through the curls, stretching them out, and commenting— probably on their length, but altogether acting reluctant to take the scissors to them. When he had finally given in, he must've wanted to do something with the cut locks because he gathered them up with care.

Keefe winced at his shorthaired reflection in the mirror. His face looked strange, and his ears stuck out. But then his heart stirred, making him certain that he'd pleased God, and he smiled.

He left the barbershop walking on air and, having had done something so radical, bursting with the desire to tell someone. He turned his phone on to check the time. Papa wouldn't meet up with him until later. But on the way to the barbershop he'd caught a glimpse of the clock tower and, though he couldn't see it now, he knew it was near. The basilica! It felt right to return to the place where he'd made his promise. Now that he decided to go there, he couldn't walk fast enough.

Stepping around the corner of the next building, the basilica came into view. Then his cell phone rang. He glanced at the caller ID. *Jarret.* Did he want to share this with Jarret? Why shouldn't he? He had never kept things from his twin. Of course, he'd never had something like this to share. Jarret almost considered their hair sacred.

Keefe shook the doubts from his mind as he answered the phone. He couldn't let Jarret's reactions influence his choices in life. He would tell Jarret. Besides, Jarret would find out soon enough.

"Hey, Jarret." Eyes on the Romanesque front door, he strolled toward the basilica.

"Hey, man, what'cha up to?"

Hesitant to get into it, Keefe said, "Must be early over there."

"Yeah, I just got up."

"Still camping?"

"Yeah."

"I've been worried about the little boy you said was lost."

Jarret made a breathy sort of chuckle that Keefe immediately interpreted. Something about that situation had worked out in Jarret's favor. "I joined the search after all. Guess who found him?"

"You did? That's great."

"Yeah, I'm a hero. All the girls love me. Even Peter likes me. He invited me along with his friends on a midnight rampage down to the river last night."

"Rampage? That sounds like trouble."

"Nah. This is Peter Brandt we're talking about. Just a bunch of hootin' and hollerin' and getting wet." He was silent for a moment. "Hey, I got a new girlfriend."

"Yeah? Who?" Keefe stepped into the shadow cast by the clock tower, his gaze still on the dark doors. He felt driven by the need to probe and counsel his twin.

"You've seen her in school. Zoe McGowan. Long, dark hair. Walks like a model. She's really hot."

"Isn't she a freshman?"

"So? She's fifteen. I'm sixteen. Saying I'm too old?" He laughed.

"No, it's just . . ." What was it? "You're respecting her, aren't you?"

He chuckled. "Yeah, sure. Don't worry. I haven't had her in my tent . . . yet."

"Roland's in your tent, isn't he?"

"Man, you sound really worried about it. So what about you? What you been up to? I tried calling a few minutes ago."

"Yeah, I was getting my hair cut." There. He said it. Quick and painless and now—he took a breath—for the aftermath.

"Oh, yeah? Did you get some new Italian do?"

"Uh, actually . . ."

"Actually?"

Keefe detected suspicion in Jarret's tone. "Yeah, I decided to have it cut short. I'll send you a picture with my phone."

"Short?" Jarret sounded shocked. "Uh, whaddya mean by short? How short?"

With his eyes fixed on the door to the basilica, he ran his hand over his hair. "Very short. The barber took a trimmer to it, you know, in the back." Keefe cleared his throat and swallowed. "It's a little longer on the top. I'll send you a picture, okay?"

Jarret didn't reply.

"Jarret? Are you there?"

Chapter Nineteen

Jarret

He could not be tied up and subdued with fresh bowstrings,
nor with new ropes, nor by weaving seven locks of his head
and tying them around a nail fastened in the ground.
The secret of his great strength lay in his hair.
When someone had shaved off the seven locks of his hair,
it was then that Samson was subdued.
It was then that his strength left him.
~Judges 16

Jarret wore his hair down, aware that he drew the attention of more than a few girls. Cigarette in hand and refusing even to glance at his admirers, he strode alone to a pavilion. Agitation had been gnawing at him since he'd spoken with Keefe in the morning. He had spent the rest of the morning alone, trying to walk it off, and then down by the river, considering going home. If not for Zoe, he would go. He had no other reason to stay.

Zoe had tried to find him in the late morning. He'd seen her searching. Not in the mood to talk, he'd gone in the opposite direction.

But she saw him now.

He stepped onto the pavilion, sat up on the railing, and leaned against a post. His gaze drifted to the woods, but he knew a group of kids approached him, Zoe among them.

Keefe was a fool to have cut his hair. No one had hair like theirs. Everyone envied it. They had Mama's dark Latin American hair, beautiful, long, and all curls. Had Keefe forgotten the significance of it? Roland didn't have it. Roland had Papa's hair.

Mya reached the pavilion first. "Hi, Jarret. We've been looking for you all day." Her voice was soft and sweet, too sweet.

"Oh yeah?" Jarret glanced at her as he blew out cigarette smoke.

She wore cut-off shorts and a long sleeved sweater that emphasized her figure. Her short blonde curls and hot pink lipstick gave her a very feminine quality. He hated short hair. Still, she was cute.

"Why were you looking for me?" He dropped his spent cigarette onto the clean platform of the pavilion.

"Well, you weren't there for breakfast." Mya stuck out her bottom lip. "And Roland said you . . ."

Walking at a leisurely pace, Zoe followed the others to the pavilion. She didn't run like Mya had. She was too dignified for that. Dressed in stonewashed straight-legged jeans, hiking boots, and a short lavender jacket with black trim that made her long dark hair stand out, she looked good. She gave Jarret a shy glance then leaned against the opposite railing, facing away from him. He liked that. She didn't throw herself at guys.

Peter, Caitlyn, Roland, and Peter's Mexican-American friend Dominic crowded into the pavilion. It was strange seeing Dominic on his feet. The kid used to speed around the school in a wheelchair; it wasn't even electric. Roland said a car accident had messed him up years ago, but—supposedly—he'd since had a miraculous healing. Whatever happened to him, Roland had been going to church ever since. But maybe he was going for another reason.

Jarret's gaze went to Caitlyn. She belonged to the Catholic youth group and probably went to church every Sunday. She'd looked good in the jeans she wore the first day camping, but she'd worn dresses ever since, a denim one yesterday and a rust-colored one today, both of them long. They looked good on her but left everything to the imagination. Not like Mya's clothes.

Mya was still talking. ". . . so we went all the way down to the river, and Peter wondered if we needed to organize another search party, but Roland—"

"A search party, for me?" Jarret said. "I'm a big boy. I can take care of myself."

"Let's get a football game going, vato," Dominic said, jabbing Peter in the side.

Peter put his hands on his hips and stepped toward Jarret. "Anyone can get lost back here. Some trails go on forever. And they aren't all marked well. And they cross over each other. Really, anyone could—"

"Not me." Jarret turned away and gazed into the woods.

Mya leaned on the railing with him and peeked around at his face. "Well, I'm glad, because we wanted to do something with you. We've wasted all morning."

"What did you want to do with me?" He said it in a flirty way and caught Roland's eyes narrowing up. Was Mya Roland's girlfriend? She was always hanging on him. He could take her away from Roland if he wanted to, which he didn't. He'd have enough fun making him jealous.

"Some of us . . ." She twisted around as she spoke, throwing a look to each of them. ". . . want to go swimming." She leaned close again. "Do you like to swim? I hear you guys went swimming in the river last night. Was it cold?" She giggled.

Jarret glanced at her sweater. "Did you bring your swimsuit?"

Peter cracked up. Dominic mumbled something, every other word sounding Spanish.

"Mya." Roland approached. He gave Mya a glance and a nod, sending her away.

Mya went to Zoe, who was now sitting on the railing with arms folded and eyes narrowed to slits.

Roland stood where Mya had been. "Where you been?"

Jarret grinned, seeing the worried slant of Roland's eyes. "Worried about me? Afraid I drowned in the river?"

"Well, no, but . . . Where've you been? It's past lunch time."

Mya must've heard Roland, though he spoke low. She hopped over again. "Are you hungry? There're still some hamburgers on the grill. Mr. Brandt kept asking where you were. You know he's so thankful for what you did for Toby. I think he—"

"You want to get me something to eat?" Jarret said.

She batted her eyes. "Do you want me to?"

Jarret gave her a crooked sort of grin. Out of the corner of his eye, he caught Zoe's jealous glance. "Yeah. I want you to."

Mya bounced. "Okay." She turned to Zoe. "Want to help me?"

Zoe shook her head, threw Jarret a cold look, and turned away. Jealousy fit her, made her look hot.

A few minutes later, a few other guys came with a football and started a game in a long stretch of grass. Roland tried to get Jarret to play, but Jarret didn't want to play that game.

He and Zoe remained alone in the pavilion, watching the game and throwing each other cold glances.

After a long while, Zoe stared him down. Then she spoke. "Are you tired of camping?"

He met her gaze. "I'm tired of a lot of things." He hated what Keefe had done to his hair, and how Roland kept tabs on him, and that he had to wait to get the car he should've gotten on his sixteenth birthday.

Her jaw twitched, but she didn't look away.

Jarret moved in. "But I'm not tired of you." He grabbed her upper arm and leaned in to kiss her. She yielded to him as he expected she would, but then Mya broke the moment with her shrill voice.

"I hope you like hotdogs. The hamburgers sat on the grill too long and turned black. So I thought you'd rather . . ."

Chapter Twenty

Caitlyn

Caitlyn stood mesmerized, gazing at the sky. Kites of all shapes and colors, long tails streaming behind them, weaved through the clear blue sky over the lake. A panda swooped toward a butterfly. An octopus floated by, its eight legs waving beneath it. A stunt kite flew alone.

She glanced at Roland, who stood flying a kite beside her.

Gray eyes sparkling in the sunlight, he concentrated on working his kite up higher.

Contented, she sighed.

"Get your freaky brother out of my way!" Jarret shouted. "He's gonna tangle up the kites."

Caitlyn snapped from her trance and looked.

Toby, clutching the string of a huge orange fish kite, had come up behind Mya while Jarret was *teaching* her how to fly a kite. Toby had come up to everyone. And why not? They were all his kites anyway, sort of. Toby enjoyed flying kites, obsessively. So Mr. Brandt, the devoted father that he was, had accumulated a ridiculous amount of kites. Now Toby wanted to *talk kites* with everyone, but he paid little attention to kite strings.

After passing his box kite off to Dominic, Peter bolted across the field for Toby.

Roland looked, too, his dark brows knitting together. He was probably trying to decide if he needed to help. He and Jarret had been *helping* the whole time. Helping Mya that is.

Jarret left Mya and strutted back to Zoe. Zoe turned her back on him. He moved in front of her, but she turned again. He grabbed her around the waist and lifted her off her feet. She laughed and, eyes on her kite, got her feet back on the ground and pried his arms away.

Roland no sooner returned his gaze to his own kite when a shriek ripped through air. Mya's shriek.

Roland shoved his kite string into Caitlyn's hand and dashed for Mya.

Oh tragedy, Mya's kite had crashed. Jarret ran to her, too.

A minute later, Zoe shuffled up beside Caitlyn, her eyes to the sky. "What are we going to do about that girl?"

Caitlyn sighed, watching Roland and Jarret argue with each other as they helped Mya with her kite. "I don't know."

"We need to fix her up with someone." Zoe eyes narrowed in a calculating glare. "They're actually fighting over who gets to help Mya."

"Yeah. Maybe they're just nice." Caitlyn struggled with the kite strings, trying to keep hers and Roland's good and tight.

"Someone else can be nice to Mya."

"Hold this." Caitlyn handed Zoe the spool of string for Roland's kite and wound in her own.

"Who do we know that she could like?" Zoe said. "Not counting Roland and Jarret."

Roland walked off from Mya and Jarret, cell phone to his ear. He headed for a picnic table in the shade at the edge of the field.

Caitlyn rolled her kite in faster, and it crashed to the ground.

Roland hadn't noticed, but Jarret had done an about-face. Grinning, he strutted toward them.

Caitlyn took Roland's spool from Zoe and strode out to meet Jarret.

"Here, hold this." She slapped the spool into his hand and walked off, not giving him a chance to object.

Roland sat at a picnic table, facing the lake and deep in conversation with whoever had called him. He glanced as Caitlyn approached and nodded for her to join him.

She sat on the opposite end of the bench.

". . . a miracle? A real miracle?" he said into the phone.

Caitlyn's ears perked.

"Blood? Wow. Like real blood?" Roland leaned forward, resting the elbow of his phone arm on his thigh. "Jesus? Not some saint? Are you sure?"

Then he was quiet, just listening and giving an occasional *uh-huh*. Finally, he sat up and said, "I can't believe you did that . . . No, not confession, the haircut . . . Of course, I won't tell him . . . Yeah, yeah. I'll try to get him to call you. Okay. Bye." He leaned back against the picnic table and pressed a few buttons on his cell phone. Then his mouth fell open, and he sat staring at his phone.

Caitlyn scooted closer. "Are you okay? You look upset."

"I'm not upset. It's just . . . Look." He turned his phone so she could see the screen. And the image of a handsome boy with a serious face and short dark hair. "That's Keefe."

"Keefe?" She squinted out at Jarret in the field. "I don't remember him looking like that. I thought they were identical twins." Examining the image again, she decided they did have the same long-lashed brown eyes, long nose, and strong jaw, though Keefe had a gentler, more mannered appearance. He also lacked the cocky sneer that Jarret always had, at least when talking to other guys.

"Yeah, they're identical. He cut his hair."

"Wow. He went from hair down to his shoulders to that?"

"Yeah."

Caitlyn angled her body towards his, hoping she wasn't about to be too bold. "I hadn't meant to be listening in on your conversation, but I heard you say something about a miracle."

He glanced then returned his gaze to the kites. "Yeah."

"Were you talking to Keefe? Did he see a miracle?"

Roland nodded.

"What kind of a miracle? Can you tell me about it?"

He faced her. "I . . . don't think so. I wouldn't feel right about it. It's not really my business to share. I . . . suppose you could ask Keefe when he gets back."

As comfortable as she felt around Roland, his twin brothers made her nervous. She didn't like the idea of asking either of them anything, but the urge to know gnawed at her. She had to find out. Miracles were meant to be shared. When her friend Dominic had been healed, no longer needing a wheelchair, it made her think about the relationship God wants with each person and the confidence everyone ought to have in Him. Somehow, she would ask Keefe about it when he returned.

Chapter Twenty-one

Jarret

The aroma of grilled fish and charred hamburgers wafted in the air. Jarret's stomach growled. He lowered his cigarette and pivoted on his shoulder to peek around a tree.

The adults prepared dinner, men standing over the grill, women placing things on picnic tables in the community campsite. Zoe and Caitlyn carried condiments to a table. Peter chased after Toby, who wouldn't stay put and kept whining about something. Did Toby just say the word *fishing*?

Jarret sneered. The kid had better not sneak off again. He was in no mood for a repeat performance. It was the last night of camping, and he had plans of his own.

Taking another hit off the cigarette, Jarret continued scanning the campsite.

Three cute girls sat in camp chairs: Mya and two longhaired, long-legged girls that Jarret didn't remember seeing before. They whispered secrets back and forth, giggling and glancing around.

Something moved in Jarret's peripheral vision.

Jarret looked.

Walking as silently as a fox, Roland strolled toward him coming from the direction of the bathhouse. Looking like he wanted to talk.

Not ready to be noticed yet, Jarret gave him a threatening glare and shook his head.

Roland, like a good boy, redirected his steps.

A few minutes later, dinner preparations complete, the white-haired priest led everyone in a blessing and people lined up for the food.

Jarret strolled from hiding.

Zoe sat between Caitlyn and Mya at the farthest picnic table, Roland, Dominic, and Peter across from them. Zoe's eyes snapped to Jarret.

He nodded, but there was no room at her table. Aware of Zoe's eyes on him, he headed for the camp chairs by the campfire, where a few other guys sat.

"Hey, Jarret," said the pimply-faced kid in the chair beside him, a kid whose name Jarret couldn't remember, a kid who talked with food in his mouth. "You're making yourself scarce."

"Yeah." Jarret tapped the chest pocket of his t-shirt, where he kept his pack of cigarettes. "I hate to light up in front of the adults."

A laugh and a good amount of food erupted from the kid's mouth. The other two boys in the camp chairs laughed, too.

Jarret gave them a crooked grin then noticed Mya approaching.

She stopped by the beverage coolers near his chair.

"Aren't you going to eat?" she said, her voice all whispery and sweet.

He watched her bend over the cooler and pull out a dripping can. "Why don't you make me a plate?"

She hesitated but then said, "Okay," and gave him a big smile before trotting off.

The guys in the camp chairs chuckled. Jarret chuckled with them, but then movement by the picnic tables caught his eye.

Zoe rose from her place at the picnic table. A plateful of food lay before her, but she tossed her hair over her shoulder and sauntered off without looking back. She headed for the dirt road, maybe on her way to the bathhouse. Or the campground store. Or maybe she was just taking a walk, angry, with no destination in mind. Except to go somewhere he wasn't.

It thrilled him to know he had that effect on her, and he wanted to go after her, but he forced himself to wait. Not yet. He would avoid her until later. Then she'd really be worked up with jealousy.

After dinner, some kids stayed to help clean up, others ran off to the lake for a last paddle-boat ride, and the kids in the Catholic youth group—after making an open invitation—left for a prayer and song-fest at their campsite.

Jarret walked alone. He strolled out to the Lexus, climbed in, and rolled the windows down. As he reclined the seat, he turned on the radio. A favorite song played, making him long for his own house, his room, his bed, and all his things. He hated sleeping on Peter's squeaky air mattress. He hated the bugs. He hated how dirty and sweaty he felt at all times. What he needed was a good long shower and to sit in front of the TV. He should just go home. Forget Zoe. Roland could find his own way home. Everyone would think he had gotten lost on a trail—as if he could really get lost out here. They'd throw together another search party and look for him. Then someone would realize his car was gone. They'd figure it out.

He dozed off thinking about it. After a good rest in the car, he strolled to the campground store and bought himself a candy bar. Going home would just remind him of Keefe and his haircut. He could stick around for the last night.

Jarret set out for a long, slow walk down a trail that should've wrapped around to the lake—but didn't.

~ ~ ~

The sun dropped behind the trees. The trail went on and on, winding one way and the other but without coming out anywhere. "Son of a rat!" Jarret thrust a hand into his hair. He picked up his pace, jogging now. His heart beat faster. The trail had no end. Roland, the others, they'd go searching for him. Peter would have something to say. He'd rub it in.

Jarret jogged. He couldn't live with that. He couldn't be lost. He'd feel like an idiot. This trail should have come out at the lake. Could it have branched off without him noticing it? Had he been that distracted?

Trees. More trees. No people. Nothing familiar.

He stopped. He would go back the way he came. The sun would soon set, so he had better hurry. He jogged alone down the trail. No one else was fool enough to be out on the longer trails at this hour.

At a fork in the trail, he stopped. A fork in the trail? No, he didn't remember seeing a fork in the trail. One way would probably bring him to the campground store. Where would the other path take him?

He stood on each fork and looked back, trying to picture the direction he'd come from. Nothing looked familiar. The sun had disappeared, though its light still lingered in the sky, so he picked a path and jogged on.

After some time, a cool sweat covered his chest and back, and still the trail appeared to have no end. *Screw this.* He was not staying another night. As soon as he found his way out of the miserable woods, he would jump into the Lexus and go home.

"Blast these woods, these bug-infested, endless woods. Blast Keefe and Roland. Shoot Peter and his whiney little brother. And Zoe—"

Jarret slowed, his gaze latching onto a distant point.

A golden light flickered, showing through the leaves. The flame of a campfire? Voices and laughter traveled to him. Had he come to a campsite?

Abandoning the trail, he crunched through dead leaves and scraped between trees and wild bushes. A few more steps brought him out into a clearing. Kids too far away to identify stood in groups and sat on blankets, laughing, talking. A bonfire blazed above him. *Bonfire Hill.*

He took a deep breath, relieved.

He'd come out behind the little hill, the side opposite most of the activity. Strolling along the edge of the woods, he took deep breaths and exhaled slowly, trying to regain his cool before anyone saw him. He wiped the sweat from his neck and pulled his hair back into a ponytail.

Moving in closer, he recognized a few people. Caitlyn's parents and her little sisters and brothers shared a huge blanket. The pimply kid who had sat by him at dinner stood by two others. Father Carston and the kids from the Catholic youth group—

Zoe. She sat with Caitlyn on a blanket at a little distance from the others. She leaned forward, her hair falling in her face. She pushed it back, lifting her head, looking at Caitlyn, saying something . . . She shook her head and jerked her hand in a way that made her seem angry. Caitlyn nodded, looking sympathetic.

They were talking about him. It was time.

Jarret strolled toward them. He and Zoe would have a talk.

Still a good twenty feet away, Zoe caught sight of him.

Maintaining a casual stride, he was about to give her a nod when a body collided into him from behind. He fell forward, threw out his hands, and caught himself on his hands and knees.

Wrath boiled over. He jumped up.

"Sorry, man." Peter shot over, hands up, offering an apology, but it was Toby who had crashed into him. "Hey, you know, Roland's out looking for you."

Toby, head cocked to one side, watched Jarret from behind Peter.

Every muscle in Jarret's body tensed. He stepped up to Peter, sneering. "I told you before to keep your freaky little brother away from me." He stepped closer, maybe too close, staring down his nose at Peter's pink face. "Keep him under control, or I'm gonna take it out on you." He slammed Peter's shoulder with his palm.

Peter brushed his shoulder as if wiping off a speck of dirt. And he laughed. "I'm not afraid of you." Then he lunged, both hands slamming Jarret's chest.

Jarret staggered back, shocked. Peter had guts. Then adrenaline surged, and he swung his fist.

Peter leaned back, Jarret's fist skimming his jaw. He came at Jarret again, this time with a bear hug.

Jarret stumbled, almost fell, but he was used to fighting. He and Keefe did it for sport all the time, and he had more than a few moves to deal with someone like Peter. He twisted to one side, throwing Peter off balance. At the same time, he slipped his foot behind Peter's calf. The two of them landed on the ground, Jarret on top.

Peter lay there, stunned for a moment.

Heart racing, seeing stars, Jarret drew his fist back.

Then someone shouted his name and hands snaked all over his arms and chest.

"Break it up, you two." It was the white-haired priest.

The boys from the Fire Starters dragged Jarret off Peter and Peter off the ground. A group gathered, Zoe among them. Before the priest let them go, he said a few things about talking it out, and he made them shake hands. Then everyone scattered, leaving Jarret, Zoe, and Caitlyn standing together.

Zoe stared at him for a long moment. Then she flipped her hair and turned away.

Jarret could stand it no longer. He grabbed her arm and spun her to face him. "Don't you be mad at me." He frowned and peered at her through sad eyes, trying to communicate without words his feelings for her.

She blinked rapidly and pressed her lips together. Then she whispered something to Caitlyn that made Caitlyn leave. She gave her eyes to Jarret again.

"Why shouldn't I be mad at you?"

"I didn't do anything to you."

With an annoyed little smile, she averted her gaze, looking out toward the bonfire.

Waiting for her to reply, he stood appreciating her beauty and watching flames reflecting in her eyes.

"I thought you liked me." Her eyes turned to ice. "But I see you like every girl. So . . . I'm not interested in you." She folded her arms and turned, but she didn't walk away.

A little worried that she might slap him, he risked a touch, brushing her cheek with his hand. She let him do it, so he risked more, turning her face toward his.

"I don't like every girl. I-I know I flirt. I can't help it. It's who I am. But they don't mean anything to me."

She met his gaze, the flames in her eyes dimming. "And I do?"

Gazing deeply into her eyes, trying to convey his desire, he nodded.

She blinked as if to break the connection he wanted to make. "So what do I mean to you?" While suspicion rang in her tone, it had softened. She had softened.

He smiled inside. He had her back. "Why don't you . . . let me show you?" He kissed her, soft and sweet at first, but he couldn't control his desire and the kiss grew deep and intense.

She pulled back.

"You wanna take a walk?" he said.

Suddenly he knew exactly where he would take her.

Chapter Twenty-two

Caitlyn

A week after the camping trip, Caitlyn sat on her bedroom floor, painting a miniature of Roland's castle-like house.

The camping trip ranked number one in her life experiences, mainly because she and Roland had become close friends. He even sat by her for the camp Mass Father Carston offered Sunday morning before they all packed up to go home. As they strolled back to the campsites, he totally opened up to her.

"Is something wrong?" she had said. "You seem distracted."

"No. I'm just . . . I'm trying to get over my anger." His eyes clicked to Jarret, who walked ahead of them. "I can't believe he went off alone last night without telling anyone. He had to know people would worry about him, I'd worry about him. I mean, I was glad when he finally showed up, but I was angry, too. Sometimes he's so . . ."

When she realized he did not intend to complete the sentence, Caitlyn said, "You went off, too, didn't you?"

"Yeah, but I went to look for him."

"Why didn't you tell anyone? We could've all looked for him."

He smiled. "Yeah, he would've loved that." He shook his head and stared at the ground as they walked, probably thinking about Jarret's pride and the explosive reaction he would've had to a party searching for him. "No, I'm angry at myself. I'm still judging him. Maybe Jarret went off alone because he misses Keefe. They were always together. I'm sure it's hard for him. I promised myself I'd stop judging him. From now on, I'll assume he has good motives . . . no matter how it looks."

Caitlyn didn't think that was a good idea, but she kept it to herself.

She had Peter talking in her other ear, telling her how mean Jarret had been about Toby. She didn't like anyone being mean to sweet, naïve, little Toby. Since the fight, Peter complained about Jarret at least once a day, although never in front of Roland.

"Do you like this color?" Mya said, drawing Caitlyn's thoughts back to the present. She sat on Caitlyn's bed, painting her toenails salmon pink. Sometime last week, it dawned on her that Roland didn't want a girlfriend. She then developed an interest in future-Marine Leo. In addition, since Zoe never came around anymore, Mya and Caitlyn had become friends.

"Sure. That's a nice color," Caitlyn lied.

She missed Zoe. It was now Zoe and Jarret, girlfriend and boyfriend. Zoe hardly came around, and she only talked about Jarret. *Jarret taught me how to ride a horse today. Jarret had me over for dinner. Jarret took me out to look at cars. Jarret came over to my house.* Jarret said this and Jarret did that. Blah, blah. Not that Caitlyn wasn't happy for her, but she was really sick of hearing his name.

Caitlyn wanted to find another way to get her friends together because she only saw Roland at school, and they only shared lunch break. Sometimes he ate with her, but on cold and rainy days, she ate in the lunchroom. He didn't.

"I have an idea," Mya said.

"What's your idea?" Caitlyn searched through paintbrushes, looking for the thinnest one. She needed it for the battlements that ran along the top of the Wests' house.

"We should throw a party. Halloween's in October." Keeping her toenails safe in the air, she rolled onto her belly and looked at Caitlyn sitting on the floor. "Let's have a Halloween party."

"You mean a costume party?" Not finding the brush she wanted, Caitlyn settled for one that had lost bristles thus becoming her second thinnest.

"Mmm-hmm." Mya was all girl, from the white-blonde curls that framed her face and accentuated her overly made-up eyes, to her shapely figure that she made no attempt to hide. So when she looked at

Caitlyn the way she did now, eyes round and a clever smile on her face, Caitlyn felt incredibly plain in comparison.

"Yes, a costume party!" she squealed.

"You could wear a white dress and be Marilyn Monroe," Caitlyn said and turned back to her painting. She steadied her hand and tapped the canvas a few times, beginning the battlements.

"That's a great idea! What about you?" Mya rested her head on her folded arms and gazed at Caitlyn's work in progress.

Caitlyn hated when people saw her artwork before it was done, but she let her go ahead and look. "I don't know. We can't really throw a party. Where would we have it? Not at my house. We barely have room to live."

"Why, Zoe's house, of course. Her house is new and big. Her parents are nice. They wouldn't care."

By *nice* Mya meant *rarely home.* Zoe's mom and dad had professional careers, worked long hours, and traveled. Zoe could get away with a lot.

"Well, I guess we could run it by Zoe. But we'd have to get her parents' permission."

Mya shrugged, sat up, and peered at her toes. "I'll ask her tomorrow." She opened the nail polish and started on a second coat. "Your castle is pretty. I thought you were painting Roland's house."

"It is Roland's house." As the words came out, she regretted saying it, though she wasn't sure why. Surely, Zoe had already told everyone about the Wests' unusual house.

Mya froze with the nail-polish brush held above her toes. Then she spun to face Caitlyn, her eyes wide open. "Roland lives in a castle?"

Caitlyn sighed. Okay, so maybe Zoe hadn't told anyone. Now, if the whole school found out, it would be her fault.

Nail polish jar in one hand and the brush in the other, Mya rolled onto her belly again. "Does Roland live in a castle?"

"Sort of. But don't tell anyone you heard it from me." Caitlyn would tell on herself. She would tell Roland the next time she saw him. Maybe he wouldn't care.

"A castle would be *perfect* for a costume party," Mya said, all dreamy-like.

Chapter Twenty-three

Roland

Roland pivoted the laundry basket to his hip and reached for the doorknob to Jarret's bedroom. He hesitated. Jarret had taken off in Papa's Lexus around noon, but he usually left the door open when he wasn't in his bedroom. He hadn't returned, had he?

He knocked. No one answered so he tried twisting the knob. It was locked. He knocked again, louder.

"Go away." Jarret sounded annoyed.

"Open the door. I have your laundry."

"Leave it and go."

"Leave it? On the floor? Really? I've got your . . ." He checked the label of the shirt on top. ". . . your two Armani shirts, your Gucci jeans, your—"

A thud and a clank sounded then the door opened but only enough for Jarret to glare out. "Use your brain. Set the basket down and go."

"My stuff's in here, too, in the bottom. Why can't you just open the door? I'll put your clothes on your bed and go."

Words like selfish, annoying, and inconsiderate popped into his mind, but he really wanted to stop judging Jarret. Jarret had more than proven he could be nice, helpful, and self-sacrificing. So he was a little rude at times. Maybe he was having a bad day. His computer could've crashed, or his credit card could've gotten turned down while he was shopping online. Or maybe he was anxious about Keefe's return. He had a different way of handling things.

"I'm using my bed." Jarret grinned, his eyes holding a cocky glint.

"So, I'll set them on your chair. Come on. Basket's getting heavy." Roland shifted the basket and re-gripped the handles. "Open the door!"

Jarret's grin grew, the look in his eyes now calculating. Then he flung open the door.

Though he hadn't wanted to show annoyance, Roland huffed and shook his head as he stepped into the room. Why did Jarret have to hate him so? If it were Keefe—

Roland stopped mid-step and his mouth fell open.

Jarret had a girl in his room!

Zoe stood facing the window, holding the curtain back with one hand and combing her hair with the other. Letting the curtain fall, she turned and smiled. "Hi, Roland."

"You can't have girls up here." Roland spun to face Jarret. "I heard Nanny talk to you about it. It was a week ago when you had Zoe over for dinner and tried to go upstairs. She was very clear. No girls upstairs."

Still grinning, Jarret swaggered to Zoe. "Yeah, Roland, I remember. So you'd better not tell. Cuz if Nanny or Papa finds out, you're gonna be toast." He threw Roland a murderous glance.

"So, what's she doing up here?"

Jarret took the comb from Zoe and ran his fingers through her hair. "You really want to know?"

A faint sound came from outside. Tires crunching over gravel? Then an ominous silence.

The stupid grin faded from Jarret's face.

A car door slammed. Then another.

Feeling a strange need to flee, Roland tensed.

Jarret spun to face the window. As he drew the curtain back, a bad word slipped out. "Papa's home! We gotta get you downstairs," he said to Zoe, then to Roland, "Go see where Nanny is."

Gripped by a sense of urgency, Roland dropped the basket and dashed downstairs. At the foot of the steps, he glimpsed Nanny working at the kitchen table. If Zoe came down now and Nanny looked up, she'd see her. If he could get Nanny farther into the kitchen, like behind the bar counter—

He dashed back upstairs. "Nanny will see you if you go down now. Give me a few seconds to distract her."

Jarret peeked out his window. "You've only got a few seconds." He spoke fast. "They're pulling luggage from the trunk."

Heart racing, Roland dashed back downstairs. A thought flitted through his mind. Why was he helping Jarret get away with something? It would probably be better for him to get caught.

He slowed to a normal pace as he entered the kitchen. "Hi, Nanny."

She looked up. "Did you get that laundry put away? Your father should be here any minute now."

Yeah, don't I know it. Roland nodded, stepped around the counter, and opened a cupboard. Not one to destroy things on purpose, his insides twisted as he pulled a glass from the shelf and let it slip from his fingers.

The glass shattered on the floor.

Nanny gasped and shot to his side. "Are you alright, dear?" She assessed the situation and motioned him away. "I'll take care of that."

"Sorry. Thanks." He stepped around the bar counter. It was just a glass. Why did he feel so—

A blur of black hair and pale clothes passed the open kitchen doorway.

Then the front door creaked open.

Roland dashed from the kitchen.

Zoe and Jarret stood frozen in the middle of the hallway. At least they weren't upstairs. Papa, Mr. Digby, and Keefe mumbled to each other as they carried luggage into the sunny foyer.

"Howdy, boys." Papa set his luggage down and opened his arms. Jarret, the closest, stepped over for a hug.

Keefe's attention snapped to Jarret and his face lit up. As Jarret backed up from Papa, Keefe moved in, lifting a hand to his twin's shoulder.

With a glance that could freeze a desert, Jarret shrugged Keefe's hand from his shoulder and turned away.

While Keefe's hand remained hovering in mid-air, his expression fell.

Papa hugged Roland then his blue eyes lassoed Zoe. "Who's this?"

"Uh, I've got a girlfriend now." Jarret returned to Zoe's side.

"Hi." Zoe swung her hand out and smiled politely. "I'm Zoe." With her silky dark hair and poise, the beige khakis and white sweater, she gave off a definite air of class.

"Nice to meet you. I'm Mr. West." Papa shook her hand and tugged his cowboy hat. He looked every bit the cowboy, hat, boots, leathery skin, and tall. "Maybe you can join us for dinner."

"I'd like that."

"Why don't we all have some refreshments?" Nanny stepped into the foyer, all smiles and cheer. Her gaze landed on Zoe, and her eyes narrowed with a look of suspicion. "I didn't know you were here, Zoe."

"She just got here," Jarret lied smoothly. He took Zoe by the hand and led her to the kitchen.

While Mr. Digby carried luggage past, Keefe came up to Roland and hugged him. "Hey ya, Roland. Miss me?" The picture of him on the cell phone didn't compare to the real thing. Keefe looked mature and clean-cut with the cropped hair, his dark eyebrows and eyes standing out.

Roland smiled, finding himself drawn to the strange look in Keefe's eyes. "Yeah, I missed you." He wanted to share how hard he'd been trying to keep Jarret out of trouble, in Keefe's stead, but that would only reveal how judgmental he'd been. So he decided to limit his comments to praise. "You know Jarret went camping with us, right?"

Keefe draped an arm around Roland's shoulders as they walked to the kitchen. "Yeah, he told me." He leaned in and spoke low. "That was before he stopped talking to me."

"He stopped talking to you?"

Keefe nodded, ran a hand through his hair, and whispered, "Doesn't like my haircut."

Zoe and Papa took seats at the little kitchen table. Jarret pulled the chair in the middle around to one side and sat next to Zoe.

"Their house is done. Looks great," Jarret said to Papa. "So when are we gonna go look for my car?"

Eyes on Jarret and mouth half open as if he wanted to say something, Keefe eased himself onto a stool at the bar counter.

Jarret threw a hostile glance in Keefe's direction.

Keefe took a deep breath and averted his gaze.

"I'll give Mr. Finn a call," Papa said. "Make sure he's satisfied."

Hearing the name *Finn*, Roland looked. Papa already knew what Jarret had done for them? Roland took the barstool next to Keefe, and Nanny slid glasses of iced tea to them.

"I've got something for you," Keefe said to Roland before sipping his iced tea. "Two things, really."

Jarret threw another glance.

Papa's voice had lowered, but Roland still heard it. "Maybe Mr. Finn has a few things that need touched up. I want him to be satisfied with . . ."

"We got a lucky break two days ago," Keefe said, glancing from Roland to Nanny. "Or we'd probably still be out there." A sentimental, distant look came over him. "I really liked Italy. Could've stayed longer."

"What was your lucky break?" Nanny offered Keefe a muffin from a basket then shuffled around the counter, her eyes on Papa.

"A gentleman Papa met with in Bagno di Romagna . . ." Keefe turned, keeping his eyes on Nanny as she carried the muffins to the kitchen table. ". . . gave us a lead which took us back to Florence. Most of our leads led to nothing."

"I worked my hours," Jarret said to Papa, sounding annoyed. "Mr. Finn kept track. I think he wrote things down: when I was there, what I did . . ."

"Most leads were dead ends," Keefe said, looking at Roland. "You know how that is."

"Yeah." Roland wanted to pay attention to Keefe but . . . It almost sounded like Papa and Jarret had had an arrangement concerning the Finns. But he shouldn't think like that; he didn't want to judge, to attach a selfish motive to Jarret's good deed.

Roland forced his attention back to Keefe, realizing he'd missed bits of what he had said.

". . . brought us back to Florence and Saint Ambrose's Basilica. They have a museum attached. You know, the tomb of Saint Ambrose is there. Do you know who he is?"

"Huh? No."

"I want to get my car," Jarret said through clenched teeth, his jaw twitching. "You're back. I did what you said. Why do I have to wait?"

"Settle down, Jarret," Papa said. "Did you two meet at school?"

Zoe answered him and said something else with a smile. She grabbed Jarret's hand, probably wanting to calm him.

". . . so two miracles took place at this church, this little basilica," Keefe said, blinking a few times. He pressed his lips together and stared at the countertop. "And when I went in there, the feeling was just the same. You remember what I told you about the miracle in Bagno? It really changed me."

Jarret spun to Keefe. He dropped Zoe's hand and scraped his chair out. "What're you talking about?" He stomped up to Keefe, the muscles in his arms flexing.

Keefe looked at him over his shoulder and swallowed hard.

Roland felt tempted to avert his gaze. He'd never seen Keefe uncomfortable around Jarret before.

Keefe straightened and turned on the stool to face Jarret. "If you hadn't stopped talking to me, you'd know all about it."

A crooked grin stretched across Jarret's face. The kitchen lighting brought out the stubble on his chin and over his lip and the darkness in his dilated pupils, giving him a sinister quality. "Does this have to do with your haircut?"

"It has everything to do with my haircut."

They stared at each other in silence, the way they had always done, seeming to communicate without words. Papa, Nanny, and Zoe stopped talking, everyone waiting the moment out.

"Do you want to know about it?" Keefe finally said.

Jarret made the slightest headshake. "There couldn't be a good enough reason." He stepped backward. "All your strength, Keefe. You gave up all your strength."

Eyes hard and jaw set, he motioned for Zoe to follow and walked away.

Life-Changing Love

Eyes hard and jaw set, he motioned for Zoe to follow and walked away.

Chapter Twenty-four

Caitlyn

The school day dragged. Caitlyn couldn't wait to talk to Zoe. Due to the nice weather, she expected to find her outside with Jarret at the picnic tables. When lunch break finally came, she snatched her lunch from her locker, tied her sweater, and bolted out the back doors of the school.

The sudden burst of sunlight dazzled her, but she didn't mind. She relished every opportunity to eat lunch outside. The cool air carried the scent of burning wood, making her breathe deep and reminding her of camping. Oh, she hoped this would all work out.

It was already the middle of October, and they still didn't know whose house they could use for the Halloween party. Mya had asked Zoe. Zoe was supposed to ask Jarret. And Caitlyn was dying to know the answer. If Jarret didn't like the idea, they would resort to the original plan and throw it at Zoe's house. Time was running short, and they needed better plans if they were going to do it.

Caitlyn had already begun work on her costume, though it wouldn't come close to what she originally envisioned. She wanted a big, frilly 17th century European dress with ruffles, embroidery, and full skirts. But she had a single old-fashioned square-dance dress to work with and no money for extras. The fabric was sky-blue, shiny, and big enough to make the pleats she wanted in the back. At the second-hand store, she'd found a white linen shirt with puffy sleeves that would work perfectly under a dark blue shirt that she had torn apart and turned into a vest. And an old white sheet would make a good enough slip. She could do wonders with a sewing machine and old clothes.

Weaving around a group of girls, the picnic tables came into view. Zoe sat facing Caitlyn, Jarret across from her. They didn't look at each other. He stared out at the farmland that bordered the school grounds. She stared ahead, without appearing to see Caitlyn.

Caitlyn reached the picnic table and climbed onto the bench on the same side as Jarret so she could face Zoe.

Zoe's eyelids flickered. She turned to Caitlyn and flashed a weak smile. "Hi."

Jarret gave Caitlyn a casual glance and a nod then returned his gaze to the farms.

"What's wrong?" she mouthed to Zoe.

Zoe shrugged, the gloom in her eyes deepening.

"Are you fighting?" Caitlyn mouthed, glancing at the back of Jarret's head. The last word came out as a whisper, but Jarret didn't twitch.

She mouthed back something like, "I might."

Caitlyn squinted. *I might* didn't make sense. She must've said something else. Caitlyn was lousy at reading lips, signs, or gestures. People always got what she said, but she never got them.

Zoe turned to Jarret. "Just go over there. Talk to him instead of staring at him all day."

Jarret snapped his attention to her. "What? Go talk to who?" He glanced at Caitlyn, his look less friendly this time.

"You know who," she said. "How long can you be mad at him for cutting his hair?"

He glanced at Caitlyn again, giving her the distinct impression he wished she would go. She wished she would go, too, but she had already dumped her lunch onto the table, and she couldn't think of a single reasonable excuse for leaving.

"You don't understand me," Jarret said to Zoe.

Zoe rolled her eyes.

His jaw twitched, and he rocked forward as if he had something to say but thought better of it. Maybe because Caitlyn was there.

Again, Caitlyn wanted to get up and leave, but she really wanted the answer to her question first. Maybe she could speak in code.

"So, Zoe," she began, slow and awkward. "Mya said she asked you a question . . . that you were going to ask someone . . . about doing something, somewhere."

Zoe and Jarret both looked at her through squinty eyes, but then Zoe dipped her head and laughed.

"Oh, I forgot to ask him," she said. "I've had something on my mind."

Jarret rocked forward again. "Ask who? Who's *him*?"

"You," she said.

"Ask me what?"

She leaned toward him, tilted her head, and spoke in a flirty way. "We want to have a costume party for Halloween . . ." She touched his arm. ". . . at your house."

Caitlyn couldn't believe Zoe asked him in front of her. He was so touchy. And now he just stared at Zoe. Maybe he needed time to process the idea, but every second he delayed giving his answer increased Caitlyn's anxiety.

"I've been working on my dress," Caitlyn said, just to have something to say.

"I can't wait to see it." Zoe's eyes lit up. "Is it fancy?"

"Fancy? No. It's nothing like what I wanted. I don't have that kind of money. I'm a peasant in real life and a peasant in make-believe." She sighed. "But it's still a 17th century, medieval sort of thing. I'm hoping Roland will want to be a musketeer."

Jarret smirked. "A musketeer?"

"What's wrong with that? Musketeers are cool." Caitlyn sounded defensive. "Don't they carry swords?"

"That's gonna be my costume."

Zoe grabbed his arm. Her eyes popped. "You and your brothers can be The Three Musketeers."

He flinched. "No. Just me. They can be waifs. I'll get your costume, too. You'll be my lady." He took her hand and kissed it.

"So, we can do it?" Caitlyn's whole body tingled with anticipation. They were going to throw a party!

"Yeah. We can do it." He sounded matter-of-fact.

"Don't you have to ask?" Zoe said.

"No. We had to skip our annual end-of-summer competitions, so this can make up for it."

"Your what?" Caitlyn said.

"It's just something we do every year," he said. "Family and friends come from all across the country, and we compete in archery, fencing, sprinting . . . That kind of stuff. We had to skip it this year due to my father's schedule." He grinned and gave Caitlyn a flirty look that made her uncomfortable. "So he owes us."

Turning to Zoe, he continued. "We'll have a pig roast and a band. Someone will have to be in charge of decorations. I like those white Christmas lights. Yeah. I want them everywhere." Smiling, he reached for the cell phone on his belt and walked away.

"Where are you going?" Zoe said.

"I'm gonna tell my father. We'll have to get started on all the arrangements." Phone to his ear, he strode in the direction of the old maple tree, but then he veered and headed for the smokers' corner of the building.

"Wow," Caitlyn said. "That was easy. And don't you love how every other teen has to ask, but he calls home to *tell* his father?"

"I don't think so." Zoe's eyes sparkled. "He's probably begging right now. That's why he's walking to where we can't hear him."

They both giggled.

"I wonder where Roland is. I can't wait to tell him." Caitlyn scanned the school grounds, her gaze skimming over groups and slowing over shadows.

"He's over there." Zoe pointed to the old, thick-trunked maple in the strip of grass between the school grounds and the farmland. "He's with Keefe. That's why Jarret's been staring over there. Didn't you notice?"

The hint of a jacket stuck out from behind the tree trunk.

"Keefe's over there, too?" She wanted to find out about the miracle he'd witnessed. She could probably walk right over there and ask him. Her palms sweated at the thought. What would she say? Would she sound nosy? Did he even know who she was? She'd have to begin with an introduction. *Hi, I'm Caitlyn, Roland's friend, but not his girlfriend because he doesn't want a girlfriend. I go to school here. You're in my study hall. Anyway, I overheard Roland talking to you on the phone one day. . .* No. That just wouldn't work.

"So, did you understand what I said, what I whispered?" Zoe said.

"What?"

"You asked me what was wrong. I told you *I'm late.*"

"You did? Late for what?"

Zoe huffed and shook her head. Then she glanced to either side, leaned forward, and whispered, "You know, *that* time."

"What do you mean, that time?"

"Of the month, dummy."

Oh. *That.* Caitlyn ripped open a bag of cookies. "I'm always late. Sometimes I skip a month."

"Well, I'm never late, so I got a pregnancy test. But I'm afraid to take it."

Caitlyn stopped chewing and swallowed the cookie dry. "Why would you be pregnant?" She grabbed her water bottle.

"Why do you think?" Zoe stared off into the distance, combing her fingers through her silky curtain of hair.

Caitlyn sat frozen. Were they actually . . . *doing it?* Her mind reeled at the thought.

Zoe broke her gaze and glanced. "We'll talk about it later. Jarret's coming back."

"Doesn't he know?"

She shook her head then smiled up at him.

Jarret sat down next to Caitlyn, grinning. "It's a go. Better make up a guest list."

Chapter Twenty-five

Caitlyn

Caitlyn loved holding little Andy. A baby in her arms stirred up all the love in her heart. She and Andy liked to stare at each other, just letting the love flow back and forth through their eyes. She could stare at him all day, but he always broke the trance by gurgling and drooling or reaching for Caitlyn's hair or nose. Today he latched onto the strings on the neckline of her dress and undid the bow that she'd worked so hard on.

Caitlyn considered handing Andy back to Mom, but Mom just stood for the Gospel reading. Besides, Mom probably appreciated having her hands free every now and then, and Caitlyn didn't really mind. Holding a baby was worth every little inconvenience. It made her long for marriage and motherhood.

Did Roland like babies?

What about Zoe?

Caitlyn hugged Andy to her chest and rested her chin on his soft head. Father Carston read the Gospel, a smooth melody in his tone.

Could Zoe really be pregnant? She'd never even let on that they had that kind of relationship. Wasn't that something a girl should tell her best friend? Did she even love him? Did he love her? Did they really even know each other? They'd only been seeing each other a little over a month. How could she be pregnant?

Everyone sat down and Father began his homily. Mom reached for Andy, but Caitlyn hugged him tighter, stuck out her bottom lip, and made sad eyes. Mom let her keep him.

Maybe Zoe wasn't pregnant at all. She still hadn't taken a pregnancy test. She carried it around in her purse but whenever Caitlyn asked, she said she wasn't ready to find out yet. What was she waiting for? Caitlyn would be dying to know. But she wouldn't be in her situation. She'd have a husband to tell. Zoe would have to tell Jarret, and he seemed like a guy who might overreact.

For the first time in her life, Caitlyn did not envy Zoe.

They would know tonight. Zoe promised to meet Caitlyn at Peter's house for dinner. She said she wasn't comfortable taking the test at her house. She wanted to do it at Caitlyn's, but they hadn't a shred of privacy in their little, one-bathroom house. And the day she'd asked, they were having another chastity/courtship meeting.

Dominic's mom gave a talk about doing things in groups and developing friendships without the pressure that comes from one-on-one dating. Caitlyn had taken the opportunity to mention the Halloween party, which she hadn't told Mom about earlier because parties made Mom suspicious. But Caitlyn stressed that parents were welcome, it would be outside, and they would have games and other things that she made up on the spot. It went over well, and she even got volunteers for snacks, beverages, set-up, and clean up. Rick, who was also in the Fire Starters, committed the whole group to hanging white Christmas lights. Jarret would like that since the lights were his idea.

Caitlyn glanced at the altar. The bells rang and everyone dropped to his or her knees for the Sanctus prayer. Unable to kneel with Andy on her lap, she scooted to the edge of the pew.

Suddenly it was time for the Consecration, the most sacred part of Mass. The bells rang again. And Father lifted the Host.

Peace flooded Caitlyn's soul. Her mind settled for the rest of the Mass, leaving her unable to concentrate on anything but the love of Jesus — until she got in line for Holy Communion.

There in the other line, a little bit ahead of her, was Roland West. He wore black dress pants and a gray dress shirt. She'd only seen him once or twice before at noon Mass.

Nearing the altar, she shifted Andy to her hip. The man in front of Roland knelt to receive Holy Communion. Her heart stirred to see such faith in a young man.

Father offered Caitlyn Holy Communion.

Her eyes watered as he placed the Host on her tongue. Did she have that faith? Did she believe in the True Presence of Jesus Christ here in this Eucharist? Did she believe that Jesus loved her so much that He wanted to give Himself to her completely, here and now in this Holy Communion? Was she willing to accept and enter into that love, to give herself back to Him in faithfulness?

"Let us pray," Father said and everyone stood.

Caitlyn turned to glimpse Roland and the man who sat beside him, the one she'd seen kneeling for Holy Communion. Her breath caught at the sight.

The young man was Keefe West. The picture of him on Roland's cell phone hadn't prepared her for the real thing. He stood with bowed head, displaying a genuine humility that moved her. Mr. West stood next to him, then Jarret, neither of whom she had seen in line for Holy Communion. But there they all were, the entire West family, in the second row on the opposite side of the church. Boy, they were a handsome bunch of men, and all dressed up . . . well, except for Jarret, who wore jeans.

Caitlyn gasped, an idea coming to her. She knew how she could find out about Keefe's miracle.

This time, when Mom reached for Andy, Caitlyn relinquished him and prepared to make a break for it. After the last word of the final hymn, but before the organist stopped playing, Caitlyn bolted for the back of the church, where she knew she'd find Peter.

Peter stood with his arms out to each side, blocking Toby from the candles at the Saint Anne's shrine. He saw Caitlyn and rolled his eyes to show his frustration.

Toby managed to reach past him and snatch one of the long matches.

"Oh, no you don't." Peter grabbed it.

"Did you see the Wests here?"

Peter gave her an amused grin. Maybe she looked a bit too anxious.

"Yeah, sure, I saw them." Keeping one arm in front of the shrine to block Toby, he faced Caitlyn.

"Can they come over to your house tonight?"

"My house? All of them? Why would I want the entire West clan at my house?"

Caitlyn stepped closer and put on a begging face, not that her effort at looking pathetic ever had any impact on him in the past. "Pleeease."

Mr. Brandt had managed to lure Toby toward the doors, and now an older woman approached the shrine, but Peter still stood with his arm out.

"I don't think so, Caitlyn." Peter must've sensed someone trying to step around him because then he lunged to the side.

The woman jumped back and shrieked.

"Oh, sorry." Peter's face turned beet red. "I thought you were—" He squeezed Caitlyn's arm and led her to the vestibule. "Why didn't you tell me that wasn't Toby?"

"Why can't the Wests come over?"

He stopped by an usher handing out bulletins. "You know how many guests we have at the B & B in the fall? With your family over and all the guests, there's no room to spare today. You and me will probably be eating in the living room." Peter's family operated a bed-and-breakfast that provided dinner as well. And he probably wasn't serious about having to eat in the living room, but they did fill up in the fall.

"What about after dinner?"

"I don't know. I'm not asking them." He strode toward the door. "See ya later."

Caitlyn followed him into the vestibule, where the gray outdoors and a steady rain showed through the propped-open doors. The Brandts, Mr. West, Keefe, and Roland stood on one side of the vestibule, the adults talking. Toby walked in circles around Roland. Roland watched him, amusement in his eyes.

Peter approached Roland and grabbed Toby by the arm. "Knock it off."

On the other side of the vestibule, Jarret West stood alone. He leaned against a waist-high cabinet, arms folded and eyelids at half-mast. He yawned. When he cast a glance Caitlyn's way, she decided to ask him to invite his family over. The Brandts wouldn't care. They expected the Summers every Sunday and always said she could bring friends.

Jarret gave her the once-over as she approached, his gaze lingering on her neck or—

Caitlyn's hands shot up to re-tie the bow at the neckline of her Bohemian style dress.

He gave her a lopsided grin. "That's a nice dress . . . for church."

"Thanks." Caitlyn refused to recognize the sarcasm in his tone. Her dress was long and completely modest. "I was wondering . . ." How should she word this? "Are you . . . are you doing anything tonight?" She stopped a few feet away and picked up a flyer on the cabinet, pretending to be interested in it.

He pulled himself up and sat atop the cabinet, next to the stack of flyers. "Why? You wanna go out?"

Her face burned. She avoided his eyes. "Don't be silly. Zoe's going with me to Peter's later, and I thought you might want to come. Actually, I thought your whole family might want to come. You know, with Keefe just getting back." Pushing past her discomfort, she forced herself to make eye contact. "Do you think they would?"

He glanced across the vestibule.

Parishioners continued to trickle out of the church. Caitlyn's family appeared in the doorway, and Dad came up to her.

"There you are." He chuckled. "One minute you're with us, next minute, I look and you're gone." Dad, shorter than average, somewhat chubby, and with graying hair that he could never comb straight, found everything in life amusing. "We have to get back to the house. Your mother wants to bake an angel food cake for tonight, and you know how long that ends up taking." He looked at Jarret. "Who's this?"

"No one." Caitlyn turned her back to Jarret and folded her arms. She did not want her parents thinking she liked him. With his long hair, ripped jeans, and attitude, he had rebellion written all over him. If they thought she liked him, they'd never let her leave the house again. "I'll be out in a minute, okay? I need to talk to Peter."

"Okay, but it's raining so make it snappy." He snapped his fingers a few times, never making much of a sound.

When her family left, she faced Jarret again.

He had another crooked grin for her. "I'm no one, huh?"

"I'm sorry. I just didn't want, um, to introduce everyone. So, will you invite your family over?"

"No. But I'll come. Zoe didn't tell me she was going over there."

The blood drained from Caitlyn's face, neck, then her entire body. What had she done? Not only had her plan failed, but now she'd betrayed Zoe. Zoe wanted to meet over there so she could take the pregnancy test privately, and here Caitlyn had just invited her boyfriend over. What a terrible friend she was.

"Why don't you come around seven?" Caitlyn said, since Zoe would be there around five-thirty. "And I'd really like it if you'd invite your family, too. Please."

"Can't. I'm not talking to them." He smiled as he slid off the cabinet. "See ya later."

Chapter Twenty-six

Caitlyn

The Forest Gateway B & B brimmed with life, loud talking, laughter, and the smell of Italian food. Caitlyn's parents and sisters shared one of the three booths in the big dining room. Peter's parents, his aunt, and guests sat around the long table in the middle of the room. More guests filled the other two booths.

Peter, Zoe, and Caitlyn ate dinner in the living room, balancing their plates on their laps. Toby sat on the floor, playing a game on the TV and whining every time Caitlyn's two-year-old brother David reached for the remote. The baby slept soundly on a blanket on the floor, between the couch and recliner. Zoe had barely touched her dinner, had barely spoken a word, and appeared absorbed in Toby's game—an old version of Super Mario.

A clock hung above the TV. Jarret would arrive in twenty-seven minutes, if he were punctual.

Hunched over her second plate of spaghetti and lasagna, Caitlyn twisted noodles onto her fork. Anxiety made her hungry.

Her gaze slid to the purse beside her on the couch. Zoe's purse. Not the little black one she usually carried. The bigger denim one. The one big enough to hide a pregnancy test kit among its contents. If only Zoe would've taken the test as soon as she got here, but she insisted she needed to eat first.

Minutes passed. Guests finished their dinners and returned to their rooms. Zoe sat holding her fork but not eating.

Caitlyn stuffed the last bite of lasagna into her mouth, set the plate on the coffee table, and shoved the purse toward Zoe. "If you're not hungry, why don't you go to the bathroom?"

Peter's head turned. "What're you, her mom?" he said with his mouth full.

"Yeah, Caitlyn," Zoe said. "Are you my mom? I'll go when I need to go." She flashed a snotty smile and turned away, flipping her hair.

Caitlyn huffed and sunk back in the couch. "Come on, Zoe. Now's a good time. Let's not wait any longer. Besides . . ." She hadn't told her Jarret was coming over, and they must not have talked all day, because she didn't seem to know. Fearing it would affect her decision to take the test, Caitlyn didn't want to tell her yet.

Caitlyn stood and slung Zoe's purse strap over her shoulder. "Well, then I'm going to the bathroom."

When Caitlyn stepped past Zoe, Zoe groaned. "Oh, all right."

"It takes two of you to go to the bathroom?" Peter said.

"Will you watch the baby?" Caitlyn headed for the steps with Zoe at her heels.

Peter shouted, "No," but she knew he would.

In an earlier discussion, Caitlyn and Zoe decided to use the upstairs bathroom, Peter's bathroom, in case someone needed the one downstairs. Peter's bedroom was the only other room upstairs in the converted attic, so they should have complete privacy.

A few minutes later, they stood motionless in Peter's bathroom, huddling over the test stick and peering through the result window.

"I see two stripes," Caitlyn said.

Zoe's eyebrows drew together. "Are you sure?"

"What do *you* see?" No matter how you looked at it, two pink stripes ran across the result window.

Zoe sighed and staggered back, bumping the towel rack. "I'm pregnant." She slid to the floor, next to a pile of damp towels.

Caitlyn sat beside her. "It's not the end of the world. It'll be okay."

She shook her head, looking like Caitlyn had lost her mind.

A thought occurred to Caitlyn. She could take care of the baby for Zoe! Mom might not like the idea, and Zoe wouldn't want to hear it now. Besides, it was too early for that kind of planning. First on the "to do" list: tell Jarret.

"Do you think the results could be wrong?" Zoe crawled to the garbage can and dug the box back out.

"I don't know. I wouldn't think so. It said something about showing you're not pregnant when you really are. I don't think it goes the other way around."

Kneeling by the garbage can, Zoe spread out the crinkly instructions and stared at them through desperate eyes.

Caitlyn wished she had words that would comfort her. "I guess you could get another—"

The doorbell rang.

Caitlyn's mouth fell open. She still hadn't mentioned that Jarret was coming over. Zoe should know so she could prepare herself. She grabbed Zoe's arm. "I have to tell you something."

Still reading the instructions, Zoe wiped her nose with the back of her hand. "Huh?"

"Have you talked to Jarret today?"

Zoe shook her head. "He was car shopping."

"Um, well, Zoe, I think Jarret's here."

Lifting her gaze from the instructions, she gave Caitlyn a blank look. Then her forehead wrinkled and her eyes got big. "What?"

"I saw the Wests at church today and I . . ." How in the world could she word it?

"You what?"

"I wanted to know what happened to Keefe in Italy." Oh my, she had no idea how to tell her without revealing what a lousy, selfish friend she was.

Zoe shook her head, still looking troubled but also confused. "I thought you said Jarret's here."

Footfalls sounded on the stairs, many footfalls, as if a gang ascended them. Then voices. Someone pounded on the door.

Zoe and Caitlyn gasped.

"Hey, are you still in there?" Peter shouted. "The West boys are here. Every. Last. One of them. And two of them are up here with me."

"I'll be out in a minute." Caitlyn meant to give the impression she was alone so no one would wonder why they were both in the bathroom.

"Let's get you fixed up." She smoothed Zoe's hair then went to the vanity to find a clean washcloth.

Zoe stood. "Jarret's here?"

Caitlyn held a washcloth under cold water, rung it out, and handed it to Zoe. "Try to compose yourself, or he'll wonder what's wrong. You don't have to talk about it now. Wait until you're ready. Okay?"

She nodded and turned to the mirror. Within seconds, she had composed herself, model perfect.

Caitlyn cracked open the bathroom door. Voices came from Peter's room. "Ready?" She looked at Zoe.

Zoe nodded.

They crossed the landing to Peter's half-open bedroom door. The door wouldn't open further, so they squeezed into his room.

Clothes lay in piles by the bed, the closet, and behind the door. Boxes of electronic projects lined one wall. Peter sat at his desk, the cleanest thing in the room, showing Roland something. Jarret sat on Peter's messy bed.

"Hey." Jarret stood when he saw Zoe.

". . . so next time I need to pick a lock, I'll be able to," Peter said to Roland then looked at them. "You girls done in the bathroom, or did you need more help in there?" He grinned.

Roland turned and gave Caitlyn a shy smile, making her heart skip a beat. He'd changed out of his Sunday best and now wore a straight black jacket over a black shirt, the hem of a red shirt showing from underneath.

"Hi," Caitlyn said to Roland. "I didn't know everyone was coming over."

"Yeah, Peter's father invited us."

Jarret came up to Zoe and rubbed her arm. "Something wrong?" he whispered.

"Mr. West and Keefe are downstairs," Peter said in his typically loud voice. "Your dad's getting the scoop on their trip to Italy."

"He is?" Caitlyn was missing it! Keefe was probably telling them all about the miracle. She had to get down there.

Zoe folded her arms and moved closer, bumping Caitlyn.

"What's the matter?" Jarret said to her, no longer whispering, sounding annoyed.

"You know our Halloween party is going to be soon." Caitlyn looked directly at Jarret, but his eyes were fixed on Zoe. "I have some volunteers. Some people offered to help with things."

"Why the heck do you want to throw a big costume party anyway?" Peter looked from Roland to Caitlyn. "Sounds like a lot of work. And what if it rains?" He spoke lower, to Roland. "Do you have a costume?"

Roland nodded.

"What is it?" Peter said. "No, let me guess. You're going to be a vampire."

"Let's get a notebook for planning and go downstairs." Caitlyn pushed past Peter to get to his desk.

"Why does everything have to be a secret with you?" Peter said to Roland. Then he shouted at Caitlyn, "Stay outta my desk."

Caitlyn found a notebook in the second drawer and bolted for the door.

Jarret stood in her way, arms folded, peering at Zoe. Eyes downcast, Zoe shook her head.

Caitlyn stepped around Jarret. "Come on, Zoe, guys, let's go downstairs." She figured Zoe would want to be around more people. But, more selfishly, she just couldn't miss the details about the miracle! Not really knowing Keefe, she would never find the courage to ask him herself.

Caitlyn's sisters and brothers romped around the living room while Toby played a game on the TV. The bed-and-breakfast guests had left the dining room, leaving only her parents, the Brandts, Mr. West, and Keefe. They sat at the long table, so Caitlyn slid into a booth.

Mr. West, seated at the end of the table, said something about paintings.

Peter and Roland strolled side by side into the dining room. Peter slid into the booth, sitting across from Caitlyn, but Roland approached Keefe.

After Roland said something to Keefe, Keefe shook his head. "He's not talking to me," Keefe said. "It wouldn't do any good."

Looking sulky, Roland came to the booth. His gaze swiveled from Peter to Caitlyn, then back to Peter, but then he slid in next to Peter.

"Where's Zoe?" Caitlyn said.

"Didn't you hear them?" Peter grinned. "As soon as we left my room, their conversation got heated."

"What about?" She hoped they didn't have an answer to her question. She hoped Jarret and Zoe weren't talking about Zoe's situation. Zoe should wait until she's had time to think it over.

Peter shrugged. "I don't know. I mean, I'm nosy, but . . ." He smiled at Roland. "Roland wouldn't let me stand there and listen. He said it's none of our business."

Roland stared at his father, who was describing a basilica in Florence.

"Wow," Caitlyn's dad said, chuckling, "that makes our church sound like a mere chapel. So, uh, tell us Keefe . . ."

Caitlyn's ears perked.

"What was your favorite part of Italy?"

Keefe rubbed his hand over his hair. Maybe the short haircut still felt odd since he'd worn his hair long all his life. "My favorite part . . ."

Someone stomped down the stairs, and all heads turned. Jarret stormed past the living room and to the front door. As he grabbed a leather jacket from a wall hook, his gaze shot to his father. "I want my car. I'm not waiting any longer."

Mr. West made no reply.

Jarret didn't wait for one. He yanked open the door. Rain poured outside, but he pushed open the screen door and stormed out. The screen door slammed behind him. He left the front door wide open.

Caitlyn's dad chuckled. "Well, he's in a hurry. Must have a hot date, huh? Or off to get that car." Dad wouldn't have known Jarret's *date* was upstairs and probably crying her eyes out. Dad just always said silly things. Maybe he thought it lightened a tense moment.

Keefe scraped his chair out and stood.

Before he could take a step, Mr. West latched onto his forearm. "Let him go," Mr. West said in a low voice.

"But it's raining. Can I take your car, drive him home and come back?"

Mr. West shook his head. "Let him sort this out on his own."

They stared at each other, Keefe standing at his chair, Mr. West clutching his arm. No one spoke until Mrs. Brandt said something about drinks and got up. Mom went to help.

A long moment later, Keefe sat down and scooted his chair in. He might've been willing to answer the question Dad had asked about his favorite part of Italy, but to her dismay, Caitlyn wouldn't be around to hear it. Zoe hadn't come downstairs yet, so Caitlyn excused herself and climbed the stairs.

Zoe sat on the windowsill in Peter's bedroom, staring through raindrops on the window to the darkness outside. She remained motionless as Caitlyn crossed the room to her.

Caitlyn wrapped her arms around Zoe's shoulders, hugging her from behind. "You told him?"

"You know me. I can't hide the way I feel." She faced Caitlyn. "He knew something was wrong. I told him we'd talk later but . . ." She dropped her gaze. ". . . that made him angry." She paced across the room, stepping over a toolbox and a book, and turned around. "Didn't you hear him?"

Caitlyn shook her head. "I didn't hear anything from downstairs."

Zoe stopped by Peter's bed, grabbed a crumpled sheet and pulled it straight, then she dropped it and sat on the mess. "He calmed down after a short rant and said he cares about me. That's why he *needed* me to tell him. So I told him."

Caitlyn sat beside her. "What'd he say?"

"He wouldn't believe it at first."

"He believes you now, doesn't he?"

Zoe nodded. "I told him I'd take another pregnancy test to be sure. He's not happy about it." She pressed her lips together as if to keep from saying more. She probably needed time to think.

"Is he downstairs?" Zoe said.

Caitlyn shook her head. "He left."

"It's raining." She glanced at the window. "And he rode with his father."

Caitlyn shrugged. "Maybe he's sitting in the car."

Zoe got up, combed her fingers through her hair, and walked to the bedroom door. "I don't care. Let's go plan the party."

As they reached the foot of the stairs, the Brandts and Caitlyn's parents burst into laughter. Mr. West sat with his back to Caitlyn, so she couldn't tell if he laughed, too. Peter and Roland sat across from each other in the booth, Peter leaning forward and saying something that became clear as Caitlyn neared.

". . . never expected to see him darken the doors of our church."

"Papa made him go," Roland said. "There was a big fight in our house this morning, or we wouldv'e gone to an earlier Mass." His eyes shifted to Caitlyn and Zoe, and he shut his mouth.

Zoe slid into the booth next to Peter, leaving the seat next to Roland the obvious choice for Caitlyn.

Caitlyn struggled to suppress a smile.

Roland scooted over then leaned close. The faintest scent of spicy cologne—maybe just deodorant—the warmth of his body, his shoulder bumping hers . . .

A bolt of electricity passed through Caitlyn.

"Everything okay?" he whispered.

Unable to speak due to the influx of emotion, she nodded.

Peter's aunt said something about ice cream floats and, in the next minute, appeared at their booth and handed one to each of them.

Regaining her voice, Caitlyn thanked her and turned to Peter. "So, what was everyone talking about while we were gone?"

"Italy." Peter grabbed his spoon and the tall frosty glass. "They were telling us about the ancient city of old buildings and basilicas and all."

Caitlyn sighed, dipping her spoon into the blob of ice cream in her glass. Keefe had probably told his miracle story, and she'd missed it. Maybe Peter knew, now. Maybe he'd tell her. She watched him eat for a second then said, "Why don't you share some of it with us? What was the most interesting thing they talked about?"

"They took pictures. Mr. West said he'd invite us over for a slideshow." He turned his attention to his float, shoveling spoonsful of ice cream into his mouth. Then his gaze snapped to Caitlyn again. "Oh." He gave a sly grin. "Keefe told us why he got the haircut."

Was it related to the miracle? She leaned forward. "He did? Why? Why'd he get the haircut?"

Peter shrugged, tossed his spoon and straw aside, and brought his glass to his mouth to finish off the float. Then he banged the glass down and wiped his mouth on his sleeve. "Eh, it sounded kind of personal. Maybe you oughta ask him yourself."

Caitlyn looked at Roland, hoping he would tell her now that Keefe had made it public.

"I'm sure he'd tell you if you asked," Roland said.

She slumped back in the seat. Of course. She'd missed the whole conversation. Now she'd never know. She didn't know Keefe. They'd never even been introduced. How could she ask something so personal? Why did she feel so compelled to know? It wasn't her business anyway. She should just let it go.

With a sigh, she sat up, dragged her glass closer, and resumed sipping the float.

Someone knocked on the front door, and Peter's dad told Peter to answer it.

"Me? Why me?" Peter said as he trudged to the door. He opened it to a drenched and sour-faced Jarret.

Jarret stepped inside, bumping shoulders with Peter as he passed.

"What'd you do that for?" Peter glared.

Jarret stopped by the coat hooks and stared at Zoe, water dripping off his curls and into his frowning face.

Zoe stared back. Then she slid out of the booth and ran to him. She hugged her drenched boyfriend for a good long time, probably soaking up his wetness. Then she helped him remove his jacket and led him to the couch.

Caitlyn didn't hear him apologize, but he looked sorry enough.

Mr. West, who sat with his back to the living room, twisted around and gazed in their direction. Throughout the evening, he continued twisting around and glancing at them. The conversation at the table went from Mr. Brandt's work as a forest ranger to Mr. West's future assignment in Mississippi. Peter, Roland, and Caitlyn got down to the party planning business. The day would come before they knew it.

Chapter Twenty-seven

Caitlyn

Caitlyn carefully slipped into the pinned-up skirt of her costume and stood before the mirror on the closet door. Drawstrings around the wrists made the shirt sleeves full and draping. A scoop neckline, midnight blue vest, and a full skirt that hung to the floor gave the outfit a totally medieval look. Yes, she was ready to sew!

"It looks great," Zoe said. She'd flung herself onto Caitlyn's bed as soon as she had come over, and she hadn't moved since. She seemed to want to talk about something, but she sure was taking her time. "I love the back of the skirt. The pleats give you a figure."

"Thank you." Caitlyn removed three pins to get out of the skirt.

Zoe sat up. "You and Roland seem to be getting close. He looks for you every day at lunch. Does he ever call?"

"Not really. But I feel like we're getting close." A pin poked her as she emerged from the skirt. "I love being his friend." She wriggled out of the slip and stepped into her denim skirt.

"Do you think he'll change his mind about dating?"

"You mean courting?" Caitlyn smiled, zipping her skirt. Zoe knew she wasn't allowed to date.

Zoe smiled, groaned, and slid off the bed. "I have to tell you something." She stood in front of the mirror, looking at herself sideways and rubbing her flat belly.

Sitting cross-legged on the bed, Caitlyn placed the medieval skirt on her lap and grabbed a box of pins.

Zoe watched her through the mirror. "Jarret wants me to have an abortion."

Caitlyn froze.

Abortion?

The word, coming from the mouth of her pregnant best friend, shuddered through her soul. "You told him you wouldn't, right?"

Folding her arms, Zoe faced Caitlyn. "You'll never have to face something like this. It's horrible. There're no easy decisions here." She covered her face with her hands and tipped her head back. "I don't know what to do." She went to the window at the head of the bed.

"Well, you can't have an abortion. That's a real live baby in you. You can't just—"

She turned around, her eyes hard. "Don't tell me what I can't do. It's perfectly legal and people do it all the time. No one wants to do it. No one wakes up and says, I think I'd like to have an abortion today. It's a terrible thing to have to think about." She returned to the mirror. "I wish this had never happened. I'm too young to have a baby." Her eyes glistened with tears.

The box of pins tipped over, spilling pins on the skirt. Caitlyn set the skirt aside and scooted off the bed. "Why don't you carry the baby and let someone else raise it?"

Zoe huffed and walked past Caitlyn without looking at her. "These decisions are so easy for people who aren't pregnant, for people who aren't even involved in a relationship." She curled up on the bed, facing away from Caitlyn.

"Maybe you shouldn't have gotten into that kind of relationship. Why did you let him do it?" Caitlyn regretted her words and her shrill tone. She blamed Jarret more than Zoe. Seeing Zoe so distraught, knowing her situation, made Caitlyn's blood boil.

Zoe moaned. "Oh, girlfriend, it just happened. I don't think he meant for it to happen any more than I did. We were both upset at each other, and we got carried away making up. He was a virgin, too, you know."

Caitlyn hadn't known. The rumors she'd heard at school gave her the opposite impression.

She sat beside Zoe and stroked her hair. "Please don't do anything right away. Take some time and think about it. Okay?"

Zoe nodded just as someone knocked on the bedroom door.

The door opened a crack, and Mom stuck her head in. "Caitlyn, Roland's here to see you."

Caitlyn's eyes popped open and she sucked in a breath. "Roland? To see me?" She jumped up—jostling the skirt and sending pins flying everywhere—and went to the mirror. She hadn't looked at her hair all day. Why hadn't he called first?

"You look fine." Zoe sat up and hugged her knees. "Don't keep him waiting. Go see what he wants."

"Come with me."

"No. He'll see how upset I am and report to Jarret."

"No, he won't." Caitlyn took her hand and yanked her to her feet. "Not Roland."

Roland, wearing a black vest over a dark blue shirt, faced the window in the living room and stood with his hands in the front pockets of his faded black jeans. He turned as they came into the room and gave Caitlyn that little smile of his.

Like usual, her heart leaped. "Hi, Roland. You came over. Would you like something to drink?"

He blushed. His eyes turned to the ground then to the door. "Mr. Digby's waiting on me. I just wanted to ask you something. I guess I should've called but—"

"That's okay." She stepped closer but not too close, since standing near him made her lightheaded. "You can stop by whenever you want. Is something wrong?"

His steel-gray eyes flickered, and he smiled again. "No, nothing's wrong. My brother . . ." His gaze flitted to Zoe and back to Caitlyn. ". . . Keefe has a problem."

Twisting her arms behind her back, Caitlyn risked another step closer. "A problem?"

"Yeah, he, uh, ordered a costume from somewhere, but they're out of the one he wants, so he went online to find another one, but . . . Well, no one can ship one in time, and I told him . . ." He gulped, his Adam's apple bobbing. "I hope you don't mind, I told him you're making your own." He pulled a folded paper from the back pocket of his jeans and handed it to Caitlyn. "Do you think you could make him one?"

Caitlyn unfolded the paper to find a picture printed from a website. It was a monk in a long brown robe with a hooded cowl.

He reached into a front pocket and brought out some bills, all folded up. "He'll pay you."

"Oh, I'm sure I could do it. I'd have to get some measurements."

"You have our phone number, right?" He stepped closer with the money. "Whatever you need, just call."

When she took the money, their hands touched. Not wanting to look into his eyes at that moment, she looked at the folded bills. "Oh, this is way too much." Caitlyn held it out to him.

He backed up, stuffing his hands into his pockets. "No, it's not. He'd pay that at a store. Just keep it."

With her spirit as light as a helium balloon, Caitlyn watched him walk down the driveway to Mr. Digby's big black car. Her heart stirred. Roland turned to her for this! They'd worked together helping the Finns, searching for Toby, putting the party together, and now he came to her for this. Feeling closer to him than ever, she couldn't wait to see where their friendship would go.

"Let's go shopping." Zoe came up behind Caitlyn. "Will you have enough money left over for a cape?"

Chapter Twenty-eight

Caitlyn

The slant of the afternoon sunlight created a magical aura around the Wests' stone castle and surrounding grounds. Among dark evergreens and bony trees, leaves glowed gold and orange on the few trees that hadn't shed their leaves.

People flitted around the grounds, preparing for the party. Caterers bustled around the spit roast, the big purple tent next to it, and the rows of tables and chairs they'd set up earlier. White tablecloths, held down by jack-o-lanterns, soon covered every table and fluttered in the occasional breeze. The boys with the Fire Starters had already come, put strings of white lights everywhere, and gone home to get into costume.

Caitlyn couldn't have asked for better weather for the party. *Thank you, Lord.* Who wanted to wear a coat over a costume? Until the sun went down, she wouldn't even need the cape she had made for herself after making Keefe's monk outfit.

She and Zoe had strolled the grounds to see where they could help. Finding nothing to do, they stood in the shade of the front porch and watched Jarret rant at the stage set-up crew in the sprawling front lawn. His musketeer tabard flapped with his every exaggerated gesture. Evidently, they had put the stage and/or the dance-floor platform in the wrong spot.

"The costume fits him well. Don't you think?" Zoe said. She wore a matching Renaissance Lady costume with a long velveteen black skirt, puffy black and white striped sleeves, and a silky white bodice.

"By *fits him*, do you mean it's the right size? Because, yes, it fits him well. He makes for a handsome musketeer."

She giggled. "I meant, sometimes Jarret can be so pompous. Just look at him."

Jarret snatched the feathered hat from his head and used it to point here and there. The crew nodded their heads at whatever he said.

Caitlyn didn't want to say, but they both fit their costumes well. The elegant silk, ruffles, and frills suited them. They both had class and poise and often seemed conceited. Not that she thought Zoe was truly conceited.

"Where's Roland?" Zoe said. "Have you seen his costume?"

"I think he went to put it on. I have no idea what it is? Do you?"

She shook her head. "He's very mysterious. What about Peter?"

"He's out back getting the bonfire ready," Caitlyn said. "He was going to come as James Bond, but Roland and I talked him out of it. I suggested he come as a farmer. Roland thought woodsman, you know, like Daniel Boone. Peter didn't like either idea, but we all agreed on Luke Skywalker."

"Before he becomes a Jedi or after?"

"Before, of course. He's wearing dingy white. It looks natural on him."

They laughed.

Jarret put his hat on and strutted toward them. Possessing a masculinity that his long tresses, frills, and lace could not diminish, he mounted the steps and took Zoe in his arms. "Hey, gorgeous. You look hot." He kissed her with a passion Caitlyn didn't expect to encounter until her wedding night. Then he whispered in her ear, "I have something for you," and he looked at Caitlyn as if just noticing her.

Hating that she stood so close, Caitlyn smiled politely. "I think I'll go find Roland." She gathered up her skirt, feeling like a milkmaid next to the two of them, and stumbled off the porch.

"He's by the hog," Jarret shouted.

Caitlyn waved to show her appreciation then half jogged, half walked toward the spit roaster, weaving around people busy about their tasks.

Nothing could compare to the rich, fatty meat smell of roasting pig. The chefs cooked other things, too, on portable grills, and the mixture of savory smells made her stomach growl. She couldn't wait to eat.

Mr. West spoke with one of the white-clad chefs. In addition to the cowboy hat, he wore chaps and a gun belt over his jeans, and spurs on his boots. He probably owned all the parts for his costume and hadn't needed to buy anything. Maybe he'd been a ranch hand or a cowboy in his younger years.

Four teens in costume strolled up the driveway, walking side by side. Two wore black robes. One carried a scythe. The other had a curly white judge wig. Then came an angel in a long flowing gown, and last, the devil himself.

Caitlyn laughed. Then her gaze landed on a figure in the driveway, just beyond the spit.

A man in black. He stood with his back to her, but her heart recognized him. *Roland!* He wore slim black pants, a black long-sleeved shirt, and a Spanish gaucho hat.

Picking up her pace, she glimpsed another figure standing in front of him. A blonde in a white dress. Marilyn Monroe Mya!

Mya handed Roland a long white fur coat, stepped back, and spun in a circle. Her white halter dress billowed out, making her look like Marilyn Monroe standing over the subway grating.

Roland just stood there, watching.

She spun and spun then stopped, swooned, and grabbed her head. His arms flew out, catching her before she fell. She laughed flirtingly as he helped her regain her balance, but she didn't let go of his arm.

And he didn't let go of hers. They stood so close, him looking down at her, her gazing up.

A sinking feeling and a deep groan rumbled in Caitlyn's chest. Jealousy, or maybe disappointment, bubbled up inside. She turned and walked away.

Roland *did* like Mya. Caitlyn saw it with her own two eyes. Well, she couldn't see his face but she saw Mya's, and Mya definitely liked him. Did he have to catch her like that? Well . . . not that Caitlyn would've wanted him to stand there and watch her fall to the ground. But did he have to keep holding her?

With her skirt draped over one arm so she wouldn't trip on the hem, Caitlyn stomped off. Her skirt, she should've admitted it sooner, hung way too low.

Caitlyn stopped at the drink table and offered to help, wanting to keep busy and to keep what she'd just witnessed off her mind, but they didn't need her. She stomped to the snack table, but they didn't need help either. So she went around to the backyard, to where Peter and his father had been for the past hour.

They weren't there. The wood for the bonfire was all set up, camp chairs surrounding it. There was absolutely nothing left to do—except to think of how Roland liked Mya.

Caitlyn plopped down in a camp chair and groaned. Then she made fists and stomped her feet, quite childishly. She took a breath and smoothed her skirt. Why should she care? No. She didn't care. She didn't care one bit.

Jumping to her feet, she spun around the chair and smacked into someone.

"Oh, sorry," Caitlyn said, stumbling back.

"Hi." Keefe West stood before her dressed in the long, brown monk outfit she had sewn. He pushed the hood off his head. "You're Caitlyn, right? I mean, I've seen you. I guess, well, we've just never met. Have we?" He stuck out his hand. "I'm Keefe."

Caitlyn shook his hand and lowered her eyes, her gaze happening to land on the hem of his costume. It was ripped! All the way around, the hem had been ripped off and much too short. Why, she could see his ankles!

Her stomach turned. The costume must've been too long on him, and he'd tried to remedy it himself. He'd paid her so much, too. In her defense, they hadn't met once during the process. She'd called Roland with questions. Roland told Keefe. Nanny measured things. Keefe should've at least come over and tried the thing on.

"I'm sorry," Caitlyn said, glancing up at him.

"You're not Caitlyn?"

"What?"

He smiled. "I wanted to thank you. You did a great job with my costume."

"No, I didn't." Not wanting to look at the dreadful hem again, she looked at the horse stables in the distance behind Keefe. "I'm sorry I bumped into you. And you should probably get some money back for the robe. You paid me way too much." She stepped around him.

"No, I-I should've paid you more. It was a last minute request."

Caitlyn kept walking, feeling stupid in every way. She did a great job? Keefe was just being polite.

"Thanks again," he shouted.

Chapter Twenty-nine

Jarret

Jarret glanced up as three zombies shuffled by with bloodstained faces and ratty clothes. He sat in the driver's seat of his new car—his deep cherry red, two-year-old Chrysler 300. He hung his legs out and smoked with his left hand, being careful not to drop ashes in the interior. He'd insisted the dealer detail the thing before he drove it off the lot yesterday. And he intended to keep that *new car* look and smell for as long as possible.

The guests had been trickling in for the past hour. He hadn't recognized half of them in their costumes: pirates, superheroes, hippies, and freaks. Most of the guys, though, had come up to him and his new car. He'd even let Dominic, Foster, and Leo sit in it for a few seconds.

Caitlyn's father, Mr. Summer, had spent the most time admiring it, him in a formal suit and hat, looking like a gangster. "Hey there, Jarret, she's a beauty," he'd said. Then he talked cars for at least twenty minutes while the sun crept lower in the sky and the party filled up. His vast knowledge of cars and engines made Jarret feel stupid a time or two, so Jarret made a personal commitment to learn everything he could about engines.

After watching Mr. Summer walk away, Jarret closed and locked his car. Then he strode toward the party and found himself face to face with four kids standing side by side: a reaper, a judge, an angel, and a devil.

"Nice costumes." He nodded and tried going around, but they sidestepped, blocking him.

He made eye contact with the judge then tried squeezing between the judge and angel, but they shifted.

"You can't avoid us," the reaper said, peering through dark eyes.

"Oh yeah I can." Jarret glanced to either side, making sure Papa didn't see, and drew his sword. "Outta my way."

The reaper stepped up to his blade. "All ways lead to me. I'm Death." He gestured toward the others. "May I introduce Judgment, Heaven, and Hell?"

"Nice." Jarret appraised their costumes, and they let him pass.

On the gravel path between the stables and the steps of the veranda, Zoe stood with a group of prissy girls from school. One wore a red hooded cape, another looked like Mary Poppins, and the other two were flappers. They all held cups of punch, threw flirty glances, and giggled.

Jarret came up behind Zoe, pushed her silky hair out of the way and kissed her neck.

She pulled him to her side. "Are you done showing off your car?"

"For now."

"Hi, Jarret," the other girls each said. He gave them nods and looked them over. No girl held a candle to Zoe with her dark eyes, jet-black hair, slim figure, and expensive dress—which reminded him . . .

He took Zoe's hand and whispered in her ear. "I have something for you." He tugged her hand, wanting to lead her to the house. He'd bought her earrings that matched her dress, but he'd left them in his room.

Zoe twisted her arm as if to break his hold. "Where are we going?"

"In the house."

"Your father said no one's allowed inside."

"It's my house. If I wanna go inside, I'll go inside. And you're with me, so come on." He tugged her more forcefully, and she came.

He led her through the veranda and the long family room, heading for the stairs. As he stepped into the great room, the front door creaked open. Squeezing Zoe's hand, he darted to the corner where they wouldn't be seen down the long hallway that led to the foyer.

Boots scraped the floor.

"Come on," he whispered, dragging Zoe back the way they'd come. He ducked into the recreation room and flipped the lights on.

"It's Papa. He's probably getting something from his office. We'll wait here."

"What if he comes this way?" Worry showed in her pretty brown eyes.

It annoyed him that she didn't trust him. "We're playing pool. Why should he care?" He went for the cue rack on the wall. "But he won't come this way, so we'll hang out here till he goes back outside."

"Okay." She took a deep breath, watching as he set the triangle rack on the table.

The spark she'd had in her eyes in the beginning of their relationship had faded. He wanted it back. It had faded the day she'd told him she was pregnant. With that threat gone, she ought to have her spark back. Why didn't she?

He racked the few balls on the table that he could reach. "Something bothering you?"

She sauntered around the pool table carelessly reaching into pockets, pulling out balls, and letting them roll to no particular place on the table. "Actually . . . I want to talk to you."

"Why's that?" He hated those words. They made his insides bristle.

She gazed at the table, still fishing balls from the pockets.

Leaning, he snatched as many balls as he could reach and dropped them into the rack. "You look serious. Are you breaking up with me?"

"Breaking up with— No." She let the striped ball in her hand fall back into a pocket and met his gaze.

He returned his attention to the balls in the rack, putting them in order. Girls were hard to read. She seemed serious, as if something were really wrong. But everything was perfect about their relationship now. What could she have a problem with? "Wanna roll me that striped ball in the pocket?"

After a brief look of confusion, she dipped her hand back into the pocket and rolled the ball to him. "I didn't do it. And I don't want to." She spoke without looking at him then pressed her lips together and folded her arms.

He hung the rack on the wall and selected a pool cue. Lining up the break, he said, "Didn't do what?"

She turned away and leaned her velvety black skirt against the pool table.

He drew his arm back and was in the middle of making the break when she answered.

"I'm still pregnant."

He jerked. The cue slid, and the cue ball popped up. "Wow! What the—Are you out of your mind?" He tossed the cue stick onto the table. "What are you waiting for? You gonna wait until you start showing? Or . . . kids at school start noticing?" He sneered. "Gonna wait till your parents figure it out?"

Still leaning against the pool table, head down, she tensed her folded arms.

With a deep breath, he tried to subdue his anger. He approached her slowly, determined to speak gently. Persuasion would work better than threats, in her case anyway. He stroked her silky hair where it fell over her shoulder, then lifted her chin and gazed into her eyes with compassion.

"Hey, we're too young for a baby. You know you don't have to be pregnant if you don't want to be."

She huffed and turned away.

"Come on," he whined. "What do you want me to say? I mean, what're you thinking? Is it the money? I don't care how much it is. I'll pay for it."

Still not facing him, she laughed. "Oh, my poor little rich boy. It's all about the money."

His jaw tensed. What did she want him to say? What did she want him to do? She was being unreasonable. Why couldn't she at least look at him and talk about it?

He touched her chin and tried to turn her face, but she resisted. "There's nothing for you to be afraid of."

"Easy for you to say." She pushed off the pool table and sauntered to the far corner of the room, keeping her back to him as she spoke. "You act like it's nothing. Don't you understand what it means when I say I'm pregnant?"

He sneered. "Of course. I'm not stupid. Don't you understand it's easy to take care of? You had health class and Sex Ed. You should know."

She laughed again, glancing at him over her shoulder. "Just like that, huh?"

"That's right. Just like that."

Boots scuffed outside the recreation room the split-second before Papa spoke. "Jarret?"

Jarret swallowed his Adam's apple, hoping his voice hadn't traveled, trying to remember exactly what he'd said, and wondering if Papa could've caught the gist of their conversation. "Yeah, what?" He picked up the cue stick and reached for the cue ball.

"The shindig's outside." Papa leaned against the doorframe, tugged the rim of his cowboy hat, and gave Zoe a nod.

"Hello, Mr. West." She had composed herself enough to give him a pleasant smile. Without a glance in Jarret's direction, she tossed her hair over her shoulder and left the room, Papa sliding out of her way.

"Everything okay?" Papa said.

"Why wouldn't it be?" Jarret tossed the cue stick onto the table and headed for the door.

He breezed through the veranda to get outside. The evening air chilled the sweat he'd worked up in the heat of the moment, arguing with Zoe. He tugged his shirt to cool off then fished his cigarettes from a vest pocket.

Before he could light up, Keefe, dressed in the long brown robe of a medieval monk, strolled up to him. "Hey, Jarret."

Fortunately, the rough cowl and hood concealed his cropped head so that Jarret could look at him. He could almost picture him with long hair pulled back in a ponytail. Jarret didn't answer though. He lit up and took a long drag off the cigarette, turning his attention to Zoe as she sauntered to her girlfriends.

She was so slim, so gorgeous. Did she really want to lose her figure being pregnant?

"How's it going?" Keefe stepped close.

Jarret shook his head and started walking. "I'm not talking to you. I don't even know you."

Keefe followed, walking in step. "Of course you know me. I'm still me. My hair's just shorter. Get over it already. It's not a big deal."

Jarret smirked, looking his twin up and down. Keefe knew how he felt about it. It *was* a big deal. And it wasn't just the hair. Keefe was different.

"Jarret, knock it off. You haven't talked to me since I've been back. Don't you think that's long enough? I got you the shirt."

Picking up his pace and puffing on his cigarette, Jarret headed for the band.

Keefe stepped in front of him, forcing him to stop. "All right, then . . ." Keefe snatched the black gloves that hung from Jarret's belt.

Jarret shoved Keefe and moved to step around him . . . when a black leather glove struck his cheek.

"I challenge you to a duel."

Jarret snickered then glanced to either side to see who'd witnessed the slap. The flapper girls with Zoe looked directly at him. He'd have to accept. "A duel, huh? Yeah, I'll take your challenge. When I win, you have to leave me alone."

"Okay. And if I win, you have to talk to me again."

"You never win. I always win." Keefe was good, but Jarret had always been better. He couldn't remember the last time Keefe had beat him at fencing.

"We'll see. I'll go get a sword." Keefe took off.

A short time later, Jarret and Keefe, carrying fencing masks and wearing swords in their belts, strode across the front lawn out past the band and the dance floor. The setting sun had turned the sky a moody pink that made for a nice backdrop and reflected on their blades. They stopped a good distance between the band and the edge of the woods.

Jarret tossed his musketeer hat.

Keefe pushed back his cowl.

They both donned facemasks. Keefe assumed the standard *en garde* position, standing sideways, right hand leading.

Jarret remained intentionally loose and casual. He engaged his brother's blade by simply dragging his own across it, grinning as he did so.

Keefe gave a nod.

Jarret stepped back and glanced away, feigning a lack of enthusiasm. Then he lunged. Keefe was not fooled. He parried with skill. The second their swords clashed, a crowd gathered.

Knowing he could end this fight within a matter of minutes, if he wanted to, Jarret lunged again before Keefe could attack. Keefe beat back his sword with a double strike and circled Jarret as he recovered.

Turning to keep his twin before him, Jarret grinned. Keefe was using *his* tactics. He had used this move countless times, getting his opponent off balance and following with a series of blows.

Adrenaline surging, Jarret advanced, lunged, and swung his blade low. Keefe jumped and stumbled back. With a laugh, Jarret continued his advance, his attack. Keefe parried and scuttled backward.

Their blades became a flurry of movement, strikes and parries, Jarret confident he had the upper hand. They inched, they lunged through the yard, one way then another, Jarret only at times aware of the onlookers that surrounded them.

Their blades crossed. "I'm going to end this now," Jarret said and shoved Keefe back. Then he attacked with all the rage he had within, all the anger at the loss of control over his life. Keefe parried but Jarret kept coming.

Then something impossible happened.

Keefe's riposte came so quick it caught Jarret by surprise, and he ended up parrying with the end of his blade instead of the lower third where he could keep control of it. The sword slipped from his hand.

"Touché." Chest heaving, Keefe tapped his blade to Jarret's ribs.

Keefe won?

Anger surged through Jarret. He whipped his mask aside and thrust his palms into Keefe's chest. Keefe fell to the ground. Jarret jumped on him and wrestled to keep him from getting up. Jarret drew back a fist and swung before he realized that Keefe still held his sword . . . and that he was about to make contact with the hilt.

Pain shot from his knuckles to his wrist. He rolled off his brother, clutched his hand, and groaned.

Keefe laughed and sat up. He tossed his sword aside and peeled the facemask off. "That was a stupid thing to do."

"Yeah." Jarret pushed himself up, breathing hard, his fist aching. "It hurts like mad. I can't believe you beat me."

"I'm sure you let me win." Keefe smiled. "You miss talking to me." He stood and reached a hand down.

At first Jarret shot hate through his eyes, but then he allowed himself to smile. Shaking out his right hand, he took Keefe's outstretched hand with his left and got to his feet. "So, what do you want to talk about so badly?"

Keefe threw his arm around Jarret's shoulders. "Let's take a walk." Leaving their swords where they lay, they headed for a path in the woods.

Chapter Thirty

Caitlyn

In addition to the black pants, shirt, and Spanish gaucho hat, Roland now wore a black mask and a cape, leading Caitlyn to believe he was either the Lone Ranger or Zorro. She hadn't asked him yet. In fact, she hadn't spoken to him at all since she first saw him with Mya, though she hadn't seen him with her since. His brothers' swordfight drew her here, to where she and Roland stood side by side in the front lawn, the closest she'd come to him so far tonight.

He acknowledged her with a glance before turning and motioning to the band. Though a good distance away, they must've caught his signal because they immediately strummed their electric guitars.

"Okay, okay," Roland said to the crowd that had gathered to watch the swordfight. "Show's over." After motioning them away, he stooped and picked up one of the two swords his brothers had abandoned.

"Was that really just for show?" She watched the West twins disappear into the woods bordering the front lawn. "Jarret seemed so angry. I thought it was real."

With one dressed in a flamboyant musketeer outfit, his cape flying dramatically as he fought, and the other as a medieval monk, their swords flashing under the setting sun, they had looked like performers. But the way Jarret moved, lunging and swinging with such force, gave the impression he meant business.

Roland grabbed the second sword and came over, peering at Caitlyn through his steel-gray eyes visible from behind the mask. "Yeah, you're right. It wasn't for show." He tucked one of the facemasks under his arm. "They've been kind of, uh, distant lately. But that's how they make up. They fight it out."

"Oh. That's terrible." She hoped Jarret wasn't like that with Zoe.

He stared again, making Caitlyn wonder what he was thinking. "Want to take a walk?" He glanced at the swords in his hands.

"Sure."

They strolled toward the house. She felt silly for having thought he liked Mya, but she could still picture them together in her mind. "Are you the Lone Ranger?"

"What? No." He sounded disappointed. "I don't have a gun. I have a sword. See?" He flipped his cape back, revealing the sword at his thigh. "I'm Zorro."

"Oh, of course." She felt bad for guessing wrong.

He gave her the hint of a smile, which would've ordinarily set her heart to racing, but her thoughts remained stuck on Zoe and Jarret.

So she asked a question which, as the words came out, she wondered if she should've kept to herself. "Does your father know about Jarret and Zoe?"

Roland glanced, his gray eyes flashing with a look of caution. "Sure. You mean that they're seeing each other? She's over here all the time."

They passed the dance floor and crossed the driveway. "No. I figured he knew that. That's not really what I meant."

They walked in silence for a few paces and mounted the steps to the porch before he looked at her and spoke again. "What *do* you mean?"

"Um . . ." Maybe she shouldn't have brought it up. Maybe Roland had no clue. "Well, I mean, your father wouldn't approve of the type of relationship they have, would he?"

A smile flickered on his lips, making him look annoyed. "What do you mean by that?"

They stopped in the middle of the porch.

"They're . . . uh . . . doing things together." She couldn't believe she'd said it. She wished she could snatch the words out of the air before they reached his ears. If Roland hadn't already known, she'd just made known the sin of another. And hadn't Roland told her, not so long ago, that he wasn't going to jump to conclusions about Jarret, that he would give him the benefit of the doubt?

His eyes flashed then blinked. He looked down. "How do you know?"

"She told me."

He turned away and grabbed the doorknob. "I'm sure my father would have no clue about that."

"Well, maybe you should tell him."

With a hand still on the doorknob, he faced her. His eyes narrowed to slits and his upper lip curled. "Why should *I* tell him?"

Caitlyn had never seen Roland look as annoyed as he did at this moment. "You're his brother. Don't you care?"

He shook his head, not so much to say *no*, she didn't think, but as a further expression of his annoyance. "Of course I care." He cracked the door open. "What good is telling Papa going to do?"

It always made her smile when he let the word *papa* slip out, because she thought it was cute, but also because it made him blush, as if he'd never meant to say it. But she didn't smile this time. His attitude hurt. She wished they were on the same side. But they weren't.

"Don't you think your father would talk to him?" She spoke softly and leaned on the doorframe to watch his face.

"What good would that do?" His jaw visibly tensed. "You think he'd stop if my father told him to?"

"I don't know what he'd do. But your father should know. Maybe he'd keep a better eye on him."

"You don't know Jarret." Opening the door further, he stepped inside and turned to face Caitlyn. "Besides, it's none of our business."

His words stung. She blurted out in a voice way too loud, "My best friend is in trouble. That makes it my business."

She spun away from him, her blue cape billowing out, and she dashed away. Maybe he hadn't known and she'd shocked him with the news. Maybe Zoe wouldn't be pregnant much longer, if Jarret had his way.

Tears pricked Caitlyn's eyes as she ran to the side of the house where fewer windows looked out, to the side with the beverage table where moms stood talking and laughing with their little kids.

Foolishly, she ran without lifting her ridiculously long skirt, the way they do in the movies, and her toe caught the hem. Tumbling forward, she threw her arms out and smacked her palms to the cold ground. People had seen her. She felt their glances, but she didn't wait for anyone to approach and ask if she was okay. She jumped up, hiked her skirts high and dashed off again, this time headed for the stables.

A horse nickered, making her want to go inside and see it. Gentle animals, especially big-eyed horses and fluffy kittens, had a way of calming her. But seeing the veranda windows not far off, and not wanting Roland to see her, she darted behind the stables instead.

A trail laden with hoof prints wound behind the stables. She decided to follow it. It was peaceful, not that any birds were singing or anything. She'd probably scared off every form of wildlife with her cloddy running. But the setting sun sparkled through the leaves, the air smelled fresh and clean, and she could barely hear the music from the band. The Wests probably rode horses back here all the time. Maybe she'd learn to ride a horse someday.

Her heart winced. She picked up her pace. She'd once entertained the idea that Roland would teach her. That would never happen now. He probably thought of her as a prying, clumsy, talkative control freak. He told Peter he didn't want a girlfriend, but maybe he just didn't want *her* for a girlfriend. Maybe he did like Mya. And why not? She was sweet, bubbly, and all girl.

A thick root stretched across the path, Caitlyn noticed too late. The toe of her shoe cracked against it. She stumbled forward, lost her balance, and took a complete dive, landing hard on her hip and right palm. Pain shot through her and jarred her bones.

Why me? Instead of trying to get up, she rested her head on the hard-packed ground and let the sobs erupt. No one would hear her. She was out too far. So she sobbed and sobbed and sobbed, and it felt good.

When she finally ran out of tears, she sat and wiped her face with her skirt. The sun had disappeared from the sky, but she could still see the trail. She climbed to her feet, gathered her skirt, and walked on.

After a while, the trail branched off. It had been curving so much to the right that she decided to take the left branch. Fifteen minutes later, noticing the dwindling light, she questioned her decision. Maybe the right branch wrapped around to the back of their property, coming out by the fire pit and lawn chairs. And maybe the path she took wound on forever.

Caitlyn stopped, blew the hair from her face, and looked around. Darkness prevented her from getting her bearings, but she was never one to get her bearings in the light either. Peter liked to say she could walk the same trail for a whole year and still get lost. He was right. She was terrible at orientation.

She sighed. The trail had to come out somewhere, so she kept on in the same direction, slower this time, because she could barely see and her feet were drawn to roots and stones. Maybe the moon would come out and shed some light. Every few yards she scanned the woods, hoping to see the party lights but seeing only shadows and darkness. Until—

A moving point of light showed some distance off to the left.

"Hello!" she shouted, hoping it was someone with a flashlight, someone come to rescue her. "Hello?" she shouted again.

The jittering light grew bigger. A branch cracked.

She moved toward the light and called again.

"Caitlyn?"

Not recognizing the voice, she replied, "I'm here." She stumbled towards him with arms outstretched to avoid walking into anything.

When he got within a few feet of her, she recognized him. It was Keefe, the monk.

"Hi. I'm glad I found you." He sounded sincere but breathless.

"Me, too." Her neck and face heated then chilled her. She thanked God for the darkness that would prevent him from seeing her blush.

"My lady has wandered far from camp," he said, using a rough British accent.

She giggled. "Yes, Brother Monk. I am most grateful that you have come to my rescue."

She wasn't sure if her choice of words fit whatever time period they ought to be from, based on their costumes, but she liked using an accent. "How ever did you find me?" For that matter, how had anyone known she was missing? Who would've noticed her absence? Roland? Zoe?

"I caught sight of my fair lady when she stepped behind the stables." He continued with the accent. "I assumed you went for a walk, but this trail is quite long. And when I didn't notice your return . . ."

"Again, I am most grateful. These woods are quite lovely. At least so I thought by light of day."

"You must see them one day in the early morning." He pointed over her shoulder and his accent faded as he continued. "There's another trail. It branches off. It leads to some cliffs."

"Oh, well I'm glad I didn't take that trail. Cliffs are not the place to be in the dark." She pulled her cape tight.

He laughed. "No, they aren't." Using the accent, he said, "But they afford a breathtaking view. And now, would my lady care for an escort back to camp?" He stuck out his elbow, which she guessed she should take if she wanted the escort.

So she curtsied and took his arm. "I would be most grateful."

With the flashlight aimed at the ground before them, they hiked down the trail.

Caitlyn smiled, a feeling of security enveloping her. Someone had found her! Keefe had found her. He was so different from his twin, so different from Roland, for that matter. Had he really been watching her? Maybe she upset him with her reaction to his costume. Who was Keefe? She didn't really know him at all. She shuddered.

"My lady is cold," he said, removing his hooded cowl.

"No, I'm fine."

He put the cowl over her head and adjusted it, hood up, the smell of his musky cologne drifting to her nose.

Enjoying the scent, she inhaled deeply. "Thank you. And I'm sorry I messed up your costume. I made it too long, huh?"

"Too long? Oh, because I . . . No. I-I wanted to give it more of a poor friar look. You know, like Saint Francis. I guess I shouldn't have ripped the hem like that but . . ." He turned and walked backwards a few steps, shining the light on himself and lifting one arm with his question. "Does it work?"

She giggled, nodding. "I'm just glad you like it."

"I do. I love it."

They walked the rest of the way in silence, finally emerging under a string of lights near the beverage table. The party was in full swing, the beverage table having turned into a popular teen hangout. The band played louder, and at least a dozen kids danced on the platform dance floor. Voices came from behind the house, too, from where the fire pit and lawn chairs had been set up. Kids stood in groups and walked in pairs.

Caitlyn pulled the cowl off over her head.

"You can hold onto it if you want," he said.

"No, thank you. I'm not cold anymore. Besides I have a sweater on the porch."

He took the cowl, and they stared at each other for a long moment. Then he smiled and dipped his head. "Shall I walk you to the porch?"

"No, really, I'm fine now. But thank you. I think I would've been wandering out there forever. I'm sorry to have been trouble."

He smiled but before he replied, someone called her name.

"Where you been, man?" Peter shouted. "We've been looking for you all over." He and Roland pushed through the crowd by the beverage table.

Roland opened his mouth but closed it when his gaze caught Keefe, who was putting his cowl on over his head.

"She was in the woods," Keefe said to Roland, adjusting his costume.

Roland nodded but barely gave either of them a further glance.

"In the woods?" Peter smirked. "It's pitch black out there. You know coyotes live out here, right?"

"Coyotes?" Caitlyn said. Was he serious?

"Isn't that what you said?" Peter nudged Roland, but Roland only shrugged without looking at anyone.

"Well, I'm going to . . ." Keefe seemed at a loss for words but finally said, ". . . get something to eat." He left, and Roland went with him.

Caitlyn stared, so confused that she wanted to go home. "Have you seen Zoe?"

"Mm, yeah. She's yelling at Marilyn Monroe for dancing with her musketeer." Peter laughed.

Chapter Thirty-one

Roland

Roland slumped back on the couch in the family room, the remote dangling from one hand, the figures of a black and white Sherlock Holmes movie flitting in the corner of his vision. His gaze rested on the armor of a German knight that stood tall and proud—though often overlooked— in the corner of the room. Fluted metal plates, a mail skirt, and the full, gothic helmet would have protected the knight in battle. Points jutted out from the elbows, knees, and feet, giving it a fearsomeness appearance.

If Roland lived in medieval times, and he wanted to be a knight, he would've been a page for the past seven years. Now, at age fourteen, he would move up to squire. Squires were considered to be young men. They learned the Code of Chivalry, bravery, and the use of various weapons. In seven years, he would become a knight.

With all that training and preoccupation with obtaining his own shining armor, would he even be thinking about girls? *Yeah. Probably.*

Roland leaned his head back, no longer focusing on anything.

He sure wasn't ready for a girlfriend, so why had it made him jealous to see Caitlyn with Keefe? They hadn't even been holding hands. But Keefe's eyes held a look. Caitlyn's eyes, too.

Why did his temperature spike, his palms sweat, and his mouth go dry, every time she got near? Why couldn't he just see her as a friend, the way he saw Peter? His temperature sure didn't spike when Peter got near. His temper did, sometimes, but not his temperature.

Was Jarret really doing it with Zoe? Yeah, he was. Why else would she have been in his bedroom? Was Caitlyn right? Should he say something to Papa? It wasn't his business. Was it? What did she mean

Zoe was in trouble? She didn't mean *pregnant*, did she? No. Zoe didn't look pregnant.

"Hey, Roland."

Roland sat bolt upright. The remote flew from his hand and cracked into the coffee table.

"You doing anything?" Keefe strolled around the couch. Socks made his steps silent.

Roland snatched the remote from the floor. "No. Not really." He shut off the TV. He hadn't been following the show anyway.

Keefe sat down beside him, rubbed his hands down his thighs, and bit his bottom lip. "I, uh, wanted to ask you something."

"Okay." Roland slumped back, waiting, wondering what made Keefe so nervous.

Keefe's eyes rolled upward, and he continued biting his lip. "Um . . ."

Footfalls came from the direction of the garage or the veranda. Then Jarret, wearing riding boots, sauntered into the room. "So, what'd he say?" He stood with legs spread and hands on hips, grinning.

Keefe jumped up, shaking his head wildly at Jarret. He rushed him and whispered, stuttering, "I-I didn't ask him yet."

Roland sighed. Once the two of them had mended their relationship, it hadn't taken long for Keefe to resume his position as Jarret's bird dog. Would things ever change? Keefe had even cut his hair as a sign of his—

"Roland." Keefe leaned over the back of the couch, his hand brushing Roland's shoulder.

Jarret, snickering, strutted past and left the room.

"Yeah?" Roland twisted to face Keefe, wishing he'd just be out with it. He always seemed so tortured when carrying out Jarret's plans.

"Do you . . . have a girlfriend?"

"Do I *what*?" Now Roland bit his lip. What kind of a question was that? "No. I don't have a girlfriend. Why?" He glanced to see if Jarret stood listening from somewhere nearby but caught no sign of him.

"Well, because . . ." Keefe came around the couch again and sat on the coffee table. "I like someone, and I know she's your friend."

Roland huffed as it dawned on him. *Caitlyn.* This wasn't about Jarret after all. "What, do you want my permission to go out with her? She doesn't even date."

Keefe glanced toward the great room, the room through which Jarret had disappeared. "Yeah, I know that. And I-I guess I do want your permission. She's your friend, right? I get the impression you're close. So I'm asking you first. I guess I'll have to ask her father next. I don't know a thing about courtship. I'll have to learn."

Keefe rubbed his stubbly hair. "I really like her. She's different from other girls." He leaned forward, his eyes intense. "Do you think she likes me?"

Roland's mouth had fallen open while Keefe spoke. He couldn't believe his ears. Keefe wanted to see Caitlyn? "I-I don't know. You're nice enough."

Keefe slapped and rubbed Roland's thigh. "It won't bother you if I ask her?"

He shrugged. Would it bother him? Yeah, it would bother him. He really liked her. She *wasn't* like other girls. In fact, he could see her being his girlfriend . . . someday. Not today. No, he really wasn't ready for that . . . But Keefe was. She probably was. It wouldn't be fair to Keefe or to her for him to stand in the way.

Fighting back feelings of jealousy, Roland took a breath and tried to sound indifferent. "I'm not ready for a girlfriend, all that drama and involvement. I'm only fourteen, you know."

Keefe bit his lip, nodded, and then smiled and exhaled a ton of air.

Chapter Thirty-two

Caitlyn

"A white car drove by," Priscilla shouted.

Caitlyn gasped, again.

"Yeah, and it went real slow," Stacey said, teasingly.

Caitlyn tossed the kitchen towel and bolted for the living room window. The street was empty. The driveway was empty.

Steam shot from her ears. She couldn't take it anymore. "Mom! Make them go away. Can't they play outside?"

"No, dear, they're all dressed up. Everyone's just anxious to meet Keefe. This is a new experience for all of us." Mom slid a pie out of the oven and set it on a cooling rack, the sweet warm smell permeating the house. "We'll all sit in the living room for a few minutes. Then they'll go play in their room until bedtime."

Caitlyn groaned and would've thrown herself onto the couch for emphasis, but she didn't want to mess up her dress or hair—or the couch for that matter. Her dress came from the second-hand store but it was gorgeous, beige and frilly with big dark-brown and red flowers. She'd spent a full hour on her hair, trying to tame the curls and get them to sit nicely. The living room, well, there was nothing she could do to make twenty-year-old furniture look good. It was what it was: a little living room with over-sized, hunter green furniture with tan geometric patterns and replete with knitted blankets. Crocheted doilies and candles decorated the glass-topped coffee table.

"Who messed up the candles?" Someone had arranged the candles into a heart shape. Caitlyn grabbed one with each hand, wanting them back in the casual pattern she'd created earlier.

She still couldn't believe Keefe West liked her. He wasn't put off by the courtship rules at all. She hadn't even had to explain how she didn't date. He just came up to her one day at lunch. She'd been sitting in the cafeteria with Mya and five other girls, laughing and having a good old time when he stopped at the end of their table.

"Hi," he'd said and nothing more, but his gaze was definitely on her.

"Hi," Caitlyn had said back.

Her girlfriends giggled.

Keefe blushed and pulled a note from the front pocket of his jeans. He started to hand it to her then pulled it back, shaking his head. "I'd like to know if I can drop by your house sometime and . . . and talk to your father."

Now that it got down to it, Caitlyn had no clear idea how this courtship thing worked. How was a guy supposed to make known his interest? It was only the reaction of her friends that made her realize Keefe was interested in her. They all giggled, Phoebe kicked her, and Mya nudged her. She had assumed Keefe needed some heating or air-conditioning work at his house, and that he'd known her Dad did that for a living.

"I'd like that," Caitlyn had said, long after he'd turned every shade of red and glanced over both shoulders.

Two days later, he'd stopped her between classes and asked if he could call her. Caitlyn said he could but never gave him her number. Roland must've given it to him. He called that very evening and had painfully little to say, but they had arranged the *meeting of her family* for tonight.

"He's here!" Priscilla screamed.

Caitlyn abandoned the last two candles, jumped up, and straightened her dress. Mom made the girls sit on the couch and—didn't it figure—David toddled into the living room with absolutely nothing on his lower half.

"Mom! Where are his pants?"

Laughing, Mom scooped him up and carried him away as the doorbell rang.

When the doorbell rang a second time, Dad shouted from his recliner in the enclosed back porch, "Somebody get the door."

Why hadn't she answered the door on the first ring? Why did she still just stand there? Worried he might take offense at the delay, she sprang to the door but forced herself to ease it open.

Keefe stood on the front porch with his head down and one hand behind his back. The driveway was empty, so whoever had given him a ride must've dropped him off and left.

As she pushed open the screen, he lifted his head and smiled. After having hoped on Roland for so long, imagining him coming over to officially meet the family, it felt a little strange having his brother at her door. She wasn't sure at all how she felt about him. Dressed in jeans and a blue-striped polo shirt under an open gray jacket, he had a clean look and a gentle demeanor, not roguish like his twin, nor mysterious like Roland.

"I, uh . . . Is it okay that I brought flowers?" He offered a little bouquet of pink and white daisies.

"Oh, they're beautiful. Thank you." Taking the flowers, she stepped out of the way to let him in.

Her sisters sat on the end of the couch, enjoying the moment with giggles and whispers. Mom returned and took the flowers, David—in pants—toddling after her. Dad's voice came from the enclosed porch. He was mumbling something about the football game.

Keefe and Caitlyn sat on the couch under the window. They hadn't said two words before Mom and Dad joined them in the living room, Dad getting comfortable in the rocking recliner chair and Mom sitting by Priscilla.

Priscilla spoke first. "Do you really have a twin brother?"

"Yes."

"Does he look like you?"

"Pretty much, except his hair is longer."

"How long?"

Keefe glanced at Caitlyn as if unsure of how to answer. "Long." He tapped his shoulder. "Down past his shoulders. But it's curly so . . ."

"Does he look like a girl?"

Caitlyn gasped.

Dad laughed and leaned forward in the chair. "Priscilla, you're a silly head. He just told you they're identical. That means they look the same. Does Keefe look like a girl?"

Keefe peeled off his jacket and wiped the back of his neck.

Caitlyn hadn't realized how much darker the twins' complexions were than Roland's, not that anyone had skin as pale as Roland's. Nor had she paid attention to the similarities, but they shared a definite family resemblance in the way their gorgeous eyes and brows dominated their features. Keefe had dark brown eyes, however, and Roland, steel-gray.

Caitlyn wished she would stop comparing them.

"I saw you at the Halloween party," Keefe said to Priscilla. "I'm sure you saw my twin brother. He was the musketeer."

The girls giggled and Stacey said, "That was his real live hair?"

"That was a nice party, Keefe," Dad said, taking over the conversation, to Caitlyn's relief. He continued talking about work and the weather for the next ten minutes until dinner was ready. Mom added a comment or two about the family.

It wasn't until everyone stood to go to the dinner table that Stacey really humiliated Caitlyn.

Mom made the girls tell Keefe *goodbye,* and Caitlyn's tension eased as she watched them skip from the room. Then Stacey stopped in the hallway. She turned around, an impish look on her face. "Do you know Caitlyn likes Roland? She thinks he's cute."

Caitlyn sucked in a breath that smacked the back of her throat with croak-like sound. She couldn't bring herself to look at Keefe and see his reaction.

Dad lumbered to the hallway, picked Stacey up, and threw her over his shoulder. "I think it's time for this little bugger to go to bed."

Mom led Keefe to the table, and Caitlyn helped bring out the food: ham and pineapple, scalloped potatoes, rolls, and steamed green beans. Dad led them in the prayer before meals. Keefe said how nice everything tasted, and Mom thanked him. Caitlyn still couldn't make eye contact.

"I enjoyed hearing about your trip to Italy," Dad said halfway through the meal. "I can't wait to see the slide-show your father's working on."

Keefe nodded. "I loved Italy."

Caitlyn glanced.

He glanced back, and she felt a warm glow inside. If he still liked her by the end of the night, if he still wanted to court her, someday, she would be comfortable enough to ask him about the miracle. She'd witnessed a miracle herself, not too long ago. She could still see Dominic getting up from his wheelchair after they had prayed over him with the relics of Saint Conrad. It changed everyone who witnessed it. It had put a hunger in Caitlyn that she didn't understand.

"Hey," Dad said. "I don't think Caitlyn was in the room when you told us about the miracle."

Tensing with anticipation, she dropped her fork and it clattered on the table.

"Why don't you tell us again?" Dad said, and Caitlyn could've hugged him. "I'll bet she'd love to hear about it."

Keefe turned from Dad to her.

Too nervous to nod or say a word, she simply stared back.

"Okay." He sipped his water, set his glass down, and gazed at the table. "We were in Bagno di Romagna, two hours east of Florence. My father needed to meet with the priest of the Basilica of Saint Mary." He closed his mouth and pressed his lips together as if some inner emotion had taken hold of him.

Mom and Dad stared, probably making him uncomfortable, so to break the tension Caitlyn said, "Was it a pretty church?"

He gave her a smile that communicated his thankfulness. "Yeah, it was pretty. They had adoration of the Blessed Sacrament going on inside. Afterwards, we were told about the miracle that had taken place in 1412."

He continued to gaze at her as he spoke.

It made her warm all over and somewhat uncomfortable, but she wanted him to keep talking. She wanted to know.

"The prior of the basilica in 1412 had doubts, doubted the Real Presence of Jesus in the Eucharist. And while he was saying Mass, at the words of consecration, the wine transformed into living blood and flowed from the chalice. It dripped onto the linen cloth on the altar. The priest was so deeply moved that, in tears, he confessed his lack of faith to the people present."

He took a breath. "They've got the bloodstained cloth preserved in that basilica. They even did a chemical analysis over five hundred years later. It still had the properties of human blood." His eyes flickered and his gaze shifted to the table. "It's Jesus's blood."

Something deep transpired inside him, she could tell. And she had questions. *What was it like to be there? How did it make you feel?* But she knew he wouldn't want to talk about it now. If they did become friends and continued to get to know each other, maybe he'd tell her more.

Chapter Thirty-three

Jarret

Jarret pulled his shirt on over his head as he stepped to the window in Zoe's bedroom. Oak trees with bare branches and well-manicured bushes separated the McGowans' tidy back yard from neighbors behind and to each side. He'd hate living like that. Like Papa, he loved his privacy.

Zoe gazed at herself in the dresser mirror while combing her silky black hair, a stately look of indifference on her face.

"I don't see why I have to meet your folks." He walked around the bed, trying to make eye contact in the mirror. "Just because Keefe went over Caitlyn's . . . Those are their rules."

Still combing her hair, Zoe paid him no attention. Her eyes hadn't even twitched.

"We don't play by those rules." He came up behind her, watching her through the mirror. "Why does anything have to change? I like the way we have it. Don't you?"

Still combing.

He grabbed her wrist.

She shot a glance through the mirror. "I want you to meet my parents."

He released his grip, took a breath, and exhaled loudly to show his irritation. "What if they don't like me?" He yanked the band from his hair to fix his ponytail.

She gave him a smile, the kind a girl makes when she sees a puppy.

"What if they won't let me see you?" With a gentle tug, he turned her to face him. "Are you gonna sneak around with me?" He leaned to kiss her lips, but she laughed, so he landed a kiss on her neck. "I need you."

She pushed him away. "You don't need *me*. You just like—"

The front door creaked open.

Jarret and Zoe spun to face the closed bedroom door. She gasped. He dashed to the window.

"Don't be silly," she whispered. "You can't climb out the window. Even if you could, the dining room is right downstairs." She pointed to her bathroom door. "Go in there. I'll go downstairs and give you a signal when the coast is clear."

Heart pounding, he did as told and ran softly for the bathroom. What kind of a man was her father anyway? What would he do if he found a boy in his daughter's bedroom?

Jarret stopped at the bathroom door. "Hey," he whispered, stopping her from turning the knob. "What kind of a signal?"

"I don't know. I'll . . . I'll turn on the hall light." She opened the door and looked back. "Don't forget your boots are down there."

"Yeah." He ducked into the bathroom and listened.

"Zoe!" A man's angry voice shook the house.

"Coming." She descended the steps, making soft footfalls. "You're home early. I haven't even started dinner. Do you remember Jarret's coming over to meet you?" Her voice quieted as she moved through the house. A cabinet door banged, a pan slid . . .

Jarret crept from the bathroom and stood by the bedroom door. She had left it open a crack so he could watch for the hall light.

"Well, where is he? Is that his car in the drive?"

"Shoot!" Jarret restrained himself from hitting the wall. Zoe had told him to park down the street, but he said they had plenty of time, and he could move his car later.

"You weren't here yet, so he went for a walk." Zoe sounded relaxed, completely in control of herself. "Maybe he's in the backyard."

A screen door slid open . . . shut. "There's no one back there. If I find out you've had a boy in the house—"

"Oh, Dad, don't be silly. Do you want a pop or spring water?"

"Water. Set it on the table." He sounded calmer but nearer. "I need to change out of this suit." A step creaked.

Jarret's eyes bugged.

Mr. McGowan climbed the stairs.

A surge of adrenaline made a jump from the window seem doable. Jarret turned in a circle, his gaze darting to the window, to the closet, to the bathroom— He dashed for the bathroom and climbed into the tub. He should've come over later, at the time they expected him. Would Mr. McGowan peek into her room? What would he think of her messy bed?

Footsteps sounded in the hall. Her bedroom door squeaked.

Jarret's heart leaped to his throat. He held his breath.

The footfalls continued down the hall. Then the door at the end of the hall clicked shut.

Jarret breathed, his mouth going dry and heartrate quickening. Every muscle in his body felt ready for action. *Time to run.*

He scrambled out of the tub and scooted to the bedroom door. He was not waiting for the hall light. Inching forward, he peeked around the doorframe.

The door across the hallway hung open, the door to the master bedroom at the end of the hallway . . . closed.

Jarret dashed down the stairs.

Zoe squatted by the pile of shoes near the front door. She stood up with his boots in her hands and her eyes round. "Get out of here. Pretend you were taking a walk."

He nodded, yanked open the front door, and stumbled onto the front porch. She closed the door behind him. He dropped a boot and shoved his foot into it. Took a step toward the porch steps. Dropped the other boot and—

A white Lincoln pulled in the driveway, parking next to his car.

"Flipping son-of-a duck!" He shoved his foot into the other boot and spun to face the front door, lifting a fist as if he had just come to knock on it.

"Hello." A petite woman with a silky dark bob peeked at him over the Lincoln. The car door slammed. "You must be Jarret." She took long steps, walking around the car.

He nodded, still trying to wriggle his foot into his boot. "And you must be Zoe's mother."

Fumbling with her purse and car keys, she stepped up and joined him on the porch. She had an attractive smile and dark eyes like Zoe's. She stuck a slender arm out, reaching to shake his hand. "Nice to meet you, Jarret."

He wiped his sweaty palm on his jeans and took her hand. "Yeah, same."

"Come on in." Mrs. McGowan opened the door and stepped in first. "Zoe, your boyfriend's here." She slipped out of her dark heels and dropped them on the pile of shoes.

Jarret pried his boots back off and followed her down the hall toward the kitchen. The house smelled of spicy chicken . . . already. Zoe was fast.

Before they reached the kitchen, Zoe peeked around the corner. "Hi, Mom. Hi, Jarret."

Mrs. McGowan washed her hands in the kitchen sink and opened a cupboard. Mr. McGowan's heavy footfalls sounded on the stairs, in the hall, in the kitchen. He stopped behind Jarret.

Jarret's skin crawled. He turned, wishing his heart would stop trying to break through his ribs. "Hi."

"Hello." Mr. McGowan was a towering figure with a grim mouth and vulture-like eyes. "Is that your Chrysler in the driveway?" He pushed past Jarret and grabbed a pile of mail from the countertop.

"Yeah. Did you want me to move it?"

Zoe stirred something in a pan and set the spoon down. Smiling playfully, she took Jarret by the hand and led him to a chair at the kitchen table. "Dad, this is Jarret."

Mr. McGowan sat across from him, glancing up from the mail. "You came over early, huh?"

"Well, I . . ." He had no idea what to say.

"I told him the wrong time," Zoe said casually. "Jarret, would you like a pop?"

Jarret nodded.

"You're kind of young to have a car, aren't you?" Mr. McGowan didn't look up from the mail this time.

"Uh, I'm sixteen. I'll be seventeen in a few months." Maybe that wasn't a good answer. Zoe had turned fifteen over the summer. Would he care?

"What grade are you in?"

"Eleventh."

"What's your father do for a living?"

"Uh—"

"Honey, stop grilling him." Mrs. McGowan carried plates to the table. "Jarret's our guest. Let's just have a nice dinner." She flashed a sweet smile at Jarret, but it did nothing to calm the violence inside him.

"Just making small talk," Mr. McGowan said with his eyes on the mail. "How does a boy your age get a car like that? Do you have a job?"

Jarret gritted his teeth. He didn't like the man, not at all. And Mr. McGowan obviously didn't like him. It was only a matter of time before the two of them butted horns. Why couldn't Zoe have left things the way they were? There was no reason he needed to meet her parents. It's not like he and Zoe planned on marrying anytime soon. They were just hanging out and having fun.

Chapter Thirty-four

Caitlyn

The weather forecast warned of snow, but South Dakota could change her mind the way a girl changed purses.

After school, Zoe called Caitlyn and they decided to take a walk, meeting in the middle. Her house sat down the hill from Caitlyn's, on one of the streets of big, newer homes. Once they met, they walked back and forth, up and down the sidewalks between their houses.

The chill in the air kissed Caitlyn's cheeks and renewed her zeal for life, though her thighs burned as they reached the top of the hill for the third time.

Her eyes locked onto the playground across the street. "Let's go sit on swings."

"Okay." Zoe strode into the street without looking first, though very few cars had passed them on their walk.

Caitlyn jogged a few steps to keep pace. "I'm surprised you're not with Jarret." A cloud drifted overhead, casting a shadow on them.

Zoe buttoned the top button of her coat and took a deep breath but gave no answer.

"Are you guys fighting?"

"Fighting? No." After a glance at Caitlyn, she bowed her head and watched her feet while she walked. "You don't see Keefe very often, do you?"

"I see him. He belongs to our Catholic youth group now, the Fire Starters."

The playground had a green climbing fort with slides, one bench, and old swings. They headed for the swings. "I've seen him twice since he met my family. We worked at the food pantry together. And we'll be planning a Thanksgiving dinner for the homeless."

"Gee, that sounds fun." Zoe sat on a swing and pushed it back but didn't let go.

Caitlyn twisted her swing one way and then the other, her leg muscles appreciating the rest. "It is fun. I like working on things with him." It was one of the courtship principles. *Get to know each other by working together on group projects.*

"Do your parents like him?" She swung forward and back a few times.

"I think so. The whole family had a great time when he came over for dinner. Dad said he could come by anytime."

"Doesn't he say that to everyone?"

Caitlyn shrugged. "I guess so. So, do your parents like Jarret?"

She smiled without looking up. "My mom does, I guess. My dad doesn't. But I don't think anyone would be good enough for his little girl. He's very suspicious of Jarret."

"He has a reason to be, doesn't he?"

She stopped her swing and shot a glare. Then she leaned on the chain and spoke in a calm voice. "You're never alone with Keefe, are you? If you only see him with groups, how will you guys talk and really get to know each other?"

"We talk. I guess there are some drawbacks to courting. We don't talk about personal things. I would love to talk to him about a few things, but it never feels like the right time. Some things you just can't discuss in front of people."

She gave an understanding nod. "Has he kissed you?"

"No."

Zoe's mouth fell open. She blinked. "You're kidding me."

Caitlyn looked at the street to avoid seeing her shocked face. "No, I'm not. He's never kissed me."

"Why not? Don't you want him to?"

Caitlyn shrugged. Of course she did. She was dying for her first kiss. She still clung to the idea that it would be from Roland, but she did like Keefe an awful lot. Maybe he wasn't sure if people did that when courting.

"I know." Zoe's eyes flashed. "Isn't your birthday coming up?"

"It's this Sunday."

"Let's have a party."

"A party? I'm not ready for another party. Mom will make me a cake. I don't need a party."

"Not a big party. A little one. Just the four of us, me and Jarret, you and Keefe, like a double date. You're allowed to do that, aren't you?"

Seeing movement out of the corner of her eye, Caitlyn turned toward the street. A red car drove by. It slowed, came to an abrupt stop, and backed up. The passenger-side window went down as the car neared the playground.

"Oh, there's Jarret." Zoe didn't sound pleased.

"Zoe," Jarret shouted through the window.

She got off the swing, stuffed her hands in her coat pockets, and strolled to him in no obvious hurry. "Hi, Jarret."

"Where you been?" He sounded annoyed.

She twisted around to face Caitlyn then twisted back to him.

"Get in. I wanna talk to you."

"No."

"I don't know what you're so mad about."

"Don't you?"

"No. You don't answer my calls. You avoid me at school. If we're over, just tell me to my face."

She stood with her head down, not replying.

Caitlyn leaned back on the swing, not wanting them to think she was listening.

The driver's door flew open. Jarret jumped out and strode around the car to Zoe. He stopped a few feet away then cast a glance across the playground to Caitlyn.

"Hi." Caitlyn tried sounding cheerful and she waved, wanting him to think Zoe hadn't told her anything, which she hadn't. Caitlyn had no idea what their problem was, this time.

Making no acknowledgment of her greeting, he turned back to Zoe. They both stood with heads down. He mumbled something to her. She nodded. He stepped closer while he spoke. She replied, peering up at him. He pulled her into a hug and kissed the top of her head. After saying something else, he walked around his car and got back in.

"I'll see you later, then," he said through the passenger-side window and took off.

Zoe sauntered back to the swings and sighed. "What am I going to do about him?"

"What's the matter?"

She shook her head, twisted her swing, and stared at the ground. "So, what do you think about my idea for a birthday party?"

"I don't know."

"Well, we wouldn't have to call it a *date*. You always spend your birthdays at my house. Remember last year?"

She remembered. Caitlyn had never spent the night before. They put their sleeping bags in the family room. Zoe's mom baked tater-tots, shrimp rolls, and pigs-in-a-blanket. They watched movies and ate chocolate cake and snacks into the wee hours of the night.

"We'll do the same thing this year, only with the guys, but not a sleep over, of course."

"I guess that would be all right."

"We'll do it Saturday. My mom and dad will be out of town."

"What! No. I can't visit if your parents aren't home, even without a boyfriend."

"Well, you don't have to mention that part. My mom will cover for us."

"I don't know. I don't think Keefe would like the idea. He's very honest."

"We won't tell him. In fact, just let me arrange it. You don't have to say anything to anyone. Forget I mentioned it. We aren't doing anything." She grinned, a sneaky sparkle in her eyes. "Just don't make plans for Saturday."

Chapter Thirty-five

Caitlyn

Caitlyn hadn't told a single lie, so why did she feel like a snake? On Friday, Mom gave her permission to go over Zoe's house with Keefe, and Caitlyn hadn't even asked. "Of course, it won't be a sleepover like last year." Mom giggled. "But if you want to stay until eleven or twelve, that's fine." No doubt, Mom assumed Zoe's parents would be there the entire time.

The clock struck seven and Jarret's red car, looking picturesque under the street light and the sprinkle of snow, rolled into the Summers' driveway. Keefe spoke with Dad while Caitlyn shoved her arms into her long wool coat and stuffed her feet into boots. Priscilla whined and complained, mad because she couldn't go, not that she had gone last year either. Mom told her they'd have a little family party tomorrow, which meant cake, ice cream, music, and balloons—probably at the Brandts' since tomorrow was Sunday.

Keefe escorted Caitlyn to the car and offered the front seat to her, but she didn't want to sit next to Jarret, not even for the short ride to Zoe's house.

"Can we just sit in the back?" Caitlyn said, a pleading look on her face.

"Um . . . okay."

When she slid into the backseat and bumped into a present with a big blue bow, she realized why he'd wanted her to sit in the front. Keefe scooted in beside her, reached past her for the box, and set it on the front passenger-side seat. What could he have possibly gotten for a girl he'd just begun courting? She hoped it wasn't something expensive.

"What, are you afraid to sit next to me?" Jarret peered through the rearview mirror.

She flashed a sweet smile at him. "Thanks for picking me up."

He backed up fast and took off faster, making her hope Dad wasn't watching through the window. Guilt gnawed at her stomach. What would Keefe do when he found out Zoe's parents weren't home?

Welcoming lights shone in every window of Zoe's house. Balloons and streamers in the living room showed through the big front window. The door opened before they stepped onto the porch.

Zoe wore a dark red dress, shorter than Caitlyn would've worn, but long-sleeved and very pretty. "Happy birthday, girlfriend." She stepped outside barefooted, hugged Caitlyn, and dragged her inside.

Pop rock blasted and smells of fried food filled the air.

"We picked up two movies." Zoe smiled and bounced on her toes. Caitlyn hadn't seen her so excited in a long time. "And I have all kinds of snacks, more than last year, and your favorite: shrimp rolls." She took Caitlyn's coat and hung it in the closet.

Caitlyn sat on a lower step of the staircase to take off her boots. "I wondered what those wonderful smells were."

As Caitlyn unzipped a boot, Jarret plopped down beside her, his leg bumping hers. He threw her a sideways glance, grinning as if he knew he made her uncomfortable. "You don't mind, do you?" He unbuckled his black boot and yanked it off.

Keefe stood by the shoe pile, kicking off his tennis shoes. "You have a cozy house," he said to Zoe as she took his leather jacket.

"Come see the decorations." Zoe led everyone down the hall to the kitchen.

Balloons and streamers decorated the front room, kitchen, and the sunken family room that came off the kitchen. A plate of shrimp rolls and paper plates lay on the kitchen table. Caitlyn had never seen the countertops more cluttered . . . a mixer, glasses, oven mitts, and cookie sheets.

"Oh, Zoe," Caitlyn said, admiring her work. "You shouldn't have."

She smiled, handing her a tall glass of a pink, slushy drink. "Yes, I should've. You're turning fifteen. That's special."

Caitlyn brought the glass to her mouth.

Before she could take a sip, Jarret snatched it from her. "That's not ready yet."

"Where are her parents?" Keefe said to Jarret. "I'd like to meet them."

Zoe turned her head so fast her hair fanned out and landed over one shoulder. She and Jarret shared a look. Then she took Caitlyn's hand. "Come see the basement. We even decorated down there."

Their basement, much like the Wests' recreation room, had a pool table and dartboard, but they also had two arcade games and a stocked bar. Zoe, or more like Jarret, had strung white Christmas lights along the top of the walls.

"This is so nice." Caitlyn sat on a bar stool and spun it around, stopping to face Zoe. "What did your mom say about all this? She's the one who called my mom, right?"

Zoe sat on the stool beside her, smiling from ear to ear. "She thought it was a great idea. You're fifteen, in one day, why shouldn't you have your own party? Do you think other kids our age are having birthday parties with their parents?"

"I don't know. Some are. Dominic, Philomena, Peter and—"

Zoe smacked Caitlyn's arm. She must've known Caitlyn knew at least a dozen kids who still had birthday parties with their families. Did a person ever grow out of it?

Caitlyn ran her toes along the smooth face of the bar. "I hope Keefe doesn't mind when he finds out." When her toes reached the edge of the bar, her foot pushed into some wires.

"That's why we're down here. Jarret can talk to him. And since you're already here, hopefully, he won't make you leave. Apparently, Jarret thinks he can get Keefe to do anything he wants."

"I don't know about that." Caitlyn bristled inside, not wanting to think about Keefe as one easily manipulated by others. She jerked her foot free of the wires, and all the little white Christmas lights went out. "Oops."

"What happened?" Zoe peered up at the lights.

Caitlyn slid her hand between the bar and wall, wanting to fix things. She must've accidentally unplugged something. She patted the wall, searching for an outlet. Her hand brushed a tangle of wires. Suddenly, lights jerked free of the crown molding along the nearest wall.

"Oh no!" Zoe jumped up, laughing.

Caitlyn ran for the wall. "I can fix this." A string of lights hung to the floor and dangled from the dartboard. She grabbed them, bumping the dartboard.

"Oh, look out!" Zoe laughed harder.

The dartboard slipped to the side.

Caitlyn smacked both hands against it, keeping it from falling. More lights fell.

Zoe doubled over, her laughter so hard it was no longer audible.

"I'm sorry, I'm sorry." Glancing from the lights on the floor to Zoe, almost on the floor, a wave of heat washed over Caitlyn. Then she saw the humor in it, too. If it didn't bother Zoe, why should she let it bother her? "You'd think a girl would outgrow her awkwardness by the time she turned fifteen."

"Don't worry about it. I'll send Jarret down here. He must not have put them up very well." She dragged Caitlyn from the dartboard. It slid down the wall and landed on its face.

Caitlyn stared at it, hoping it didn't break.

Zoe draped her arms over Caitlyn's shoulders and pressed her forehead against Caitlyn's. "Caitlyn, it's okay. It's your fifteenth birthday party, and we're going to have fun. You'll get a chance to talk with Keefe without people all around. You can cuddle on the couch watching a movie, eating snacks, cake, more snacks . . ."

They giggled.

"Okay, I'm just sorry for the mess. It looked so nice."

"These decorations are here for you. If you want to tear them all down, tear them all down." Zoe took Caitlyn's hand and turned toward the stairs. Then she stopped. "Oh, there's something else I wanted to ask you, a favor."

"Sure."

"Please don't say anything about me being pregnant."

Caitlyn knew she looked dumbfounded. "You already told Jarret. Oh . . . Keefe doesn't know? You don't want him to know?"

"Jarret doesn't know."

"What? But you told him the day we—"

"No, he thinks I had the abortion."

"What?" Caitlyn's stomach turned.

"He thinks that's why I haven't been talking to him all week." She glanced at the top of the stairs. "I never told him that. He jumped to the conclusion, and I didn't correct him. I figured it would be easier. He was really hounding me, but when he assumed I did it, he was real sweet, comforting. He'll do anything for me right now."

"But, Zoe, you're going to start showing. Don't you think he'll be mad then?"

"I don't care. Maybe I'll break up with him. He shouldn't push me to do something I'm not comfortable doing. Come on."

As they stepped into the kitchen, Jarret handed each of them a slushy pink drink. He kissed Zoe on the lips and whispered something in her ear.

Keefe came to Caitlyn. "I need to talk to you." A hint of displeasure showed in his eyes. He glanced at Jarret, who stood in the kitchen.

"Aw, not again," Jarret said to Zoe. "I'm not fixing it. Someone else can fix it."

Keefe, who had yet to hold Caitlyn's hand, took her by the arm and led her into the front room. Someone had turned the lights off in the front room, hall, and formal dining room, so they stood in semi-darkness with only the dim light that traveled from the kitchen.

"Zoe's parents aren't here." His soft tone and the shadows on his face kept her from knowing if he blamed her. "They're out of town."

"I know."

"I think we should go."

At this moment, Caitlyn realized distinctly that she had a choice. She really wanted to stay, but she agreed with Keefe. They should go. Suddenly, a million reasons for staying came to mind and a few tumbled out of her mouth. "It's my birthday. I come over here every year on my birthday. My parents aren't expecting me home until midnight."

"But your mother thinks Zoe's parents are here."

"Does she? She never told me that. Is that what she told you?" This was true, although she figured Zoe's mother had sort of lied to her mom about who would be here.

"Well, no, but . . ." Something in the foyer drew his attention.

"Hey, there you are." Jarret carried two more slushy drinks. He made Caitlyn take one, trading it for her empty glass. The other he gave to Keefe. "Zoe's mother talked to Caitlyn's. You aren't still worrying about that, are you?" A grin flickered on his lips. "Maybe Mrs. Summer trusts her daughter."

Keefe's jaw twitched.

"It's not like we're completely alone," Caitlyn said. It felt strange being on the same side as Jarret.

Keefe nodded and his face softened into a look of resignation. He sipped his drink. "This is good. What's in it?"

Jarret gave a satisfied grin that annoyed Caitlyn. "Why don't you ask Zoe? She's in the basement. Besides, she needs help with something."

Keefe narrowed his eyes at his brother. "What does she need help with?"

"Your girlfriend here . . ." Jarret smiled at Caitlyn playfully. ". . . went and knocked down all my lights, all my hard work."

Keefe laughed.

Caitlyn hid her face with one hand, glad that the attention was now on her clumsiness. "I did. It was an accident."

"You don't mind fixing them, do you?" Jarret said to Keefe. "I just can't do it again."

"Yeah, sure." Keefe squeezed Jarret's shoulder as he passed.

Standing in a dimly lit room with Jarret, and no one else, made Caitlyn want to crawl out of her skin. Eyes to the floor, she walked past him, planning to return to the kitchen.

He followed.

Once in the kitchen, she picked up a dirty cookie sheet and set it in the sink. She could clean until Keefe and Zoe came back up. It was a bad habit of hers, and Zoe wouldn't approve, this being Caitlyn's party and all.

"You guys afraid to be alone together?"

Jarret stood closer than she realized, making her jump. "What? No. Why would you say that?"

"He hasn't even kissed you yet, has he?"

She gave him a none-of-your-business glare and kept cleaning, dumping onion rings onto a plate, peeling foil off the cookie sheet, putting the cookie sheet away . . .

"Maybe you're both afraid of your feelings."

Caitlyn tensed, her armor coming out. "Not everyone does things the way you do. You put the horse before the cart, or cart before the horse, or whatever."

"What does that mean?"

"You know what it means. You're too fast."

Grinning, he went to the blender and returned with a slushy pink drink that he poured into her half-empty glass. "Why don't you take your drink and your onion rings and go sit at the table?"

"I don't want to sit at the table." She wiped the counter with a damp washcloth.

"Where do you want to sit, on the countertop?"

"Maybe." She dried the counter with a hand towel, then turned and pulled herself up onto it, giving him a smug grin and folding her arms.

He looked pleased and swaggered closer. "I bet your parents put the cart before the horse. That's what happens when two people are into each other. They know what it's like. Maybe that's why they set all these silly rules for you."

A comfortable fog had entered her brain and every muscle in her body felt smooth and relaxed. "My parents did *not* put the cart before the horse."

She studied his face. It was amazing how two people, just because they were twins, could look so alike. Keefe and Jarret had the same high cheekbones, curvy mouth, dark brows, and heavy-lidded, long-lashed, Coca-Cola eyes.

The eyes . . . Now that she really looked into them, there *was* a difference. Perhaps it was a reflection of what lay behind them. Keefe had nothing but pure and kind intentions, while Jarret seemed bent on annoying her.

He handed her a drink then rested his hand on the counter, next to her, a leering look in his eyes. "So, tomorrow's your birthday, huh?" While he scrutinized her entire face, his thumb touched her skirt at the thigh.

"Yes, it's tomorrow." She glanced at his hand but couldn't tell if the touch was intentional, so she decided not to draw attention to it.

"Okay, and when were your parents married? Their anniversary? When is that?" With eyes glued to her face, his thumb moved an inch down her thigh.

Could that have been accidental? "Um . . ." She broke from his gaze so she could think. Where was Keefe? How long did it take to re-hang lights? He wouldn't like that Jarret had her trapped on the kitchen countertop where she couldn't get down without sliding into his arms . . . *Okay, what was the question?* "My parents . . . They got married in April, I think. Yeah, April."

A slow grin spread across his face. "April, huh? How long they been married?"

She glanced at the ceiling, trying to remember. *Oh yes, the cake.* She helped make their last anniversary cake. *Let's see . . . which anniversary was it?* "Fifteen years."

His lips parted and a breathy chuckle came out. Then he nodded and rested his hand on her thigh.

"Stop it." She shoved his hand and clutched his wrist so he couldn't touch her again.

He twisted his arm until he had her wrist, but she didn't release his. "So you're turning fourteen tomorrow?" He smirked.

"No." She wrestled her wrist from his grasp and rubbed it with her other hand, not that it hurt. His touch disgusted her. "You know how old I'll be. I'll be fifteen."

As he snickered again, he pushed off from the counter. "Yeah. Told you. Takes nine months for a baby." He stepped backwards. "You do the math. Your parents did it in February and married when they found out about you." He jabbed his index finger at her and turned away.

She watched him swagger through the dining room and into the sunken family room. He couldn't be right. April was their fifteenth anniversary. May, June, July . . .

She counted months on her fingers but only came up with seven. Any chance she was a premie? That had to be it. As strong as her parents felt about waiting for marriage, there was no way they—

"Hey." Keefe came through the basement doorway. He glanced at Jarret, who now lay on the couch playing with the TV remote, then came to Caitlyn. "Why are you sitting on the countertop?"

"What? Oh. I don't know." She slid down, into his arms—that he withdrew as soon as her feet landed on the kitchen floor. She sighed and picked up her drink, wishing he wanted to kiss her.

He took the drink from her and set it on the counter. "I think these are spiked."

"What?"

Keefe opened a cupboard, closed it, and opened another. "Can't you feel it? I'm starting to feel sort of fuzzy."

"Oh. I guess I am, too." She eyed the drink suspiciously then stomped to the family room.

Zoe had also returned and now lay beside Jarret on the couch, with her arm draped across his chest. Jarret only seemed interested in flipping channels.

Caitlyn stopped, intentionally blocking Jarret's view of the TV, and folded her arms. "Did you really put alcohol in our drinks?"

He craned his neck to one side. "You're in my way."

"Aren't you going to answer me?"

"You figure it out." He grinned, his eyes sparkling with his cocky attitude. "That'll give you two things to figure out tonight."

"What's the other thing?" Zoe asked.

"Caitlyn, let's just go." Keefe came up beside her and offered his hand.

"What?" Jarret shoved Zoe aside and jumped up from the couch. "You can't leave. This is your girlfriend's birthday party. We've got cake, music, drinks, a movie. Or . . . you can go upstairs."

Keefe's face flinched. He drew back a fist.

Jarret glanced at Keefe's fist and grinned, looking pleased that he'd managed to rile up his ever-calm twin. "What're you gonna do with that?"

Keefe lowered his fist, took Caitlyn's arm, and tugged her from the room.

Jarret followed. "Man, you're a wimp. She knew Zoe's parents weren't gonna be here. She wants you to lighten up."

"Don't speak for me," Caitlyn said.

Keefe led her down the hall, stopping at the pile of shoes by the door. He stooped for her boots and handed them to her. Then he faced Jarret, stepping toward him as he spoke. "Listen, brother. You put yourself in situations like this where you end up doing something stupid, something wrong." He continued inching forward though Jarret stood his ground. "All my life, I've tried talking you out of bad decisions." They stood face to face now, closer than two guys really ought to stand. "But I've also gone along with you . . . too many times. I'm done doing that. You're on your own."

Jarret's bottom lip jutted out, his eyes sulky. "I've been on my own since you went to Italy. You went to Italy, and a stranger came back. You're not my brother." He turned away, to where Zoe waited in the hall, and the two of them walked arm in arm back to the living room.

Caitlyn picked up Keefe's tennis shoes and stuffed her feet into the boots while Keefe yanked their coats from the closet. Eyes downcast and shoes in hand, he opened the door and motioned for her to go out first.

"I'm sorry about all this." Caitlyn buttoned her coat as the door squeezed shut.

"It's not your fault." Keefe shoved his foot into a shoe, stumbled, and sat on the patio chair under the window to finish the job. "I have a different way of looking at things than I had in the past. He doesn't understand that. He doesn't respect that. I don't blame him. He's right about me coming back a different person. To him, I'm a stranger." He stood and gazed through Caitlyn, perhaps recalling a memory or thinking of Jarret.

She wanted to take his hand and wished he wanted to kiss her, but she shoved her hands into her coat pockets instead.

As they walked, the cold air and sprinkle of snowflakes did her good. She took long, deep breaths and soon the cloud in her head dissipated. Guilt and joy crept into her mind, a confusing and uncomfortable combination. She knew where she went wrong. But she marveled to see the strength in Keefe. She hoped he wouldn't change his opinion of her over this.

"Keefe . . ." It took a bit of courage for her to speak. "Jarret was right."

Keefe didn't look or reply. He pulled a stocking cap from his pocket and put it on.

"I knew her parents weren't going to be there. I let Zoe talk me into this party. I'm sorry. Now we have to walk back in the snow, and I'll have to tell my parents." The last thought troubled her the most. She'd always been trustworthy. This was her first lie, and she hated to let them down.

He turned and in his eyes, she saw only compassion. He smiled. "We all make mistakes, me more than others."

Caitlyn couldn't imagine why he felt that way. She gathered it had something to do with what he had said to Jarret before they left, about going along with Jarret's bad ideas.

They walked to the sound of their feet crunching in the snow. Snowflakes danced like ballerinas in the sky and gathered on their shoulders.

As they climbed the hill between Zoe's and Caitlyn's house, Keefe broke the silence. "Jarret was right about me, too. I did change in Italy. I changed when I witnessed that Eucharistic miracle."

Her heart skipped a beat. He was going to tell her more about it, and she didn't even have to ask.

"I tell you, Caitlyn, when I walked into that church, I had no idea what was about to happen to me. I was just looking for my father. But as soon as I laid eyes on that cloth, on the blood, I just . . . I fell to my knees. I knew in my heart it was Jesus. At that moment, I could think of nothing else. It was my Lord, Creator of the universe, Redeemer of the world, and He loved me. It overpowered me."

Keefe dipped his head and wiped his nose with his gloved hand. "Feeling His amazing love made me want to . . . I don't know, try to love Him back. I decided things in my life had to change. I made promises. That's why I cut my hair. It's a sign of my promises." His expression showed sadness but also joy. "Sometimes, I still feel His love strong like that, especially at Mass. Not that I have to feel it to believe it, but . . ."

"I understand." His words struck her deep within, making it difficult for her to speak.

"I'm so weak, Caitlyn. Part of me wants to be who Jarret wants me to be. I ache thinking how alone I'm making him feel." He shook his head. "I have faith but my faith is so . . . weak. When I was in Italy, I drew strength from the churches, museums, all the religious artwork, even just walking down the streets of that ancient city. But now, I'm on my own."

"You're not on your own. The Lord is with you. You said so yourself."

He nodded.

"I'm with you, too," Caitlyn said. "We can help each other, like you helped me tonight."

Chapter Thirty-six

Jarret

Two weeks later, Thanksgiving morning, Jarret leaned against the doorframe, admiring Zoe's slender figure right before she hid it with her coat. "Why didn't you wear that red dress I like on you?"

"What's wrong with this dress?" She held her coat open and wiggled her hips. "You don't like black on me?" She gave him a sophisticated glare that instantly turned him on.

He grabbed her, wanting to pull her into his arms, but she twisted away. "Fine. Let's go before your parents get here." Her parents had gone to her grandparents' earlier in the day and probably wouldn't return until late, but why take chances.

She slung the skinny strap of her black purse onto her shoulder. "Why don't you like my parents?"

"You got that wrong, babe. They don't like me." He opened the front door and led the way to his shiny red Chrysler. He loved that car. Just seeing it could lift him out of a mood.

She got in and closed the door. "I've always had Thanksgiving at my grandparents' house." She stared at her fingernails. "And I could understand going to your house. That would've been nice. Your dining room is gorgeous, the long table, the chandelier. It would be perfect. But the Brandts'? Why is everyone going over there?"

Everyone meant his family, her, and the Summers.

Jarret shrugged and cranked the engine to life. "I don't know. The Brandts invited Papa. He said *yes*. Who cares? We won't stay that long. We'll go back to my house. No one will be there." He backed out of the driveway and shifted into drive.

"You always want to be alone."

"Yeah, well, how much fun do you think we're gonna have at Peter Brandt's house? I hate that kid. He's so rude. Every time I see him, I wanna punch him."

She sighed, her breath making a cloud in the cold air. "You're sooo not nice."

He grinned, satisfied with her reply.

When they reached the Brandts', he pulled into the two-car driveway and parked beside the Summers' van.

"I'm glad Caitlyn's here," Zoe said.

"You're pretty close to her, huh?"

She nodded, staring placidly at the front door.

"You don't tell her everything, do you?" He shoved his keys into his jacket pocket.

"She's my best friend."

"So, you don't have to tell her everything. I don't even tell Keefe everything." He still hadn't decided if he wanted Keefe to know how intimate he and Zoe were.

"What don't you want me to tell her?" The look in her eyes showed annoyance and amusement.

"Well, you sure the heck didn't tell her you were pregnant, did you? I mean now that we're past that . . . There's no reason for anyone to know. Right?"

She pressed her lips together, turned away, and gave a little headshake. "Jarret, now might not be the best time to tell you, but we're not really past that."

"Sure we are. I'm not gonna make that mistake again. Haven't I been careful?"

She huffed, still not facing him.

"Well, haven't I?" Realizing his teeth were clenched, he took a deep breath and tried to relax. She was probably just toying with him. She had a way of doing that.

"Jarret." She faced him, a hard look in her eyes. "I'm still pregnant. I didn't get the abortion, and I'm not going to."

Unable to move, he stared at her hard eyes.

I'm still pregnant . . . didn't get the abortion . . . not going to . . . pregnant . . . pregnant . . . He saw her saying it in his mind, over and over.

Every muscle in his body tensed. It couldn't be true. His hands curled up into fists. It *was* true.

He slammed the steering wheel one, two, three times, a harsh curse word ripping out each time. Then he turned and punched the back of his seat. A deep groan came from somewhere inside, then he sat still.

"Are you kidding me? You said— I mean, what were you doing when you stopped seeing me? I thought you— Didn't you say— Look, we talked about this. There's no other way. You're not doing this. You're not doing this to me."

He couldn't make himself look at her. She had betrayed him. "Get out of the car."

"What?"

"You heard me."

"I don't want to be at the Brandts' if you're not going to be here. Take me home."

"You're not going to wanna be here if I am here." He looked at her with disgust.

Her eyes held the same look. Then a tear welled up and rolled down her cheek. First one. Then another. They traced a path down her face, taking some of her mascara with them.

He swooned inside. Hating how her sadness weakened him, he turned away. "Just get out, will ya?"

"Are we . . . through?" Her voice wavered.

His chest tightened. Why was she doing this? Didn't she care what he wanted? Didn't she love him? Did he love her? He didn't want her to leave. He didn't want to see her walking away from him. She filled a void no one else could.

She cracked open her door. "Goodbye, then."

He didn't watch her get out. Didn't watch her close the door. He would've slammed it, but she only shut it. He caught a glimpse of her as she walked around his car, then he allowed himself look.

Hands in her coat pockets and head down, she walked in her high-heeled boots through the Brandts' front lawn, headed for home. She'd have to walk in the street or in grass for over a mile. There weren't any sidewalks in this part of town.

Jarret jumped out of the car. "Hey!"

She stopped.

"Hey!"

She turned to him.

He nodded for her to come back but she only stared. Maybe he was making a mistake, but he jogged to her.

The nearer he got, the softer her expression became until she was blinking back tears. She threw her arms around his neck.

He pulled her to himself. "Don't leave me," he said. "I need you. I-I-I . . ." His mouth had gone dry.

"Zoe, I think I love you."

~ ~ ~

Loud talking and laughter rang out in the Brandts' house, creating a mood that rubbed Jarret raw. The women hung out in the kitchen, clanking dishes and pans, the men in the dining room, commenting on food and football. Caitlyn sat alone in a booth, her back to the door. Peter, Keefe, and Roland must've been upstairs. The little kids shrieked and played in the living room, all except for Toby, who zipped around the place bugging one person after another with repetitive questions.

Watching everything but not wanting to join anyone, Jarret stood in the middle of the living room waiting for Zoe to get out of the bathroom.

The glass door to the backyard and guest rooms slid open and Roland came through. He weaved past the men and sat down opposite Caitlyn.

"I haven't seen much of you lately," she said to him. "How have you been?"

"You don't go outside for lunch anymore," Roland said.

"It's cold. Do you still go outside?" She sounded shocked.

Even though Keefe had returned from Italy, Roland still hung out with Jarret and the other smokers on lunch break, not that he smoked. Jarret had even let him sit in his car twice.

Toby waddled to Jarret and stood gawking. "Hello, some-un."

"Scram," Jarret said, looking as unfriendly as possible.

"Today is Thanksgiving dinner." Toby shook his hands in the air while he spoke. "You are eating Thanksgiving dinner?"

"Yee-up, that's why I'm here." Jarret tried to walk away but Toby stuck to him.

As he neared the booths in the dining room, he caught Roland saying, "I'm sorry I got mad at you at the Halloween party."

Jarret laughed to himself. So those two had a falling out, huh? Had they been a couple? Had Keefe come between them? He couldn't resist saying something. "Hey, Roland," he said so loudly that Papa, Mr. Brandt, and Mr. Summer turned, too. "You trying to steal Keefe's girlfriend?"

Roland turned beet red.

"You are eating Thanksgiving dinner with us?" Toby said.

"Uhh-huh." Jarret turned his back on the kid, glad he didn't have to put up with him twenty-four hours a day.

Toby jumped in place, so close that his flapping hand hit Jarret's chin.

Jarret's temper spiked. "Look here, you little twerp—" Out of the corner of his eye, he caught sight of Zoe.

She sauntered down the hall, looking gorgeous in her slim black dress, all traces of tears gone from her flawless face. "Toby, I hear you have an *Alice in Wonderland* video." She gave him an exaggerated smile.

Toby went right to her, and she redirected him to the living room.

Jarret just watched. Yeah, he loved that girl. She knew his moods as well as Keefe ever had. She knew what he could bear and what he couldn't. If only she wouldn't be so bull-headed about ending her pregnancy. She was scared. That had to be it.

She left Toby in the living room.

"I love you," he mouthed as she neared. This was a new level for him. He never imagined he would say those words to a girl until he was, well, older.

"I know." She wrapped her arms around his neck.

Her hug sent him to another world, far away from Toby and the Brandts, far from all his problems. He didn't want to let go.

"I know how hard this is on you," she whispered in his ear. "I love you, too. I'll set the appointment next week."

His breath caught then he exhaled hard on her neck, emotion kindling a flame inside him.

Chapter Thirty-seven

Keefe

Papa paced the family room from the blazing fireplace to the window overlooking the snow-covered back yard. Whatever he had in mind to say, it couldn't have been easy for him. He'd called everyone together over ten minutes ago.

Roland and Jarret sat on one couch, Keefe on the other. When they had first gathered in the room, Keefe had taken the spot next to Jarret, the way he always had. Jarret had actually gotten up and gone to sit by Roland.

Melting with a sense of loss, Keefe gazed at his twin. The words of his promise returned to him. *I will listen to your voice. I will live knowing You are with me and that You love me, knowing that You shed your blood for me. I will not forget, no matter whom I'm with or what temptation I face.*

Sometimes he struggled to keep his promise. Temptations came daily. Jarret wouldn't speak to him, acted like he hated him. What pain did Jarret suffer over their separation? What pain would he continue to suffer? If only Jarret would change. After Jarret had forgiven him and they'd started talking again, he'd returned to his old manipulative ways. Resisting his will felt impossible sometimes, as if Keefe had an inner need to protect and please his twin. Standing against him even felt wrong, like rubbing against the grain.

Keefe had thrown himself into prayer, begging for strength, seeking the Lord in everything. He'd asked in every possible way, yet he still couldn't understand what the Lord wanted of him, the meaning of his restless heart. He'd only grown in the awareness of his own weaknesses.

Papa stopped pacing and propped a boot on the coffee table. "I wish your mother were alive. I admit, when it comes to talking about some things, I'm at sea." He removed his cowboy hat, wiped the shine from his forehead, and put the hat back on. "I don't know, maybe I'm too late with this talk."

"Oh no, not the birds and the bees." Jarret snickered.

Roland's eyes popped open.

Papa slammed his boot to the floor, stuck his thumbs in his belt loops, and faced Jarret. "Yep, Jarret, that's the talk."

Jarret smirked. "Uh, we got that in Sex Ed. It was very detailed. Very." He paused, probably waiting for a reaction, but Papa only stared. "So, if that's all . . ." Jarret stood.

"Sit down, son. It ain't the school's job to teach you this."

Jarret's cocky grin faded. He sat down and glanced at Keefe. They'd always sat side by side for family talks. Keefe had done a good deal of telling Jarret when to shut up and sit down. He looked a little helpless all on his own. Roland wouldn't say anything to him. He'd be too unsure of himself.

A twinge of guilt struck Keefe.

"You've got a steady girlfriend now," Papa said to Jarret then looked at Keefe. "And you, though it's a different situation, I guess, but still . . ." He exhaled loudly. "I want to make sure you boys are respecting your girlfriends. I don't know what they learn you in . . . Sex Education. But I don't reckon they learn you any morals. I don't want no boy of mine eatin' supper before he says grace."

When Papa's *cowboy talk* slipped, they all knew he was serious, and he would go on talking until he thought he was understood. If he thought he wasn't, he'd start throwing in swear words. But that didn't happen often. Papa had a good amount of self-control.

"Twice now I've seen you on the Brandts' couch, Jarret. You're all over Zoe."

Jarret threw shifty glances around the room. "So? I like her."

"You need to use a little self-control there, son. Show her some respect. What are you up to when no one's around?"

Jarret blinked a few times, glanced at Keefe, then at Roland, then . . . dropped his gaze?

Keefe studied Jarret now as Papa spoke. Jarret never dropped his gaze. He would stare down anyone who challenged him, unless . . . Jarret had something to hide.

"Now your mother was a fine looking woman, and let me tell you I was mighty attracted to her. And I know waiting can be a hard row to hoe."

"Paaapa." Roland squirmed, sliding to the edge of the couch. "I don't have a girlfriend. Can I go?"

"No. You will someday in the not too distant future, I'm sure."

Roland blushed, slumped back, and folded his arms.

Jarret's fingers and thumb tapped out a rapid beat on his thigh.

"As trying as it was, we waited. That's the right thing to do. I want you to have that in mind when you're keeping company with a girl. I know Hollywood paints a different picture, but God means for a man and a woman—"

"Okay, screw this." Jarret jumped to his feet. "You married Mama two weeks after you met her. You waited? Huh!"

It was an exaggeration, but they hadn't waited long to marry. Papa met Mama in Arizona when on an assignment for a friend. He hadn't meant to stay in Arizona after the work was done, but he'd fallen in love and didn't want to leave without her. So Papa made Mama his wife within a matter of months.

"We married right quick, but we still followed God's rules." Papa raised his voice. "I want you boys to show your girlfriends respect. If I find out that you're taking advantage of a girl . . ." His eyes stayed on Jarret. "I'm gonna tan your hide."

Chapter Thirty-eight

Caitlyn

Wind whistled through Caitlyn's bedroom window. A single snowflake swirled past twiggy branches under a gray sky.

Warm in her terrycloth bathrobe and vintage flannel nightgown, Caitlyn sighed.

She never much cared for dreadful South Dakota winters and often dreamed of living in one of the warmers states when she grew up, but the way South Dakotans celebrated the winter holidays made it bearable. She especially loved Christmas and all the preparations that went into it. She and Mom had already planned the menu for their family Christmas dinner and the treats they'd eat throughout the season. She and her sisters had decorated the house, David helping with the Christmas tree.

Every year she painted a few miniature pictures to give as gifts to friends and relatives. This year, she hadn't completed nearly as many as she'd hoped to by this time.

A miniature canvas sat balanced on her knee. She dipped a tiny paintbrush into a bit of pale blue acrylic paint to add the final touches to her painting of the Wests' castle-like house. She mostly painted South Dakota scenes: farms, bison in big fields, the buttes of the Badlands, Sioux on horseback . . . Sometimes she made historical paintings, like the one of the Alamo. She never ran out of ideas.

Keefe would receive the painting of his house. She dropped the paintbrush into a jar of water and examined her work. Sun gleamed on a dusting of snow on evergreens, turrets, and battlements. A light shone from one window. The others remained dark to create a lonely mood. She added a horse and rider in the distance, deciding it was Keefe.

When she began the painting in October, she'd had Roland in mind. She'd wanted to give it to him as a gift between friends. She'd never imagined she'd be closer to his brother by the time Christmas rolled around. She missed the friendship they had developed over the camping trip. He stayed shy of her now. Maybe he felt obligated to avoid her since Keefe was sort-of courting her.

Caitlyn stood to stretch her legs and propped the painting on the back of her cluttered dresser. Keefe would like it. He'd like it because she made it. He was so sweet, appreciating the little things. She was blessed to have him for a boyfriend.

Courtship had not turned out the way she'd expected, even after monthly meetings on the subject. She'd had a more romantic notion in mind. Keefe rarely held her hand. He never kissed her. And they only saw each other with the Fire Starters. Their relationship felt more like friendship. She enjoyed it, though. She liked when he drew near and spoke low as if sharing a secret. He did that often. It reminded her of the way he and Jarret used to talk in the school halls, before they stopped talking to each other.

She shouldn't complain. She would rather have their relationship move too slowly than too quickly. She felt safe with him.

Too bad Jarret wasn't more like him. Zoe had lost her joy. Would Jarret stay by her throughout her pregnancy, especially since he had wanted her to . . .

Caitlyn's mind wouldn't complete the thought. It wasn't something she could understand. She loved life. She loved babies.

She carried the paintbrushes and dirty paint water to the bathroom and turned on the water. Priscilla's and Stacey's voices came from their bedroom. The baby was quiet, probably still napping. Something banged in the living room, probably David.

A stream of bubbly white water brought blue, green, and brown paint from deep inside the brushes, washing them clean.

Did Keefe know about Jarret and Zoe or about her pregnancy? Caitlyn had almost mentioned it a few times. Someone ought to tell their father. But she couldn't get herself to bring it up after Roland's angry reaction at the Halloween party. Maybe he was right. It was none of her business.

She dried the clean paintbrushes on a towel and shuffled back to her bedroom.

Keefe's experience in Italy, his encounter with Jesus, had sure changed him. The way he stood up to Jarret at her birthday party . . . As close as he and Jarret had always been, it had to have been difficult. But that's when it mattered. "When doing the right thing is a challenge, and a person does it anyway, that's when it means something," Mom always said. "That's when your character is proven."

Caitlyn dropped the art supplies into her old toolbox and shoved the box between the dresser and the wall. Then she sat on the bed and gazed out the window at the gray sky.

She wanted to possess that kind of character, to know that life-changing love. She wanted to love Jesus more than herself so that she would do the right thing, especially in the hard times. Her sheltered life gave few challenges. Though the one time she was measured, she'd failed. She shouldn't have agreed to the party at Zoe's house knowing that her parents wouldn't be home.

Caitlyn stretched out on the bed, her body relaxing.

In a way, Keefe had become her role model. Now that she thought about it, maybe Keefe already knew about Jarret and Zoe. Maybe Keefe already discussed it with Jarret. He would never share another's private business, so he wouldn't have told her about it.

Even if he had talked to Jarret, Zoe still seemed miserable, her smiles not reaching her eyes and her walk lacking its usual model-like quality. With Christmas on the way, it was totally unlike her. If only Caitlyn could cheer her up. She had tried inviting her to the parish Christmas festival. "We have teen bands all weekend long," Caitlyn had told her. "And I'm going to be Mary in the live Nativity."

Caitlyn sat bolt upright, her gaze snapping to the digital clock on her dresser. "Mary! That's this afternoon." She had less than an hour to get ready for her shift. Stripping off her robe, she dashed to the closet to find something warm to wear.

Zoe's rejection echoed in her head. "I can't go. I have an appointment." It was an excuse. Zoe had never even asked the time of Caitlyn's shift.

Caitlyn should call and try one more time to convince her to go. Zoe would have fun. She loved watching live bands.

After putting on a corduroy dress, a turtleneck sweater, and thick stockings, she headed for the phone in the kitchen.

Mrs. McGowan answered, sounding rushed and out of breath.

"Hi, Mrs. McGowan. This is Caitlyn. Can I talk to Zoe?"

"Caitlyn? Zoe left already. She's on her way to your house. I'm not sure when she left." She paused. "I'm surprised she's not there yet."

"Oh. Don't worry. Maybe she stopped at the playground along the way. Sometimes we like to sit on the swings. I'll go find her. Thanks." As Caitlyn hung up the phone, she shuddered. A dread feeling passed through her.

Caitlyn stuffed her feet into her boots, shrugged into her coat, and shouted, "Mom, I'll be back in a minute," as she yanked the front door open.

The cold air smacked her face, and her breath made clouds before her as she sprinted down the sidewalk. Gray clouds hung over the empty street and sidewalk. Maybe Zoe climbed the hill between their neighborhoods.

Alternating between jogging and walking, Caitlyn neared the top of the hill. More empty streets and sidewalks lay before her. Not a soul on the playground.

Caitlyn jogged, heading for Zoe's house. As she neared the edge of the last treed lot that blocked the view of Zoe's house, she stopped. She peeked around tree trunks and glimpsed Zoe's house.

Okay, where was Zoe? She must've lied so her mother wouldn't know where she went. Maybe she met Jarret somewhere. Her parents didn't like him, right?

"I have an appointment," Zoe had said. Could that be true? Could she have an appointment she didn't want her mother to know about?

For the past two weeks, ever since Thanksgiving at the Brandts', she hadn't been herself. Their conversations never went deep anymore, and Caitlyn often got the feeling Zoe wanted to avoid her altogether. Maybe Jarret had talked her into doing something she hadn't wanted to do. Maybe Jarret had talked her into—

Mind reeling, she bolted home and stopped on the front porch to catch her breath. Her coat trapped her body heat and sweat, overheating her, so she ripped it off before she flung open the door.

"Mom." Caitlyn stepped inside. "Did anyone call me?"

"Not that I know of." Mom moved from the refrigerator to the counter, stepping over David, who lay stretched out on the floor. "Why don't you help me get lunch together?"

Caitlyn dashed to the kitchen phone and called Zoe's cell. It rang once then a recorded voice said, "Your call has been forwarded to an automatic voice message . . ."

Caitlyn slammed the phone down. Zoe shut off her phone?

"Peanut butter jelly," David said, pulling himself up with Mom's legs. "Peeenut butter jelleeee."

Mom stood over four pieces of bread, dealing out slices of chicken roll, dipping a butter knife in mayonnaise, ripping up lettuce leaves . . .

"I'll make his sandwich." Caitlyn grabbed the loaf of bread. Zoe could be with Jarret, but why would she shut her phone off? She didn't usually do that.

She pulled the jar of peanut butter from the cupboard and opened a drawer for a butter knife. Maybe Zoe's troubled mood stemmed from a decision to . . . to have the abortion. Today? Now?

The knife slipped from her hand and clanked to the floor.

"Be careful," Mom said. "David's on the floor."

"Mom, I have to go." Caitlyn snatched up the knife and tossed it into the sink. Keefe and Roland were supposed to be at the church. Maybe one of them would know more, or one of them could ask Jarret.

"Where are you going?" Mom sounded annoyed. "I want you to help me get—"

"I have to go up to the church. Remember? I'm supposed to be Mary." She grabbed her coat and stuffed her feet back into her boots. Mom wouldn't be able to drive her right now, so she'd have to walk.

"That's not for half an hour. It'll take less than five minutes for me to get you to the church."

"I'll walk." Caitlyn flew out the door before Mom could object and bolted down the sidewalk, pulling her coat on as she ran.

Zoe had an appointment to get an abortion. Every step increased her certainty. She ran faster, her open coat flapping behind her.

If Zoe took the time to think it through, she wouldn't want to do this. She would regret it, and her depression would deepen. Caitlyn had learned that many women who've had abortions get suicidal. She had to find a way to stop her.

Caitlyn regulated her breathing to keep up her pace, inhaling through her mouth with every other step. Her eyes watered from the cold. Her heart pounded.

If Zoe recently left for the appointment, it might not be too late. Caitlyn could talk to Keefe. If he didn't know the type of relationship Jarret and Zoe had, she'd have to tell him. He and Jarret were once close, he had said. Keefe had kept Jarret out of trouble before. Maybe he could say or do something now.

Lungs burning and sides aching, Caitlyn slowed.

Cars lined the streets near the church. Families walked down the sidewalks. Keefe had volunteered to set things up and help for a few hours. He wanted to be there when Caitlyn stood in as Mary in the live Nativity. Roland and Peter had taken the shift before hers, so they should be standing out in the cold right now.

Reaching the church grounds, Caitlyn weaved around groups of chatting parishioners then stepped inside the community hall. A band of five teenage boys stood in the far corner, the leader talking into a microphone to a group of about thirty people. Snack and beverage tables lined one wall, children's games another. Dominic, Greg, and Doug from the Fire Starters stood near a partially set up fabric dartboard game.

She ran to them.

"Have you seen Keefe?" She looked at Dominic since she knew him best.

He straightened and tossed his shiny black bangs from his eyes. "No, chica. I think he went to get something, but he will be back." He turned to Greg and Doug as if for confirmation.

"Yeah." Greg glanced at his watch. "He should be back soon. He's gonna help get the next team out to the Nativity."

Doug gave one of his silly smiles. "He'll be back. He's got to escort his Mary to the stable. He wouldn't miss it for the world." He pointed to a nearby folding chair. "Wait with us. Maybe you can tell us what we're doing wrong with this dartboard."

Caitlyn couldn't wait. Zoe couldn't wait. She tore through the side door, heading for the live Nativity. And Roland.

Chapter Thirty-nine

Roland

The cold bit Roland's fingers as he adjusted his gold crown. He tugged his purple and black robe closed and made a sweeping gaze of the church grounds, scanning for Jarret. How had he gotten himself into this predicament?

The Fire Starters got the wise idea to make a live Nativity this year. Now three smelly sheep, a calf, a donkey, and a goat stood on piles of hay in the front lawn of Saint Michael's church. Behind them, a heater kept *Mary* and *Joseph* warm in a makeshift stable. One shepherd had crept inappropriately close to the manger, no doubt to keep warm.

Roland and the rest of the adorers were left to freeze and consider, for their hour-long shift, whether or not they would be warmer cuddling up to one of the smelly animals. The angel had the hardest job, standing up on the platform behind the stable, the north-wind blowing her hair and turning her lips blue.

At least they still had the sunlight. The kids on the evening shifts would have it worse.

"I can't believe I let you talk me into this." Peter's cheeks had turned as orange as the puffy hat and the long robe he wore over his clothes. "It's freezing out here. And I've gotta pee." Clutching a gold box in one hand, he hugged himself with the other and bounced on his toes.

Roland took his eyes off baby-doll Jesus, the only *fake* part of the live Nativity, and glared at Peter, bumping him. They stood so close that they bumped by accident every few seconds. "Me? I didn't talk you into anything. I'm not even a member of the Fire Starters. This is your fault."

Peter had talked Roland into taking one of the shifts. Roland only wanted to listen to the bands playing in the community hall. He always wished he'd learned to play the electric guitar.

"Aren't you a Fire Starter?" Peter squinted at him. "Your brother is."

"Keefe? Yeah, I know. That's because of Caitlyn."

"Yeah. Where is she anyway?" Peter craned his neck. "Isn't she supposed to be Mary for the next shift? Hey, you got a watch?"

"I got my cell phone." Roland set his gift down and wiggled his hand into the oversized sleeve of his robe. He slid his hand into the back pocket of his jeans wishing he'd worn gloves. His numb fingers felt weird as they wrapped around the phone and eased it from his pocket. Then his phone slipped.

"Shoot."

"What?" Peter turned his eyes to the people milling around. "Jarret here already?"

"No. I don't know. I dropped my phone. Help me find it." Roland stooped and pushed through sweet-smelling hay.

Maybe Jarret wouldn't come for him. "Let 'em walk," Jarret had told Papa. Papa had replied in a voice too low to overhear, saying something that had changed Jarret's mind. Jarret's mood had been foul all day. Roland almost said he'd find his own way home, but then he got to thinking that they could talk. Jarret still hadn't let Keefe back into his life, and he grew more distant and moody every day.

Peter set his gift down and joined Roland in searching through the hay. "Are you and Jarret gonna hang out here awhile? Why don't you just let my folks take you home? You can hang out with me instead. I smell popcorn every time someone opens the doors to the community hall. I'd love to shove my hands into the popcorn machine."

Roland jabbed his icy fingers into a mound of damp hay. The phone must've slid way down. "Are you helping me look? I don't want to lose my phone."

"Hey!" Monica Wellsford, aka *Mary*, whispered in a tone unbecoming of the Virgin Mary. "You guys are supposed to be looking at us. Get. Up. People are watching."

"I dropped my cell phone." Roland stood, glanced at the family of five that had stopped nearby, and then faced Monica. Bending down and moving his limbs had actually warmed him a bit.

Mary wouldn't understand how cold the adorers got. She had it made, kneeling there next to the heater.

Peter stood and wacked Roland's arm. "Chill out. Here it is." He handed him the phone. "Are you calling Jarret?"

"No. You asked me the time."

"Oh, yeah." Peter bounced on his feet.

Monica-Mary grunted and gave a disgusted sigh.

Another family stopped next to the first family and pointed things out to their kids. Then a redhead pushed through the two families and bolted recklessly toward the Nativity.

Monica-Mary gasped. "Caitlyn! You're supposed to wait for the guys to bring the curtain. You can't just barge up here." That was how the kids changed shifts. Two guys held up a big blanket, and the new crew traded places with the frozen crew.

Caitlyn, ignoring Monica completely, ran directly to Roland. Judging by the slant of her eyebrows, something bothered her.

Roland's face warmed a bit, which under the circumstances he didn't mind. "What's up, Caitlyn? I think we've got five more minutes here."

"Oh my gosh," Peter shouted, his eyes bugging at Caitlyn. "People are watching. This is supposed to remind them of the first Nativity. I'm sure no one charged up to the stables to chat with the wise men. Can't you wait?"

Caitlyn turned her back on Peter and grabbed Roland's shoulder. She leaned in, her hair tickling his face, then whispered in his ear. "I have to talk to you. It's an emergency."

"What's wrong?" His heart thumped like mad at her closeness.

She pressed her lips together as if unsure of how to answer. "I have to talk to you. Not here. And it can't wait."

Her gorgeous green eyes did something to a guy, whether or not he wanted them to, whether or not she was his brother's girlfriend. He abandoned his post and followed her, Peter and Mary calling after him, kids commenting, and parents fumbling with excuses for why one of the three wise men had taken off. On the good side, embarrassment had caused a spike in his temperature, thawing him even before they stepped foot inside.

Christmas music blasted. People of all ages crowded around a boy band in the community room. Teens stood in groups. Little kids ran around their parents. The smell of hotdogs and buttery popcorn filled the air.

Caitlyn led Roland to an empty corner and faced him. Then she grabbed his upper arms, tugging the robe tight around his neck, and pushed his back to the wall. Worry clouded her eyes. "I think Zoe's going to have an abortion."

Roland pulled away and cracked his head on the wall. "What?" The music drowned out other sounds, but he'd heard her all right, and his stomach had dropped to his feet.

He hadn't allowed himself to believe Zoe was really pregnant. When Caitlyn had said she was *in trouble*, she could've meant anything. He hadn't wanted to jump to conclusions. And it still annoyed him that she expected him to interfere in Jarret's business. If Jarret and Zoe had decided to do this . . . to do this . . .

He swallowed hard. An abortion?

She threw a worried glance over her shoulder. "I'm afraid she's doing it now. I invited her here yesterday, but she said she had an appointment today. I only realized today what that probably meant."

"Maybe you're wrong." He straightened and pushed away from the wall, forcing her to release his arms and step back.

"I'm not wrong." She wrung her hands. "She's been quiet lately. Something is bothering her, something big, but she won't talk to me about it."

Roland shook his head, not wanting to believe it. He scanned the crowd and caught sight of Jarret near the back of the audience. His stomach returned to its place. "Wouldn't Jarret be with her? Wouldn't he take her?"

Caitlyn looked in the same direction. "I don't know. I wanted Keefe to ask Jarret, to talk to him. But I can't find him. Someone needs to talk to Jarret."

"Uh, not me. He doesn't listen to me. And he's not talking to Keefe now anyway."

She let out a frustrated groan, grabbed his arms, and shoved him against the wall again. "We have to do something. Maybe we can save the baby. Please, go ask him." She did that thing with her eyes again, gazing right into his soul.

He pushed off the wall, heart pounding in his throat. Could he? Should he? "I don't know—"

"You have to." This time she spoke with a stern voice and with eyebrows low over flaming green eyes. "This is yours to do."

A verse from Scripture came to mind, and the Word spoke to his heart. *Go and tell him his fault between you and him alone.*

Roland peered inward and shuddered. Fear motivated him. He was afraid to talk to Jarret, afraid Jarret would accuse him of being judgmental and intolerant.

"Caitlyn." Doug, one of the boys with the Fire Starters, came up. "Time for your shift. Better get into the blue." He wiggled a finger at her dress.

Caitlyn gave Roland one last desperate glance and stormed away.

Roland watched her go then directed his gaze to Jarret.

A guitar played. Another joined in. The band began a slow, emotional song as Roland weaved through the crowd toward Jarret.

Jarret hadn't wanted to give Roland a ride, so he was probably anxious to get out of here. What could Roland say to him? How could he ask anything without sounding judgmental?

No. Roland steeled himself. He was past that. He wasn't judging Jarret's eternal soul but his actions. If he cared about Jarret at all, he needed to confront him.

A mother holding a baby stood in front of Jarret, the baby peeking over her shoulder at him. Jarret's face contorted as if he saw something horrible rather than the cute little baby before him.

Roland drew near.

Jarret remained statue-like, his eyes on the baby, his face frozen with the morbid expression.

"Hey there, Jarret." Roland slapped his arm to get his attention.

Jarret jerked to face him, his expression unchanged. "What d'ya want?"

"Uh . . . Aren't you giving me a ride home? Isn't that why you're here?"

"Oh. Yeah." The horrid expression faded though he faced the baby again. "I need to get out of here."

Roland's stomach turned. Why would it bother Jarret to see a baby . . . unless he had a guilty conscience? He had to ask him. No matter how Jarret would take it, he had to ask.

Jarret turned to go.

Roland grabbed his arm. "Before we go, can I talk to you?"

Jarret glanced at the hand on his arm then shook his head as he turned away. He pushed between the couple behind him, though he could've easily gone around them, and plowed through another group that hadn't really stood in his way.

Roland followed. "I need to talk to you for a minute. I have something to ask you."

Jarret headed for the door, but when a clear path opened, he veered away from it as if unaware of his surroundings. He pushed through two women and stopped dead, the disturbed and fearful appearance returning to him.

Before him on a chair by the wall, Mrs. Finn sat nursing her newborn. She glanced up.

Jarret stood gawking down at her or at the baby.

"Did you want something?" Mrs. Finn said.

Jarret's eyelids flickered, but he didn't answer.

"No, Mrs. Finn, he was just on his way to the . . ." Roland shoved Jarret toward the hall that led to the bathrooms. "Uh, Jarret, are you okay? You're acting a little strange."

Jarret offered no resistance as Roland dragged him down the hall and into the boys' bathroom.

"How old do you think that baby is?" Jarret staggered to the first stall and pushed open the door. Metal smacked against metal.

Roland stood by the bathroom door, prepared to send away anyone who would try to enter. "Gosh. You mean the one Mrs. Finn was nursing?"

"Yeah." Jarret pushed open the second and third stall doors, banging them.

"Don't you think it's rude to stare like that?"

Jarret said nothing.

Considering how to word what he had to say, Roland stepped closer to his brother. As the last stall door flung open and before Jarret had time to turn around, Roland blurted out, "I, uh, need to ask you . . . Is Zoe really pregnant?"

Jarret froze. Then he reeled around, hands reaching for Roland's chest and fury written on his face.

Roland backed up to avoid contact but not soon enough. Jarret gripped his shirt at the chest, spun him around, and rammed him into a half-open stall door. The door gave way and Roland's feet slid out from under him.

"Who do you think you are?" Jarret spit, glaring down his nose.

"I'm only asking because—" Roland struggled to get up, but Jarret's boot landed on his shoulder.

"I know why you're asking. You're all the time following me, thinking I'm up to no good, trying to get something on me. You're so good. I'm so bad. You're already Papa's pet. Isn't that enough?" Jarret paced to the mirror.

Roland climbed to his feet. This was none of his business. Maybe he should keep quiet and leave it alone, but—

No! *I am sending you out as sheep among wolves. So be as shrewd as snakes and as innocent as doves.*

Bracing himself for another hit, he said, "I know you think I judge you. And maybe I have. But that's not what this is about. While Keefe was gone, I only followed you because I was worried about you. I'm not trying to get you in trouble."

Jarret smirked at him through the mirror. "You trying to keep me out of it? You're too late. Yeah, she's pregnant. I mean . . . she was." His mouth curled, his bottom lip trembling. He grabbed the hair on the top of his head, groaned, and flung himself against the wall. "I . . . told her—"

The bathroom door opened and some young kid stepped in.

"Hey," Roland said to the boy, his voice like gravel. "You can't come in here."

"But I have to go," the boy said, eyes wide, backing up.

"Use the girls' room."

The boy took off.

Roland faced Jarret again, determined to get straight to the point. "Caitlyn thinks Zoe's having an abortion today, right now."

Still clutching his hair, his face hidden by his arms, Jarret made no reply.

Maybe he didn't realize the gravity of it all, but Roland knew a secret from the past that might bring it home. "I heard Mama talking once . . ." Roland came close. "The doctors said her pregnancy had complications."

Jarret eased his hands down from his face and looked.

"She'd had a miscarriage before, so they advised her to abort . . . one of her twins."

He stared for a moment, looking like he hadn't understood one word. Then he groaned and turned toward the wall. "Oh God, I'm killing my baby." He slid to the floor.

Roland's heart stopped cold. Then anger bubbled up inside. Jarret was a coward. He couldn't face the consequence of his actions, so he chose to kill someone else. An innocent baby.

Face buried in his hands, Jarret sobbed on the floor.

Roland stood over him, his heart like stone. He'd never seen his brother shed so much as a single tear. Had he even cried at Mama's funeral when he was just a ten-year-old boy? Papa said Jarret's cold attitude was his way of handling the pain. Maybe it was.

Body convulsing, Jarret groaned and wept. He seemed unaware that Roland stood over him, unconcerned that anyone might see him. What he'd done, he regretted.

Roland squatted and squeezed his shoulder. Sympathy seeped in, melting the stone in his heart. "Jarret, get up. Maybe we can stop her."

"It's . . . too late."

"Maybe it's not too late. Let's go try."

Jarret lifted his head, moving in slow motion, until his gaze rested on Roland. The look in his eyes showed he couldn't believe Roland wanted to help. "I . . . don't even know where she's having it done. I just . . . I told her to do it."

Roland took his brother's arm and helped him stand. "I know how to find out. There aren't a lot of places that do that around here, and I hear the Fire Starters go out there with signs. Come on."

~ ~ ~

A minute later, Jarret sat behind the wheel of his red Chrysler, speeding down the highway. Roland rode shotgun, and smiling Doug Baxter sat in the back.

"Okay, take this exit." Doug knew the way. Roland had spotted him first when they'd left the bathroom, so he'd asked him for directions. If he'd had time to choose, he wouldn't have asked Doug. Doug was a clown. Always cheerful, ever ready with a joke, liked to make people laugh. To his credit, though, he'd asked no questions when Roland said he needed to know how to get to the abortion clinic. The look on Jarret's face probably said enough. Doug started giving directions but then said, "Why don't I just ride with you? It'll be easier." So, the three of them set off together.

"So, who drove her?" Roland glanced warily out the rear window. He'd been praying that a cop wouldn't stop them as Jarret pushed seventy-five on a sixty-mile-per-hour road.

"I don't know. She didn't want me to go with her." Jarret's gaze remained fixed on the road.

"Do you know what time her appointment was?"

"No." Jarret shot him a cold glance. "Shut up and pray."

Roland smiled inside. Another first. Jarret had never asked anyone for prayers.

Roland prayed for a miracle, that the abortionist would be converted or that his car would break down, that the power would go out in the clinic or that lightning would strike, that Zoe would change her mind or that someone would change it for her. God worked in mysterious ways. God could do all things. *Please, God, save the baby!*

All the while, sorrow hovered in his soul. He knew that the deed might already be done. If that were the case, Jarret and Zoe would both need God's help and healing. They'd have a long, hard road to recovery. And pain that would never go away.

The abortion clinic sat on a busy street in a big old building with many steps out front. Across the street, a small group of people held signs and prayed, rosaries dangling from their hands.

As Jarret pulled up to the curb, he stared out the side window and muttered something under his breath.

Zoe sat on the steps in the arms of a gray-haired woman, both of them crying.

Jarret threw open his door and bounded up the steps. When he reached Zoe, he said something, gesturing wildly, then fell on his knees. Whatever she said made him slowly raise his head. The two embraced. The gray-haired woman wiped her eyes repeatedly.

"Are we too late?" Doug said, Roland almost forgetting he was there.

"I guess so." It hurt to say it, to face it, and his eyes welled up with tears.

A long time later, the three on the steps got to their feet and headed down. Jarret and Zoe walked arm in arm, not speaking until they reached the bottom of the steps. Then Jarret hugged the gray-haired woman. She smiled, hugged Zoe, and after a few words, headed across the street towards the group with signs.

Roland opened his car door, ready to let Zoe have the front seat.

"Get in the back," Jarret said to Roland, emotionless.

Before Jarret pulled onto the road, he and Zoe hugged each other again. He kissed the top of her head then looked over his shoulder. "The baby's okay."

"What?" Roland shook his head in disbelief, a tingling sensation washing over him. Relief scattered his sorrow. He took a deep breath and slumped back in the seat.

Zoe turned around, joy in her eyes. "Those people changed my mind." She pointed at the people with signs.

The gray-haired woman had rejoined the group and stood in a huddle with the others. As Jarret drove past, they cheered, waved, and blew kisses. Jarret gave a double honk. Zoe waved. They all had a reason to rejoice. A baby was saved this day.

Chapter Forty

Jarret

"Do we have to do this?" Jarret desperately wanted a cigarette, but he wouldn't compromise his car, so he drummed his fingers on the steering wheel instead. He couldn't peel his eyes from the front door of Zoe's house. It would be a while before he'd get the chance to smoke.

Zoe leaned against his arm and moaned. "We already waited for Christmas, then New Year's. We can't wait for Valentine's Day. I'm four-and-a-half months. I was lucky to get past the morning sickness without anyone catching on, but I'll start showing soon. Besides, don't you think this is the responsible thing to do?"

"No. I think we should run away, raise our baby bohemian style."

She giggled and looked up at him.

He gave her a little kiss. Sure, he was kidding, but part of him wasn't. He'd do anything to avoid telling Mr. McGowan he'd knocked up his daughter. The man looked mean, probably had a temper. What would he do when he found out?

"Come on. Let's do it before I chicken out." Zoe patted his thigh and slipped her fingers around the passenger-side door handle.

Jarret tensed. He forced himself to open his door and emerge from the car. Should he hold her hand? Should he put his arm around her? Should he keep his hands to himself? Did it matter what he did? He was a dead man.

Zoe gave him a determined look and reached for his hand.

Taking her clammy hand into his own, he walked with her to the door, each step increasing his desire to run. She opened the front door. As he crossed the threshold, he resigned himself to his fate.

Mr. McGowan sat hunched over a magazine at the kitchen table, sparing them a glance as they took off their shoes in the foyer. Zoe hung her coat in the closet.

"I didn't know we were having company for dinner," Mr. McGowan muttered.

Jarret put his mouth to Zoe's ear and whispered, "We're not staying for dinner."

She patted his arm and gave him a reassuring nod. "I know."

"Oh, Zoe, you're home." Mrs. McGowan peeked around the corner of the kitchen, a spatula in her hand and a smile on her face. Something sizzled on the stove. "Hello, Jarret. Will you be joining us for dinner? I'll have to put more—"

"No. Don't worry about me. I won't be staying." He followed Zoe to the kitchen.

"Why don't you sit down?" Zoe nodded toward the table, the determined look still in her eyes.

Eyes wide, Jarret shook his head and wanted to whisper a protest to Zoe, but Mrs. McGowan looked at him. So he took the chair across from Mr. McGowan.

The man hadn't looked up from the magazine since his first beady-eyed glance. He was a big man, a good two-fifty or more pounds, but he didn't look like he worked out any. His dress clothes, the tie on the table, and the business magazine in his hands probably told it all.

"Want to give me some help here?" Mrs. McGowan handed Zoe a head of lettuce and other things from the refrigerator.

Zoe took them to the sink. "Mom, actually, Jarret and I have something serious to tell you and Dad." She turned on the water and stuck the lettuce under the stream.

"Serious, huh?" Mrs. McGowan pushed something around in the skillet. Her lazy tone of voice made her seem distracted.

Mr. McGowan's gaze snapped from his magazine to Jarret.

Jarret looked away, trying to appear unfazed, though beads of sweat rolled down his back. Maybe he should've taken off his leather jacket. No. He did not intend to stay longer than necessary.

Zoe set the vegetables on paper towels then turned and leaned against the countertop. "You're not going to like what I have to say."

"Oh?" That got Mrs. McGowan's attention.

Jarret could feel Mr. McGowan drilling a hole through his head with his eyes, but he wasn't ready to meet his gaze just yet.

"I'm pregnant." She said it. The words were out. Just like that.

Mrs. McGowan gasped and smacked her chest.

Mr. McGowan stood, his chair scraping the floor, his eyes still on Jarret. "Is that so?"

The blood drained from Jarret's head. He got to his feet, meaning to make his exit. She said it. They were done. A wave of heat hotter than hell washed over him.

"Boy, I'm talking to you." The man's voice boomed. "Did you get my daughter pregnant?"

Jarret met his gaze and forced himself to answer. "Yeah."

"You've been taking advantage of my daughter?" Red faced and eyes blazing, he stepped to the end of the table, the end Jarret would have to pass to get to the door.

"Dad!" Zoe grabbed his arm. "Don't worry. We're not keeping the baby. We're going to see a social—"

"You're daggone straight you're not keeping the baby. You're a child. How long has this been going on?"

Zoe scowled and folded her arms. Mr. McGowan turned to Jarret for the answer.

"Look, I'm sorry." Jarret threw his hands up, palms out. "We messed up. I didn't, I didn't want her to get pregnant. We'll take care of it. We're gonna put the baby up for adoption."

"When hell freezes over!" Mr. McGowan grabbed Jarret by the front of his jacket, whipped him around, and slammed him into the wall.

Unsure of the man's strength and not wanting to rile him further, Jarret only glared, tempted though he was to peel the man's hands from his Hugo Boss dirty-black leather bomber.

"You stay away from my daughter, boy." He shoved Jarret again as if for emphasis. "If I ever catch you near her—"

Zoe and Mrs. McGowan grabbed Mr. McGowan's arms, both shrieking for him to stop.

Mr. McGowan backed off and dusted his shirtfront as if he had soiled himself by touching Jarret. "Get out of my house." He turned to his wife and ranted, "Take your daughter to get an abortion. You're too lenient with her. You let her run wild . . ."

Mrs. McGowan turned her back on him and put an arm around Zoe, saying something to her about being so young and wondering how it happened.

Jarret's head reeled. Anger or fear brought stars to his vision. He backed away from everyone, taking a few steps down the hall. He wanted to take Zoe and leave, or be shut of the place, as Papa would say. What would Papa say when he found out? He wasn't going to find out. There was no reason he should have to know. Zoe just had to stay away from the house, that's all.

Mr. McGowan kept ranting. He faced the glass doors to the patio now. Mrs. McGowan, her arm still around Zoe's shoulders, spoke low. "I understand what you're feeling . . ." Her eyes showed worry though she smiled. "I'll be there with you. It'll be okay . . ." Her voice dropped too low to overhear, but it sounded like she said *abortion clinic*.

Jarret's fists and jaw tightened. He stomped back into the kitchen. "We're not killing our baby." Grabbing Zoe's arm, he yanked her to himself.

Zoe was saying something about making an adoption plan but neither of her parents listened. Mr. McGowan stormed over, yanked Zoe's other arm, and shoved Jarret back.

Jarret's shoulder hit the wall.

Mrs. McGowan shrieked.

Zoe was crying.

"She'll do what I tell her," Mr. McGowan spit. He said something about lawyers.

"Not to my baby," Jarret spit back then ducked as the man swung at his face.

"Just go, Jarret," Mrs. McGowan shrieked.

Zoe grabbed his hand and dragged him to the foyer. "It'll be okay. Dad just needs to calm down. Don't worry . . ." She pushed him out the door.

Hands trembling, Jarret groped his jacket pockets for his cigarettes as he walked alone down the driveway and to his car.

Chapter Forty-one

Caitlyn

The turquoise blue dress from the second-hand shop, while totally 1980s, didn't look half-bad on Caitlyn. Short, loose sleeves and a wide cummerbund waist with pleating above and below gave the impression she had a feminine shape.

Caitlyn turned to see the back of the dress in the mirror on her closet. She wanted to look nice for Keefe. Would he wear a button-front shirt and tie? A suit jacket? Could her five-dollar dress possibly complement his outfit?

Butterflies danced in her stomach whenever she imagined how tonight would go. Even though they spoke every day at school and saw each other at the youth center with the Fire Starters once or twice a week, Keefe had blushed when he invited her to his house for dinner. He'd said Nanny would be making something special.

She slipped out of the turquoise dress and reached for the brown tie-dye dress she'd worn to school. Her sisters screamed at each other in the hall. Caitlyn hoped they wouldn't barge in while she changed.

After hanging the turquoise dress in the closet, she stretched out on the bed and lost herself in thought, imagining how the evening would go.

Someone bumped her door then the voices quieted. Her sisters had probably stopped arguing and resumed their game.

After a moment of silence, a knock sounded on the front door, and the baby let out a wail.

Caitlyn pushed herself up and glanced at the clock. It was only a little after four. Keefe wouldn't come to the door today anyway; Dad said he'd drive her over.

Someone knocked on the bedroom door, then the door opened a crack and Mom stuck her head in. "Zoe's here." She opened the door the rest of the way.

Zoe carried a suitcase and her black and hot-pink duffle bag. "Hi." She smiled as she stepped into the room, but the fakeness of her smile spoke of trouble. She set her suitcase against the wall.

"Are you running away?" Caitlyn giggled.

She frowned. "I can't stay at my house." She sat on the bed and scooted back against the headboard. "Do you think your parents would let me stay here?"

"Really?" Caitlyn crawled across the bed to sit facing her. Something banged against the wall in the hallway. Someone whined. Her sisters must've launched a new battle in the hall. Caitlyn couldn't imagine anyone unrelated wanting to stay here. "What happened?"

"My dad. He insists I have an abortion. He says he'll drive me there himself."

"Oh, Zoe, how terrible. You can stay here. I'm sure they'll let you."

"Do they know I'm pregnant?"

"No." It wasn't something Caitlyn wanted to share with them knowing how they worried over her choice of friends.

"Well, I have to do something. If I can't stay here—"

"You *can* stay here. I'll go get Mom." Caitlyn jumped up and stuck her head out the door. Stacey and Priscilla had gone. "Mom," she hollered then turned to Zoe. "You can sleep in my bed. I'll sleep on the floor or the couch."

"Oh, your bed's big enough for two. It's a full-size, right?"

They both looked at the bed with its flat pillows and old blue and yellow quilt. The headboard partially blocked the window. The bed took up so much space that it allowed just enough room to walk past the dresser and get to the closet.

"What's up girls?" Mom bounced into the room, a cloth diaper draped over her shoulder. Her eyes slid to Zoe's suitcase.

"Mom, sit down." Caitlyn sat sideways on the end of the bed so she could see Zoe. She patted the mattress until Mom joined them. "Zoe needs our help."

Zoe scooted forward so that all three sat in a little circle. She fidgeted with her sock then looked directly into Mom's eyes. "I'm sorry you have to find this out, Mrs. Summer. Please don't think my mistake has any reflection on Caitlyn. You have a very good daughter."

Mom gave them both a funny, narrow-eyed glance. "What's this about?"

Zoe and Caitlyn exchanged glances. Then Caitlyn said, "Zoe's pregnant."

Mom's eyes popped open wide.

"I know." Zoe dipped her head, and her silky black hair fell forward, hiding her face. "I made a mistake. But I don't want to make another one." She lifted her head. "My dad wants me to have an abortion, but I won't do it. He keeps after me about it. I can't stay there. I need someplace to live . . . at least until he calms down."

"Oh my heavens, Zoe." Mom's face turned white. She snatched Zoe's hand and squeezed it. "You dear girl. Of course we'll help you."

Zoe lunged forward and fell into Mom's arms. Mom squeezed her and stroked her hair, a strangled smile on her face.

"Thank you, Mrs. Summer," Zoe whispered and sat back.

Mom pushed Zoe's hair off her face, draping it behind her shoulder. She sighed. "If you don't mind me asking, who's the father?"

Caitlyn gasped. What would Mom do, knowing that Keefe's twin brother got Zoe pregnant? Would this revelation change her life, too?

"Um . . ." Zoe turned wide-eyes to Caitlyn.

They could always say—

No. Caitlyn wasn't going to lie again. "Jarret's the father. Jarret West. That's still Zoe's boyfriend. You saw them together on Thanksgiving. Don't you remember?"

Mom's forehead wrinkled but she smiled. "Oh. Keefe's twin brother?"

Caitlyn swallowed hard and nodded.

Mom stood. "How far along are you?"

"Nineteen weeks." Zoe smoothed her sweater over her belly, revealing her little baby bump.

"I'll talk to your father," Mom said to Caitlyn then left the room.

Caitlyn exhaled.

Zoe slumped back on the pillows. "I hope they let me stay. I have no one else to ask. I can't stay with Jarret. He doesn't want his father to know. Do you know I only see Jarret at school now?"

"Really?" Caitlyn got up to listen by her bedroom door but couldn't hear Mom or Dad at all.

"My dad started working from home in the afternoons. And if he has to go anywhere when Mom's not home, he actually has one of the neighbors keep an eye on me. It's embarrassing. I feel like a child." She propped herself up on her elbows. "No, I feel like I'm in prison. I'm allowed to go to school and home. Anywhere else and I have to go with Mom or Dad."

"It's like that for me. I don't mind."

"You're going over to the Wests' house for dinner, aren't you?"

"Yes."

"I can't see Jarret at all. My dad hates him with a passion. I'm not allowed to visit friends because he thinks Jarret will show up. I bet I wouldn't even be allowed at your church with that youth group of yours." She grimaced with emotion, forehead wrinkling and eyes glassy. "This is my fault. I feel so broken, so mad at myself. I . . . I feel like I've lost myself."

Unable to think of one word of comfort, Caitlyn leaned and hugged her. Two seconds later, someone knocked on her bedroom door.

"Caitlyn." Dad opened the door. "Can you spare a minute?"

Leaving Zoe in the bedroom, Caitlyn followed Dad to the enclosed patio through the dimly lit and surprisingly quiet house. Mom sat on a cushioned patio chair nursing Andy.

Dad propped his hands on his hips and gazed at the backyard where David and the girls played. "Caitlyn, we're a little concerned about this situation." He didn't chuckle, laugh, or use his silly intonations.

"Okaaay." She hoped he'd get right to the point. It made her uncomfortable seeing him so serious.

"Jarret is Keefe's twin brother, eh?"

"Yes." Her eyes narrowed. He knew the answer. Why ask?

"I guess it surprises me that one of the West boys would . . ." He made a face as if struggling to find the right word.

"Get a girl pregnant?" she said.

Dad chuckled and rubbed his head, making his hair stand up on top. "That's right. I guess I assumed all the West boys had the same high standards I see in Keefe. But I realize, I don't really know Keefe that well. I've only spoken with him the few times he's been over here or, uh, at the Brandts'. What do I know?" He dropped his gaze.

Caitlyn shuffled to Dad and touched his arm so he would face her. "Look, Dad. Sure they're twins and they look alike, but they don't act alike. Keefe's nothing like Jarret."

Dad nodded. He and Mom held each other's gazes for a moment. "Well, I don't know if that's good enough for me, Caitlyn. I don't want you . . ." He rubbed his mouth in a nervous way uncharacteristic of him. "Maybe you and Keefe need to slow things down. Maybe you should get to know some other nice boys. When we talked about courtship, I never thought you'd only be seeing one guy at your age. You're only fifteen. It's not like you'll be getting married anytime soon. What's the rush?"

Jarret's accusation at her birthday party came to Caitlyn's mind. Had Dad gotten Mom pregnant on Valentine's Day? That may have explained his over-protectiveness now. "It's not fair." She folded her arms. "I never see him anywhere except at church or with the Fire Starters or at school. He never comes over, and I never go to his house. How much slower can we take it?"

"Who's going to be over there tonight, at the Wests'?"

With a huff, Caitlyn threw Mom a look to get some help.

Mom's eyes remained fixed on Dad, a show of their unity in the matter.

"I already told you," Caitlyn said. "Mr. West will be there and so will Nanny and Mr. Digby. We won't be alone. And stop thinking of him as if he's just like Jarret. He's not."

Dad rubbed his mouth again. "Well, Caitlyn—"

A knock sounded on the front door. Everyone looked.

"I'll get that." Dad, never one to worry about his appearance, combed his stringy gray hair with his fingers on the way to the door.

Caitlyn dropped to her knees by Mom and rubbed Andy's smooth head. "Mom, please don't do this. I feel like you guys don't want me to see Keefe at all. We're more like friends anyway. You have nothing to worry about."

Mom gave her a love-filled smile though her eyes held a distant look. "Honey, we can't help but worry about you. This is a very important time in your life. You're nearing adulthood. Some questions don't have clear answers. It's easy to make mistakes." The baby had fallen asleep and Mom handed him to Caitlyn.

Caitlyn's heart calmed, holding him close. She loved his baby smell and the way his body molded into hers, his eyes so peaceful, his mouth so perfect . . .

Voices traveled from the living room.

Mom stood. "I'll just go see . . ." She crossed the enclosed patio and stepped into the house.

With her eyes on the treasure she held, Caitlyn got up and followed.

Jarret and Zoe sat side by side on the couch under the living room window. Zoe held a bouquet of red roses on her lap. She brought a hand to her mouth, her eyes emotional. Jarret smiled, gazing at her. He leaned and whispered.

Dad sat in the rocker-recliner saying something Caitlyn couldn't make out until she stepped through the dining room. ". . . spoke with your mother, Zoe. You're welcome to stay here. But we'll have to ask that you follow the same rules as our own daughter."

"Okay." Zoe nodded. "I can do that."

Mom opened a cupboard in the kitchen, but she was no doubt listening and watching everything over the counter.

Caitlyn stood in the dining room, holding Andy and swaying from side to side, decidedly staying out of the living room and out of the conversation—but close enough should Zoe need her.

Jarret squirmed a bit then bounced one knee. "What does that mean?"

"That means, Jarret, I don't want her sneaking off to see you. That's how she got this way, huh?" Dad chuckled. "I like you, Jarret. We've all made mistakes, and I sure don't hold anything against you. I don't have a problem with you coming over here. But I'm sure Zoe will have homework and other things to do. So I wouldn't want your visits to be an everyday thing."

"Do I need to ask permission to take her to dinner tonight?" He used a sarcastic tone, a cocky expression on his face.

Dad laughed, not in a cruel way, but as if he thoroughly enjoyed the conversation. "Yeah, that's what I'm saying. I don't let my own daughter run around. As long as Zoe wants to stay here, she's not running around either."

Jarret's sneer grew. "She's not your daughter."

Dad leaned back in the rocking chair and chuckled. "Oh, Jarret."

Zoe took Jarret's hand. "Why don't we just go to your house with Caitlyn? That would be nice for Valentine's Day. It doesn't have to be a restaurant." She said to Dad, "Is Caitlyn allowed over there tonight?"

"Uhhh . . ." Dad twisted to look at Mom in the kitchen.

Mom had half the spice cupboard emptied as if she intended to sort out the cabinets at this time. "I suppose it'll be all right." Her gaze shifted to Caitlyn. "I want you to call when you get there, and I'll speak with Nanny, too. And remember, you're to slow down after this."

"Okay." Caitlyn frowned. They had no right to judge a boy because of his brother's mistakes. And what did this say about their trust in her? Granted, she was wrong to have gone to Zoe's when her parents weren't home, and she did want her first kiss, but she wouldn't have done anything inappropriate with Keefe. She had every intention of saving her virginity until marriage—unlike her parents.

Chapter Forty-two

Jarret

They had the house to themselves. Papa had taken off a couple days earlier for a job. Mr. Digby had taken Nanny shopping at an outlet mall an hour away. Keefe said he was going to try to see Caitlyn at the Brandts' house. And Roland, wherever he was, kept to himself.

When Zoe had shown up at the door wearing stretch jeans and the ivory, wool-cashmere Michael Kors coat he'd given her for Christmas, he couldn't have wished for a better surprise.

"Hey, come on in." He stepped aside to let her in and watched her take off her coat, admiring her jeans. Her long sweater hid her six-month belly well enough, but she shouldn't come over when Papa was home.

"Can we talk?"

He slid his arms around her waist and kissed her, enjoying the scent of her perfume. It reminded him of desert flowers. "We can do anything we want," he whispered. "There's no one home."

"Oh."

Did he detect a hint of boredom in her tone? Maybe she was upset about something.

She sauntered down the hall, so he followed. "Can I have something to drink? Some juice?" She strode into the kitchen, talking to him over her shoulder and batting her eyes.

"Yeah, sure." He went to the refrigerator while she seated herself at the little kitchen table. "We'll take it upstairs." He grabbed a Coke for himself and an orange juice for her.

"Can't we sit here?" She stretched her arms out on the table, inviting him to join her.

"No. I'm downloading songs." Drinks in hand, he headed for the stairs, not looking back until he reached the door of his bedroom.

She had followed at a distance, head down, gait slow. Something bothered her.

He wavered between concern and annoyance. Maybe he would sit at his computer and ignore her for a few minutes. She'd get around to sharing her problem. He wouldn't have to ask. But he couldn't remember the last time they'd been alone, and he longed to hold her. He set the drinks on his dresser, pulled her into his room, and wrapped his arms around her.

She usually melted in his arms, but her body stiffened. She lifted a hand to his chest and pushed him back.

"What's the matter?" He leaned to kiss her neck.

She turned and stepped away. "Jarret, I want to slow down." She ran her hand up the bedpost, her eyes on the bed.

He snickered before he thought how mad that might make her. "What does that mean, slow down?"

Clinging to the bedpost, she rounded the corner of the bed and met his gaze. "I don't want to do this anymore."

"Uh . . . What're you worried about? You're already pregnant." He leaned against the bedpost she held.

She withdrew her hand and crossed her arms.

His body tensed. He couldn't help glaring. What was she thinking? Caitlyn must've been getting to her, filling her head with nonsense. "It's not like you can—"

His cell phone rang and confused his thoughts. He glanced at it over on the dresser. "It's not like—"

It rang again. He couldn't figure out how to word what he wanted to say. What did he want to say? Something about not getting her virginity back. The phone kept ringing.

Zoe must've seen his confusion. She laughed.

He hated being laughed at. He stomped to the phone, meaning to check who called before answering it but instead bringing it to his ear. "Hello?"

"Jarret?" Papa said. "I'm on my way home, and I want you boys to be there when I get there."

"Uh, I'll try. When are you gonna get here?" He glanced at the window, his heart thumping. Papa didn't mean immediately, did he?

"A couple hours."

Jarret exhaled. "Good, I mean, why do you want us here?" He shouldn't have answered the phone. If he would've known it was Papa . . . Papa never called him. What could he want? Could he know? Who would've told him? Roland? Jarret gritted his teeth.

"I need to talk to you boys tonight."

That didn't sound good. "Yeah? What about?" Papa was the last person he wanted to talk to. Did Papa know? Man, he'd faced enough people over this already. He just wanted to do the right thing by not having the abortion, but now he had to own up to everybody and his brother. *So what* if he was doing it with Zoe? Was he the first sixteen-year-old boy to do it with a girl? Everybody did it.

"I have a trip coming up, and I need you boys to go with me."

"All of us?" He watched Zoe play with something on his nightstand. "Where to?"

"Mississippi."

"Count me out."

Papa breathed into the phone. "I'm not counting you out, Jarret. I said I need you boys there. That includes you. I need to organize an archaeological dig. You've all helped with this before and I—"

"No. I said *no*. Count me out." Jarret ended the call and tossed his cell phone onto the dresser. He should've turned it off. Papa would probably try to call again. Did he know?

Jarret returned to Zoe, who was still messing with something on his nightstand. "Are you mad at me?" He took her by the arm, turning her to himself and pulling her close.

Her honey-brown eyes sparkled with their natural beauty, but they had a definite coldness about them. "I'm not mad at you. I've just been thinking. I don't want this kind of relationship. I think we went too fast."

Feeling the slap of her words, he released her and went to the window. "You don't like me anymore?" He clenched his jaw.

"I like you, Jarret. Why can't we just do things differently?"

"Differently? You mean like Keefe and Caitlyn?" He spun around and took slow steps toward her, speaking with an annoyed tone. "You want me to court you, see you only with my father around or with your parents?" He came up behind her and spoke over her shoulder. "In case you've forgotten, your daddy don't like me much. He said he'd kill me if he found me with you."

He grabbed her arm and forced her to face him. "Do you really like having to tell Mr. Summer everywhere you're going? You sure didn't tell him you were coming over here. Where does he think you are?"

She yanked her arm from him, flipped her hair over her shoulder, and sauntered to the window. "Yes, I lied to Mr. Summer. He thinks I'm visiting my family. And I was, for a while, so it was partly true. I had Mom drop me off at the Brandts' and I walked here. I really wanted to talk to you about this."

"I don't want to talk. I haven't been alone with you in over a month. No one's here. We don't get chances like this anymore. And . . . Papa just said I have to go on a trip. I'll probably be gone for a time. I'll miss you." He paused, giving his words time to sink in, looking as downcast as he could. "You know I love you."

She cast him a sad and sympathetic glance.

He went to her and pulled her into his arms. Before she could break away, he kissed her, good and long, trying to communicate how desperately he needed her.

Her hands went to his shoulders, and she melted in his arms.

Chapter Forty-three

Keefe

Winding tea-colored streams and fresh-scented pine trees covered the gently rolling terrain of the 500,000-acre De Soto National Forest, but the West family had come for the mud.

Muddy and weary, Keefe slumped back in a camp chair and cracked open a pop. He took a deep breath and relaxed.

The late afternoon sun lit up clusters of needles on the tall and stately longleaf pine behind the excavation area. Days upon days of spring rain had made the site muddy and miserable to work, despite the tarps that hung over each of the dozen three-by-four-foot holes. A few members of the excavation team wandered between sites and team leaders, others dug with trowels and sifted dirt with mesh screens. They'd found animal bones, pottery shards, and a few points already.

On the opposite side of the site, Roland carried a . . .

Keefe did a double take. *Uh oh* . . . a bucket of water toward Jarret? Roland must've had revenge on his mind.

Papa may have noticed the tension between the three of them ever since the trip to Italy. This family trip may've been his way of forcing them together, hoping they would all reconcile. Papa seemed to think taking one or the other of them on a trip would help with this or that problem. Maybe he was right. Keefe had definitely changed from his visit to Italy.

But this trip seemed to have made things worse.

Roland set the bucket behind Jarret, next to an excavated hole, and walked off. Jarret was too busy flirting with a cute blonde to notice.

From day one in De Soto, Jarret and Roland had been at each other, bickering and pulling pranks. Earlier today, Roland said something to Jarret about a secret. Then Jarret shoved Roland into the mud pile where everyone dumped the excavated dirt. Papa had come around before Roland could retaliate.

But Papa wasn't around now.

Keefe looked again.

Roland pushed two buckets of . . . mud? . . . on a wobbly cart.

Then it all happened at once. Someone shouted, "Look out!" Jarret turned toward the voice. Roland let the cart go, and it barreled into Jarret.

Keefe slapped his forehead. Jarret hadn't seen it coming.

The buckets of mud, the bucket of water, and Jarret all disappeared into the hole.

Roland stood at a distance watching, the hint of a smile on his face. If he were wise, he'd run. Any minute now, Jarret would—

Jarret clawed his way out of the hole and darted for Roland. Roland neared the mud pile. Jarret lunged . . .

Keefe scooted to the edge of his chair, spilling pop onto his shoe. Then he laughed, watching his brothers wrestle in the mud.

A twinge of jealousy stabbed him. He'd always known Jarret's secrets, always been the one to try to convince Jarret to do the right thing. Where had Roland gotten the courage? He would've never confronted Jarret before. He had rarely ever defended himself against Jarret in a fight. Maybe the secret was that important.

"West boys!" Papa's voice thundered, and all heads turned. "You'd better cut dirt on over here."

Papa and Miss Anna Meadows, both in cargo pants and multi-pocketed vests, walked together into the excavation area. They stopped a good distance away and watched while Roland and Jarret, both muddy from head to toe, sulked up to them.

Miss Anna Meadows, a head shorter than Papa but tall for a woman, stood with her hands on her hips and a stern look in her eyes. Like Papa with his cowboy hat, she always wore a white sunhat with a wide brim. Thirtysomething, with sandy blonde hair worn in a ponytail, and a make-up free face, she was pretty.

Keefe got up from the camp chair and headed over to them.

Miss Meadows always made him nervous. He avoided speaking around her unless he had something intelligent to say. Her gaze penetrated right through a person. And it sometimes seemed like she could read minds. He'd seen her softer side a few times, too. It showed when she ate meals with Papa or in the evenings. She had a nice laugh and a comfortable way.

"What's all the fuss about?" Papa's eyes went to Jarret.

"We fell." Avoiding eye contact with Papa, Jarret gave Roland a sideways glance.

Roland rolled his eyes.

"Looks like I got me a couple of chuckleheads frolicking in the mud," Papa said between gritted teeth. Then he ranted about work ethics, being an example, and wasting time, all in cowboy-speak. "Scoot off to the motor coach and get yourselves cleaned up before I set about you with my belt."

Jarret only glared, but Keefe and Roland said, "Yes, sir." The three of them headed down the trail that led to the campers and tents.

Once out of hearing distance, Jarret said, "Papa's just trying to look smooth for his lady friend. If not for her, we wouldn't even be in this mud hole." He shoved Roland as he said *mud hole*.

"No, he's not," Keefe said. "You two have been at each other since we got here." He glanced at each of them but turned away to keep from laughing at their muddy faces. "I wish I knew what your fight was about."

"I bet you do." Jarret smirked.

Keefe ignored him. "You've really got some courage, Roland. What's come over you?"

Roland exhaled, shook his head, and rolled eyes.

"Yeah. Courage. If you want to call it that." Jarret walked backwards, facing Roland. "Wait and see what I'm gonna do to you later."

Jarret was the only unchanged one of the three of them. What would it take to get him to grow up?

They neared the motor home. Papa had been very particular when he selected one to rent, and it had seemed roomy enough at first. But with the three of them and Papa, it didn't take long for them to feel cramped. Papa got the bedroom. They had to sleep on the two sofa beds, Roland and Keefe sharing one. But they all stored their clothes in Papa's closet, since there was nowhere else to store them.

"Get me some clothes." Jarret kicked off his muddy boots and flung open the door to the motor home. He climbed in first and went straight for the bathroom. "I'm taking a shower." The bathroom door clicked shut. The shower blasted.

Roland stood motionless facing the bathroom door. He gave Keefe a wary glance. "Was he talking to me? Does he expect me to get his clothes?"

"I guess so," Keefe said. "He doesn't boss me anymore, since we aren't really talking. But I'll get them. I know what he'll want to wear and, besides, Papa won't like to see your muddy footprints in his room."

Keefe grabbed a pair of Jarret's faded designer jeans, clean underwear, and a dark green hoodie. Then he joined Roland in the kitchen, taking a seat at the dinette, a booth for four. "So he shares things with you now, huh?" Wanting to look outside, he pushed the curtain open but it slid back.

Roland stood in the middle of the kitchen, hands in the front pockets of his jeans, probably trying to avoid spreading more mud. "Not really. I don't guess he talks to me any more than you."

"So, what's the secret? What doesn't he want Papa to know?"

Roland shrugged, gazing at the bathroom door. "Nothing I can talk about."

"Why not? He used to tell me everything. Sometimes I can help him sort things out, do the right thing."

"It's too late for that. Some things happened while you were gone, and Jarret needs to . . . to cowboy up." They both grinned at his choice of words.

"So, you're trying to get him to tell on himself. Will it change anything? I mean, is it something really bad?"

Roland nodded. "It's really big."

The shower shut off and something bumped in the bathroom.

Keefe twisted around to reach the drawer in the kitchen cabinet where he kept his notebook. He had something he wanted to finish but never found the time.

Roland smiled. "Are you doing school work, now?"

"No. I'm writing Caitlyn."

"Why don't you just e-mail her? Papa gets online. I think the connection's at Miss Meadow's trailer, since that's their office." He paused. "Do you think they like each other?"

Keefe chuckled. "Papa and Miss Meadows? I don't know. Seems like it. But I don't want to send an e-mail. I'd rather write. It's more personal that way. Don't you think?" He started to reread what he had written.

The bathroom door flew open and Jarret came out in a towel. He sat across from Keefe at the dinette and grabbed his clean clothes.

Roland stepped into the bathroom but shouted before closing the door, "You left all your muddy clothes on the floor."

"So take care of it." Jarret stuck a foot through the leg hole of his underwear. "Put mine with yours. You can wash them together."

Keefe wanted to tell Caitlyn about the De Soto Forest and the feel he got when taking walks, so he worked with a sentence in his mind.

"When are you going to write my English composition?" Jarret pulled the hoodie on over his head and stood to zip his jeans. "What's yours about?"

"I'm not doing school work for you."

Jarret tossed his towel at the closed bathroom door and slid farther into the booth. "Why not?"

"You know it's wrong. I'm not doing it anymore."

Jarret grinned and leaned forward on his folded arms. "Aw, come on. I'll totally forgive you for everything. I see you're letting your hair grow back. You got a good couple inches on you."

Keefe's hand shot up, and he stroked the back of his hair. He had been meaning to see a barber but never got around to it. He hadn't meant to grow it out. Whereas Jarret felt his strength came from leaving it long, Keefe's came from keeping it short. It reminded him of the promise. "Actually, I've been meaning to—"

"Things can go back to the way they were between us." Jarret used the low, soothing voice that he used when trying to manipulate someone. "You'll know all my secrets before everyone else. I'll know all yours. What kind of secrets are you keeping lately?"

"No, Jarret." Keefe leaned back and dropped his pen. "I don't want things the way they were. You're my brother and I love you, but I can't do everything you want me to do. I have to do what I think is right, and if that means—"

"Goody two shoes." Jarret sneered. Then he snatched Keefe's notebook and spun it around so he could read it.

"Hey." Keefe tried to grab it.

Jarret jumped up and blocked Keefe with his body. "Dear Caitlyn," he read in a soft, mocking tone. "It's only been a week, but I miss you sooo much . . ."

"Give it back." Keefe cornered Jarret by the driver's seat and yanked the notebook away. He stuffed it under his arm and returned to the dinette.

"That ain't no report. You're writing a love letter. You've been apart for a few days and you miss her already?"

"Sure I miss her. Don't you miss Zoe? Why don't you write Zoe?"

Jarret leaned against the kitchen counter, a smirk on his face. "If I have something to say to Zoe, I'll call. I ain't writing no love letter. I think you're just trying to make sure she don't cheat on you while you're away."

Keefe huffed. "I'm not worried about that. I have complete trust in her."

"You trust her, huh? Your girlfriend goes over another guy's house to study Algebra, granted it is only Peter, but I've seen them come out of his bedroom, just the two of them. That doesn't bother you? And you know Roland's still hot for her."

"I respect and trust her. Don't you trust Zoe?"

Jarret chuckled. He peeked into Papa's bedroom at the back of the motor home then sat across from Keefe at the dinette. He grinned. "Zoe's seven months pregnant, or haven't you noticed? What's she gonna do?"

Keefe shook his head to clear his mind. Did Jarret say— "Zoe's .. . *pregnant?*" He could hardly get himself to say the word. "Seven months? I, uh . . . I hadn't noticed."

"She hides it well. It's cold out, so big sweaters don't draw attention."

"But seven months?"

Jarret shrugged. "Yeah, I think, or just about."

"You got her pregnant? I didn't even know you were—"

"Come on. You can't be that naïve. Roland even knows." His gaze shifted. ". . . but maybe someone told him."

"It's just that . . . Well, I used to know you so well. I could read your every mood on your face, in your attitude. I didn't know you were . . . *that* close."

"Get over it." He pulled back the window curtain over the dinette, but it slid closed again.

"So, that's why you don't trust her. If you can't use self-control together, why would you trust each other apart?"

Jarret called Keefe a bad name as the bathroom door flung open. "I don't have to trust her. Who's gonna want her?"

"You told him?" Roland said to Jarret before darting into Papa's bedroom. He slid the closet door open and spoke with his head in the closet. "You're talking to Keefe again? Maybe Keefe can convince you. You need to talk to Papa. He's going to find out anyway."

"You need to butt out." Jarret's jaw twitched. "If I find out that you . . ." He jabbed a finger at the bedroom though Roland had closed the door. ". . . say a word about it to Papa, or if you keeping bugging me about this, I'll make your life a daily hell." He stood and shouted at the door. "No, I know. I'll go after Caitlyn. I can make any girl like me. Give me a couple of months and she'll be—"

The bedroom door flew open and Roland came out in jeans and a black sweatshirt. "You're wacked." He squeezed past Jarret and slid into the booth. "She'd never fall for a guy like you. And besides, how's that going to get back at me? She's Keefe's girlfriend, not mine."

Jarret leaned his palms on the table. "We all know you're still hot for her."

Roland blushed and tried to open the curtain, but it slid back. "You don't know anything."

"Is that true, Roland?" Curiosity rather than jealousy moved Keefe to ask. "I've always felt I sort of stepped in on you."

"No. I told you I don't want a girlfriend. I'm not ready to date. I'm fourteen."

"You'll be fifteen soon."

"So? Who wants the pressure of that? I like being friends."

Jarret leaned back against the counter, stretched his arms along the countertop, and laughed.

"It's not like dating with her," Keefe said to Roland. "It's more like courtship. We're always around family or we're with a group, so you don't have to wonder what a girl expects you to do." He liked getting to know Caitlyn this way, working together on projects and hanging out with kids who shared their faith. No pressures. He had enough on his mind.

When he prayed, lately, and even at times when he least expected it, the Lord moved his soul in a dramatic way. God wanted something of him. He felt it with every cell of his being. Maybe he ought to stop seeing Caitlyn until he figured out what God wanted. *No.* He didn't want to stop seeing her. She helped him focus, the way she listened to him, the things she brought to his attention.

"Courtship." Jarret threw his head back and let out a hearty laugh. "You guys are killing me. What's the point of it? Where's the fun? You really want to spend all your time around her family? Ew. Romantic."

"Your romance has gotten you in enough trouble," Keefe said. "Zoe's not your wife, but she's having your baby."

"La de da." Jarret paced to the front of the motor home. "You're never alone with your girlfriend. Have you even kissed her?"

"Roland's right. Papa should know. Are you afraid of what he'll do to you?"

Jarret twisted one of the front seats around and sat in it. "I'm not afraid of anything. It's just not his business."

"You're wrong," Keefe said. "You really need to tell Papa."

"Who needs to tell Papa what?"

Keefe jumped.

The door was half-open when Papa spoke, and now he swung it the rest of the way and stepped inside.

Jarret spun the front seat around to face the windshield. "Nobody needs to tell you nothing."

Keefe stood. "Get some clean shoes," he said to Roland. "Let's take a walk."

Papa leaned against the counter, eyeing Jarret.

Jarret spun the chair back around, chuckling and glaring at Keefe. "Smooooth." He watched them leave, mouthing a bad name just before the door closed.

Chapter Forty-four

Keefe

Sunlight broke through the canopy of pine needles, making beams of orange light that illuminated clumps of wiregrass. Keefe and Roland made their own path, crunching over pine needles and strolling through well-spaced trees.

Keefe took a deep breath and pushed past the apprehension he felt, making himself say, "Roland, if you like Caitlyn, you can see her, too."

Roland didn't even glance.

"You guys hardly seem like friends anymore. And it's not like we're going steady. Besides, I get the impression her parents don't want her hooked on just one guy."

Head down, Roland kicked a pinecone. "What makes you think that?"

"Um, Mr. Summer said so. He wouldn't even let me see her before we came out here."

"You're kidding." He finally looked up.

"No, I'm serious. But I understand where he's coming from. We're just kids. Who knows what plans God has for us, right? No point in rushing things."

"I guess." Roland went out of his way to kick another pinecone. "I'm not ready to have a girlfriend. Maybe next year. I just wish Jarret would slow down. I can't help but think I could've changed things if I would've told Papa earlier." He pulled a black rosary from his front jeans pocket and let it dangle at his side.

"How long have you known?"

"I don't know. Sometime in October. It was before the Halloween party. I caught Zoe in Jarret's bedroom."

"Mid-October?"

He nodded.

"Jarret said she's almost seven months pregnant, so it happened before then. You couldn't have changed anything. I'm guessing it happened when you guys went camping." He remembered the phone call. Jarret had said he planned to make Zoe his first.

Keefe sighed. "If we had still been talking, if I hadn't cut my hair and ruined our friendship, I could've stopped him. I could've talked him out of it." He stopped and reached out for the scaly bark of a pine tree. The guilt hit him hard. Was there something he should've said or done differently? Could he have helped Jarret? Was he being selfish with his new way of looking at life?

"Nah, don't blame yourself." Roland stopped, too, and stared at his rosary beads.

"I guess you're right. Papa always says Jarret needs to make up his own mind to do right. He knows what he should do. He's just used to doing what he wants. Who knows what it'll take for him to change?" Keefe pushed off the tree trunk and draped his arm over Roland's shoulders. "You and I have to do what's ours to do, even if it's hard, and leave the rest to God."

He sighed heavily and strolled on. Part of him rebelled at the truth. Love was tough. Sometimes it meant saying or doing something that the other wouldn't like. It could even mean losing the other or accepting the other's hatred for a while. That was the hard part. He didn't want to lose Jarret. They had been close, uniquely connected since their first moment of existence.

"I'm glad Papa came to the motor home when he did." Roland swung his rosary at his side. "Do you think Jarret's telling him?"

"I don't know. I hope so."

"When we get Papa alone, should we—"

"No. Let's give Jarret a chance."

~ ~ ~

The rest of their time in De Soto went peacefully. The rain had lessened and the work went smoother. Jarret and Roland hadn't exchanged so much as a single rude word, not that they had been friendly either. Papa now took his meals with them or with the entire group of students and volunteers, rather than alone with Miss Meadows. The only one who showed signs of tension was Miss Meadows. She snapped at Papa once and threw him cold glances from time to time, for whatever reason.

Chapter Forty-five

Caitlyn

Easter break came and the Wests had still not returned from Mississippi. Zoe had spent the past few days at home, her father having finally calmed down and her mother missing her dearly. Earlier today, Caitlyn broke down and invited Mya over, but she had other things to do.

So, utterly bored and lonely, Caitlyn went to check the mailbox. There in the middle of the bills, she found a letter addressed to her.

She ran from the mailbox to Mom in the kitchen, squealing and pressing the envelope to her chest. "He wrote me! He wrote me!"

Mom turned from the sink, smiling and drying her hands on a dishtowel. "Let me guess. *He* means Keefe?" She stepped to the bar counter, grabbed a bag of potatoes, and opened a drawer.

Caitlyn ripped open the envelope, yanked out the letter, and brought it to her nose. After a deep breath, she read to herself: *Dear Caitlyn, It's only been a week but I miss you so much.*

"Wow, he started writing me a week after he got there."

"It sure took a long time for the letter to get here."

Caitlyn continued reading.

I know how you enjoy nature, so I think you would love these De Soto woods. The pine trees are tall and smell good in the early morning. There is a stream nearby. I like to go there by myself, when I can, and think and pray. God speaks to me out here. I'll tell you about it when I get back.

Caitlyn sighed and pressed the letter to her chest. What had God said to him? The way Keefe prayed, the way he searched for God moved her. He seemed so willing to change his life, even to the point of sacrificing relationships and his reputation to follow the Lord. Could she do that?

She walked to the dining room table and sat in a chair where she could see Mom over the counter. She read more.

I don't get much time for walks, though. My father keeps us busy digging in the mud. We work with a good group of people. Many are volunteers and they take their work seriously. Plus, schoolwork keeps me busy. You should see the list of assignments my teachers gave me. They must think I've got nothing better to do than write essays. I really have to force myself to do them.

The other day, Jarret told me something that I'm sure you already know. I was really bummed to learn about it. I feel like somewhere I went wrong, let him down. Please keep him in your prayers. I hope Zoe is okay.

I wanted to write you once a week, but already three weeks have passed, and I'm still working on this same letter. Sorry. It's not that I don't miss you. I do.

Things are starting to wrap up around here. The woman running things told my father we could go soon. She and my father had been good friends, but I think there's some friction between them now. I don't know what that's about, but it's too bad because I thought my father liked her.

I can't wait to see you again. Keefe.

Caitlyn sighed, flipping the page over. "He didn't sign it *love*."

The potato peeler slipped from Mom's hand and landed on the far edge of the counter. "Well, that's fine. Does he tell you he loves you?" She snatched the peeler and continued peeling potatoes.

"No. But we're always around other people. When would he tell me?"

Mom smiled. "Maybe he's too young to be in love. You're both very young. There's no reason to rush things. Maybe God has someone else in mind for each of you. And what about Roland? Weren't the two of you good friends? What happened to that friendship? This is a time for friendships. Why limit yourself—"

"How old were you when you started seeing Dad?"

Her pale eyebrows twitched. She wiped her forehead with the back of her peeling hand. "Oh, we've known each other since grade school."

"When did you start dating?" At this moment, Caitlyn decided she wanted answers. She wanted to know everything. How could they insist she follow so many rules when they obviously had not?

Mom glanced then turned away, taking the peeled potatoes to the sink. With the water blasting she said, "We saw each other in high school."

"When did you fall in love?"

"Some time in high school. I feel like I've always been in love with him."

"Did you guys date like everyone else? Because I think I'd like to go out on dates." Caitlyn's eyes watered and her voice came out high with her frustration. "I'd like to go to the movies, or to dinner, or even just take a long walk in the park with Keefe, just Keefe and no one else. I'd like to be alone with him. I know I shouldn't have gone to Zoe's knowing her parents weren't there, but that's why I did it. How can I really get to know someone without having any private conversations? It's not fair. It's not the way you did it."

Mom shut the water off and shook her head, her face to the window over the sink. "I wish you understood."

"I understand more than you think."

Mom turned, drying her hands on the dishtowel with intensity.

"Mom, you were married fifteen years in April, and I turned fifteen in November. That's only seven months."

Head down, Mom set the dishtowel aside and wiped the front of her shirt. Then she came around the counter and sat cattycorner to Caitlyn. Mom looked younger in the dim light, with strands of red hair falling out of the ponytail and framing her face. She gave Caitlyn a sad smile and touched her hand, the one holding the letter. "I wondered when you'd figure that out." Still smiling, she looked at the letter. "I was nineteen when we married. Your father and I had only made one big mistake. It was on—"

"Valentine's Day."

Her smile grew, the look in her eyes showing surprise. "Wow. You're right. We were already engaged. Your father had an apartment of his own by then, and he wanted to cook dinner for me." She winced, still smiling. "He's no cook. He found a recipe in a magazine. Filet mignon." She giggled, gazing off in the distance, her eyes glistening.

"We made many small mistakes, Caitlyn." She met Caitlyn's gaze. "I can't help but think we fell because no one had warned us. Growing up, those things just weren't talked about in my house. I guess we always knew we should wait for marriage. But my folks sat in front of TV shows with characters that didn't share those values. It sent the message that maybe some things were okay. Everyone in the shows who fell in love or even just dated made out, necked. I just thought that's what you did on a date when you liked someone."

Caitlyn had seen Mom and Dad kiss before. But making out? The image popped into her mind for a shocking split-second. She tried not to think about it.

"No one ever told me that one thing leads to another. Maybe that's common sense, but it wasn't to me. I had no intention of giving myself away before marriage."

Mom rubbed Caitlyn's hand. "Protect your virtue, my dear. Save yourself for your future husband. Looking back, I wish someone had talked to me about true love and about the reasons sex belongs in marriage. I wish I had been given guidelines. I wish I would've seen the bigger picture, how the union of husband and wife is an expression of permanent, self-donating love. It reveals God's plan for us, how He desires for us to become one with Him."

Seeing the sincerity in her eyes, Caitlyn's heart went out to her. "I hadn't thought about it like that."

Mom shook her head. "I'm not trying to excuse my behavior. For all that, I knew it was wrong. It's just . . . I want you to have the guidance I didn't have. You'll give your virginity away only once. It means a lot more to give it to your husband on your wedding night than to let it slip away accidentally in the heat of a moment. Our culture has cheapened the gift of sexuality, separating it from true, permanent, beautiful love."

Her eyes hardened as if revealing some inner strength. "You can judge me if you want, just, please . . . don't make the same mistakes I did."

"You're not saying I'm a mistake?"

She let out an exasperated groan, slapped Caitlyn's hand, and hugged her. "Oh, my dear little girl. Of course, you're not a mistake. *We* made a mistake. We let passion pull us over the boundaries that God sets. But God does not make mistakes." She kissed Caitlyn's forehead and returned to the kitchen.

Chapter Forty-six

Jarret

Jarret stepped through the doors of River Run High, and his stomach soured. Having had a tutor up until high school, he'd liked going to school, getting away from home, and being with kids his age. Today, however, he did not want to be here. In fact, if he could have a tutor again and avoid the gossip . . .

"Problem?" Roland walked with him and must've noticed his disturbed expression.

"No. Scram." Jarret took a deep breath and headed down the hall for his locker.

Kids crowded the halls. He knew at least half of the ones he passed. Most gave him a nod or a *hey*. Another third gave him strange looks as if they didn't recognize him, or didn't expect him to return . . . or something.

He checked his fly.

A few steps from his locker, his gaze traveled to the end of the hall to where three girls stood in a circle. Only one of them mattered to him. *Zoe.* Her shiny black hair hung halfway down her back and bounced as she shook her head. Her bare slender arms moved gracefully when she gestured.

He couldn't wait to hold her. She'd be surprised to see him. They had gotten home late, so he hadn't called her yet. He passed his locker and strutted a little faster, deciding to see her first.

Then she turned, and he stopped dead.

Zoe wore a sleeveless purple shirt that fit snugly around her big rounded belly. No one would doubt she was pregnant. Was she crazy? How did she get so big in just one month?

Jarret shrunk back.

Roland came up to him. Hadn't he gone down the hall a minute ago? His gaze seemed fixed on something in the distance behind Jarret. One of his eyes narrowed. He combed his fingers through his hair. "I wonder what *he's* doing here."

Jarret peered over his shoulder. The blood drained from his face, neck, body . . . His life flashed before his eyes. "What's *he* doing here?"

Papa stood by the door to the principal's office, talking to . . . to the principal. If Papa were to turn around, he'd see them. If he were to really look, he'd see Zoe.

"Yeah," Roland said, "that's what I said."

Keefe joined them in the middle of the hall. "What's up? What's the matter with you two?" He turned and looked in the same direction. "So Papa's here. Is that a problem? Let's go see what's up."

"Uh-uh."

Realization flashed in Keefe's eyes. "You didn't tell him? You said you told him. What did you and Papa talk about in the motor home?"

"I lied. I told you guys that I confessed so you'd leave me alone." He spoke through gritted teeth. "Of course I didn't tell him. We talked about Miss Meadows."

"Miss Meadows?" Keefe said.

"Yeah. I said we all knew they liked each other, and that you and Roland elected me to talk to him about it."

Mouth open, Keefe shook his head. "What'd you say about it?"

"Yeah." Roland folded his arms and narrowed his eyes.

Jarret gave a crooked grin. "I said we didn't like it. Now, if you'll excuse me . . ." He pushed Keefe out of the way so he could get to Zoe.

Papa stood at one end of the hallway and Zoe at the other. If he could get her to duck into a classroom for a minute or so—

Jarret dashed down the hall.

Zoe smiled when she saw him coming, her look soon changing to one of confusion. "What's wrong with you? Why are you running?"

He forced a smile but it felt all wrong. Grabbing her arm, he tried to drag her along, but she wriggled free.

"What are you doing?" She put her hands on her hips.

Boy, was her belly big.

"Aren't you even going to say *hello* and tell me how you missed me? We haven't seen each other in—"

"I'll tell you over here." He felt his eyes bugging, but he couldn't control it. He darted into the nearest classroom, hoping she'd do the same. "Come on, come on, come on," he muttered, waiting a few long seconds.

She finally appeared in the doorway.

He couldn't help but gawk at her belly. "You look big."

"Wow. Did you think I wouldn't? I'm due in a little over a month." Arms folded and agitation showing in her every move, she stomped to the front of the empty classroom and examined the white board.

"I, uh, I missed you." What else had she told him to say?

"Really?" She didn't sound convinced.

Papa had to have seen her. *He saw her. He saw her.* Jarret's mouth went dry.

Chapter Forty-seven

Caitlyn

The school bell rang. Caitlyn groped under her desk for her books while everyone else bolted for the door. She should've gathered her things sooner, but she couldn't copy down the homework assignment fast enough. Was she the only one in history class who did homework?

She arranged her folders, notebooks, and science and history textbooks into a neat stack, hugged them, slung her purse strap over a shoulder, and scooted for the door. The West boys had returned from Mississippi, but she had yet to cross paths with any of them. She couldn't wait to see Keefe.

As she stepped through the doorway, her history book slipped out of place. She glanced at it and . . . Bam! She smacked right into someone.

"Oh, sorry." She backed into the door and looked up. "Keefe!"

She hadn't seen him in nearly a month, and he looked different: a little taller, his hair longer. Curls surrounded his gentle face. But his brown eyes still glowed with sincerity. He gave her a pleasant smile, bent towards her, and stuck out an arm.

She leaned forward to hug him but found his arm wrapping around her books. "Oh." She backed into the door again, embarrassed.

"I missed you," he said, still smiling and now holding her books on his hip. "You on your way to study hall?"

"Oh. Yeah." A frown threatened to steal her smile. Why hadn't he hugged her? It felt like the natural thing to do after having been apart for so long.

They strolled side by side, kids rushing past them.

"I can't wait to hear about your trip." Caitlyn finally mastered the ability to smile.

"Yeah." He glanced. "Maybe we can talk in study hall."

"Or you could come over for dinner." She meant to work up to the invitation, not just blurt it out.

"Um, I don't know." He glanced again as they rounded the corner. "Not tonight. I've got something . . ."

"Oh." Her face warmed. "It doesn't have to be tonight. My parents said, well, you know, you can come over sometime."

"Yeah, that sounds nice." He stepped into the cafeteria, *study hall* after the lunch times, and led her to a table against the far wall.

She sat across from him. "The Fire Starters meet tomorrow. We're organizing a spring card party for senior citizens. If you want to—"

"I don't know. I-I can't." Keefe shook his head, his brows drawing together. He turned away, his gaze bouncing from face to face as kids filled up the study hall.

Caitlyn opened a notebook and flipped to a blank page, trying to keep from looking offended. He didn't seem to want to do anything with her. Didn't he miss her? She glanced. "So, uh, is something wrong?"

"No." His eyes snapped to her. "You got my letter, right?"

"Yes." She'd read it at least a dozen times. It had made her feel close to him. Was there something in it that explained his cold attitude? There was that one part . . . "You have something to tell me? You said you'd tell me about it when you got back."

"Yeah," he breathed. "I uh . . ." He glanced over his shoulder at the exact moment Jarret strutted into study hall. Jarret acknowledged him with a nod but sat at a table clear across the room.

Keefe bit his lip, rested his arms on the table, and fidgeted with a ring on his little finger. "I um . . ." He leaned toward her, smiled, frowned, and finally whispered with his eyes on his ring, "It's like this: every day when I pray, sometimes I'm not praying, I get this feeling." He glanced. "It's so strong, overpowering at times. It's like—"

"No talking." Mrs. Packwood tapped her bony finger on their table and narrowed her heavily made up eyes. "This is study hall. Get out some work."

Caitlyn cracked open her history book. She had pages to read, questions to answer, terms to write . . . . Not that she intended to do them now, not with Keefe here. Keefe had brought nothing with him, so she slid her open notebook to him.

He gave a look to show his appreciation then snatched her pen. He scribbled something down, ripped the page out and folded it once. After a glance over his shoulder, he slid the page to Caitlyn.

She opened it and read: *God is trying to tell me something.* It moved her to see a guy so open to God's inspirations. He'd given his heart to the Lord, and it affected every aspect of his life.

Lifting her eyes, she found him staring at her. "Trying to tell you what?" she mouthed.

He took the paper back and wrote something. Sliding the paper to her again, he smiled, almost playfully. His note: *I don't know. But He won't leave me alone.*

Wow. God really wanted something of him. Keefe had told her that before. Maybe she needed to make a sacrifice. She pulled the pen from his hand and scribbled a note on the bottom of the page, but she folded the paper before he could see it. Did she really want to give this to him? She'd written it on impulse, hadn't thought it through, didn't even like the idea—

He reached across the table and put a finger on the note, ready to take it. She did not release it. He looked at her. She gave a look to show her uncertainty. Then she let the note go.

He slid it to himself and flipped it open. His gaze swept across the note, once, twice, three times. His cheeks flushed. He pressed his lips together. Then he looked at her and shook his head.

Holding his gaze and trying to appear strong, she nodded. He might not have liked it, but he probably knew she was right.

Her note: *Forget about me. Focus on God.* If the Lord had been speaking to him with such intensity, he needed to dedicate himself to listening. They could see each other in the future.

She took the note and added: *We'll still be friends. You need to do this. And I understand.* Though the thought of not seeing him disturbed her, she refused to show any emotion. She wanted to be strong for him. Would she be able to keep her resolve?

Chapter Forty-eight

Jarret

Jarret pulled up the circular driveway to drop Roland and Keefe at the front door of their house. As Roland and Keefe got out, the front door opened and Nanny stepped outside. She said something to them. They both nodded.

Jarret threw the car into drive. Movement in his peripheral vision made him look. He shouldn't have. He should've just stepped on it.

Nanny charged down the steps of the porch waving both hands and saying something Jarret couldn't make out. Judging by her urgency, he wasn't gonna like whatever she had to tell him.

He lowered his window. "Yeah?"

She came over with the frown she used whenever she tried to boss him. The stern face never looked natural on her. "Your father wants to see the three of you this evening. He said you're not to go off after school."

"What for?" He didn't really want the answer. It had to be about Zoe. Papa must've seen her.

"Well, I don't know, dear." She patted her short gray curls and gave him a sweet smile, an expression more natural to her. "Come inside and let me get you a snack. I made lingonberry muffins." That was Nanny's way. She liked to serve, clean, and cook. She hated having to tell anyone what to do, though Papa made her do it all the time.

Jarret parked his car and went inside. Papa wanted to see the three of them, so maybe he hadn't seen Zoe. If he had seen her, why would he want to talk to the other two? He wouldn't. He would just want to talk to Jarret, right? Papa didn't know.

~ ~ ~

No matter how hard Jarret tried to assure himself that Papa didn't know, he couldn't relax so he invited his brothers to a game of pool.

"I can't remember the last time the three of us played pool." Keefe leaned against the wall, resting his hands on a cue stick.

"Two summers ago." Roland sat on the arm of the couch. He held Jarret's cigarette and smoke trailed up past his pale face. He *would* remember. He'd lost every game. It was the end-of-summer competitions that had become a family tradition, but which they had to skip last year because of Papa's work.

Jarret leaned over the pool table for an awkward shot and scratched. "Shoot." Straightening up, he snatched his cigarette from Roland.

"Papa's got maps and blueprints out on the map table already." Keefe edged around the pool table, eyeing the balls.

Jarret sat on the desk in the corner of the room and took a long drag off the cigarette. "Oh yeah? What of?"

"I don't know. I just passed by his office. I didn't get a good look." Keefe lined up a shot.

"Why not?"

"Do you just go in Papa's office without permission?"

"That's a dumb question." Jarret smirked. Keefe knew he did.

Keefe made his shot and grinned. "Do you think Papa saw Zoe?"

Jarret's stomach flipped. "I don't really care. What's he gonna do about it? What's done is done. He can't make me stop seeing her."

"Why can't he?" Roland handed the chalk to Keefe.

"I'm sixteen. I have my own car. I can do what I want." He said it more to convince himself than them. Papa would surely do something if he knew. What was it he'd said in the last family meeting? If he found out Jarret wasn't respecting his girlfriend, he'd tan his hide.

Keefe aimed for a striped ball but sunk the solid next to it. Only a few balls remained on the table, most of them striped. The glance he gave Jarret as he stepped out of the way showed he knew he was about to go down.

"Hold this." Jarret passed Roland his cigarette then stepped up to finish the game. "Corner pocket." The ball shot straight in. "Side pocket." He was lined up perfectly. Couldn't miss. "Eight ball." He tapped the edge of the table to indicate a corner pocket. As he lined up his shot, Papa's boots sounded in the family room.

Roland jumped from the arm of the couch and bolted for the desk drawer where Jarret kept a hidden ashtray. Keefe froze with wide eyes.

Jarret scratched the eight ball and sunk the cue ball. He cursed aloud as Papa stepped into the room.

"Boys." Papa glanced about as if he saw a swarm of gnats. "I'm glad you're all here." He went directly to the wall rack and reached for a stick. "Why don't you rack 'em up?" He tossed Jarret the triangle rack.

Roland helped fish balls from the pockets.

"You wanted to talk to us?" Keefe said.

Jarret shot him a glare. Couldn't he wait? Couldn't he let Papa get to it on his own?

"That's right." Papa chalked his stick. "I'll make the break."

Jarret racked the balls and stepped back.

When Papa made the break, balls typically went everywhere and one or two always went in. This time he sunk two solids. With a tug of his cowboy hat, he straightened but kept his eyes on the table. "I'll be leaving on another trip in a matter of days."

Jarret held his breath. Keefe and Roland looked like they held theirs, too.

"It'll be another long trip, and one of you needs to go with me."

Okay. Cool. He's asking for a volunteer. Jarret exhaled louder than he would've liked. "You can count me out. I'm not going anywhere." He grinned at Papa. "I got school work to catch up on."

Papa sunk a ball in the corner pocket and reached for the chalk. "Oh yeah?"

"Yeah." His voice squeaked, making him sound uncertain. He hated coming across weak. "You're the one who decided we should go to public school. Then you took us out of town, made us miss school for how many days? So uh . . ."

Jarret glanced at Keefe then Roland. He did a double take. Smoke seeped from the drawer in the corner of the room. Roland must not have put the cigarette out all the way. *Idiot.* Was everyone trying to get him into trouble?

He strolled casually to the drawer while he spoke. "I mean, you're sending us to school now, and we don't have the tutor, so why do you keep taking us out?" He reached into the drawer and snuffed out the cigarette, throwing Roland a wicked glare.

Roland shrugged.

"You want to take someone on your trip," Jarret said, loud and with confidence, "take Roland. He always wants to go."

Papa had taken another shot while Jarret ranted, and now he stepped back and leaned against the wall. "Your turn."

"What!" He couldn't believe it. It wasn't fair. Papa knew. He must've. This was his way of punishing Jarret. Every other parent would have a heart-to-heart talk or ground a kid. Not Papa. No. He took them away. He thought taking them on trips would fix things. "Mississippi was enough for me. I don't like going places, not in our country anyway. I've been everywhere I want to be. You wanna take me overseas? I'll go overseas. Is that where you're going? Huh?"

Papa nodded toward the table. "Your turn."

Jarret's heart raced. He looked at the table. "Oh." Papa must've scratched. He breathed and stepped up to find a shot. Was he stripes or solids? Fewer solids lay out, so he must've been stripes.

"We're going to California. Northern California."

"We?" he squeaked. He couldn't have sounded more desperate, and he hated himself for it. He looked to Keefe for help.

Keefe stared at the table. Didn't he care? Why didn't he say something? Why didn't he offer to go?

"Take your shot," Papa said.

Jarret leaned over and lined up. He missed. He knew he'd miss. Biting back a bad word, he straightened and turned away from Papa.

A ball cracked. Papa probably sunk another one. "Don't worry, Jarret. You'll be back in time."

Jarret glared over his shoulder. "In time for what?"

Papa squinted at him. "You know what."

Chapter Forty-nine

Caitlyn

Surrounded by a dozen sock-balls, wearing only a diaper, and lying on his back, little Andy took his fist out of his mouth and patted Zoe's cheek. At that moment, his eyes closed. Zoe and Caitlyn lay on either side of him on her bed. For close to an hour, they'd been trying to get him to take his nap, but he only wanted to throw sock-balls.

His hand slid from Zoe's face and he lay still, breathing easy.

Zoe and Caitlyn looked at each other.

"We did it," Caitlyn mouthed. As much as she enjoyed putting Andy down for his naps, she wanted to talk to Zoe. Had she been wrong to suggest to Keefe that they stop seeing each other? It seemed like the unselfish thing to do, like the thing God wanted of her, but she was beginning to change her mind.

"He slimed me," Zoe whispered, wiping her cheek with a sock. "But he's so sweet." She watched him a moment then rolled onto her back. "The doctor said my baby weighs about four pounds and is seventeen inches long."

Delighted, Caitlyn gasped. "They can tell?" She crawled to the window to close the curtains though the flowering bush that grew nearby kept out most of the light anyway.

"I guess so. Her organs are completely developed, except for her lungs. She has fingernails." Zoe smiled, rubbing her round belly. "But her brain is still developing—Oh!" She jerked her hand to the underside of her belly. "She's kicking."

She motioned Caitlyn over, grabbed her hand, and placed it on the spot.

Something pushed against Caitlyn's hand. She sucked in a breath and laughed. "That's so awesome. How wonderful to feel a life growing inside of you." She'd learned from Zoe all the stages of the developing baby. "I can't wait to be pregnant."

Zoe moaned. "Yes, you can. I wish I would've waited. I was so embarrassed when kids figured it out at school. Most kids were cool with it, but there're those few."

"Oh, they have something to say about everyone." Caitlyn ran a hand up and down Andy's smooth, bare leg, and then she gathered sock-balls. "Just ignore them."

"I know. I tried not to let it bother me. Then I decided not to hide it anymore, and I started wearing whatever I wanted. I don't think Jarret liked that."

"Why do you say that?" Caitlyn carried an armful of socks to her dresser.

"I only saw him at school for a few days before his father whisked him away to California, but he must've asked me five times why I was wearing *those kinds of shirts*."

Caitlyn laughed. "What are *those kinds of shirts*?"

"Any shirt that doesn't hide my big ol' belly, I suppose." She rolled onto her side again, facing Andy, and propped her head up with her hand.

"I bet you miss him," Caitlyn said.

"Yeah. I hope he gets back before the baby's born. I want him to be there."

"Do you know where he went? Keefe doesn't even know, except that they're in California."

"Jarret didn't know either. He assumes his father is taking him somewhere to teach him a lesson. He thinks his father discovered I was pregnant that day he saw me in school." She smiled as if she knew better.

"Keefe thinks that, too. It's not true?"

"No. After we told my parents, Dad was so angry. He said he was going to call Jarret's father. I don't know for sure, but Mr. West took them away to Mississippi after that. What do you think they did there?"

"Jarret didn't tell you?"

She shook her head. "He was very sarcastic about the whole thing, said they dug and fought in the mud."

"Keefe said they found old artifacts like anvils and cutting tools, bones and pieces of pottery, even a figurine of some sort. When they analyzed them, they discovered that the site was occupied from 360 BC to 110 AD or something. I guess they learned a few things about the connections among different Native American groups. I don't remember exactly. He said they'll put the collection in a museum when they're done. I'd love to go with them someday. I bet Jarret's at another site, digging in more mud."

They giggled.

"I can't picture it," Zoe said. "He's so vain."

A light knocking sounded on the door. Caitlyn figured it was Priscilla. Priscilla wanted to be around Zoe and her big belly every second she could. But maybe she came to relay a message. Maybe Keefe had come to speak with her. He hadn't given Caitlyn an answer yet. She almost regretted asking him to end their relationship. Maybe she was being silly.

"Who is it?" Caitlyn said in a singsong voice, leaning close to the door.

The door inched open and Priscilla peeked in. She wore one of Caitlyn's dresses, one that dragged on the floor, one that she hadn't asked to borrow. And she had a pillow stuffed inside over her tummy.

"Come in, silly." As the door opened, the aroma of fresh-baked chocolate-chip cookies wafted in. Caitlyn's stomach growled.

Priscilla tiptoed toward the bed. "When will your baby come out?"

Caitlyn sat on the end of the bed to admire Zoe and the way she interacted with Priscilla.

"I told you already. Don't you remember? It'll be summer." Zoe smiled, barely turning her head to watch as Priscilla neared. Her pregnancy did nothing to diminish her grace and beauty. If anything, it magnified it.

"As soon as school's out?" Priscilla sounded hopeful. She crept toward Zoe, her eyes glued to Zoe's belly.

Zoe peered at Priscilla. "Well, no, not like *the day* school's out. A few weeks later."

"Can I see the baby then?"

"Not unless you come up to the hospital." Zoe sat up and took Priscilla's hand. "You can touch my belly, if you want."

Priscilla grinned from ear to ear, her eyes round and bursting with joy.

"Is the adoption plan all ready? Did you pick the couple?" Caitlyn couldn't imagine carrying a baby for nine months and never seeing it again. She admired Zoe's strength and sacrificial love.

Zoe nodded, still smiling at Priscilla.

Priscilla's eyes popped and she cooed. "The baby moved."

Zoe laughed and rubbed Priscilla's hair. "Are those cookies I smell?"

"I'll bring you some." Priscilla took off.

"I chose the couple yesterday," Zoe said. "They were the first ones I met: in their thirties, he's a financial advisor like my dad, she wants to be a homemaker. After talking to them, it just felt right."

"I remember their profile. I had a good feeling about them, too." While the Wests had been in Mississippi, Caitlyn and Zoe had looked through a dozen profiles of prospective adoptive parents. Most had no other children, one had an older child, and several had pets. Zoe met with three different couples.

"I thought Jarret would want to help choose," Zoe said, "but he wasn't interested. He doesn't like the idea of giving the baby up, but he agreed neither of us could raise it. He hasn't signed the papers. Says he's not ready, that he might not ever be ready. He's so confusing. I never know what he wants."

Jarret was selfish. Caitlyn wouldn't dare give her opinion to Zoe. But what else would keep him from doing the right thing and letting go?

Letting go . . .

The thought pierced her like a spear to the heart. She needed to let go, to let Keefe go. Why did she hesitate to go through with it? Now that she thought about it, she had never felt for Keefe the way she had for Roland. She only liked being in a relationship, feeling like someone wanted to be close to her.

Mom had told her something that only now began to make sense. *God desires to be one with us.* God wanted to be close to her!

Caitlyn's heart stirred so violently she had to close her eyes. When Keefe had encountered the Lord, he'd changed. He lived life differently, put God first, sought His will, and let nothing stand in the way. Caitlyn had only been seeking a boyfriend. What about God? Where was He in her life? What changes would He work in her?

The answer came with the question, a feeling so strong she could not deny it. The Lord would teach her love and make her ready to truly love another.

Her desire for love, for a relationship, wasn't a bad thing. The love between a man and a woman was an image of God's love, Mom had said, of the eternal love that He calls everyone to. But in her pursuit for love, she'd offended God. She offended love. She tried to pretend to be someone she wasn't—dressing in jeans—in order to get Roland's attention, then she lied to be alone with Keefe at Zoe's house.

"Lord, forgive me," she prayed. *God desires to become one with us. God desires me.*

She would let Keefe go. She would seek God first. Besides, she was too young to marry. High school was the time to find her bridesmaids.

"I never told you," Zoe said.

Caitlyn opened her eyes and focused on Zoe, who lay back on the pillow and now stared at the ceiling.

"Some time ago, I told Jarret I didn't want our relationship to be so . . . physical. I wonder what it will be like between us after the baby's born. I want things to be different."

"Good for you," Caitlyn said. "You can always start over." *Yes, that was it. Start over. Seek God first.* "I'm starting over."

"What?" Zoe threw a worried glance, her brows high on her forehead.

Caitlyn smiled to reassure her. "Keefe and I aren't going to see each other for a while. No more courtship."

"Why?" Her brows continued to show her concern.

"It's not a big deal. It's just that Keefe has a lot on his mind. And I've come to realize a few things about myself."

She shook her head. "Wow. Well, I guess it's just you and me for now."

Caitlyn scooted closer, draped her arm around Zoe's shoulder, and rested her forehead on Zoe's head. "Good. Just the way I like it." She would be free to focus her thoughts and time on her very best friend during the last two months of her pregnancy. When Jarret returned, she knew she would see less of Zoe. But for now, it thrilled Caitlyn to experience this with her.

"I want to be here for you. And always remember, it's never too late to start over." Caitlyn wanted to say more, but her bedroom door creaked open and Priscilla tiptoed in with a plate of cookies.

Chapter Fifty

Jarret

Jarret decided to stop going back and forth for water and snatched the pitcher from the fridge. With a glass tucked under his arm, an energy drink in one hand and the pitcher in the other, he strolled down the hall, through the great room, and back to Zoe in the family room.

Since his return from California, she had all but moved in. And she had a hundred and one needs. Papa didn't seem to care that she was here every day, sharing their meals, loafing on the couch, or even up in his bedroom. Of course, they never closed the door and someone else always came upstairs, too. Papa had never spent more daylight hours in his room across the hall than he had in these past couple of weeks.

"Oh good," Zoe said as Jarret rounded the couch.

He set everything on the coffee table and poured her some water. When he went to hand it to her, she waved it away.

"I need the bathroom."

"Again? Didn't you just use it ten—"

She chastised him with her eyes, shutting him up. Then using her hands and some awkward movements, she scooted to the edge of the couch.

He stood and took her arm to help her, since she really seemed to need it. "Isn't this baby due yet? How much bigger can you get?"

She smiled and kissed his cheek before waddling around the couch and to the bathroom near the mudroom.

He plopped down on the couch, twisted the lid off his energy drink, and snatched the remote. Flipping to a baseball game, his muscles relaxed. She once told him she liked baseball, but since the season began, she hadn't wanted to watch a single game with him. Soap operas in the daytime and stupid reality shows in the evening. That was all she wanted to watch.

The bases were loaded and a good hitter came up to bat. Then Zoe returned.

"You turned off my soap?" She lowered herself onto the couch.

With a sigh, he surrendered the remote and took a swig of his drink.

"It's getting dark in here. Why don't you open a blind or turn on the lamps?" Her eyes stayed glued to the TV even though a commercial had come on.

"It's not dark in here. It'll just make the place hot. It's a hundred degrees outside."

She shot him a glare. Maybe her head hurt or something.

"How're you feeling?" He tried to look compassionate, but his limit had drawn near and it probably showed in his eyes. For the past few days, he had to keep reminding himself she had only two more weeks. The baby would come and life would return to normal. He would never let this happen again, at least not until he was older and ready for it.

"I still get lightheaded every now and then," she said. "But I'm fine now."

The other day she had totally freaked him out, telling him she thought she was having contractions. His heart had stopped. He'd wanted to call an ambulance or rush her to the hospital, but she'd only wanted to call her doctor. He forgot what the doctor had called the contractions but, apparently, they didn't matter.

"Are you hungry?" she said.

They'd eaten lunch an hour ago. "No."

She clicked her tongue. "I wish you wouldn't look at me like that all the time. I'm not crazy, I'm pregnant."

He snickered. "That'd make a nice slogan on a t-shirt. Maybe a bumper sticker."

She didn't laugh. "Ever since you've gotten back, you've been so grumpy and anxious around me."

He rolled his eyes and sighed. *Here she goes again.*

"You don't show any compassion for what I'm going through."

"Sure I do." He got up to get her drinks fifty times a day, fixed her food when Nanny wasn't around, brought her pillows, rubbed her back . . . *What more did she want?*

"It's not easy being pregnant, you know, especially at this stage. Maybe this is all a shock to you, I mean, we were together when it was easy to hide, but then you left—"

"Not my fault."

". . . and when you return, my belly's grown. It's not my fault either."

"I mean, it's not my fault that I left. I didn't want to go."

"I know. But it's not my fault that I'm pregnant. It's not *all* my fault. You were there, too."

His chest muscles tightened. "Do we have to do this?"

"I'm just tired of you acting so put out by everything. I feel like you force yourself to put up with me, like I'm so unattractive to you because I'm pregnant." Her voice wavered and her breath caught in her throat.

He found himself reaching for her, rubbing her shoulders, leaning his face close to hers. "Don't feel that way, baby. I don't want you to think that. Things will go back to the way they were soon. I'm just— I'm scared. This is too much for me."

My gosh, did he just tell her he was scared? He pushed away and breathed deep to compose himself. He pulled out the band in his hair and remade his ponytail, wishing he'd taken a shower in the morning and vaguely aware that she was sniveling.

"You still need to sign the adoption papers," she said.

"I'm not ready." He finished his drink.

"When are you going to be ready?"

He shrugged, refusing to look at her. "Maybe never."

"I think you're just being possessive. You're not thinking about what's best for the baby. Are you going to raise the baby yourself?" Her tone had taken a sarcastic turn.

He glanced at her and got up. "I'm gonna go have a smoke."

She huffed. "Whatever."

He opened the veranda door and stepped from the dark of the house. The noon sun reflected off the sidewalk and driveway by the garage, making him blink and squint. Inhaling a deep breath of warm, fresh air, he brought out his cigarettes and lighter.

The stables called to him. How he'd love to take Desert for a ride . . . go off down the longest trail, maybe even cross over a distant neighbor's land and see where he'd end up. It would feel good to have a horse under him, the reins in his hands, and the wind on his face.

With a sigh, he returned to the steps outside the veranda and sat in the shade. He lit a cigarette and relaxed as he took a puff. Maybe he needed a break from Zoe. If he took a few breaks now and then, maybe he wouldn't rub her the wrong way. She was right. He did put up with her now, not that he loved her any less, but he wanted things back the way they were. He almost hated having her around, knowing that the baby could come any day. What if something went wrong?

At the far edge of the backyard, a horse and rider emerged from the woods. It was too far to see if it was Roland or Keefe. Not wanting to speak with either of them, he considered going back inside. Then he got an idea.

With his eyes on the rider, Jarret pulled out his cell phone.

The horse clomped through the yard toward the stables. Keefe was the rider. *It figured.* For whatever reason, he'd been taking the horses out a lot lately.

"Hey, Keefe." Jarret jumped up from the steps and jogged over to him.

"Yeah, what's up?" Keefe brought the horse to a standstill and stared down at Jarret, genuine concern showing in his eyes.

The look gave Jarret the urge to back off, although a part of him longed to open up to his twin. He needed someone lean on. He had no one anymore. "Hey, I . . . Give me Caitlyn's phone number."

Keefe hesitated, so Jarret told him why, revealing only enough to influence him. He needed a break, and since Caitlyn loved to be around Zoe and talk pregnancy and baby things, he wanted her to come over.

A moment later, he had it arranged, and he jumped into his red Chrysler to get his liberator.

Chapter Fifty-one

Caitlyn

Zoe moaned.

At first, Caitlyn thought she did it in reaction to the chaos in the house. Andy flung himself about on the couch, throwing pillows and whatever he could reach, refusing to take his nap. He wanted Mom to nurse him and would settle for nothing less, but Mom had left Caitlyn in charge while she ran to the store, and Dad wouldn't get home from work for another hour and a half. The whole time, Priscilla kept bugging Zoe, trying to get her to decide on a baby name and look at her dolls. Stacey kept bugging Priscilla, wanting her to play in the backyard. Caitlyn wanted Stacey to watch David, who made her long for his terrible two's again. He had become markedly wilder once he'd turned three, the innocent gleam in his little, rectangular eyes having morphed into a sneaky, calculating look. Nothing satisfied him except for speed, destruction, and dirt.

The screen door off the enclosed patio scraped open.

"Stacey!" Caitlyn shouted.

Andy jumped at her voice and let out an awful cry. Stacey peeked from around the reclining rocker where Zoe sat sprawled. Stacey held a water pistol in each hand. One of them leaked.

Caitlyn sat on the floor by the couch, holding Andy with one hand to keep him from falling as he cried. She craned her neck to look at Stacey. "Go get David. He ran outside."

"No. I want to play with Priscilla. Make her play with me."

Priscilla, who sat on the floor with her dolls, turned her back completely on Stacey.

"You can play with her after—" Caitlyn twisted around and slammed her palms on the coffee table to get up. One palm slipped in the spilled milk she'd forgotten about. "Go get David, or I'll tell Mom you ate your lunch in the living room."

"I did not. I ate at the table."

Caitlyn jumped up.

Stacey ran.

It was true, she had eaten at the table, but Priscilla finished first and Stacey came out with her milk to be with her. While Caitlyn cleaned lunch from every inch of David's body, Stacey had spilled her milk but never bothered telling Caitlyn about it.

Zoe moaned again.

Caitlyn froze. "Are you okay?"

It was two days past her due date. Jarret had stayed by her side on her due date and the following day, questioning her every sigh and moan and asking if she thought it was time. Zoe said he wouldn't sit down. When his pacing drove her nuts, she had sent him to the next room to take a few deep, calming breaths. It must've worn him out. Today, he'd told Zoe he had something to do and to call if anything happened.

"I'm fine. I'm just having contractions."

"Contractions?" Caitlyn laughed. She squealed. Tears filled her eyes. She dropped onto her knees and grabbed Zoe's hands. "What should I do?"

Zoe peered down at Caitlyn through tranquil brown eyes, barely seeming phased. "First of all, calm down. The doctor doesn't want me rushing off to the hospital the second the contractions start. They need to come closer together. Do you have a clock with a second hand?"

"Oh." Caitlyn jumped up, wanting to run to the kitchen for a clock. But Priscilla had crept near, and Caitlyn hadn't noticed until their bodies collided.

Now Priscilla lay on the floor crying, not like the eleven-year-old girl she was but more like little Andy.

"I'm sorry." Caitlyn stooped and took her hand. "Want to help me get the clock?"

She stopped crying and nodded. "The baby's coming?"

"I think so." Smiling and giddy, they raced to the kitchen. Caitlyn helped Priscilla climb onto the countertop.

Priscilla jerked the big white clock—and the nail that held it—from the wall.

Zoe had moved to the couch and sat hunched over Andy, brushing his face with a lock of her hair. He'd calmed some, his sobs coming out as intermittent snivels.

Caitlyn set the clock on the coffee table and sat down beside it, right on the milk spill. "Now what?"

As calm as the eye of a hurricane, Zoe rubbed her belly and looked at Caitlyn. "Do you know where my cell phone is? I think I left it—"

"Priscilla!" Caitlyn shouted though her sister stood right there. "Check my room. On my bed."

Priscilla ran.

"I need to call Jarret. I hope he has my overnight bag in his car." Zoe winced and closed her eyes. When she opened them, she giggled. "It's going to be today."

Joy rippled through Caitlyn, leaving a wake of tingles. She flung herself at Zoe and they hugged, giggling.

Priscilla returned with the phone. Zoe eased herself up and took it.

Andy, eyes closed, let out a sleepy cry. He lifted then dropped his hand.

Caitlyn sat down and gave him a lock of her hair. "Priscilla, go check on David and Stacey. Make sure they haven't run away."

Zoe turned around, frowning. "He's not answering his phone."

"Maybe he's talking to someone."

Glaring at her phone, Zoe paced to the couch under the window. Then she looked outside. "For the past month he's been going somewhere."

"What?" Caitlyn stopped rubbing Andy with her hair. He'd fallen asleep anyway.

"He says he's just going for a drive, but he's gone for an hour, sometimes more." The faintest smile flickered on her lips. "I checked his miles a few times, and it's always the same. He goes somewhere ten or eleven miles from his house. Do you think he's—"

Caitlyn jumped up and rounded the coffee table. "Oh, don't be silly. You aren't thinking he's got a new girlfriend? He really cares about you. I see it in the way he looks at you."

She smirked. "That's not love you see. It's fear."

Caitlyn took Zoe's phone and hit redial. "Maybe he goes shopping. He likes to shop, doesn't he?" The phone rang and rang. "Maybe he has a favorite store. You shouldn't think he's—"

Zoe snatched the phone, pressed it to her ear, and then tossed it to the recliner. "Where *is* he?" Hugging her tummy, she peered down at the clock on the coffee table.

"I know. I'll call the Wests' house." Caitlyn went to the kitchen for their cordless phone and carried it back to the living room as she pressed buttons. She expected to hear Nanny's voice, since Nanny had always answered when Caitlyn called, so the sound of Roland's voice made her lightheaded and temporarily forget how to speak.

"Hello?" he said for the third time.

"Oh, hi, Roland. I was wondering, I mean, is Jarret there?"

"Um, no, I don't think so."

"Well, it's time."

"Time?"

"You know, Zoe, she's having . . ."

"The baby?"

"Yeah."

"Wait. Hold on. I-I'll go check."

The screen door slid open and broke the trance Roland's voice had put Caitlyn in.

Priscilla burst into the house. "Caitlyn, Caitlyn, come quick!"

Caitlyn covered the phone with her hand. "What's wrong?"

"David saw a bunny. It was eating the plants in Mrs. Hathaway's garden. And Stacey tried to get him to come inside . . ." Priscilla could take forever to get the point.

"So, what's wrong? Why do I have to come quick?"

"David got inside their fence."

"What? Mrs. Hathaway's fence? How?" A three-foot-high wooden fence surrounded Mrs. Hathaway's back yard. She recently installed a foot-high metal garden fence. To keep the rabbits out, she claimed. Caitlyn suspected it had more to do with their roaming David.

"Where's Stacey?" Caitlyn said just as a voice sounded through the phone.

"What?" It was Peter. "We don't think Jarret's here."

"Stacey's in the garden with him," Priscilla said.

"Oh my." Caitlyn smacked her forehead. "Go watch them." She grabbed Priscilla by the shoulder and turned her around.

"Go watch who?" Peter said, then he said something about Zoe having her baby, but Caitlyn's attention was on Priscilla as she dragged her to the screen door.

Priscilla stopped and folded her arms. "But I want to stay with Zoe. Mom told *you* to watch—"

"Go!" Caitlyn scrunched up her face and flung an arm out, pointing. Priscilla bolted out the door.

Peter was still talking. ". . . only one horse missing from the stables. So then Roland was like *reading sign*, he said, looking at hoof prints outside the stables so he could see which way the horse went. He was like Aragorn in *The Lord of the Rings*. Remember that, when he was, like, crouched down—"

Caitlyn slammed shut the screen door that Priscilla had left open and shouted, "Peter!" Sometimes a person had to get angry to snap Peter out of his rambling. "Zoe's having a baby."

"Oh, gosh, yeah. What do you want me to do?"

Caitlyn sighed, trying to think.

Zoe paced the living room floor, her hands on her lower back.

"Where's Roland?" Caitlyn said into the phone.

"Weren't you listening to me?" Peter sounded annoyed. "I said, he took a horse out to see who's riding Desert. It's probably Keefe, but that's Jarret's horse. And Keefe might know where Jarret is."

"Well, is Jarret's car there?"

"I don't know. I'll go check. I'll call you back."

Caitlyn carried the phone into the living room. "Do you want to call your mom?"

"No." Zoe didn't stop pacing. "My mom will tell my dad, and my dad will come and get me, and he won't want Jarret anywhere near the hospital. I'll tell them after Jarret takes me there."

"Okay. Well . . ." Caitlyn hated to ask. "What if we can't find Jarret in time?"

Zoe stopped. She glanced, her face blank. "When will your dad get home?"

Caitlyn peered at the wall in the kitchen, forgetting she had taken the clock to the living room. "Sometimes he's late. I don't want to count on him being here. And my parents don't have cell phones, so we can't exactly call them."

The phone in Caitlyn's hand rang, making her jump. "Hello?"

"Yeah, it's me," Peter said. "Jarret's car is gone and Roland caught up with Keefe, brought him back to the house. Now what do you want us to do?"

"Oh."

Zoe stopped pacing and clutched the back of the recliner rocker. Having a contraction? A moment later, she fumbled for her phone and pushed a few buttons.

Shielding her mouth, Caitlyn whispered into the phone, "We need to get Zoe to the hospital, and my parents aren't here."

"Call an ambulance," Peter said.

"I don't think she'll like that idea."

"Well, I'll call my dad. He can come and get her."

"Okay." It sounded like a good idea, but she doubted Zoe would agree. "I'll call you back. Don't call him yet. Let me tell her first."

Caitlyn told Zoe—who didn't like the idea. So they went round and round with the same suggestions, none of them agreeable to Zoe. She had her mind set on Jarret taking her.

The screen door flew open and Stacey bolted inside, an evil smile on her dirty face. "Priscilla's skirt is stuck in Mrs. Hathaway's rabbit fence. She's crying." Oddly, that seemed to amuse her.

Frustrated beyond belief, Caitlyn sighed and tossed the phone onto the recliner rocker. "Okay."

She hadn't taken more than two steps when Zoe gasped.

"What's wrong?"

Zoe's eyes snapped open big and round. "It's time. We have to get to the hospital NOW."

Andy, perhaps sensing the tension in the air, awoke from his nap and let out a long, loud cry.

Caitlyn lunged for the phone on the recliner, deciding to call for an ambulance whether Zoe liked it or not. Then, out of the corner of her eye, she glimpsed something through the front screen door.

Mr. Brandt's big green truck pulled into the driveway. The driver's door flew open, and he got out. Peter must've told him anyway. Caitlyn could've hugged him!

"Come on, Zoe. Your ride's here."

Peter's aunt Lotti, who Caitlyn had always called Aunt Lotti, even though they weren't related, bumbled out of the passenger side. She followed Mr. Brandt to the front porch where they all now stood, Zoe and Caitlyn holding hands and looking panicky, them smiling.

"I'm so glad you're here." Caitlyn glanced from one to the other. Then she mouthed to Aunt Lotti, "It's time."

"Well, you'd better get this girl to the hospital," Aunt Lotti said.

Mr. Brandt took Zoe by the arm. Caitlyn had to peel Zoe's fingers from her hand, but then Zoe allowed Mr. Brandt to escort her to the truck.

"I'm so glad you came, Aunt Lotti. I hate to think of her being alone. Take good care of her." Caitlyn's heart ached to go with her, but she had responsibilities. Their voices traveled through the screen door, Andy bawling and Stacey talking. Caitlyn imagined Priscilla still stood crying with her skirt stuck in the fence, and David . . .

"No, my dear." Aunt Lotti patted Caitlyn's arm. "You need to go with her. That's why I'm here. I'll watch your brothers and sisters."

So thankful she could've burst, Caitlyn gave Aunt Lotti a quick sketch of her siblings' various predicaments and dashed for the truck.

Mr. Brandt—being a forest ranger—happened to have a flashing yellow light, which he put atop his truck. Then he barreled down the road, getting them to the hospital in no time. He dropped Zoe and Caitlyn at the main doors and went to park. Caitlyn walked Zoe through the glass doors, took the elevator, and relinquished Zoe to a nurse who led her down a hallway.

Caitlyn paced in the second-floor waiting room, anxious to be allowed back. Mr. Brandt soon joined her, taking a seat in a corner to make phone calls with his cell.

Sometime later, the elevator opened and three of Caitlyn's favorite people stepped out. She couldn't have been happier to see them. As they drew near, she realized what each of them meant to her.

She and Peter had grown up together, and she'd always thought of him as an older brother. She enjoyed his company and felt comfortable sharing most anything with him. Sure, his jokes and babbling could get on her nerves, but she never doubted he would be there if she needed him.

Though Keefe and Caitlyn hadn't spoken much in the past two months, they had developed a friendship that changed Caitlyn forever. His faith and courage in facing challenges impressed her deeply, making her want to imitate those virtues, though she hadn't figured out how yet.

And Roland . . . Seeing him gave her goose bumps and stirred something deep inside. He had lost nothing of his mystery and appeal. She loved that he'd come up here to help and support them. She thought of the many ways they had worked together in the past nine months. Mom's words came to mind: *Now is the time for friendships.*

Caitlyn approached the three of them. "How did you guys get here?" She looked at Keefe for the answer since he was the oldest and the only one with a driver's license.

"I called a cab."

"Oh." Caitlyn felt stupid. "Why didn't I think of that? We could've called a cab."

Keefe squeezed her hand, anxiety in his eyes. "Jarret's not answering his phone. Did he show?"

"No. But we have to find him."

"What should we do?" Roland looked from Keefe to Caitlyn.

Peter went to the corner of the waiting room, to where his dad sat.

"We could call his friends," Caitlyn said, hopeful. "Do you know who his friends are . . . and their phone numbers?"

"I do," Keefe said, he and Roland drawing their cell phones simultaneously. "I'll give you some numbers, Roland." The two of them took seats in the corner opposite Peter and Mr. Brandt.

Remembering what Zoe had mentioned about Jarret taking drives and her checking the miles, Caitlyn said, "Are any of his friends ten miles away?" Keefe and Roland looked at her as if it were a strange question, but she decided not to explain.

While they sat with phones to their ears, and Peter and Mr. Brandt discussed trivial things, a nursing assistant finally came to get Caitlyn and led her to Zoe's room.

Zoe, looking clean, comfortable, and poised, wore a pink hospital gown and sat in an adjustable bed surrounded by monitors. "Please tell me Jarret's on his way." She smoothed the sheet around her belly and arranged her hair.

"Keefe, Roland, and Peter are here. They'll find him. Don't worry." Caitlyn dragged a chair to the bedside. "Is your doctor here?"

In the corner of the room, a nurse set up equipment and made notes on a clipboard. Wires stuck out from under Zoe's sheet, running up to monitors.

"The doctor's on his way. I have a while yet, but my contractions are getting . . . a little uncomfortable." She leaned back and breathed out her mouth. "Mom's coming up." She continued exhaling.

"You called her?"

She nodded. "I'm sure Dad will come, too. He'd better not try to stop Jarret from being here. I told Mom Jarret was going to be here and if they didn't like that, they shouldn't come."

Zoe reached for her pillows, so Caitlyn helped adjust them.

Her discomfort showed and Caitlyn really wanted to help. "Can I get you anything?"

She nodded. "Get me Jarret."

When Caitlyn returned to the waiting room to check the progress, Roland and Keefe stood up. Peter approached them just as Caitlyn did.

Caitlyn hoped they had good news. Seeing Zoe alone in that bright room of wires and machines, of things beeping and making strange noises, gave her a sense of desperation. They needed to find Jarret.

"Did you find him?" she said.

Keefe said, "No."

But at the same time, Roland said, "I know where he is."

And judging by the look on his face, Caitlyn believed him.

Chapter Fifty-two

Roland

Roland gazed out the window, listening to the rumble of Mr. Brandt's truck and watching houses and trees pass by. He considered how sometimes life goes in a full circle. Nine months ago, he and Peter had been following Jarret, trying to find him and wondering where he'd been going. Here they were, with even more urgency, searching for him again.

"I wonder if they make a tracking device the size of a pill." Peter, who sat in the middle, bumped Roland's leg with his own whenever he spoke.

Roland didn't bother looking at him or responding.

"Of course, it would probably come out when he, uh . . ." He glanced at his father and must've decided not to complete his sentence. "Hey, Dad, have you ever seen Jarret's car at the campground, you know, since last September?"

"No, I haven't." Mr. Brandt stared at the road. "But I don't spend a lot of time in parking lots. When I'm not at the office or giving talks or whatnot, I'm usually deep in the woods, working."

"We should've put something in his car," Peter said to Roland. "You know, when he first got it and was showing it off to anyone who came near. I could've easily dropped a tracking device in there. Except, he keeps it so clean, he might've found it. Oh wait, I know, they have those kinds you can stick underneath."

Roland shook his head. Peter was nuts.

"Really, man, I'm serious. That brother of yours needs a permanent tracking device. He might not keep his car forever, so maybe that's not a good idea. How about his cell phone? Does he upgrade his phone a lot? No, no, I got it. Jewelry." He waved his brows. "Something expensive, maybe a watch. He'd never take it off. He'd probably wonder why you and me would give him something. We'd have to make Zoe give it to him."

"Peter." Roland, not one to raise his voice, felt his temper spike and snapped, "Get with the real world, will you?"

Peter chuckled. "What do you know of that, oh man in black?"

He stopped talking awhile, but as they neared the park entrance, he started up again. "So, why not a friend's house? Or just driving? What makes you think he'll be here?"

Roland shrugged. He hoped he was right. It'd be a shame, them getting all the way out here and not finding him. Mr. Brandt had been nice enough to offer to drive when Keefe was about to call a cab, but he probably had his own things to do today. Roland would hate to be wasting Mr. Brandt's time, all the while getting no closer to finding Jarret. Keefe elected to stay at the hospital and make phone calls, saying he'd call if he got any leads.

"Come on," Peter whined. "You've gotta have a reason. You think he's with someone at the campground? A girl?"

"No." He hated talking about people, especially his brothers, but it wasn't anything bad that led him to his conclusion. "Jarret's sentimental."

Peter quirked a grin. "Sentimental, huh?"

"Yeah. This is where it all began."

They turned down the long winding road that led to the campsites. Mr. Brandt shut off the air-conditioner and lowered the windows. Warm campfire-scented air blew into the truck.

"This is where Jarret met Zoe and, um . . ."

"Got her pregnant," Peter said.

"Right. And Jarret was here when he learned about Keefe's haircut, which you probably can't understand, but that hit him hard because . . . well, Jarret's sentimental. And it was here that people started seeing him differently, thought of him as a hero for, um . . ."

"Yeah." Peter's grin faded and he gazed at the dash. ". . . for saving Toby."

"Right. So, people didn't just think of him as a bad boy." They exchanged a glance that let Roland know Peter finally understood. "Plus, it's about ten miles away. Isn't that what Caitlyn said? Who do we know that's ten miles away? He's here. I'm sure of it."

Mr. Brandt parked the truck near their old site. "Let's go find him, boys. I'll look for him up on Bonfire Hill."

"I'll go with you." Peter jogged with his father toward a trail.

Roland headed for their old campsite.

The campground hadn't changed much. As he passed from site to site, he remembered it all clearly: the layout of the sites, the way they had arranged several tables in one site, and even the things they had done. He let his mind linger a moment on the memory of sneaking around the woods with Caitlyn and her sisters. He missed her friendship.

"What're you doing here?"

Roland exhaled at the sound of Jarret's voice. *Thank you, Lord.*

Jarret leaned against a tree, a cigarette in his hand. He blew out smoke, making it swirl above him, looking like he hadn't a care in the world.

"You have to come with us. Zoe's having the baby."

Jarret's eyes flashed. He dropped the cigarette. "Okay." He set off at once, taking long strides. "Now? She's having it now? Where is she? Why didn't she call?"

"She's at the hospital. Check your phone. We've all been trying to call you."

Jarret jogged down a different path than the one Roland had taken, coming out on the dirt road where his Chrysler sat. To leave the campground, they had to pass through the parking lot where Mr. Brandt had parked. As they did, Peter dashed out of the woods.

Jarret slowed and unlocked the doors.

"Thanks, man," Peter said as he slid into the backseat. He waved at his father before slamming his door. "Dad's gotta get back to the bed-and-breakfast. I guess Mom's out with Toby, and he left the place unattended. Let's get to the hospital."

Jarret sped down the road at a speed that again had Roland praying a cop didn't come by. Roland sighed, thinking how Jarret had better change his ways or he'd always find himself racing from one emergency to another.

God answered Roland's prayers. They hadn't met with a single hitch until the elevator doors opened to the maternity ward.

Five people sat in the waiting room, three strangers, Keefe . . . and Mr. McGowan. They hadn't taken four steps when Mr. McGowan lumbered over, his beady eyes locked on Jarret. "What do you think you're doing here?"

Jarret shrunk back.

Chapter Fifty-three

Caitlyn

Zoe's contractions came harder and with less time between them. Her parents had come up, but only her mother had ventured into the room. After her last contraction, Zoe sent Caitlyn to check the waiting room, as if she sensed that Jarret had arrived.

And there he was! He stood near the elevator, Roland and Peter on either side, Mr. McGowan in front of him.

It sounded like Mr. McGowan said, "I warned you that I'd kill you if you came near my daughter." But Zoe had told her parents that Jarret was going to be here, so Mr. McGowan shouldn't have had a problem.

Jarret's eyelids fluttered and his face turned a shade paler. He turned away from Mr. McGowan and toward the elevator as if he were just going to leave. Then Roland grabbed his shoulder and turned him back.

Keefe approached Jarret, smiling. "Hey, you're here."

Caitlyn sprinted to him. "Zoe's been asking for you." Trying not to let her anxiety show, she smiled and reached out to welcome him.

Mr. McGowan jerked his face to her and gave her a hard stare. "Jarret will not be going to her room."

"What?" Caitlyn's hope deflated. "But Mr. McGowan, sir, your daughter, she—"

"He is not her husband," Mr. McGowan boomed. "He has no right—"

"Arthur." Mrs. McGowan came up behind Caitlyn using a stern voice that didn't fit her petite stature. "Your daughter is in pain right now. If she wants to see this boy, she's *going* to see him." She pushed through the group and latched onto Jarret's arm.

Jarret's mouth fell open. He glanced up at Mr. McGowan.

Mr. McGowan growled and stepped aside.

Mrs. McGowan yanked Jarret forward. "You'll say *hello*, tell her everything will be okay, and return to the waiting room."

Jarret dragged his feet at first but soon kept step with Zoe's mom. Caitlyn trailed behind.

The instant they reached the doorway, Jarret stopped dead.

Zoe spun to face him. The contraction monitor went wild and Zoe looked at him with fire in her eyes. "Where have you been, you pig? I hate you!"

A nurse said something about getting the doctor and ran for the door.

Jarret backed up. When he turned to make a break for it, he smacked into Caitlyn, panic in his eyes.

"It's okay. It's the contractions making Zoe talk that way. Really, she wants you here. She's been asking for you." Caitlyn grabbed his arms to keep him from escaping. But she hadn't needed to.

His eyes rolled up, and his face went white. A nurse bolted for him as he fell to the floor like an abandoned marionette.

~ ~ ~

Zoe had asked Caitlyn to stay, so she'd watched the miracle through watery eyes and with a heart elevated to God the Creator. She would never take the gift of life for granted. The agony of the labor gave way to the birth of a healthy and beautiful little girl, all nineteen inches and seven pounds of her.

Hair disheveled, skin glistening with sweat, Zoe lay back on her pillow and laughed for joy.

Caitlyn pressed a damp washcloth to Zoe's forehead, squeezed her hand, and laughed with her. "You did it."

The message of love shined so clearly to Caitlyn. Love is about sacrifice, about laying your life down for another. In married love, a man and woman forsake all others and cling to one another. Then their love bears fruit which a woman brings forth through travail and sorrow. But which fills her heart with inexpressible joy.

Caitlyn couldn't wait for the day she would know such love and bring children of her own into the world. *Well, no . . . that wasn't true.* She could wait. First, she would have to find the man God had prepared for her, her future husband. But she wasn't ready for that either. God would send him in due time.

A few minutes later, a peaceful joy filled the room. The baby had been cleaned, wrapped in a pink blanket, and placed in Zoe's arms. Mr. and Mrs. McGowan hovered over their daughter and granddaughter, teary eyed and humbled. Jarret, who had recovered at the nurses' station, had been allowed back in. He sat in a chair by the window, watching Zoe and the baby at a distance.

Caitlyn couldn't stop smiling. She gazed out the window, hoping this moment would never fade from her memory.

When Mr. and Mrs. McGowan finally left the room, Jarret whispered to Caitlyn, "Hey."

She looked at him, blinking away green afterimages from having stared outside for so long.

With a shy look in his eyes, he nodded in the direction of Zoe and the baby.

Caitlyn smiled. It struck her as funny how this vain, confident, even arrogant boy was, in this situation, as uncertain as a child. "Why don't you go over there? Hold your little girl."

With a deep breath, Jarret got up. Tears streamed down his cheeks as he took his daughter in his arms. "I don't . . . want to give her away," he said to Zoe between sniffles.

Zoe scooted over, making room for him on the bed. She smiled as she watched him, her tranquil and self-possessed demeanor having returned.

Caitlyn tiptoed from the room, leaving the couple some privacy on this, their first and last night with their little girl.

Chapter Fifty-four

Caitlyn

Zoe and Caitlyn sat on swings in the playground across the street from Caitlyn's house. The sun peeked through the leaves of tall trees and cast long shadows, making houses and landscaping picturesque.

"I can't believe you walked all the way to my house," Caitlyn said.

Zoe laughed and leaned forward, her silky black hair sweeping over her face. "I always walk to your house. You don't live that far."

"Still. You just had a baby. Not that anyone could tell by looking at you."

Zoe wore a sleeveless flowered top and white shorts, the same white shorts she'd worn last summer. She patted her flat stomach, smiling. "I was glad it went right back after a couple of days. Mom said it was like that for her, too."

"Do you miss her?"

"No. Why would I miss her? I see her every day."

"Not your mom. I mean—"

"I know." She gazed off into the distance and sighed. "Of course I miss her, especially at night. I wish I could hold her again. Those three days in the hospital, I felt so stunned, like it wasn't happening to me. Other times the tears wouldn't stop."

"Oh, Zoe, I'm so sorry."

She smiled. "I'm okay now. I still cry, even though I'm home. She'll always be in my heart, and it'll hurt now and then. But I know I did the right thing. Do you ever have that feeling? You have to do something that you don't want to do. And it seems almost impossible, but you just do it."

Caitlyn nodded, though she felt more like a child who had yet to be challenged. Keefe could relate to Zoe. Maybe even Roland, but not Caitlyn . . . not yet.

"I really like the couple I chose, and I'm happy for them. You should've seen their faces when they held her." Zoe smiled at the sky. "They sent me a dozen pink roses yesterday." She paused, her smile fading. "I'm glad Jarret finally signed the papers."

"When did he do that?"

"The same day she was born." Zoe leaned back and eased the swing forward as she spoke. "The social worker came up, and he just did it. Well, I shouldn't say he *just* did it. He still didn't want to. The social worker and I both had to talk him into seeing that it was best for the baby. She needs a mother and a father. And a stable life. Poor Jarret. He even said we should get married."

"He did?"

"I'm sure he didn't mean it. It was just his reaction to the situation. It's hard to let your baby go."

"I'm sure it would be. How's he doing now?"

"I don't know." Zoe stopped her swing. The look in her eyes said she had something important to say.

Caitlyn stopped her swing. "What?"

"We aren't seeing each other."

"Oh." Though Zoe didn't look troubled, the news upset Caitlyn. They had been through so much together. "Why not?"

Zoe took a slow and deep breath, walking the swing back a few steps. She exhaled as she lifted her feet and let the swing go. "I'm starting over." She swung back and forth a few times. "I think it would be too hard to start over with him. I don't want to be the girl he knows. I need to find out who I am before I can really share myself with someone else."

That, Caitlyn understood. The same idea had motivated her to decide something, too. "I don't want to have a boyfriend anymore."

"Really?"

"Really. I've decided I'm too young. I mean, a part of me feels ready for more, but part of me just wants to be a kid. I'll practice courtship when I'm older, closer to being ready to marry."

Having said it aloud, cemented it for her. This was what she wanted. She appreciated the practices of courtship, practices that had kept her, and in the future would keep her, from rushing things and thinking only with her unruly emotions. But for now, she wanted friendships.

"A new phase of life begins," Caitlyn said with a smile. They both leaned way back and worked their swings up high.

Let the bees stir among the flowers and make honey in their hives. Let the birds build nests and sing while they swoop and play in the sky. God held Caitlyn in His hand, helping her to understand and drawing her closer to true love. She trusted Him. She would have plenty of time to find her future husband tomorrow. Today, she only wanted the freedom to live what God had put in her heart, to search for Him, and to find herself. She did not mind at all being the sole unbusy thing.

After a while, they slowed their swings and Zoe said, "Do you miss him?"

"Who?"

Zoe tilted her chin in the direction of the sidewalk.

Caitlyn turned to see.

There he was—Roland West—strolling across the grass toward them, looking fine in black jeans and a plain white t-shirt. She couldn't remember seeing him in anything but dark colors. The white brought out his dark eyebrows and, the closer he got, his gorgeous gray eyes.

"Hey." At first, he only had eyes for Caitlyn, but then he noticed Zoe and made a sweeping gaze of the playground. "Where's Keefe?"

Caitlyn jumped off the swing and walked toward him. She stopped a few feet away and clasped her hands behind her back. "Are you looking for him?"

He shrugged. "Just taking a walk."

"All the way over here? Did you walk from your house?"

He glanced back the way he came and nodded. "I'm bored. I wanted to do something with Peter, but he's not home. I thought he might be over here but, uh . . ." He averted his gaze.

Caitlyn reached out and took his hand, not quite believing she did it. "I'm glad you came by." She led him to a bench under a tree. "I miss you."

As they sat down, he pulled his hand from hers. "Where's Keefe?"

"I don't know. We're not courting anymore, haven't been for a while."

"No? Something go wrong?" His gray eyes probed hers.

"No. I've decided I'm not ready for all that boyfriend-girlfriend stuff. I just want to have friends. He feels the same way, I think."

Disbelief showed in his eyes then he gave a little smile. "I know what you mean. And I'm glad. I . . ." He swallowed. "I miss you, too."

They sat in silence for a few beautiful minutes, watching Zoe twist her swing to the left and right. The scent of pine and dirt carried on a warm breeze. Leaves rustled in the nearest tree.

He looked at Caitlyn again. "I'm glad you made me confront Jarret back in December, when Zoe was going to, uh . . ."

Caitlyn smiled. "I feel like we saved the baby, but I know it was the people praying outside the clinic that changed her mind."

He nodded, his eyes thoughtful and downcast. "We saved Jarret."

A tingling sensation ran through Caitlyn. "Jarret?"

"He needed to *want* to stop her, to try to save his own baby, to save her, to save himself."

Caitlyn understood. *Abortion destroys more than one life.*

They both turned to Zoe again. She was too far to hear them, but she looked up and smiled.

"They're not seeing each other anymore, are they?" he said.

"No. She wants a do-over. It's probably hard to start over when you're seeing someone who expects you to act a certain way."

He nodded, still staring at Zoe.

She must've taken his nod as an invitation because she jumped off the swing and approached. "What're you up to, Roland?"

"Just wasting time."

"You know Caitlyn's not seeing Keefe anymore." Zoe sat on Roland's other side, hogging the bench and making him scoot toward Caitlyn.

"Yeah, that's what she said."

"Keefe didn't tell you?"

"Um, no."

"You West boys don't talk to each other much, do you?"

He shrugged.

"Did you know Keefe never kissed Caitlyn, not even once?"

"Zoe!" Caitlyn's face flashed twenty degrees hotter. She reached past Roland to smack Zoe's arm. "Why would you say that?"

Zoe leaned back, tilted her face to the sky, and closed her eyes as if she had no idea she had totally humiliated Caitlyn. "It's true, isn't it? I don't know how many times you told me you were dying for your first kiss."

"I can't believe you!" Caitlyn got up and stomped to the shady side of the big green climbing fort, where no one could see her. *Why would Zoe say that in front of Roland?*

Caitlyn folded her arms and leaned against the steps. Zoe and Roland talked, but she couldn't make out what they said. She didn't want to know what they said. Or did she?

She shuffled to the corner of the climbing fort and peeked.

Roland came from around the corner, and they bumped.

"Sorry." Caitlyn stumbled back then leaned against the fort.

He smiled, one of those sweet smiles that moved her, and leaned a shoulder against the fort. Close to her. "What're you doing back here?"

"Oh." Nervous now, she glanced away. "Standing in the shade."

He pressed his lips together and dropped his gaze. "I, uh, don't want to confuse you." A glance. "I know you just told me you only wanted friendships, and I do, too. That's what I want. But, well, Zoe said . . ."

Then he leaned into her space and pressed his lips to hers.

Warmth. Sweetness. Caitlyn swooned. Then it was over and she breathed. It hadn't lasted more than a second, but she'd never forget it. Her first real kiss!

He stared at her through clear gray eyes. Then he gave her his sweet little smile.

Chapter Fifty-five

Jarret

Leaves swayed in a warm breeze. Sunlight pulsated through them. Jarret lay on his back with his eyes closed, his shoulder blade digging into the gritty surface of the boulder he'd climbed onto for refuge. He turned his head to avoid the light, but it followed him anyway, not allowing him to sulk in darkness. Somewhere high above, a falcon made a shrill cry.

Then a shadow fell over him and something scraped the boulder. He was not alone.

Irritated at the intrusion, Jarret popped up and leaned back on his elbows.

Keefe stood a yard away with his hands at his sides and leaning his weight on one leg. Sunlight framed his short, curly hair.

"What're you doing here? Why are you standing over me?" It annoyed him that he hadn't heard Keefe approach. He should've heard a few twigs snap, or something, as Keefe came down the path from the house.

"I didn't mean to scare—" He gave a quick headshake. "I mean, *startle* you. The sun was on your face. Seemed like it bothered you."

"What do you care? The sun wasn't bothering me as much as you are now."

The rock formation he'd climbed to be alone had a wide surface, big enough for a whole group of people, but it offered only a few ways up and down. Keefe blocked the easiest way, and it was too high to jump down comfortably.

"You think I don't care about you?" Keefe sat down and wrapped his arms around his knees.

316

Jarret avoided meeting his brother's gaze.

"You don't talk to anyone in the house, you've come out here every day for the past few days, and you stay out here for hours."

He gave his brother a sulky look. "You know I don't like you anymore."

Keefe smiled. "Yeah, I know."

"I ain't got nothing to say to you."

With a sigh, Keefe turned to the canopy of leaves. The falcon shrieked again and Keefe's head swiveled as if he'd caught sight of it.

Jarret peered off in the opposite direction, and they sat in silence for a long moment, until he could take it no more. "Look. I know why you're out here. You think I need to talk to someone."

Keefe hadn't bothered to face him, so Jarret lay back on the cool rock again and flung his arm over his eyes. "I don't need you. I don't need anyone. I can get along fine all by myself."

Keefe didn't respond, didn't make a sound. Maybe he had snuck down and gone away as quietly as he had come.

Pretending that Keefe had gone, Jarret sought the darkness again and enjoyed the whisper of the leaves as a breeze blew. How could nature remain so calm while his heart whirled in turmoil?

Suddenly words erupted from him. "She dumped me. I stuck by her through all this, then—" His eyes watered, so he pressed his arm hard against them. "She made me sign our baby girl away. Two days later, she dumped me."

Emotion bled out in his tone, but he needed to say more. "She said she wasn't sure if she loved me, if she even knew what *love* was. She has things she needs to sort out, and she can't do it with *me*. Said she doesn't like the person she's been, and she wants to start over. But not with me."

Pressing his arm to his eyelids, he rolled onto his side, facing away from Keefe. "I need her. I really love her. And I want my little girl. I see her . . . when I close my eyes. Her little face. Her little fingers. She had black hair like Zoe's . . . Did you see her?"

"I saw her. She was beautiful."

Jarret curled up on his side. Within nine months, he'd lost everything, all starting with the trip to Italy. He should've gone to Italy. If he had gone, none of this would've happened. He wouldn't have met Zoe camping, gotten her pregnant, and gone on that emotional rollercoaster with her. He wouldn't be lying here feeling like his heart had been ripped out and trampled by a herd of wild mustangs. He wouldn't have a little girl out there somewhere in the world, a little girl he'd never know.

"I'm here for you, Jarret."

"Yeah, you're here unless I really need you. You used to be on my side, no matter the side I took."

"No, I'm here for you. I won't go along with everything you do, but it doesn't mean I'm not here for you. What good does it do you if I go along with things that are wrong?"

Jarret pushed himself up and wiped his face with his wet arm. "What's that supposed to mean? What happened to you? You're so different. You're like a stranger to me. If you wouldn't have gotten all righteous on me, maybe none of this would've happened. I don't like you, Keefe. I don't like you at all."

"I know, Jarret, but I'm here for you anyway. I hope you'll understand someday. Your day will come. God has a plan for you."

Jarret shook his head, staring at his twin with disgust. "Until then, I've got no one and nothing."

"You've got more than you know. You just can't see it right now."

"Yeah. I've got my deep cherry red Chrysler 300, still in show-room condition." He grinned.

"That you do."

A silent but companionable moment passed then his cell phone rang. *Zoe?* He snatched it and glanced at the number. Not Zoe. Papa. He tossed the phone onto the rock, to a spot between him and Keefe. Before his conversion, Keefe would've taken the gesture as a sign that he should—

Keefe snatched the phone and answered it. "Hey, Papa . . . Yeah, he can't talk right now."

Appreciating Keefe's response, Jarret took a deep breath, scanned the surrounding woods, and relaxed somewhat.

With the phone to his ear, Keefe mumbled, "Uh-huh," a few times and, "Ohh," a few more times. He ended with, "I'll tell him. We'll let you know."

"Papa said he's taking a vacation." Keefe set the phone down and picked up a stray twig.

Jarret looked. "Vacation?"

"Yeah. He's going back to the place where he grew up, somewhere in southern Arizona. He said it was a vacation, but I get the feeling there's more. I think there's something Papa has to do there." Keefe drew patterns on the rock using the twig like a pencil. "Anyway, he wants to know if we want to come along."

"I ain't going on another trip with him. I'm still trying to recover from the psychological damage I got from the last one."

"You never talked about that trip. What happened? Where'd you go?"

"Uh . . . I'm not ready to talk about that one. That one's getting filed in the deep recesses of my mind, and hopefully it'll stay there." He grinned.

Keefe laughed. "It must've been bad."

"Bad ain't the word. I think Papa was trying his hardest to cast the devil outta me."

Keefe shook his head, still laughing. "Well, as much as I'd like to see where Papa grew up, I'm not going either. Do you remember visiting when we were little?"

Jarret shook his head, not really trying to recall any memories. Mama would've been alive then, another person he had lost.

"We stayed with Papa's rich Mexican friends. They have a huge house, like a mansion, way bigger than our house. I mostly remember the chandelier in the foyer, for some reason, and the swimming pool."

"They have a pool? I thought Papa grew up in a trailer-sized ranch house."

"Well, Papa did. But his neighbors were rich. They come from a long respectable line of landholders from the time that Arizona was part of Mexico."

"I guess I do have some memories of that place." He remembered dust and heat and a squirrelly man Papa's age who cared for the horses. "Do they have horses?"

"Yeah. I remember the horses, too."

"Maybe I'll go. It's a hot time of year to be vacationing in Arizona. But I guess I got nothing better to do. You're not going?"

"No. I um . . . I have something I need to sort out."

"Girl trouble?"

Keefe smiled. "No."

"Roland going?"

Keefe shrugged.

"You gonna let that hair grow out?" Jarret smirked. "We ain't got the face for short hair."

"Speak for yourself." Keefe threw a twig at him.

Jarret stretched out on the rock again. It would be a long hot way to end the summer, but maybe he'd go. There was nothing for him here. Maybe there was something for him there . . . in the desert.

1. Caitlyn's parents had made mistakes in their youth that made them wary of allowing Caitlyn to follow the culture's dating practices. Were they just being overprotective or did they have good reason? What problems do you find with the dating practices in today's culture? What guidelines do you think would allow teens to get to know themselves and each other without opening the door to temptation?

2. At the beginning of this story Caitlyn seems almost envious of Zoe. Pretty and popular, she seems to have it all. Is it a common temptation among teens to feel like others have everything while failing to see one's own gifts? What can you do to help yourself or a friend to recognize the "beauty" within?

3. When Caitlyn discovered Zoe's pregnancy, she wanted to be there for Zoe in every way possible. She briefly fantasized about raising the baby herself. She risked her budding relationship with Keefe by asking her parents to allow Zoe to stay with them. And she was "there for her" throughout her pregnancy. If a friend or classmate of yours becomes pregnant, how can you be there for her? Do you know what pro-life pregnancy resources are available in your area?

4. Roland wanted a friendship with his brother Jarret. And he didn't want Jarret to think he was judging him, so he ignored a few of Jarret's suspicious behaviors until Caitlyn forced him to face the situation. If you suspect someone, especially someone close, is doing something detrimental to their soul, how willing are you to say something to them about it? Is a person being judgmental when they judge another's actions, or is it false compassion to ignore the

situation? Discuss the application of Matthew 18:15 "If your brother or sister sins, go and point out their fault, just between the two of you."

5. The details in this story about the Eucharistic Miracle of Bagno di Romagna are as accurate as possible. Throughout the years, numerous Eucharistic miracles have taken place and have been approved by the Church. What is God saying to us when he performs these miracles? If you witnessed one yourself, how might it affect your faith?

Every month I send out a newsletter so that you can keep up with my newest releases and enjoy updates, contests, and more. Visit my website www.theresalinden.com to sign up. And while you're there, check out my book trailers and extras!

Facebook: https://www.facebook.com/theresalindenauthor/
Twitter: https://twitter.com/LindenTheresa

Did you enjoy this book? If so, help others enjoy it, too! Please recommend it to friends and leave a review when possible. Thank you!

About the Author

Theresa Linden, an avid reader and writer since grade school, grew up in a military family. Moving every few years left her with the impression that life is an adventure. Her Catholic faith inspires the belief that there is no greater adventure than the reality we can't see, the spiritual side of life. She hopes that the richness, depth, and mystery of the Catholic faith will arouse her readers' imaginations to the invisible realities and the power of faith and grace. A member of the Catholic Writers' Guild, Theresa lives in northeast Ohio with her husband, three boys, and one dog. Her other published books include *Chasing Liberty* and *Testing Liberty*, books one and two in a dystopian trilogy, and *Roland West, Loner,* the first in this series of Catholic teen fiction.

www.ingramcontent.com/pod-product-compliance
Lightning Source LLC
Chambersburg PA
CBHW060942120726
47910CB00002B/451